I0760570

Of Deeds Most Valiant

A Poisoned Saints Novel

Sarah K. L. Wilson

For Mom and Dad -- Vagabonds, both.

This book is a work of fiction. Names, characters, places and incidents are the product of the author's imagination or are used fictitiously. Any resemblance to actual events, locales, or persons, living or dead is coincidental.

Cover Illustration: Bastien Jez

Cover Design: Sarah K. L. Wilson

Interior Art and Special Edition Case Art: Alice Duke

Figure Sketches: Sarah K. L. Wilson

www.sarahklwilson.com

First Edition: June 2023

ISBN: 978-1-990516-45-0

Praise for Sarah K. L. Wilson

"This is the paladin tale we have been waiting for.

Religious knights have been a staple in myths and legends and fantasy for centuries, but THIS story is how I've always wanted them done. Religious vows aren't treated as a punchline or a weakness to overcome, but the idea of being dedicated to a higher power is handled with all the nuance and complexity such a vow deserves.

The religious aspects of the different paladin are showcased in all their glory and corruption, all their divine strength and very human weakness.

And it's all couched in a gripping story of puzzles and lies, treachery and devotion, doubt and faith.

Victoriana and Adalbrand, (and even the enigmatic Hefertus) have reset the standard for paladin.

I loved every minute of this tale."

— J. A. Andrews, Author of *The Keeper's Chronicles*

Author's Note:

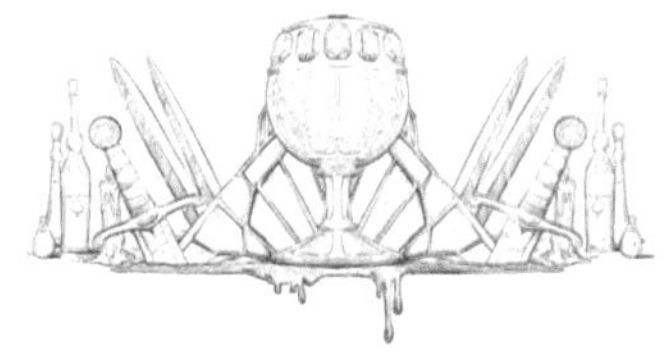

In summer of 2020, my best author friend suggested we read Tamsyn Muir's "Gideon the Ninth" together, and as I raced through that book and the following book, I was in awe of the ability of Muir to trace the various lines and musings of what it would be like to live in a world dominated by necromancers. Her deep dive into that magical bent was masterful. And from my admiration of it was born the desire to write my own deep dive — not into those who dance in death but those who dance in faith.

From these two inspirations, came the makings of this book and the others that will follow it. They are not an ordered series but rather individual tales of valiant bravery and terrible magic. I hope that by them I will do paladins justice.

Some books I write for readers. I know what they want and I try to give it to them. This book is not one of those. This book is written for one, and I hope it is pleasing.

Sarah K. L. Wilson
March 8, 2023

Cast

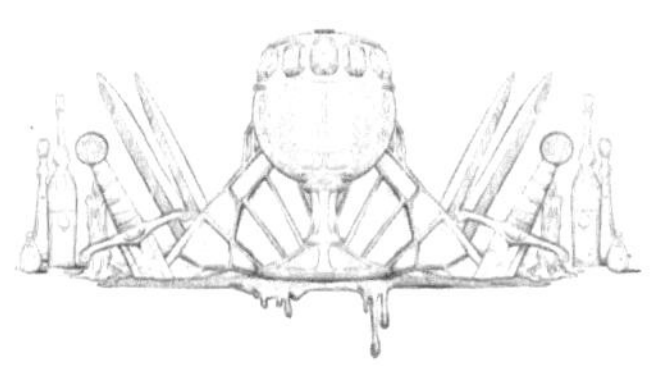

Aspect of the Rejected God — Vagabond Paladins

Victoriana Greenmantle
Sir Branson
Brindle

Aspect of the Sorrowful God — Poisoned Saints

Adalbrand Von Menticure

Aspect of the Benevolent God — Prince Paladins

Hefertus Shannamara

Aspect of the Creator God — Holy Engineers

Sorken Driftalan
Ceriand Parterio
Cleft
Suture

Aspect of the Sovereign God — High Saints

Joran Rue

Aspect of the All-Seeing God — Holy Inquisitors
Plenum Hexilan

Aspect of the All-Knowing God — Seers
Blanta Ecember

Aspect of the Majestic God - Majester Generals
Roivolard Masamera

Aspect of the Holy God — Penitent Paladins
Owalan Cantor

Aspect of the Vengeful God — Hands of Justice
Kodelai Lei Shan Tora

AND SO IT BEGINS ...

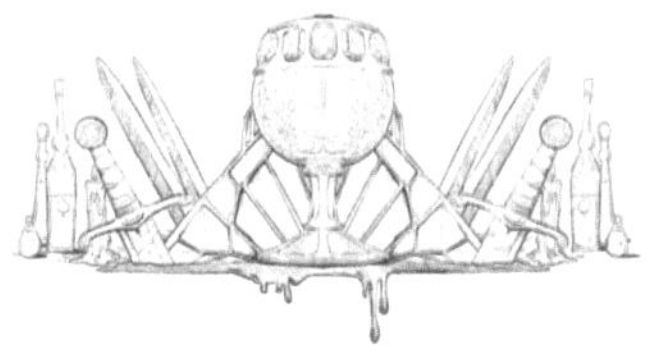

"Take into thy heart noble brother,
Take into thy heart great pain,
Bring with thee the hand of no other,
Or call all your efforts vain.

Drink down each poison offered thee,
Drink it right down to the dregs,
Now weep till your tears fill the myriad seas.
And we'll barrel them up in kegs.

Let faith hold you fast, noble brother,
Let faith hold you tossed and spent,
Fix your eye or never recover,
Fix your eye — and quick! — repent."

- Songs of the Poisoned Saints

Chapter One
Vagabond Paladin

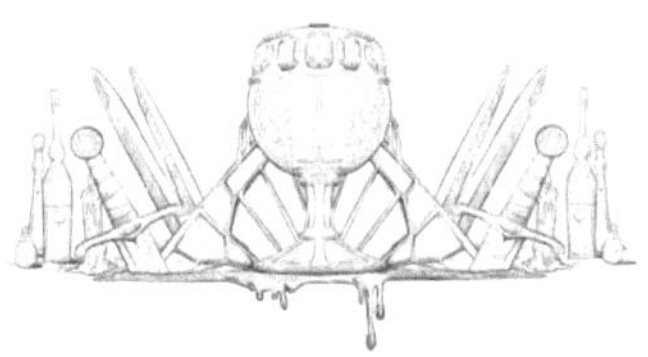

I fiercely opposed killing the dog. I was not entirely sure I could commit so black a deed, no matter how much it was warranted.

"Now you do what I say, unholy fiend," I growled as I jammed his snapping jaws into the wet clay.

Brindle's teeth had never seemed overly large when we played tug-of-war. Now, their dreadful size held an ominous threat.

The dog scrabbled hard against the ground, his claws tearing gouges into the hardpan just as they'd torn gouges through my flesh. Desperation shot hot through my limbs, granting me strength to hold him in place. It was a burning brew when it mixed with my hot tears.

"Hold, curse you. Just hold." My voice was raw — of course. Screaming will do that.

I cinched the rusted chain tight around the dog's neck. Already it was slick with spittle and blood. It painted my hands ruddy.

Here's my advice: never fight a dog unless there's no other choice.

Brindle's huge body — easily as large around the rib cage as my own — thrummed under his short fur and his wild eye rolled up, searching, the whites gleaming. The moment his gaze met mine, he snapped again, and I had to lean even harder onto his round skull with my greave to hold him in place. This was a battle of will alone and I wasn't sure which of us was winning. Or even if I wanted to win. I'd raised this dog from a pup. Every hurt to him hurt my heart.

He barked roughly, teeth snapping at air, and strings of drool flying outward like seeds of a blown dandelion. They clung to the pewter earth, adding to the churned slickness of the clay.

Let me be clear. Of all the places to fight three opponents, I'd chosen the worst. If you could call it a choice. I didn't feel particularly like someone who had been offered options.

I was trembling straight through when he finally stilled and I could ease back. The chain was securely rigged through metal loops on the long pole. It had been a lantern pole affixed to my paladin superior's saddle before I forced it to serve this way. Likely that was why his horse continued to throw dark looks my way from where he hid among the shadows of the surrounding trees — he saw me as a robber.

Yes, I know, Dandelion. I'm a traitor to us all. By all means, judge away.

Brindle swung to snap at me, stymied by the pole but undaunted. I jammed it hard against him, a reminder that just because he couldn't reach me didn't mean I couldn't reach him. I knew the look of betrayal in his eye was my imagination. It didn't make me hurt less.

I took each step backward with absolute caution until the length of the pole was between us. Former friend or no, he'd turned on me, too, and if I wasn't going to kill him outright then I'd need to secure him.

My breath sawed through the sudden stillness of the evening, loud and uneven.

How long can you keep this up, Victoriana? You must dispatch the dog, or what will you do with poor Brindle when you finally stop to bury my remains?

Yeah, there was a voice in my head talking to me. And it knew my name. This was a new development and I was not grateful for it. It might be part of our creed to "accept with gratitude that which we do not understand" but I'd never really been very good at keeping the creeds. Or at accepting things I didn't understand.

I was pretty sure it was some kind of shock or trauma or something that had me hearing my mentor's voice in my head when he was very clearly dead.

Well, I'll be the first to admit I'm not quite well, but I'm not sure I'd go so far as to say "dead."

Swallowing down a wave of unease, I spared a miserable glance for the corpse whose voice echoed in my mind.

Sir Branson lay sprawled in the clay not far away, limbs akimbo, my longsword pinning him through the chest, and quite neatly to the ground. Which, I might add, had done little to stop him when he tried to tear out my throat before the demon leapt out of him and into his beloved dog, Brindle.

Remember when I said I was fighting three opponents? That's them.

One mentor. One dog. One demon.

There were swirls of clay all over Sir Branson's armor and thick tracks and whorls scored into it around him, as if a potter had been forming a pot and set him in the wall of it as a grisly stamp. I'd seen worse things pass for art in our time journeying through the great cities — Dancartia has a grotesque statue that looks like children formed it from blobs of mud — but I'd never seen anything that wrenched me in two like this did.

Beyond my mere sorrow, this was terribly unholy.

I made the sign of the Aspect of the Rejected God — a holy tap of knuckle to forehead and then sword arm.

God forfend my spirit be stained by communing with the dead.

God forfend the demon jump to me next.

I'm doing my best to prevent that, dear girl, but if you'd stop with all the doom and gloom, I'm sure it would be easier. You've cast out demons before. Just do it again, quickly now, my cheerful — and very dead — paladin superior Sir Branson said in my mind.

Look, I know it's because I've gone mad. I'm under no illusions about this.

Sir Branson had been a Vagabond Paladin of the Forsaken Aspect in life and now, even in death, he did not seem to have a set course to take. It was disheartening, really, to think that I might suffer cold and loneliness all my life only to have it continue past the gates of death.

Well, I'm not exactly staying here for me. It's just that I may possibly, sort of … well, it pains me to admit it, but I may have skimped just a little on your training and this death situation has brought that screaming realization to the forefront and it feels just a tad irresponsible to sidle off now.

The dog crouched low, growling with a vibration so deep that I felt it more in my bones than heard it in my ears.

"Are you still in there, Brindle?" I coaxed. Who knew, maybe there was an epic dog-versus-demon battle going on within. Maybe the dog would win. He'd nearly beaten *me.* "Who's a good boy?"

A flash of red rolled through the dog's eye and then an eldritch voice — the demon, no doubt — replied, "*NOT ME.*"

Send the denizen to hell, girl. One deep strike to the throat of the dog! I think you know how stories like this end. No need to turn them on their heads.

Sir Branson was very confident for a man I'd been forced to kill. If he couldn't cast out the demon, how did he expect me to do it?

Well, I didn't want to murder a human. A dog is different.

Was it though?

I hesitated. It should be stated most adamantly that I am not a dog murderer and did not wish to become one.

You didn't have such qualms with me.

I hadn't had time to *think* with him. It had been mostly instinct.

Of Deeds Most Valiant

You *really have no option here, my squire.*

I had *some* option. Seeing as I was the one holding the sword.

The dog sat on his haunches and whined.

"I don't suppose you'll dig the grave?" I asked him hopefully. I was bleeding far more than I liked. My blood alone might soften the clay — though not enough to make any headway. In hardpan like this, I'd be digging all day. And I'd be doing it with a demon-possessed dog watching me and a dead man talking in my head.

Don't you fuss. I'll be right here the whole time, Sir Branson said gamely. *Just, do me a favor and maybe turn my body so I don't have to look it in the, well, not the eyes, obviously. In the place where eyes once were.*

"Go with the Rejected God, Sir Branson," I intoned the sacred words, trying to dismiss his ghost while swallowing bile. Look, don't judge, it's hard to give last rites to a man with no face.

I stumbled over to his horrific corpse and made the holy sign on the place where his forehead used to be and where one of the bends in his arm that I was relatively sure was the elbow was located. I touched a second one just in case. The God would forgive me ... possibly.

"Blessed Lord take from me this knight, consecrated by water most holy, dipped in the cold of sacrifice, given now into thine —"

Blessed Saints! Wait. I'm not taking last rites!

"You are extremely dead, and you should take last rites," I said aloud to the miserable corpse. I refused to speak with him in my mind. He had no right to be in there with me.

I shot a sad look at Brindle. We were both possessed. He, with a demon. Me, with a dead knight. What a sorry pair we made.

Except I will remain with your mortal coil, though I am bereft of my own, while Brindle will be relieved of his haunting spirit.

Remain?

I'd hardly abandon you when you need me the most. Like I was saying ... there are things I forgot to mention that you probably should know ...

I closed my eyes and sucked in a long inhale. It was how I handled frustrating situations — that and prayer — although this time I got a nice whiff of dog and death for my trouble. Wonderful.

"Rejected God, I beg thee send to me some means by which to bury Sir Branson with honor," I prayed aloud.

Good. Prayers. This is excellent. Your faith is unblemished!

He sounded so cheerful at this that I didn't want to point out that desperate prayers were hardly a measure of godliness.

I pushed him aside to look at the situation reasonably.

I had three problems now.

Night approaches.

Fine, I had four problems now.

First, I had a demon to deal with.

Second, I was bleeding badly from multiple lacerations and they needed to be cleaned and tended.

Third, my former paladin superior was now a paladin excisis and he was haunting me.

Rude.

I must prioritize.

I squatted down on my haunches in front of the dog.

"Perhaps we could make some sort of a deal," I said coolly. "I have you by the neck, after all."

"AND I HAVE YOU BY THE BALLS." The demon laughed — or at least, I took that stone-crunching sound in my brain to be a laugh.

"How unfortunate for you, as you'll find that means you have nothing at all," I said acidly. "I could kill you right now, but I'm fond of the dog."

Kill it! Kill it now!

"SILENCE, REVENANT! LEAVE ME WITH THE MORSEL."

I paused. Was it possible that the demon could hear Sir Branson and Sir Branson could hear the demon? The only thing worse than two voices in my head was two arguing voices in my head.

"Wuff?" Brindle asked, tilting his head.

I find myself in an embarrassing position, Sir Branson said in a tone I had never heard when he was alive. *It seems I can no longer possess my body, as it has expired.*

"Indeed," I agreed. "I bid you farewell as you enter the heavenlies. Go now, with my blessing and gratitude."

Cough.

"Did you just say cough instead of coughing?"

Dogs, it would seem, don't cough on command.

I blinked at Brindle. He blinked at me and then yawned one of those bone-cracking full-body doggy yawns. One of his eyes was still glowing red, but the other ... the other shone with a heavenly light. And it was the watery blue of an eye I'd looked into every morning over breakfast for the past ten years.

"Blessed Saints."

That curse was not ladylike at all. So, it was fortunate I was no lady.

You are a supplicant squire of the Paladins Rejected and, as such, it befits you to act in a way both godly and dignified. Sir Branson always sounded more formal when he was miffed. *Additionally, you know I don't like that curse. And I have asked you not to use it in my presence. Repeatedly.*

I glanced at my dead paladin superior, who looked anything but dignified. It would be best not to speak of what happened to corpses upon the flight of the soul to glory. That he was a knight remained obvious in that armor. The holiness, however, had evaporated with his soul.

I turned my eyes to Brindle. A dog now possessed of three souls: his own, my dearly departed mentor's, and a demon of questionable origin.

And that reminds me, Sir Branson said stiffly, *you have five problems.*

Wonderful. I now had more problems than I did gold coins.

There are four gold coins in my left boot.

I stood corrected.

Tonight, you must stand vigil and accept my cloak as my heir apparent, the anointed successor chosen by the God and the journey. Well, I say stand, but you must kneel in vigil throughout the night until the first blush of dawn. On your knees. Where it hurts.

"Great. Great. Great," I said as if considering.

You should probably take the cloak now. If you can wiggle it out from under me.

He paused as if waiting for me to obey, and when I didn't move, he went on.

And if the Aspect of the Rejected God speaks to you on this night and puts his mark on you, then you, too, will be a paladin blessed in the Holy Order of Vagrant Knights — the Paladins Rejected. And I'm sure he will, so no need to be skittish about that. It will work out, is what I'm saying.

If it wasn't obvious by the fact that all my armor was sub-par and my cloak was ragged, or that little hint about the distinct lack of gold, my master and I were beggar paladins. Knights Vagrant. The God's Own Rejected. Vagabond Paladins. Etc. Etc.

Only, Sir Branson, unlike me, was God-touched. He was a paladin called to the small places of this world, and if I were lucky — wait, we are not to say lucky — if I were *blessed* then I could be one, too. And I could join him in everlasting poverty and duty. Which might sound like hell to some people, but what can I say? I chose this. I actually want it. And if that didn't make me God-touched then who knew what would.

Okay, problem one. Nighttime. I limped to where the gnarled, ghastly trees edged the clay riverbanks, hauling poor Brindle with me.

"Were it my choice, I'd set you free, Brindle," I told the lanky dog as he looked at me with sad, liquid eyes. "I don't like keeping you tied like this, but I do not know who controls your furry form and I do not want to have to kill you, too. Gifting death to Sir Branson was bad enough."

I think I nearly have the dog under … aislhtrpoetn.

HHHTHERLJFPSDLKNG.

I gritted my teeth, falling to my knees as the two voices screeched over one another, whatever they meant to say lost in the tides of their private war. The sound was like the tearing of metal — a sound I'd heard once when the massive Oakencrest drawbridge closed over one of the Oakencrest guard, pinning him in its great jaws and tearing his steel plate chest guard in twain. I will not say what it did to his remains. It is enough to note that I've seen sorrier corpses than poor Sir Branson.

The pain in my head from the sound split it so hard that I forgot momentarily that I had a dog to mind and I dropped the chain, covering my ears as if I could block out the internal maelstrom.

Beside me, Brindle sat down, whined, and then shuffled forward, shuffling a little farther and a little farther until he could lick my hand.

When — at last — the screeching subsided, I was gasping and trembling. I blinked, the world buzzing with the sudden absence of sound. Brindle put his round head into my lap.

Blessed Saints.

Well. It must be the dog in charge of the body.

For now.

So, that was nice.

It's hard to control another creature's body for long even if one possesses it. Drains the strength.

I froze. The voice that had spoken just now was neither Sir Branson's nor that of the demon but some terrible combination of the two, and it rang in my head with the terrible certainty of a hanging-day bell.

"Which are you?" I asked, shuddering.

Which, indeed, the voice replied, and then followed it up with, *I'd think you would know, even if our voices have somehow merged into something new.*

"How would I know?"

Well, you could hardly confuse the thoughts of a most holy paladin and a demon.

It would seem that I could easily mistake them. I did not know which was speaking to me now. This was like one of those puzzles where two keepers guard two gates, and one always tells the truth while the other always lies, and the puzzler must form the perfect question to discern between the two. I did not yet know the perfect question, but at least Brindle wasn't currently trying to kill me.

I can tell you're very upset and that's understandable. Maybe you should take a moment.

I didn't have a moment. I swiped away the tears still wet on my face. Useless things. They hadn't protected any of us. Not the dead knight, not his devastated squire, and not the dog currently infested with a demon.

Brindle snuffled against my palm and I pet his head absently. This was hardly his fault.

"I suppose this will go more quickly now that you're not about to rip my throat out," I told him. "But what am I going to do with you?"

Obviously, you must keep him by your side.

Devil or Branson? Branson or devil? Either way, he wasn't wrong. Demons could jump to other creatures — a fact I had been made well aware of when this one hopped from the beggar who had found us on the derelict bridge over the Wendilclay River and into Sir Branson, and then from Sir Branson into the dog.

The beggar was dead, too, or I assumed he was, since Sir Branson had been trying to cast the demon from him and been dragged waist-deep into the water by the ravaged man. When the demon had leapt from the beggar to Sir Branson, my mentor had drowned the poor soul he'd been trying to save, before coming after me. The poor beggar's corpse had washed down the river. Were I not bleeding from multiple places, I would be honor-bound to find it and offer last rites. Given the current circumstances, I'd have to leave that to whatever priest was near the shores where he washed up.

I'm starting to suspect that you shouldn't cast the demon out.

That had to be the demon.

Cough.

I was terrible at this game.

Well, from what I can tell now that I'm elbows deep, as it were, had you tried to cast Hxyaltrytchus out without killing me first, he would have leapt from me to you, necessitating that I slay my supplicant squire, and killing a friend is not a thing a man gets over easily.

I glanced over my shoulder at the broken corpse behind me. He was not wrong on that last point. Abruptly the tears tried to surface again. I throttled them with all the heartlessness I had left.

There, there. It will be fine. I'm not really gone, am I?

From someone else that might have sounded sweet. From him it sounded dry and impatient.

But I was wasting time, even if I'd finally brought my shaking hands under control. With haste, I gathered the dead wood from the peeling trees along the edge of the forest and then hurried to light a fire.

Problem one under control.

Problem two. I was still bleeding badly and now it was making my vision shiver and darken, and if I did not deal promptly with that, then I may find I'd dug a grave only to collapse dead in it myself.

That would be such a waste.

Thank you, Sir Branson.

Cough.

Blessed Saints!

Listen, it's all in the tone. When I speak, it's in a humorous tone, and when he speaks, you can hear the clang of hell's gongs in the background.

Hell had gongs?

Did I forget to teach you that, too? I hope I remembered to warn you against going *to hell. Terribly dreadful place. An eternity without a drop of tea. I shudder at the thought.*

He'd warned me often. He had no need for guilt on that count. I struggled not to roll my eyes.

Well, he said with the air of one holding up his hands in innocence, *that really was the main thing.*

Removing the trappings of a knight or paladin requires patience and laborious care. Fortunately, we Vagabond Paladins do not wear quite as many accoutrements as some of the other aspects are known to do. I didn't regularly wear a helm and wasn't wearing one now, but the light breastplate I usually wore was removed, along with my pauldrons, and gauntlets. This way I could get to my wounds.

Sir Branson had the same advantage I had when the two of us faced off — each of us was well aware of the other's strengths and weaknesses. After all, he'd literally taught me everything I knew. And I'd lived with him for a decade.

He'd taken advantage of that to bleed me with neat cuts in every vulnerable spot. I'd taken a different approach and simply jammed my sword straight through the patchy mend in his breastplate that I knew was there from polishing to gleaming every day. I'd put all my weight behind the blow and all my prayers for his soul behind the force that kept going right through his body. It was a tidy death in the end.

But not before *the end. I swear I thought we'd end up beating each other to a pulp until both were nothing more than feasts for crows, and all we'd left behind us were some very unusual designs in the hardened clay. That would have been tricky to explain.*

To whom?

Anyone, really. Take your pick.

When I'd been taught my commandments at the knee of my mother and she'd taught me that murder was a great sin, she had waxed eloquent on the family of the victim mourning his loss, on the great guilt one must bear, and the stain upon the soul. I think she felt she'd impressed the need to not be a little death windmill upon me with great effect, although she had been disappointed that I was less moved by holy fear than she would have liked. Now, I think she may have missed a great opportunity. If she'd told me that I'd have to discuss the murder with the victim afterward, she'd have had the terrified devoutness for which she'd been angling.

It is rather inconvenient, isn't it? Can you not cast him out and leave me here alone?

Demon. That time I knew it. Sir Branson could leave any time he wanted.

Cough.

"Really?" I muttered. I would need to clean and stitch these wounds. And water and thread were both with my horse. "Are you trapped in there, Sir Branson?"

Not trapped, exactly, though it may seem somewhat undignified that I remain. It's rather like being a paupered houseguest with nowhere to go. I must tread a little longer on the patience of my host.

He was worried about his dignity when he'd already lost his face?

An apt metaphor, to be sure. But I really don't feel I can abandon you at this juncture. And I do think I might be able to keep the demon in check. For a time.

"Just stay," I told Brindle miserably, making the sign with my hand. I hoped he'd listen.

I could hear my horse snuffling just past the tree line. She was a good mare, Halberd, well trained in what to do in a crisis. We saw a surprising number of crises as Vagabond Paladins. Beggar demons were really just the tip of the spear, though this time the tip had stuck deep. Halberd had followed her training and stayed close by but away from danger.

I found her cropping up small plants and trailing her loose reins not far into the forest. She rolled an eye at me and gave me a horsey snort. To my humiliation, I buried my face in her ochre mane for a moment before leading her out to the fire. Touching another living thing that was not currently possessed by a demon was more of a relief than I would have credited.

Meanwhile, cleaning and stitching your own wounds is not for the faint of heart — a lesson Sir Branson had taught me my first week with him when I'd slashed my arm with his knife, and he'd handed me a sewing kit and started to brew a cup of tea.

"It works best if you can keep from fainting," he'd said helpfully as he'd sipped his lavender tea. "Tea helps, too."

"To clean the wound?" I'd asked, determinedly piercing my own skin with a needle and trying not to pass out. Sir Branson had been awkward with children. He never seemed to know whether to treat them as adults or dogs.

"Oh, no, for the nerves. Your stitches are too wide just there. Closer will give you less of a scar."

I never said Sir Branson was a Saint. He most certainly was not that, though he said his prayers very regularly, gave to the poor — ironic, since there were few poorer than those of us dragging around our vow of poverty — and kept to the precepts of the Aspect of the Rejected God. Or at least, I thought he did. Since he was the one who taught them to me, I could be all wrong and I'd never know.

That day he taught me two important lessons, though. How to stitch your own wounds, and that you can't even rely on kind people to be there when you really needed them. They might decide to brew tea instead.

The demon took that moment to remind me of its presence.

I'd help, but I'm afraid I'm missing the thing you'd need most. Opposable thumbs.

I was nearly done stitching. One of my shoulders was quite tender. One of my legs didn't like taking my weight but could do it. As far as the paladins of the Aspect of the Rejected God were concerned, that was fighting-fit.

We don't take whiners or the callow. Or people who are too picky about who we do or don't take. Or anyone overly fussy about dietary restrictions. Or anyone who doesn't like tea.

Maybe it would be nicer if the demon spoke more.

When I leap from the dog to another human, I will flay you slowly and then roast you alive over a pit of coals, little morsel, tasty snack, tiny bite, delicious ... oh yes, delicious ... also, I love tea. Especially when made from eyelashes.

On second thought, Sir Branson was clearly the more cheerful of the pair. But that did leave me with a problem. If I couldn't bring Brindle near people, then I would need to kill him after all, or vow to live far from humans for the rest of my life.

But that was a problem for tomorrow morning. Right now I needed to dig.

Right now you need to stand vigil, my girl. Night falls. Fail to stand vigil this night and all chance of being touched by the God will be lost. You will be forever supplicant and never paladin — forever unblessed. Your fate will be like this demon's — to wander the earth with no hearth, no home, no purpose, no reward.

It seemed I would stand vigil.

On your knees, of course.

On my knees.

I'd best get on with it.

Chapter Two
Vagabond Paladin

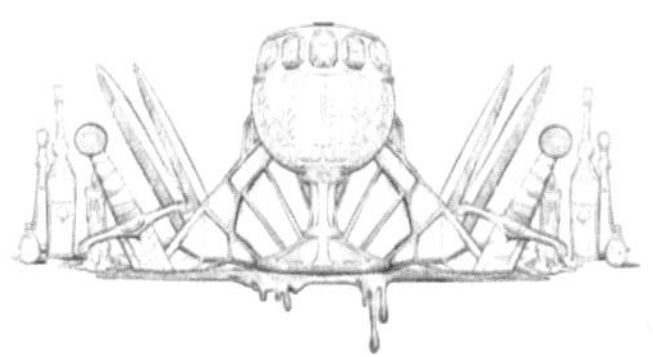

They found me while I was filling in the grave. Which was lucky for them because time had not improved Sir Branson's corpse.

I'm endlessly embarrassed about that.

Their silence was the loudest thing along the river. Louder than the murky trickling water or the fierce blast of the growing storm peppered with ice pellets. Louder, even, than the harsh scrape of Sir Branson's shield across the half-frozen lumps of clay and hardpan I was dragging into the hole to fill it.

I heard them in that silence, and when I stood they flinched as one man, though there were three. Their eyes were wide. Their shared gasp clouded the air around them like triplet hearths in the late-spring air.

No wonder they fear you, you terrifying thing, the demon paladin dog reminded me. *You stand as a warning to anyone fool enough to tangle with the power of the demonic. It's a wonder they don't run screaming from you to their wives and sweethearts. I set a woman on fire once and made her dance and she looked better than you do before the end.*

I set my hand in its wet, tattered glove upon Brindle's head in warning, and he whined loudly, sitting back on his haunches.

The lead man watched this, swathed in a deep grey cloak, his beard torn by the edges of the wind, and his eyes trailing up my arm from the dog's head to my unbound hair, likely thick now with clay, or blood, or snow, or the God Himself knew what. A ripple of terror ran over his lined face, but he clenched his jaw hard and it subsided enough for him to snap sharply.

"Revenant. We seek the Vagabond Paladin, Sir Branson the Rejected."

"Good for you," I said between huffing breaths. I was winded. I'd lost feeling in my hands and feet sometime during my vigil in the night. I had not slept and my belly ached with hunger.

As the newly minted Lady Victoriana the Rejected, can you not show more dignity? You look like you crawled out of the river and forgot that algae hasn't been in fashion for a few thousand years.

I pushed aside the voice.

I believed in the God, that he revealed to us his Rejected Aspect, and that he called paladins to his service. Even so, from the outside, I couldn't imagine a formula better designed to induce hallucinations and the belief that one had "heard" a call than to make one kneel in metal armor on hard ground with a storm whirling around them, blood still leaking out to mix hot with the cold, indifferent clay. Adding to that the horror that I had "stood" vigil beside the cold body of my only friend in the world only made my recollections more suspect. And yet, I'd seen no hallucinations during my vigil. Or at least, I didn't think I had.

It's fine that you haven't had a blessing. You're with me. And I am blessed. Always have been, really. Did you notice I didn't lose my hair? Old as pond scum but I kept it all.

"Have you seen the good paladin, Ghost of Our Fathers?" the man behind the first asked me with a quaver in his voice. He was, perhaps, ten years my senior and thick across the shoulders. Stout, and while not exactly beautiful, the strength of youth made him seem so. How delightful that he thought me a dead woman walking.

"I'm no ghost," I said shortly, jamming the shield in the

ground. It would suffice as marker for Sir Branson. Bent and sullied as it was from serving as shovel, it was still the only piece of his armor above ground. I'd buried the rest with him — including his sword — and I was already sorry I'd done that. I could use a second sword, and his had been a good one, but it was disrespectful to bury a knight without his weapon. The dog had views on the matter.

Might as well bury him without his feet. Or his hands, it had said when I hesitated over the matter. *Or his hair.*

Or at least I thought it had. I was not at full mental capacity at the moment. To say that the night had been long was a wicked understatement. It had been nigh on a decade.

"But you know where Sir Branson might be?" the second man pressed.

"I do," I agreed, pointing to the shield. "And now you do, too. And may this marker remain in his memory for many years to come."

It's a terribly sweet gesture. Honestly, I really can't thank you more. It's rare for one of us to get any kind of a marker when we die.

The looks exchanged between the three men showed a marked concern. Perhaps they knew, as I did, that the shield would last about as long as a marker as the road remained empty. Sir Branson was no decadent, but he hadn't skimped on steel when the shield was made and it would fetch a price for whichever thief found it first. The God forfend.

I certainly hope he does forfend!

I ought to say a prayer by rote, but after an entire night of them, my mind came up empty of suggestions.

When, sometime in the middle of the night, the snow started to swirl around me, I had redoubled my prayers, certain that they were my only hope of remaining still as the cold leached into every bone of my body.

"Cast upon the lake of sorrows all your hopes and gathered dreams, Let the ancient waters cover 'til hope is not as it seems," my thick lips had chanted in the darkness.

An owl had hooted in response and the small things that fled from it in terror made the grasses rustle. My horse huffed an annoyed breath from where he slept standing. Perhaps, as the horse of a soon-to-be-paladin he was doing vigil, too, but on his hooves rather than on his knees. They were likely better suited to it.

The wind had picked up, making the trees creak and groan their annoyance and whispering so intently that I heard a thousand possible voices with a thousand possible messages, but since all were echoes of my internal monologue, I didn't credit them. If the God called to me, I doubted he'd use my own voice.

"This is madness," they had whispered through the trees.

Perhaps you are not called at all. Your prayers are feeble, the demon in Brindle had suggested. *If I were a god, I'd reject you, too.*

Not everyone is called, dear girl, the paladin in the dog had said later. *And when they are, sometimes it's hard to hear. Or it's not in the way they might think.*

Which was a solid point, because how was I supposed to hear anything at all when I would not stop speaking? In conversation, one didn't natter on and on and expect that the other would speak over them. If the God had remained silent, mayhap he was merely tired of waiting for his opportunity.

"Lady? Lady?" The third man's voice burst into my memories. I was swaying on my feet, my mind wandering sinfully.

"I am no lady," I told him. I wasn't nobility, that was certain. And I may not be a paladin either.

"Would you grant us your name, then?" he asked. He was the youngest of the three. He looked almost like a royal messenger. Or a church messenger. But they didn't come so far into the wilds.

"I am Victoriana Greenmantle, Squire Supplicant —"

Cough, Brindle said.

I cleared my own throat. "*Paladin* of the Aspect of the Rejected God."

It was my first time saying it aloud. It felt like a lie, and that twisted something deep in my gut like a festering wound.

We demons know more about religion than you'll learn in your short mortal lifetime, delicious morsel, the demon had told me last night, when it seemed I could no more hear the God than I could ignore the terrible pain in my knees. *And I can tell you with certainty that you are not called to anything other than a swift death and perhaps my amusement.*

Demons knew nothing about faith. Which meant this one knew nothing about the God's call.

Perhaps the calling was within, a firm certainty of spirit that this was the right course. Perhaps the light from heaven and the voice were just ... symbols ... of what was occurring, like how a lover might offer his beloved his heart. He did not mean to cut it beating from his breast. It was merely a metaphor.

That's an adorable loophole you've found. Now, find one for me. Excuse the God's silence to me the same way, the demon had snickered. *Tell me all is forgiven and I am free to follow my heart.*

I had hoped it was the demon snickering and not Sir Branson. If my mentor was so bereft of belief, it would throw an uncomfortable light upon our shared history.

My prayers stuttered again and went out like a guttering candle.

"I offer up this well body and this quick mind, honed by faith and service, and presented for your use," I had said aloud.

And is this a bargain, then? You give the God something and he gives you something? You're closer to demon than Saint. We're the ones who do everything by transaction.

"It's not a transaction," I'd said aloud, considering. "Perhaps I must open myself up to receive the blessing."

Just listen. It will come if it will come. You can't make demands of the God like you're negotiating with a stingy fishwife.

And what if he didn't call me?

I explained that part, didn't I? I'm pretty sure that I did. Do you remember Sir Lysander? We stayed in his father's loft once just outside Saint Hermake's Rim?

I did remember him. A rough man, hard and cold, but he

softened when Sir Branson started talking horses and breeding lines, and the pair of them had been up all night debating which sire had got a foal who had grown up to win a race in some city I'd never heard of.

Yes, that's the one. He didn't hear the call. Pity, really, he was such a nice fellow. But I suppose it makes sense that the God didn't require him. He didn't have much compassion, and it's hard to be a good Beggar Paladin without compassion.

I wished he wouldn't call us that. It was a slur.

It's not a slur if you say it yourself. Or something. I've always thought it had a nice ring to it. Anyway. When the God didn't call him, he left his full kit behind, walked to the nearest town, and submitted himself to the magistrate to be assigned where he could be useful. The magistrate had him fed and shod and sent to the nearest keep, where he was kitted up and made a knight to serve the local lord. That's the way for those the God passes on. They're far too valuable to just be left drifting in the wind. But they can't keep anything from the old life.

Nothing at all? Not even their underbritches? Quite the audacity there, ghost knight, to claim your underthings are holy.

That's not what I said!

I had not wanted that future, and having him lay it out for me only made me more determined.

I wanted this future.

The road forever open before me, the past forever at my back, the goodness of the God in my actions, and the certainty of his favor in my thoughts. Loyalty, duty, and service. The want of it felt like a hunger. It howled long and intent within my chest.

Well, the wanting alone might be enough, you never know.

Bold words for a knight who has just been arguing about underbritches.

Desperately, I had opened myself up, clearing my heart and mind of all else, ready to accept whatever came to me.

And at that moment, the demon struck, leaping from the dog and attempting to leap into me, and had I been anywhere but on my knees already, I think it would have knocked me off my feet entirely.

I shuddered again at the memory. I could still feel his fingers, like thick oil, trying to seep into my heart.

"You're a paladin, then?" the first man asked, shaking me out of my memories the way Brindle would often shake a caught mouse.

To my surprise, the light in his eyes was pure relief. The other two sagged with him at my nod.

"Thank the God in all his aspects," the broad-shouldered man muttered.

"I have a message for Sir Branson," the third man said. "Or the nearest God-touched representative of the Rejected Aspect."

"That would be me." My voice rang in a way it never had before. Which was comforting, since I still wasn't entirely sure I was telling the truth.

Look, when the demon leapt, clawing into me, *something* had stopped him. To me, it had appeared as if the heavens opened and a glory shone forth, struck the demon, and washed me of all guilt. In that moment, a bell rang in my head, bright and resonant.

But I would have been remiss if I did not point out that the demon's leap had startled me, flinging me to the side, where I struck my head on a rock. It was entirely within the realm of reason that I could have seen a bright light and heard a ringing bell because my head was injured and now — when I declared myself to be what I was not — the God himself would strike me down.

So far, he had not done it.

I waited.

But perhaps he had merely stayed his hand.

Rejected God, throned in the glory men do not see, have mercy.

That prayer is a bit redundant if you're a paladin, and if you are not, you deserve the fires of hell for your blasphemy.

Demon or mentor? Mentor or —

I'm really getting annoyed by how you harass her. Is it not enough that she's stuck guarding the dog because of you? You have to also taunt her constantly?

One must pass the time how one can. I could practically hear the demon shrug. *I've made a bet with myself that she will cut her own hand off before the full moon. And when she does, I will leap, and then I will feast on the inside of a pretty, tormented faithful one instead of a dog. I can hardly contain my excitement. She's going to taste sooo good. I think I'll make her last a very long time, consume her a single lick at a time, like nougat. Have you had nougat, knight? Do they give it to beggars? Or is it just one more way I best you?*

"I'll take your message," I told the trembling youth, pushing my thoughts free of the two bickering in my head. The messenger was about my age, if I was any judge, his beard wispy and eyes furtive, but he nudged his horse forward and drew a missive from within his coat.

I stepped forward, hand out for the letter, but all three backed their horses up as if unconsciously wanting to be away from me.

"I don't bite," I said acidly. "Though you're making me reconsider that stance."

Trembling, the youth offered the letter a second time, and this time I snatched it from his pale fingers while I could.

It was elaborately sealed and ribboned. The feel of the fine parchment through my clay-smeared, torn gloves was so elegant that it made my skin crawl. Whatever this was, it was not good news.

You're doomed, girl! And we get to watch! Brindle crowed in my mind and then dissolved into spine-tingling laughter.

I was pretty sure he was the one who was doomed. I wasn't trapped in a dog.

I froze.

Trapped. In a dog. I looked from Brindle to the men and back again. The demon had not jumped to one of them.

Yet.

God forfend. God grant to me that this demon remains trapped, unable to savage another soul, I prayed.

It was in the hands of the God now. Though, in my experience, he never acted as I expected.

"I'm chief man of Loxburn," the first man said, misunderstanding my silent prayer as hesitance. I smeared my hands on the only bare patch of cloak I could find to clean them. "When the messenger came from Saint Rauche's Citadel"—he nodded at the trembling messenger—"and announced his purpose, we set out at once."

"Sir Branson stayed in my inn night before last," the second man said, frowning. "I don't recall another paladin with him."

I cracked the seal, barely listening. The letter was addressed to "Rejected Paladin," which could be any of us, and I was far too worried about what contents were so urgent as to send a messenger riding off to find any random paladin to feel the thrill I should have that I now qualified.

"I was attending to the horses," I said simply.

The letter was written with great care and sealed with the holy seal of the Paladins Rejected. A smaller letter — also sealed — fell out of the first into my hand. It was not addressed. My breath caught in my throat as I read the words on the opened letter.

"With my own hand, I write this, I Verdictian the Third of the name, Paladin Rejected, from our seat in Saint Rauche's Citadel. I send out five letters on all the roads that go north and pray to the God that the first to find hands belonging to us will have found the right destination. May those hands take up this burden. And may all the other missives be as dust."

Perhaps I should pause here and tell you that each aspect of the God granted his paladins certain dispensations that were for them and them alone. As much as he demanded, so he also gave. For our aspect, we were forsworn to wealth and required to live in poverty. But the God was merciful. If we asked a boon of him with a pure heart, he would grant it to us — though sometimes he chose to hear that request in his own way. That's why it was not all that odd that the leader of our aspect had simply jammed five of these letters into the hands of messengers and then prayed they were delivered to the right person for the job.

He had — in the way of our aspect — given the whole matter into the hands of the God. And the God had — apparently — decided to delegate it further into the very muddy hands of the paladin who had just trapped both a Saint and a demon within a dog.

I am no Saint, though the sentiment is appreciated. You'll recall that you often washed my socks. They were not Saintly socks.

Truly, the God worked in mysterious ways.

Back to the letter.

"I cannot impress upon you enough the urgency of this moment." As if to press the point home, he wrote the next sentence on its own line of the map. *"The rim has moved. It is confirmed by moon map. Have you any doubt, you have only to look up into the night sky to verify my words."*

I had been slightly preoccupied last night, to tell the truth, and had barely noticed the moon.

"The movement has exposed a key remnant of the past — the Aching Monastery. A place of legend and much speculation. It is to this monastery that you must journey immediately. I charge you, do not pause to eat or drink or wash. Do not pause to sleep."

For the love of ...

I could hear the demon cackling in my mind. Or maybe that was Sir Branson. Could this Verdictian really make these demands of me?

Well ... sort of.

I didn't like the sound of that.

Well, he can't take the God's blessing from you, or your role as a paladin, but he did *send you a divine assignment. We know it's divine because it reached you and he blessed the letters to only reach the right person.*

Solid reasoning.

Don't think I don't hear that sarcasm, my girl. But no, he can't take the blessing. But he can *put you in stocks for a year and a day, which ... well, I've yet to hear of someone who survived that, and I don't want it for you.*

That was a severe understatement. I read on.

"Take from those who delivered this missive whatever supplies they will give, and ride as if this is a quest from the God himself. I have included a map, though a prayer will serve you better. There is also an amulet. Wear it. If the monastery contains — as we believe — the most holy cup that once held the tears of our God, then it is essential that our aspect claim this artifact, for who knows tears as the Rejected do?"

This was highly suspicious. If there was one thing we were not prone to as an aspect, it was the hoarding of treasure. Our God would never allow it.

"But far worse, we fear that our quest will be found out immediately and you will need to deal with that to which the Rejected dedicate their time and service — the eradication of demons. For they will be drawn to such a place. Trust no one. Anyone you meet may be in their thrall."

Or anyone you bring with you might be in their thrall, I supposed, in the case of Brindle. I gave him a long look out the side of my eyes. He whined dramatically.

"Go with the God, my child."

How trite, coming from a man in the safety of a southern city.

"What does it say, Lady Paladin?" the messenger asked breathlessly, as I ripped the seal from the other paper and unfolded the vellum map and the amulet within.

I donned the amulet and then looked up, calling my horse with a whistle. She trotted up smartly and I mounted her, still covered in mud and my own blood. By the looks on the faces before me, I was a hideous sight indeed.

Beauty is as beauty does, Brindle told me tritely, before cackling and adding, *And beauty often does terribly cruel things.*

"The letter bids me beg you for any supplies you may be carrying and be willing to part with," I say grimly.

I expected them to shake their heads and show me empty hands, but to my surprise, they hurried to give me all that they had, which was three water skins, a few small loaves of bread, some dried meat jerky — I was careful not to ask what kind of meat — and a carrot. The messenger, with a sigh, offered me a multi-colored patched blanket. It was surprisingly soft.

I made the sign of the blessing for each offering.

"Did Sir Branson find the demon?" the chief man asked, and when my eyebrows rose, he felt the need to clarify. "The one we begged him to dispatch at the bridge?"

Well, then. Sir Branson had some explaining to do. He had not told me that he knew of the demon before we rode up upon it.

Cough. Yes. Well, I thought maybe this would be your first solo exorcism.

In the end, I supposed it had been. Though I wouldn't be asking myself back if I'd been the one with the request.

"It won't trouble you again," I assured those who had come for me — truly it was the kindest blessing I could offer them.

I turned my horse, whistled to Brindle, and rode like hell itself was at my heels — because apparently, it was.

Chapter Three
Poisoned Saint

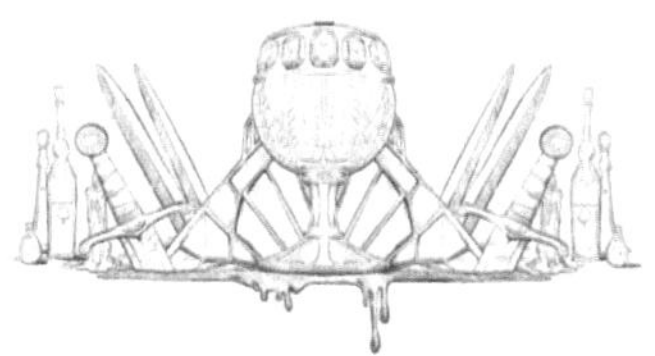

He finds me curled in a ball and shaking so hard that my teeth chatter together. I have ways to deal with this. Prayers, mostly. I run the beads through my fingers, murmuring prayers in three distinct languages as I try to distract myself from the feeling of my bones breaking again and again, twisting in my body one after another, the seizing of my guts, turning hard and sharp within me, the terrible blurring of my thoughts as time leaks out from every crevice.

I do as I always do. I call to mind the faces. A whole village taken by bone-break fever. Tiny children with pixie faces. Anxious mothers, slick with the sweat of their own fevers while they labor to help their babies breathe, to comfort them through the agony. Fathers collapsed on floors or woodpiles, trying to haul wood and water for their families while the world spins around them.

I was guided here by the God just in time. Most of the village was taken with it, but none had perished yet. I went from house to house, healing the sickest first, but going back afterward to heal all the rest. Not one slipped by me. Not one grave is being dug today. Not one.

I cling to this like a man clings to a faltering sapling as he clutches the edge of a cliff.

I remember it in the cold of night when nothing can warm me, as my stomach twists within me like one of the great boas of the southern jungles I saw when I was a squire supplicant learning at the feet of Sir Augussamana. He'd been a kind knight. Tender in every way. Washed over the side of the ship in a storm, I could not save him. I miss him yet. Miss his wise council. Miss his gift of joking with the young ones. He had a way of slipping sugar treats into tiny palms that made a whole room light up.

Were he here now, he would brew me something for the pain. Something to warm me. Or just say prayers with me, begging for courage, begging for endurance.

I've taken all their pain, Lord of Sorrows. I have taken it into myself. I have taken their ills. Bless me with endurance. Put your hand on me. Bless me with faith. I want to die. Give me the strength to live.

I'm not sure how long my visitor is there before I hear him, but he's not one for compassion. We were called about the same time, we two. Both from high houses. But he was called by the Aspect of the Benevolent God while I was called by the Aspect of the Sorrowful God.

Even so, he knows my name and he says it, and the name itself is a salve.

"Adalbrand. It *is* you. When the villagers told me some fool Saint had taken all their illnesses at once, I knew of only one so great in pride that the God must humble him."

"Hefertus." His name falls from my lips like a groan.

I feel his hand on my head. His fingers dig into my hair like questing worms.

"Father, I beg thee, grant this poor servant of thine the peace to ignore all pain this night."

"Blessed Saints," I gasp.

The pain is suddenly gone. The relief is so good it is a physical sensation. Like the feeling of cool water going down the throat after a long run. Like the feeling of a warm bed on a cold night. It births tears in my eyes. I let them fall as my breath gusts out, my limbs unfurl, my mind suddenly clears.

"Hefertus," I say again, and this time it is the closest thing to a prayer I can make it and still be reverent. "You fool of a knight."

"Paladin," he corrects me, turning away to examine the room. "Is that a set of stag's antlers? Someone has inlaid them." He makes a hum in his throat. "Gorgeous things."

"Hefertus, you know the consequences of your pronouncements."

He waves an idle hand. He's sitting in the rocking chair by the fire, feet kicked up on the top of a chest, a flagon of wine in his hand. He's made himself at home.

"Lovely place the chief has here. Wasted on you when you're like that. I told them as much. 'Next time,' I told them, 'just throw the fool in any hovel. He's feeling all the sickness he took at once. He doesn't know he's ruining your best furs on your only clover mattress.'"

I hope that isn't true. Furtively, I smell my clothing. I smell like sickness.

"Yes, you've a lovely stale scent. I very nearly dumped a bucket of water over you, but I didn't want to ruin the mattress further."

"You've only given me tonight," I say, forcing myself to think rather than to sink into slothfulness or relief. "Which means you need something from me right now."

He barks a laugh and shoves a medallion into my chest.

"We've been called," he said. "And I'd rather get a head start, especially if you'll be playing invalid most of the way."

Hefertus is a god of a man, towering at nearly seven feet, his entire body a mountain of muscle, his face bearing a short-trimmed beard, and his hair tawny. He has a smile formed in a way to make women swoon, and his order is *not* celibate, so he makes use of it readily. He is my opposite in every way.

"We've *both* been called," he says shortly.

"By the God?" I ask, suddenly breathless.

He shrugs. "Perhaps. By the church, certainly. We must ride

and ride hard. I'll ask these peasants for rope. Go saddle your horse. I'll tie you on for when the God's blessing wears off and then lead your horse from there. We ride for the Rim."

He slaps me playfully on the chest. I try not to take it personally.

"The Rim?"

He quaffs the rest of his wine in one go and then shakes his face with his lips relaxed like a great dog, spittle and flecks of wine flinging out in every direction.

"I'll explain on the way. Wear the medallion. Gather your things. Get into the saddle. I promised your Bishop I'd get you there no matter what state I found you in, and I mean to keep my word."

"Is that why you wasted your blessing on me?"

"Not a waste," he mutters, but his answer is proof enough that he has been at this too long. The paladins of the Aspect of the Benevolent God — Prince Paladins, as the rest of us fondly know them — can't serve long, or at least can't serve long on their own. For every favor they beg of the God, he takes from them some of the sense he gives the rest of men. Perhaps he spins it as an alchemist, not by transmuting lead into gold, but by forming sense into something more serviceable and breathing his breath of life into it. That's how I've always seen it, though Sir Augussamana had a different explanation.

"Overweening arrogance," he'd told me. "If you could speak a word and make it so, you'd be just as bad."

"But they don't stop," I'd argued. "Surely that is a curse."

He'd laughed. "Doesn't seem like one to me."

Perhaps he'd been right. Had he been blessed with the same, he would never have drowned. He could have simply asked the God to make his armor float and not drag him to the depths.

"Any hints on where we ride, Hefertus?" I ask.

"When we get outside, take a good look at the moon."

Chapter Four
Vagabond Paladin

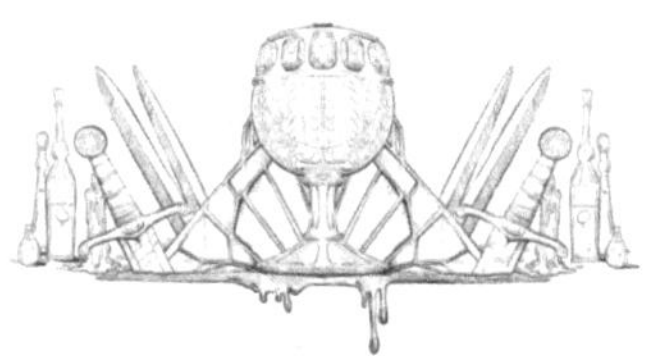

By the time I reached the edge of civilization — a place where farms and tiny hamlets dotted the landscape like freckles — most of the clay had dried and fallen away, leaving only stains where once I was coated in muck. If you think it's ridiculous that I had done as bidden and not stopped to rest at an inn, then you aren't the only one, but here was my dilemma: I had with me a dog possessed by a demon. I dared not leave him anywhere, so that left inns out — the inns of Northwark were not inclined to let their rooms to people who bring beasts within their doors.

Though I followed instructions on taking no rest, I broke the precept on disdaining supplies. Look, I could only go so far on the few things that the village men and messenger offered. They lasted me a whole seven-day and then I'd paused at a small hamlet and spent all of my paladin superior's gold coins on hardy supplies — mostly dried meat and oats, a few slabs of trail bread, and a thick fur robe. I'd never been so far north before, but I was aware that cold could kill.

A thoughtful person watching all of this might wonder how a sensible and generally cynical person like me had become a follower of the Rejected God in the first place — much less a dedicant intent on the role of paladin. After all, a life renouncing all wealth and living out of saddlebags and on the road is hardly the choice most people would make.

Those people have misunderstood me. They do not know what commitment and dedication are. They do not realize that I am subject to them every day. I know my place in the world and that place is serving the God in this way — the way of the Vagabond. Without it, there is no point to me at all.

I had left Sir Branson's mount in the first town we came to — the God gives and he takes away and we give back with open palms. The friar there promised me he had the means to keep a horse well.

I wouldn't have it any other way, but I already miss sweet Dandelion.

Cough. So do I, demon. As she was my horse. Keep on trying to imitate my voice all you like, but you won't fool Victoriana long. She's a skeptical girl with a skeptic's caution.

When night had fallen once more, I had looked at the moon and my mouth had gone dry with the certainty of what I saw.

The scholars call our moon "The Great Mirror," and she does, indeed, reflect. Some would say she reflects the sun. But others say she reflects the surface of the land, and from my earliest infancy, the adults around me would point to the sky when the moon was full, and trace out Tiberia to the south and the great Madriiveran Plains to the west, all right there reflected on the moon's surface.

"There," they would say, "is the Opal Sea, and just there is the Sea of Storms to the north. See how the Spine of the Forest ends abruptly at the edge of the moon? That is the Rim of the World, made entirely of ice. Impenetrable by even hammer and chisel, blade, axe, or fire. It awaits the turning of the age."

And I would say what every child was taught to say: "And that will be the beginning of the next age, when the wisdom and follies of our forebears will be unhidden and the secrets of another age laid bare."

And everyone would "hmmm" their agreement. It's easy enough to agree with a story when it is only a story with no relevance at all to you. After all, who would believe that in their lifetimes the ice of the Rim might recede and open new places, while it advanced in others to cover whole cities in ice too thick to break through? It is hard to accept that you are about to see the results of the turning age with your own eyes. I had not yet quite made peace with it.

Some paladin aspects put their squire supplicants into many years of training in which they stoop low over scrolls and books. My aspect believed in action, so scholarly knowledge was passed through oral traditions from paladin to supplicant. I found I wished I'd had more book training for this quest. It felt awkward indeed that those others who set out on this journey would know the lay of the land much better than I, and all from their books.

Don't worry about it. I'll be there to tell you whatever you need to know, one of the spirits possessing Brindle told me that first night as I rode deep into the darkness, mulling on what I had read in the letter. *Book learning isn't very attractive in a beggar anyway. People don't give freely to those who seem superior to them. It feels wrong. Makes their palms itch. They want that warm feeling of having blessed a lesser person.* The demon — I hoped it was the demon — paused for a round of mad laughter before he continued. *Do you know anything about the Aching Monastery?*

It had been mentioned to me once, grimly, in a long list of those places lost with the turning of the second age, long ago.

And?

And I'd been told little else that I recalled.

The Aching Monastery was a place renowned for its ability to impress upon men the holiness of the God and their own insufficiency.

Well, thank you for that, Paladin Superior.

The hollow laugh that sounded told me I'd guessed wrong again.

One day I entered that place — I recall little except I made a monk speak in tongues until he was thrown from the top of the highest tower. He was tasty, but not as tasty as you, snackling. I'll be feeding off your drama for years.

A wave of sickness washed over me. That did not sound like a thing monks would do to one of their own. Even if speaking in tongues could be … hard to interpret.

I think it was how I demanded he take the tongues of anyone who didn't *speak in tongues that sealed his eventual fate,* the demon said casually. *But I remember that — ahem — monastery being an opulent warren of puzzles and holy smells. We're going to have some fun, little snackling. The kind of fun you tell about for years to come. Well — the kind of fun I tell about. You'll likely be dead well before that. Your kind is delightfully fragile.*

Well. That settled it.

I leapt from my horse, caught Brindle by the scruff of his neck, and brought his doggy face up to mine under the light of the moon. His eyes were glowing again. They didn't do it all the time, only when the spirits were in full ascendency, but it lit the darkness in an eerie way that called to mind stories of fairy rings and magic trickery.

"We need to talk," I said firmly as the dog tried to lick my face. "I cannot bring you as you are to a place where other humans dwell. Not for supplies, and most certainly not on the task given us by the Aspect of the Rejected God."

Brindle whined, his huge doggy eyes rolling up into mine trustingly and sending a pinch of nerves through my heart. He put a paw on the arm holding him by the scruff and I sighed.

"I have told you already that I am no dog murderer. But what shall I do? I dare not risk this demon jumping to a poor, innocent soul."

I believe I have the other soul under control. I just need to tweak a few things …

"Then you are the demon speaking."

The laughing response confirmed it.

"So I put it to you. I will hear vows from you twice. Once from each soul within this doggy body. I have no need of a vow from Brindle, who is a good doggy, yes you are." Here, I chucked the dog under the chin, for this was hardly his fault. "And I know that Sir Branson will pledge without hesitation and will not allow himself to pledge a second time to free you, demon, from having to answer. So, I will hear the pledge twice. Once from each of you. You will vow to me that you will not leave this dog unless you are crossing on to realms beyond this bodily plane. You will further vow to accept my dominance over you in all things until that time has come to pass."

What good will a vow do you?

"I know as well as you do the power of words to bind. While you have no honor, your word will bind you."

Not as well as you think.

"I'll have it all the same. It is you and not I who will dance to the tune of the other, or our paths end here."

I thought you loved the dog.

"My soul I dedicate to none but the God," I quoted. "And he, only, will I serve." I cleared my throat. "As I said, I don't want to end poor Brindle."

I allowed Brindle to lick my face, feeling like there was a brick in my belly. Despite the cold of the evening, I felt feverish but I forced myself to keep going.

"One dog for the sake of many innocents? I will wear the stain of his death on my hands, if I must, to achieve that end."

I swear I will not leave this dog until I am crossing to realms beyond this earthly one. I will accept your hand as master over me in all things until then.

That was certainly Sir Branson. I swallowed miserably. I'd been working very hard to try not to think of him, but it was hard. I missed him brewing tea in the morning. I missed his rambling chatter about people he'd known and things he'd done. I missed how he fussed over how I pitched our tents and tended our horses and the absent-minded way he always forgot to tell me about details or deadlines until it was almost too late.

I was mourning my best friend and the man who had been father to me since I was eleven years old. It wasn't just the road-weariness, exhaustion, and the worry of having a major undertaking shoved into my hands while I was still coated in the earth of his burial place that was making my throat thick and eyes wet. It was also a wound deep and bleeding from losing someone who mattered.

I had the strangest sensation of being a boat set adrift without a port to which I might return.

I didn't want to kill the dog his ghost had taken refuge in. Not just because Brindle was an innocent, trusting dog, but because he was the last link to the man I knew.

And yet. If I must render this one black deed to stop a thousand others, I would.

It's adorable that you're waiting for me to surrender. If only I had a painter here to record it and a few weeks to watch him depict your caught-fish gape. That would please me enormously.

I clenched my jaw until it ached, but I couldn't see another way forward. With a sigh, I drew my belt knife as Brindle rolled onto his back and put his doggy head in my lap, begging for affection. I rubbed his belly as I seated the blade in my palm. My heart was in my throat, choking me, making my breathing painful. I wasn't ready to do this. But I dared not flinch from it. Hesitate, and I'd make the poor boy suffer more than he needed to. I must be quick and certain.

Sometimes I still had nightmares about a child we found early in my time with Sir Branson. He'd been only a few years younger than I had been. He'd killed his parents in the most grisly of ways. I do not like to speak of what the demon did with him and to him after that, or of how it ended.

"I didn't mean for you to be seeing that," Sir Branson had said at the time with a heavy sigh. His gaze had trailed me for a week after that as he clutched at his hair and beard distractedly. I could never tell if he was more distraught by what we'd both seen or by the fact I'd seen it with him. Now that I was grown, I thought maybe it was the latter.

There are nights even now when I relive pieces of that day and wake retching.

So, would I kill our beloved dog to prevent that from taking place again? A dog whose only goal had been to love me? Yes, I would. Even if it meant crying over it for the rest of my life.

My vision was blurry as I set the tip of the blade against Brindle's neck and prayed for strength. I drew in a long, sawing breath.

The vow tumbled into my mind, words said with the steaming snap of the demon's original mental voice.

I swear I will not leave this dog until I am crossing to realms beyond this earthly one. I will accept your hand as master over me in all things until then.

Well then. My breath whuffed out, unshed tears spilling with a suddenness I hadn't expected. I swiped them away violently, put my knife away, gave Brindle his belly rub, and then got back on my horse.

Don't think it will hold me for long, snackling. Words are just words. I have no honor to hold me.

But I knew that was not entirely true, for the God heard them, and his listening made them powerful.

Best to stop whining about it. She's bested you and you can't even make coy jokes about underbritches to hide your pain.

The demon retreated into sulky silence after that and I could only hope it meant he was fenced in adequately.

We traveled long through the darkness, and if Brindle seemed lively and untroubled, I was the opposite — haunted by memories and too troubled to pitch camp and sleep.

By morning, I was wrung out and past exhaustion. I built a pitiful fire on the side of the road, curled up in my small tent with Brindle, and fell asleep to the irony that my last friend in the world was a danger to anyone but me and would have to stay by my side for the rest of his natural life whether he liked it or not.

Brindle, for his part, seemed largely unconcerned. He merely yawned, tucked his nose under his tail, and went to sleep as he had every night of his life.

You did the right thing. God-touched or not. Don't let that red-eyed demon tell you otherwise. You should never trust anyone who treats you like a banquet dish rather than a human.

Good advice. The ladies I'd seen riding through great cities could use the same advice.

I went to sleep that morning not sure if I were clinging to words from my old master or from a demon. Not even caring, I was so exhausted.

When I woke, it was with relief.

The dog remained with me. The vow must have taken. And if I was stuck now for the rest of Brindle's natural life with the most concerning of companions, well, at least I had not been forced to kill a dog. We must count our blessings.

And now can we get on with this quest? I am itching to learn more and you haven't even looked at the maps, bite-sized confection. Are you as allergic to knowledge as you are to coin?

The maps, it had turned out, had envisioned us riding almost straight north — not a problem, since I'd known that already — though we'd veer slightly easterly to avoid rough country and a large lake. From what records we had, and though those records were ancient we believed them true, we knew that the old monastery was located along the side of the sea on a rocky peninsula called, portentously enough, the Saint's Finger.

The Saint's Finger. The voice in my head practically purred. *It's been a long time since I heard that name. What do you think Saints use their fingers for, snackling? Nothing fun, I'd wager.*

I shivered when he said that. I had no desire to know what demons would use a finger for. And I shivered again when I heard the purr every time I opened the map again on the way north.

He purred again when we reached the last huddled hamlet to the north, a sorry place where the thatch was thin, the chimney smoke thinner, and there wasn't a single village dog to be had. I felt so bad for them that I didn't even beg, just rode through town where the villagers were celebrating Break Fast Day with loud singing and rather more alcohol than was likely wise for people whose village was now on the frontier of newly revealed territory.

I was wearing the thick fur cloak over my armor and sometimes I put the patched quilt underneath it when the wind howled on the lonely parts of the road.

"This road peters out just north of the last farm," the old man in the street had told me over the hubbub when I leaned down to see why he was gripping my stirrup. "The others are a day or two ahead of you. One group went through around noon today."

"Others?"

"The other paladins," he said, nodding knowingly.

He was missing an eye and two fingers, though the fingers looked like they were lost to frost and not to accident. I was surprised he wasn't celebrating with the rest. With the Rim moving, the sun would change courses as it always had, and this village would grow warmer. No more lost fingers for this old man. Probably.

"It does the heart good to know the God's holy warriors are defending us from the north."

I wondered if I should set him straight. I was no holy warrior. Nor were we about any business that would benefit him.

Do not reveal the truth to this man. Why cause him distress for no reason? Let him enjoy a little hope. A little taste of joy on a sour tongue.

Good advice, Sir Branson.

The hollow laughter within me made me grit my teeth in annoyance.

Saints take it!

Don't fuss yourself, my girl. The hellion is good at pretense. Imitation is all the devils have. They cannot create or reproduce on their own. They require men for that. And so they will always be pale shadows and wavering echoes.

"Can I help you, Father?" I asked the old man with what

kindness I could manage. It was hard to focus on what was before me when there was a constant tussle inside my own mind.

In the background, Sir Branson began to recite the creeds. Sort of. He tended to get creative with them, adapting them to the situation or his own preferences. I was reasonably sure there was no actual belief that tea was from the table of the God and should be treated as such.

At least it was less distracting than direct conversation.

"No, it's how *I* can help you," the man said, pulling on my stirrup so hard that my poor mare danced to the side.

"And how is that?" I put a little steel in my voice. It was as much my duty to keep a fear of paladins in the hearts of the people as it was to aid them in need. Failure meant the next paladin might see her armor stripped away and her horse stolen.

"I had a vision," he said, his milky eye on me. "A vision of hands reaching out — hands that looked like tree roots — and they held within them a bitter cup. Do not drink the cup."

"I'll be glad to avoid it," I agreed. "Blessings be on you for your prophecy."

He laughed then and shot a look at Brindle, who I'd laid across the front of my saddle for our walk through town. I still didn't trust him near people, even with the vow in place. He did that thing dogs do that is half whine and half yawn, ending it with a snap of his jaws. If I squinted, I could still remember what those jaws had done to Sir Branson's face. Fortunately, his eyes weren't glowing demonically. Even a half-blind man might be startled by that.

"You think you can avoid it, but some of us carry our own evil around with us, don't we, Lady Paladin?" His gaze looked like it was trying to light Brindle on fire. "And yours might yet tear your throat out."

I gritted my teeth harder as the old man rolled his good eye. My belly rolled along with it. How did he *know?*

Well, he is a seer. Look carefully, pretty Seer. Enjoy your stolen glance before I rip out your throat.

Pretty? Who would have thought the demon had such odd taste.

He cackled in my mind and I gritted my teeth. If an old man had known, what would prevent the other paladins from knowing?

If they do, then they'll know also that you have chosen to bear a burden for the sake of mankind. There's no shame in that.

I had considerably less faith in my common man. You heard stories, after all. Stories of people being burnt at the stake.

You're too damp to light up easily. A true wet blanket among women. You should have more fun, enjoy a little fire. Taste the world a little — as I shall taste your flesh.

Or you heard of them being hung up in crow cages. Was that worse or better? I wasn't sure.

Your imagination is too small, snackling. Think of what I'll do to you when I take over your body, the demon purred in my mind. *I will make you dance unspeakable paths. I will baptize you in cruelty and wash you in heartlessness and make your name a byword of terror whispered in the darkness. You shall be the sweetest dainty I ever feasted upon. Your dearest dreams I shall twist until they choke you.*

I shivered.

"There were two paladins in that last group that went through here," the old man said, suddenly clear-eyed and sober-speaking. "If you aim to follow them, mind the tracks. Beelder, the hunter's boy, says they're clear and easy to follow from the end of the main road, though what fool would follow a dozen paladins is the real question. The church wouldn't have sent so many on a mission of peace, yes? No sane man would go to new lands without the paladin's blessing first. No sane man would follow holy knights into the blind night, either." He opened his mouth as if he'd say more but then shut it with a snap and said curtly, "Go with the God."

"And you as well," I told him, and then I rode out from the thin village as quickly as my horse would take me, taking care to light a lantern and hang it from my lantern pole before I was far beyond the feast lights.

I did not want to stop anywhere near that hamlet. Or any hamlet. People made me nervous. And now, I felt as though my sin was writ large upon my forehead for anyone to read.

Maybe I'll make your eyes glow to betray you, too.

I didn't think he could do that. Probably.

My eyes drifted several times to the sorry clumps of white snow along the path, hoping that any glow might be reflected there. I saw nothing.

By the time I left the hamlet behind, I found myself at the end of the road. My map showed all the details of the rest of the route with question marks added to the ends of names and the features sketched vaguely by an uncertain hand. Unhelpful.

The other map was a suggested layout of the monastery, though it seemed to me that any map of a place that existed ten thousand years ago would likely bear little resemblance to reality. It was the typical collection of cloisters, cruciform main floor, bell tower, and sanctuary. I'd seen the same pattern a hundred times before.

"It was a great civilization that lived there," someone had scrawled on the bottom of the scroll. "We know little of it beyond this single monastery and a few scraps of recorded history that depict this place as devout and possibly more advanced than we in both technology and faith. One historian claims it was the source of 'miracles and powers beyond anything seen in this world before or since.'"

We would see about that.

Look, and not to be morose here or anything, but I don't like the sound of that, Victoriana. If they're so powerful, why are they not around today? Why did they not bring such wisdom elsewhere with them? I have no recollection of these people even mentioned.

When the Rim moves, no man may stay the change of the shape of the world, the other voice in my head argued.

But the God may stay it.

Certainly. But why would he? There's no fun in that.

The God does not exist for fun.

Are you completely certain of that? If so, I've certainly slipped a lot in under his nose.

I blocked them out as I set up my tent at the end of the road with no light except the faint luminance of my lantern. An inn could have been three steps from the road and unless the windows were lit, I would not have seen it, so deep were the clouds.

I offered Brindle a second night sleeping in the tent with me. He used to sleep in the tent of Sir Branson, from the time he was so small that he rode in a saddle bag. It had always puzzled me why an impoverished knight who could barely keep himself fed, never mind curb the appetite of an enormous dog, would keep one with him, but I was starting to understand his thinking now. Even possessed, the dog eased the loneliness of the road. I had expected him to be nervous and anxious with the idea of sleeping with me instead of the old knight, but he had adapted without complaint.

He turned a circle, spreading the scent of doggy wetness everywhere, and then plopped down, panting and huffing.

Tomorrow the true fun begins, the voices in my head reminded me. *Don't forget your prayers.*

And thus, I spent my last night in a land touched by men and aspects in prayer. And if it helped with what came next, then I dread to imagine what it might have been like had I not prayed at all.

Chapter Five
Vagabond Paladin

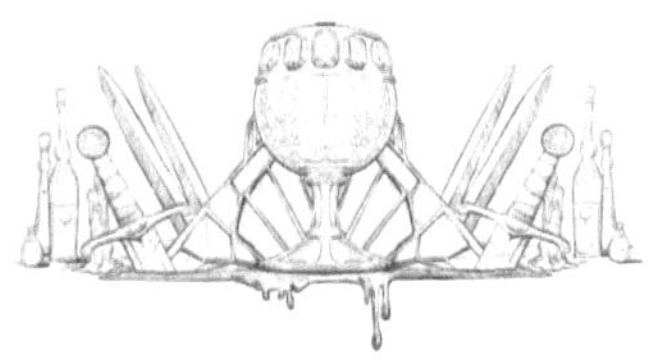

I would be the first to admit that my education was slapdash at best.

Well, yes, do excuse me for that, my girl. There was just so much to show you, and the things people think of as education are ... well, sometimes they don't seem like a real priority when you can be looking at how a blue jay puffs in the cold or how to best make a fire draft well. I mean, seriously, one must enjoy life a little.

One must. In fact, could I suggest enjoying it right now? Maybe find a nice treasure to steal and break all your vows, hmm?

While I knew one hundred and forty prayers by heart ...

See? I did teach you some things. Though, most of the rote prayers came from your dearly departed mother.

And while I could sing both the melodies and harmonies of the Hymnal Vox, and could recite the thirty-seven ways to ceremonially cleanse a site of demonic influence and the twelve great castings for the removal of a demon, along with the four ways of discerning between spirits, and the smoke rites of the dead and dying ...

I did better than I thought. That's a prodigious list. I wonder if I could be awarded a posthumous medal of some type ...

I knew all that, but I knew very little of ancient architecture and geography.

Stuffy nonsense, anyway. Which Vagabond Paladin need know those things? Tell me the name of the puffed-up fool.

Me. I was the puffed-up fool.

The geography of the current world is enough to keep our feet on the path and the quick reading of other humans tells us whom to help and whom to fear. You may yet thank me that you learned those lessons well.

When I pushed my way out of the tent, it had snowed in the night. I bit my lip so hard in my effort to control my frustration that I drew blood.

Not confident of your ability to track in the snow?

There was a mocking note to that.

It was not tracking in the snow that was the challenge. It was following tracks *under* the snow that was problematic.

This close to the Rim, it was still winter, though south of here it was deep into spring.

The sun rose in that strange way it sometimes does in a snowstorm, where a snow mist has risen up, cloaking the world around you in a fog of ice particles thick as milk, but glowing so brightly in the area close to you that it seems nearly as golden as the heart of an egg.

It was almost heavenly. Almost divine.

Hardly. Your theology knows perfectly well that heaven is not merely a golden haze but the next adventure for the righteous.

That was certainly Sir Branson. He had lectured me on the same often in life, since the day I found him in the village square and begged to be made his squire supplicant. I had eleven years to me at that time. My parents were taken by the grippe quite suddenly. I was lucky to have survived it. When I came to Sir Branson with my request to join him as squire, he sold his second pair of boots to buy me a teddy bear. I was far too old for it. But I kept it anyway until I gave it to another child just last year. I wished now that I'd not gifted it away.

That's not a sniffle I hear in my mind, is it?

It's harder when you're distilled to just your heart. You lose the outer shell. Defenseless as a newborn babe. Don't look. It's embarrassing.

There was nothing to look at but Brindle, who was occupied with cleaning his underside with a thick pink tongue.

Ha! Don't lie, old knight. You're hardly defenseless or you would have caved to me by now and relinquished this agonizing stalemate. Tell me then, where is this soft point? Where ought I to send my next barb? What pity shall I twist and ply you with until you beg for merciful relief?

Well. I guess that explained a few things. Their battle was not settled. At any moment, I might find I had only my former paladin superior following beside me ... or I might find I must contend with a newly escaped demon. He'd made vows to me ... but I couldn't rely on that.

Have no fear of my valor. I will stay the course.

I wanted to sigh. But what would be the point?

Instead, I packed camp, tended poor Halberd, who liked the snow no better than I, ate a meager breakfast of a small handful of oats, and offered a piece of jerky to Brindle, who snapped it up in a bite and nuzzled my hand for more.

"You'll have to hunt on the way," I told him sternly while I rubbed behind his ears. "I'm low on supplies and have no way to get more."

Brindle put his nose to the ground and made a solid job of sniffing anything available before making his mark on a fallen tree. It was hard to believe that such a very doggy dog could be anything else.

My side ached, and I possibly should tend it, but I hadn't been warm in days, not even with the tiny cook fires I was kindling, or the quilt, or the cloak, and I didn't want to take off even one layer of clothing if I didn't really have to. Besides, my orders said no delays.

By the time I had everything packed, Brindle was dancing

back and forth across what I could only guess was the trail. I hoped he was right. It would be enormously embarrassing to have to confess to my superiors that I had been misled by a demon.

I rested one hand on the head of my dog as the wind tore at my long, loose hair and my tattered cloak and tabard. The land behind me was all I'd ever known. The land ahead, a crooning mystery.

It was maybe an hour after we set out that the fog began to lift, and by the time it was clear enough to see, I drew Halberd up in shock.

We were moving through a forest, alright, but not a forest of trees. The land here was strewn with ancient grave markers — the type I'd only ever seen when Sir Branson drew them in the dirt for me during a lesson.

Yes. Gravebars, he said now in my mind as I swallowed. *They used to decorate them with dangling strings of bones sometimes.*

The uprights were tall and carved precisely of stone that was probably older than anything I'd ever seen, barring the bones of the earth herself. At least two-thirds of the lichen-etched markers had been pushed over — all in the same direction, I noted — and some crumbled to chunks of rock or even nothing more than a depression filled with broken debris.

As if the ice slid across them and tumbled them. Which, obviously, it did.

But then why were any still standing?

Let some things be a mystery.

I didn't like unsolved mysteries.

Then life will be difficult for you. How grand.

I rode between the denuded grave markers, Halberd's hooves squishing into pale sod as the snow quickly melted to rubble-strewn pools. Everything had gone grey. Sky. Markers. Path. I misliked it. It made this place feel dead.

I almost felt relief when I stirred up a flight of crows. They screamed their annoyance as they launched into the sky. Something lived, at least, though they'd find little carrion here so soon after the Rim moved.

I looked around me nervously. This world had been thickly encased in blue ice not a turning of the moon ago. Did that mean that even now, the Rim was moving somewhere to the south, eating up lands we would not hear were gone for many months and — possibly — trapping the people of those lands in place, dead, yet preserved in grisly perfection?

It's not our problem one way or another. The sun rises and sets over the plane of the earth. Beneath us, the great depths of hell lie cold and uncomprehending in the darkness beneath the earth.

I waited to see if there would be more "wisdom." There was not.

Blessedly, the fog cleared quickly, revealing a trail beat into the long, damp grass where about a dozen horses had recently passed, and since it was well-trampled and clear, I kicked Halberd into a solid pace and called to Brindle to follow. We covered ground as quickly as it was possible to cover it.

The graveyard was dotted with pools of standing water and it was not long before Brindle was dripping with it, shaking it from his coat and running impatient loops around me.

Was it possible that the ice rim had melted rather than withdrawn?

It doesn't melt. It doesn't scrape the land either. It simply moves in ways known only to those not mortal. Fancy you thinking otherwise. Magic is magic, girl. The sooner you accept it, the sooner you can use it.

I made a sound of annoyance at the back of my throat. I was not fond of mysteries.

I wouldn't take a devil's explanations too seriously anyway.

I peered into one of the ponds for clues. It was simply the yellowish color of snowmelt, bits of surrounding foliage floating in the otherwise glass-smooth surface. My reflection looked back at me. What a sight.

I looked exactly as I was — a woman who had only barely

won a battle against her own paladin superior and a demon, and then ridden for days on end without stopping anywhere that possessed a bath.

If there was one thing I knew about appearances from my travels, it was that first impressions were important. Arrive at the meeting point looking unkempt, and the other paladin aspects would immediately disregard me, or worse, pity me. I was too young to afford that.

I chewed my lip in thought.

There was no way to clean up properly. But what if I chose to purposefully mark myself?

They'd think I was crazy. Unpredictable.

That could work. It's hard to bully people who make you nervous.

At the next puddle, I grabbed a handful of grey clay from the edge of the pool and spread it thick through my hair where it sprang at my forehead, and then carefully swiped it into wings at either side. Without washing my hands, I plaited my hair to one side, letting the clay form around the strands of the braid. I rubbed my fingers in the clay again and then spread them like a fan across my chin and swiped downward.

There.

Saints and Angels, but I looked hideous now. Exactly as I intended. I looked fearsome and worthy of respect rather than lost and forlorn.

Are you forlorn? Sir Branson asked me.

Are you lost? The demon sounded eager.

I refused to admit to either.

I clenched my jaw and rode on until eventually, the graveyard ended. The road curved between tall rock cliffs and shot out between them to the edge of a furious grey sea. Not so much as a gull rode the cold winds, and I felt almost as if I were the last living person in all the world.

Amazing, isn't it? Remember this. You are nothing and you

never will be. Submit now to your betters. Submit or find yourself ground down to the nothing you are.

I clenched my teeth firmly and refused to listen or to let the loneliness of this place seep into me.

I could hardly hear Brindle's alert barks over the sound of the waves crashing hard on the stone. Without any other choice, I followed the winding road after him. It cut first one way and then another around foreboding rock cuts and over crumbling arch bridges. Statues still lined the road in unpredictable places. Some, sheltered by the stone, remained standing, though their faces and details were worn away to pocked obscurity. Others were nothing but feet or legs affixed to stone pedestals.

I think I knew that one there.

The one with no face? How unlikely.

Yes, that one. Most of my victims end up without faces.

In the back of my mind, Sir Branson growled and Brindle growled with him.

I swallowed nervously, when finally — late in the afternoon — the rock curved sharply and I saw the hulking shape of a ruin up on a steep stone rise.

The Aching Monastery.

We had arrived.

A map would have done me little good. Though a few arches and buttresses remained jutting into the sky, the rest was a mass of tumbled stone architecture. There was even what might have been a large tower lying in five distinct chunks at the bottom of the cliff face, half covered by the pewter water of the sea and grown all over with barnacles.

It was with stomach-twisting trepidation that I kept riding.

I had orders to follow. I had a quest to complete.

And besides, the sun was low on the horizon and there was nowhere to camp on this harsh, narrow road or the jagged rocks between it and the sea. When tide was high, I would guess it nearly licked over the road. It would be a very watery sleep.

I'm going to love this place.

I was sure he would.

It's like it was crafted for me.

That gave me pause. Which of them was saying those words? Not the demon, I hoped. Was this not a monastery? A place dedicated to the God himself?

It sings to me.

That came out like a purr.

And it was on that tense note that I finally caught up to a laughing Brindle and then wound my way up the rocky cliffside path until I crested the last turn. Halberd strode out between the two broken halves of what had once been a charcoal grey arch carved with intricate weaving strands. It gaped like a mouth, cloven as if a great axe had been slammed into it right at the peak and then pulled out again, leaving a deep wedge of stone missing on one side and a torn upright on the other complete with grooves as deep as my fist.

Even if it had not felt like I was being swallowed by a beast, I would not have liked riding under such a cursed sign as a broken arch. With no other way in or out, I had no choice and I was forced to bend double over my horse and ride through. For a moment, I thought I smelled spices foreign to my senses, and I will not pretend that sat well with me. If there were ghost scents here, then what other scents might there be?

Brindle shot out before me with a concerning suddenness. My heart was in my throat as I called him back with a stern command.

"Brindle!"

An icy hand gripped me. What if he fell into a hole or over the side of an embankment? Or worse — what if the demon took him over here and I had to give chase, only to become lost in the ruins?

But it wasn't the demon. Brindle pranced back to me, tongue lolling, doggy jubilance in every step. I drooped with relief and a flicker of a smile was already teasing around the corners of my lips before I realized we were not alone.

We'd burst into a courtyard grown over with sopping moss and twisted umber vines. A tall female statue remained intact to one side of it, posed for grace and beauty and carved of white granite. If she represented what other beauties and wealth could be found here, then it was considerable.

The courtyard was large enough for twenty knights on parade, but where once there might have been balustrades and terraces, now there were tumbled rocks and broken statuary and a lone door stood, closed and locked and still set in its doorposts even though it was surrounded by no walls at all.

I pulled Halberd up hard, breath sawing in my lungs.

Someone had lit a sulky fire opposite me. Crouched on either side of it were a pair of elderly paladins wearing amused expressions.

One paladin had silvery hair that met his pauldrons and the other wore tight pewter curls all over his head. They had the overly large noses and ears of old men, and sported hair growing out of both. Together, they seemed to be brewing a pot of tea.

But it was not these two barrel-shaped men who caught me off guard, frozen though they were in apparent amused horror at my arrival. It was the two hulking forms behind them that hooked the words of greeting in my throat before they could slip out.

Red-eyed and frozen in place — though frozen seemed the wrong word to use in a place where actual living ice had just receded; let us say preternaturally still — were a pair of hulking golems standing just behind the elderly paladins as if they were shadows cast tall and wide by the teasing flames of the tiny fire.

One of the paladins reached slowly up and, with a sound like the snicking of a well-oiled catch, the matching golem reached down, and placed a needle — no, wait, a long sword — into the hand of the paladin.

The foursome blinked at me.

I blinked back.

At my feet, Brindle yapped a single, excited bark, and then paced back and forth in front of Halberd, restrained from his clear joy only by my command.

"There's only ever one in a murder," the paladin at the fire said in the kind of voice that does not know how to be quiet. His confidence was only eclipsed by his sheer volume. "I did warn you of that."

Sometimes there are two. Or even twenty, my demon reminded me in blood-soaked thoughts. *Or even a thousand. At least when I'm doing the murdering.*

He means "murder" in the way you refer to a group of crows, Sir Branson corrected him. *A cruel nickname for Vagabond Paladins is "crow."*

Doesn't seem very cruel to call someone a crow. Crows are smart. And they always eat.

"So you did, indeed," the other paladin said cheerfully. "Brew the tea, would you? We'll need one more cup. Did any of you bring extras?"

If Sir Branson still lived, he'd scold me for missing the others. I'd been so preoccupied that I hadn't seen a single one of them.

You'd be dead by now if they were enemies and I wouldn't need to scold you at all. Watch those Engineers. Something about them makes me feel itchy all over.

Was it that they were offering me tea? Yes, kindness truly was suspicious.

No, that's not it...

Quickly, before my embarrassment was complete, I ripped my gaze from them to scan over the rest.

Ringing the courtyard were tents, and in front of the tents, forming a circle about as whole as the arch I'd just ridden through, were such a collection of paladins as I had never seen before. There were no two alike, from apparel to looks to demeanor. But they all shared one thing in common. They were staring at me aghast.

They've been here, what? Three days at the most? And we know two of them arrived just before you. Which means they're waiting for something. Try to see if it's you, little delicacy.

One of the paladins cleared his throat and I turned to him, tilting my head to one side as if in question.

He was dressed entirely in black, a cup traced on his tabard in careful stitching. His eyes were narrow and dark as shadows, not helped by the deep circles under them that made him look twice his real age, which couldn't be more than ten years my senior. His hair was precisely cut and his face nearly clean-shaven, as if he attended daily to it. He was extremely clean for someone so far from civilization and his pale skin had a greenish cast to it. There were fine lines around his eyes that I was willing to bet most people missed.

I couldn't have said why, but there was something behind his eyes that arrested my attention. Something like meeting an old friend again. I found in his gaze the precise feeling in my heart that I might feel if Sir Branson were standing in that armor looking back at me.

Well that's certainly not me. I was never that trim. Even in my thin days. Even in my youth. And I don't like the way he straightened when he saw you. He should either stand straight all the time or have the confidence to keep slouching.

Sir Branson sounded testy.

Wary. Not testy. I don't like the way he looks at you like he thinks he could possibly own you, given the chance.

I knew without an introduction that this man was a paladin of the Aspect of the Sorrowful God, forsworn to affection, a drinker of pain. They called these ones Poisoned Saints — and this particular Saint looked as though he'd been poisoning himself all morning precisely so he wouldn't have to credential himself now.

Maybe he has *been drinking poison. I knew a bishop who did that once. Said a tiny bit safeguarded him from succumbing to larger doses.*

Did it work?

He should have tried drinking souls instead if he was trying to inure himself to the coming grief. He had fifteen demons in his mortal coil when I found him. I extracted three readily, but by the fourth he was clawing his own tongue out and by the sixth, I could not continue to torture the man. I gave him the gift of a clean death. That was long ago, of course.

You could have just left him with the demons. I'm sure he was happy with them.

Their crosstalk was making me feel nauseated.

"Are you ill, Lady Paladin?" the Poisoned Saint asked quietly. His voice was surprisingly musical for a man who looked like he was in the grip of fever, and his eyes — too bright, too dreamy — met mine with something that seemed to be concern.

A thrill of something that bit like fear but held an almost pleasant burning aftertaste shot right through me from sternum to toe.

It's called attraction, girl. Have you felt it so rarely that it surprises you? I could suggest a few things to you in the depths of the night. There's more than one way to feast.

I'd really rather the demon did not.

"I am well," I answered curtly. Remember? Insane, not pitiful. Fearsome, not — definitely not — attracted. "Am I the last to arrive?"

"Do you have the amulet?" the loud paladin at the fire asked me.

I fished it out from inside the cowl of my tunic and when it caught the light, a collective sigh swept over those assembled.

The loud paladin smiled.

"And so we begin."

Chapter Six
Poisoned Saint

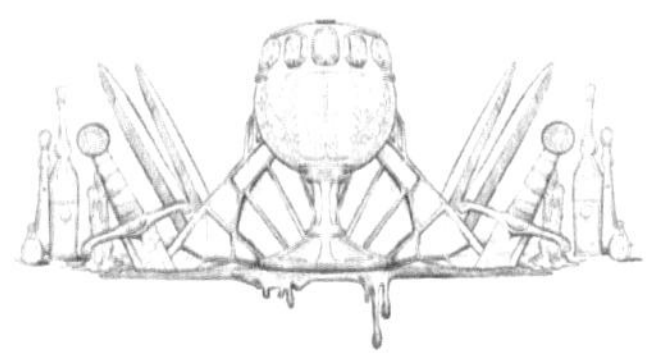

As a Poisoned Saint, I'm used to being noticed. But it is not really me that people see when they look at me. Rather, I am like the moth whose true eyes are hidden while the false eyes on his wings draw attention. People see the cup on my tabard and their faces grow grim. They see my trembling hands and pale face and their expressions cloud with sympathy or calloused hardness. I am not the pain I drink for others, but I can never convince them of that. To them, the man is the role.

Oddly, Hefertus has never been affected by that. He ignores my pain like he ignores the cold, the wet ground, and the snow. He does not acknowledge it and thus, somehow, it has no power over him.

We arrive at the Aching Monastery in his usual flurry of good humor and delight for adventure and I must admit that I feel the same even though the lingering effects of the plague I took still ravage me. Through bouts of crippling cramps and bloody spew, I feel the roar of the unknown in my ears, lifting me up and brightening my eyes. This landscape, harsh and unforgiving, is enchanting. In a world where all feels known, this slice of it is brand new. And achingly ancient. And seductive as a warm fire on a cold night.

"Don't know how you do it," Hefertus says at one point as he peers up at a circling bird. "Doesn't seem worth the trouble."

"I take their pain and ills," I say lightly. I'm no crusader. I don't need to be understood or to see others conform to my path. "Is that not enough?"

Hefertus laughs. "No, Saints and Angels, it is not. I think you've made a raw deal."

There's no rancor in my response. "I was called by the God, just like you were called. He calls the poisoned as well as he calls princes."

"Doesn't he just? And I thank him every day for calling me to Princehood." Hefertus picks his teeth irreverently as he studies the ruins above us. "A dread place, is it, this Aching Monastery?"

The Prince Paladins — as his aspect is affectionately monikered — disregard learning. He has never poured over old tomes in study or been made to memorize events from thousands of years before. When I was reciting the kings of the nations and their antecedents going back ten generations, he was being taught to tell good from bad wine and rubies from colored glass. I find this charming in the way that you can't help but smile at a spoiled but adorable child.

"Not at all," I reply, intrigued by the structure ahead of us. It's a shame that it is so crumbled by time. I read that in the past, the soaring architecture drew people from other realms to simply marvel at the lines and curves that seemed beyond the ability of man to have created. I would have liked to see that. "The Aching Monastery is mentioned often and with reverence. The priest who lectured on it when I was a squire was certain that a path to Sainthood lay here."

"I thought you lot were the ones called Saints," Hefertus says, taking a moment to braid the nearest part of his horse's mane.

He looks exactly like a prince when he does this, but there's something haunted in his eyes. It makes me feel a little ill, and I wonder if that's simply emotion or if I'm accidentally taking his pain from him. I do that sometimes and entirely by accident.

Prince Paladins do not age. There is no magic to it, nor does the power of the God preserve them more than other men. It's simple enough. They trade sense for miracles. And eventually, they lose their minds and become children trapped in the bodies of men, or they die by their own foolishness. I do not relish the thought of my lighthearted friend losing himself before his golden hair turns silver. I have grown fond of Hefertus and his innocent view of the world.

"They also call you a prince, and yet here you are riding with me," I reply and I think he might answer, but he sees a coney in a tuft of grass, and quick as gasping he has a sling out, places a deadly shot, and is all joy when — a moment later — he can present to me the fresh meat that can be our lunch.

I'm not sure I want to eat meat taken here. I can feel this place in my bones. The graveyard we passed through to get here will need a dozen of my brethren to walk the fields and soak the land in prayers and tears to clear it of the haunting feeling it gives off. It makes my skin itch on the inside.

"This place is a trap, then," Hefertus says firmly. "A trap for the godly who want to be more."

I grunt. I doubt this is a trap. But everything is an epic tale of deeds most valiant to Hefertus. Sometimes I see a look of longing mixed with ethereal joy on his face as he tells a tale of his doings and I know that in his mind he is a great hero sweeping across the landscape of this life. I am not quite so enamored by myself as to see the same.

Besides, if they call us Saints affectionately when we eat and drink suffering, what kind of tasks would a true Saint face? I am not sure I would want to know. My work seems enough of a calling for one man as it is.

We pick our way up through mist pale and whimsical as a bridal veil around jagged rocks like the ridges of a dead dragon's spine. Something in the stones stings me inside, like biting into an arrowhead chip while eating your evening meat. But it is sweet to the taste despite the pain. Sweet and beguiling.

"Kind of pulls you in," Hefertus admits as he leads me forward, tossing his wave of blond hair back over his shoulder. He is wearing two strings of pearls around his throat today — one pale as milky blind eyes and the other pink as the blush of a maiden. He fiddles with them constantly. Perhaps they are a charm he's made against an unknown foe. If so, I wish he'd give one to me.

I grunt again, but I am watching everything. I don't know what it is I'm feeling, only that it's familiar and yet foreign, far, far too powerful, and it's everywhere.

"Think the others will be there yet?" Hefertus asks when we finally get close enough that the road begins to swoop upward. "Pretty important task, looking for the Cup of Tears. We all need to be there before the search begins."

"Do we?" I ask.

I'm not certain of that. The Poisoned Saints don't jockey for position the way some of the other aspects do. No one wants to take our place. I could see other aspects wanting to make use of this kind of advantage, though. Some of them play politics in the same way that they eat bread.

"Of course. Can't have that kind of power going to just one aspect. It needs to be shared," Hefertus says. "Have you seen what the High Saints are doing in Estavia?"

I have not, but to my surprise, Hefertus *has* noticed and is able to give me a brief primer on the shifting politics of the region. I watch him as I chew a mint leaf.

My friend always surprises me. Who would have thought he knew which kings the church had pulled into power and which they'd subtly chopped at the roots and why? But as he speaks, it becomes clear that he knows better than I do what is happening.

"I'm surprised you don't know this," Hefertus says as we finally crest the peak of the hill, passing between the stones of a crumbled, broken arch. I make the sign of the Aspect of the Sorrowful God as if to ward off the curse of it. An arch is made with wholeness in mind and a crumbled arch is a terrible omen. "Your lot was there to clean up afterward, I thought."

"We don't clean up political messes," I say absently. "Unless there was a battle."

"Oh, there was. Killed a dozen men there myself. Nasty business. The king there had a predilection that shouldn't be named. We smoked him and his men out like skunks under a foundation. Didn't realize they had innocents with them. I've said a hundred prayers for the poor souls, and it still feels like not enough."

I shiver at his confession. Subtly. No need to offend. But the sidelong glance I send my friend is instinctual and I can't quite help that.

He's surprised me again. He has a tendency to do that. Never think a book is finished being written while the pages are still turning.

Even if the story appears a simple one.

"Going back to the point, the Cup would help nail that situation down. Subtle reminder not to mess with the decisions of the church. And especially the Benevolent Aspect."

He levels his gaze at me then, and I'm suddenly reminded that he's a head taller than me, his reach is at least ten inches longer, and he's double my bulk in muscle. I'd need to be fast as an eagle choking a snake to get the better of him if he drew on me. I could possibly manage to kill him, but I would certainly lose my horse in the process. I like this horse.

There's steel in his voice when he says, "We don't expect difficulties from the Poisoned Saints."

I huff a laugh, watching him, picking my words carefully.

"I think we should stay friends, Hefertus. Why break up a good thing? Especially when we don't know the others."

He claps me on the shoulder and grins. "Exactly my thoughts. And that's what I told my arch-general when he sent me out. 'Tell those dark mourners to send Adalbrand with me,' I said. 'He'll know how the tide shifts,' I said."

"Mmm." I don't commit either way. He's not wrong that we

of the Sorrowful Aspect rarely involve ourselves in politics. But he's been a fool to show his hand this clearly.

I pause.

Or maybe not.

Maybe he's clever enough to know that I'm more likely to back a play I understand than to put my trust in good faith. Maybe he's betting on me to not only walk away from glory myself but also to take it from others so he might possess it.

In our calling as Poisoned Saints, the motives of man are important. They shade everything. And on this particular quest, the motivations of man could mean life or death. I would prefer that we all walk away alive. There's no need to shed blood here.

I say that part out loud and he laughs.

"Indeed. Glad to have you at my back, Poisoned Saint."

"Mmm." If I must ride into danger with Hefertus, then I'd rather be at his back, too. Far better than being in front of his blade.

We turn a last corner and there they are — the rest of the valor of the nine kingdoms, banners flapping, tents set, fire smoking damply. The wood must still be wet.

I count them. Eight others. I have not met any of them before.

There are no servants, squires, pages, clerks, or retainers. Only the paladins themselves. That alone is shocking in a world where most paladins have retinues of dozens.

I look the others over. I don't have a sixth sense — though some attribute that to us. What I do have is a lifetime of dealing with people's hurts. I catalog everyone through that prism.

I see the Seer first and I immediately shutter my expression. Her senses are nearly entirely gone. She cannot see any longer — her eyes are a dreadful grub-white. She holds her head in a way that tells me she is struggling to hear. Her fingers fumble senselessly over her wooden cup. Hers are infirmities I cannot take. A gift to the God that her aspect requires. I neither understand it nor like it, but it isn't my place to speak on what obeisances another aspect performs, or how the God calls them.

I don't look at her for long. I do not enjoy watching the misery of others. Usually, I have the right to draw it out from them. It feels like spittle on my cheek that I cannot take hers.

She's the only female paladin sent so far. The others are men. And we are missing one. Ten aspects. Ten paladins required. There are ten here, but two are Holy Engineers. I can see the aches in their elderly joints by how they hold their bodies brittlely.

Don't misunderstand. They can still fight. Even against a trained soldier in his youth, they'll likely win, just as the Seer would, even though she can hardly hold her sword. We are paladins. We may age. We may molder. We never fail.

The others are more what one would expect as representatives of their aspects.

The High Saint of the Aspect of the Sovereign God hurries to greet us with a blessing. He's healthy and bright-eyed, his hair perfectly trimmed, face perfectly shaven. He's so homely he could be a priest, but I know plenty of simple-looking men who are masters of blade and war. His perfectly oiled and polished kit doesn't impress me, but it does speak to a mind ordered and disciplined. He bears no signs of pain or illness. A blank slate ready to be drawn upon.

"The Aspect of the Sorrowful God and the Aspect of the Benevolent God," he says, pleased. The High Saints rarely use our slang names for one another. They find it beneath them. Crass.

Personally, I don't like High Saints. I find their rigidity frustrating and their careful observance a bit convicting. After all, were I a better paladin, my observance would be more like theirs, wouldn't it? But it is not, nor will it be. And I am guilty of so much more than a few missed prayers or broken creeds.

"We welcome you here," he says, spine straight, looking down his long nose at us. He has no chin, but the collar over his chestpiece digs into the flesh in a way that constructs one for him. It must be terribly uncomfortable.

"There doesn't seem to be much of this Aching Monastery

left," Hefertus says, looking around while I make the holy sign of greeting to the High Saint and then peer past him at the others.

There's a Holy Inquisitor who has resumed training exercises. His long hair is stark white and the front is tied back in a silver clasp. He works his sword forms with speed and accuracy, careful to keep his blade facing the west, as is fitting. He's narrow as a whip and his muscles are long and lean. This exercise is designed to make him fast and accurate — but not bulky, never bulky, for physical strength is forbidden to the Aspect of the All-Seeing God. I watch him for a moment. He has an injury somewhere in his ribs — a strain, I think. Old and recurring. I could help him with it if he wants that. He may not. Not everyone wants help.

I know Kodelai Lei Shan Tora by reputation. He's the Hand of Justice here. I recognize him at once by the red horsetail in his helm. Not many Hands of Justice wear ornamentation, and everyone has heard of Kodelai. He's a legend. Called out of a kingship, called from majesty to service, strong as an ox and twice as charming as he ought to be, there are stories of him in every town and city. Hands of Justice are not called before they are at least forty and he's closer to the end of his fifties, I would think. I heard he was challenged on a judgment just last year — challenged and won, obviously, since he's still alive. If I get the chance to ask him about it, I will. He has something wrong in his guts. Age, perhaps. It plays nasty tricks on everyone from peasant to king to ... ahem ... paladin.

"The monastery was always mostly underground," Sir Kodelai says easily. His voice is like gravel. "It's why everyone is so excited. Down there, most of it should be intact, though the outer facade fell into the sea."

He gestures around at the tumbled masonry and chunks of riven stone that had once been buttresses and beautifully worked doorways. They look now as if a giant child lost his temper and flung the last bits of it about.

There's a single statue left whole, a woman with an innocent expression still obvious on her white, marble face. I almost find it unsettling that she remains while the rest is devastated.

"And you haven't gone to look?" Hefertus asks. "Not even a single step?"

"Not one step until all are assembled," another voice orders. It's deep and thick. A voice for commanding others. That's a Majester General or I'm a stuffed owl. My lip curls before I can prevent it.

This one is arrayed like a general, sitting in a camp chair, and eating a roasted pheasant. He must have made it himself, as there are no servants here. Impressive. The best I can do over a fire is fresh fish.

He sees me looking. "Pheasant? Might make you less pale."

"I thank you," I say coldly. Nothing will make me less pale except time or the expulsion of the magic the pain is generating within me. "But none for me. Hefertus?"

My friend waves it away. "Who are we waiting for? Let's see." He points at us as he speaks — or rather, he points at the medallion each one wears. "Engineers, General, High Saint" — the Saint in question flinches — "Inquisitor." He gets a salute for that. "Seer, Hand, Penitent." He waves at the last fellow, a man cloaked head to foot in a cassock that disguises all but his beardless chin. He's kneeling on the rock in prayer. I can feel the ache in his knees from here but if you're going to pray like that, there's little I can do for you. The hunch in his shoulders is worse. He's disguising old pains and new. So many that I can almost feel the constant buzz of them. "Poisoned," Hefertus says, flicking a finger at me, "and Prince." He lays a hand across his chest. "Missing the Beggars, then?"

The High Saint clears his throat. "The Aspect of the Rejected God," he corrects, "has yet to send a representative."

"Well, beggars can't be choosers," Hefertus says lightly.

"Generals can," the Majester General says calmly. "And I say we wait."

At his words, I feel it again. That terrible draw to dive deeper into the ruins here. It pulls me almost like the call of the God. It pulls me so hard, in fact, that I lift my head and ask.

"Has Terce been said yet?"

"It has not," the High Saint says with grim enthusiasm. "We heard your hooves on the rocks and determined we would wait."

"Hooves," the Majester agrees through another mouthful. I'm certain he would gladly postpone prayers well past Vespers. Most of us are not so observant as the Aspect of the Sovereign God.

"Let us gather," the High Saint says, making chivvying motions with his hands.

Hefertus shoots an accusatory look at me, annoyed that I've stirred this up. He may be good-natured, but he's not as easily entertained as I am by the quirks of others.

"At least let us tend our horses first, brother," he says.

The others give us brief directions and I follow him to where the horses are tethered a little ways from the camp.

Which is where we find the golems.

There are two of them. I am well acquainted with the shambling creatures that the Holy Engineers pour the gift of the God's own life into. In cities across the earth, they are commonplace enough, but somehow out here on the very edge of man, these seem more than unnatural. They seem as though they loom.

"Oh, don't mind Cleft and Suture," the less ugly Engineer says, hopping up from behind us as quickly as a man can when one of his knees is no longer functioning well. His longish white curls tumble in the breeze as he hops and skips to join us. The top of his head is bald, but he's making up for it with the bottom. He bears a friendly grin.

I am not feeling quite as friendly.

I disapprove of golems on principle. I do not think the God ought to let men breathe life into stone. Especially not when they are then allowed to command that stone to fetch and carry and do it all mutely. It feels too close to slavery to me.

The church allows the kings of the east to keep slaves. I find the practice appalling.

"What does it matter," they say. "We are all slaves of one thing or another. Slaves of the God, slaves of our appetites, slaves of our circumstances. Who is to say it is worse to be slave to our betters?"

"Who is to say who the betters are?" I'd countered, and been cuffed across the face for it. Not by my paladin superior. He was not given to violence, but he turned his head when a Majester General cuffed me and he offered no healing for the wound.

I still feel my lip curl a little whenever I see one of those red-tabarded devils.

Which brings us back to golems. They have no mouths. No way to protest how they are treated. They have glowing bright eyes, as if demons reside within them churning out the fires of hell in inner furnaces. If looks could kill, they would level cities. But their bodies are massive and crudely formed. They're made of metal and rock and bone — whatever the engineer fancied.

These two are very different from one another. One is entirely constructed of animal bones — Saints and Angels, I hope they are animal — and its joints are made of ball-and-sockets formed of metal and screwed into the bone. Someone has whimsically laced ragged strips of cloth between the bones of the rib cage to offer a bit more of a feeling of a body. I can only hope it was an Engineer who did it and not the poor creature itself.

"Wonderful construct, my Suture!" the Engineer says, gesturing at the poor devil. "So much better than a horse. No need to feed it, no end to how far he'll go, and three times as strong as your strongest draft horse."

It's not shaped like a horse. It's shaped like a man. I think that if I watch it being ridden, I might be ill.

"Cleft is twice as strong because I wasn't the bloody daft fool who chose bone," the other Engineer announces, striding over to us to lay a meaty palm on the haunch of the second golem.

I channel my rage into efficiently removing tack from my stallion and tethering him where the grass grows in wide tufts. The other paladins weren't fools. They found a place where runoff is draining down in a steady, if thin, stream and they've tethered the horses there. If, for whatever reason, we are delayed in the ruins below, our horses will have water and food close by. I appreciate the common sense in that.

"Cleft is made of rock," the first Engineer objects. "He's too heavy to be efficient. You lose adaptability with that weight and it causes more wear and tear. That's why you have to bring all those extra ball joints with you. You don't see me hauling around spare ball joints, now do you?"

"Cleft" is indeed made of stone. Someone has carved a grim face and suspicious eyebrows around his glowing eyes. He looks an awful lot like the High Saint.

So much so that I ask, "When did you carve the face?"

The second Engineer smiles. "I put the finishing touches on it this morning."

His gaze meets mine. He knows I know. I know he knows.

"Do you like it?"

"It's a strong look," I say. Not an answer. He wouldn't like the answer I have to give.

I am still on the fence about whether such golems experience sorrow or pain. If they do, I have an obligation to relieve it. If they do not, it's possible that a Vagabond Paladin has the obligation to end them, as they must then be demonic apparati.

"Don't keep them next to the horses," Hefertus orders. "They'll spook, and then it will be up to you to round them up."

I expect the Engineers to object. Paladins are, by nature, bull-headed. We are used to ordering ourselves, to making judgments in the field. To leading forces. We don't take kindly to being ordered by others. But these two don't object; they merely smile, make chirping sounds to their golems, and then amble back toward camp, their golems shambling behind them.

Hefertus leans in close. "I don't like this place and I don't like the company."

I tilt my head in question. I have been acquainted with Hefertus for most of my adult life. He is not naturally a suspicious man. Rather, I've found him too open and affable. Seeing this dark cloud settling over him leaves me edgy.

"We can't all look amazing in pearls," I say, trying to turn the barb.

It doesn't work. He grimaces and heads for camp, packs on his back, still clearly troubled, his fingers spinning down and around his double pearl string as if he is counting out rosary beads.

Perhaps he is. Perhaps this is some new, decadent Prince Paladin rosary.

"You'll camp with me," he says over his shoulder when we're almost back. "Won't hear of anything else."

Ah. He does not fully trust me. But he trusts me not to kill him in the night. And he does not trust the rest of them even that much. How very interesting.

By the time we've finished setting up Hefertus's tent, the High Saint is practically jumping from foot to foot.

"Please, we must observe Terce, brothers."

The Engineers are making tea and refuse to be budged. They seem put out that their golems are here with them instead of with the horses.

"Just start the prayer and we'll join in for the important bits," Sir Sorken, the uglier Engineer, says.

We form a ragged circle and begin the prayer.

"We confess our deepest weaknesses, we bring them to your door," the High Saint begins. "Let the Lord of Order set them right and make them be no —"

But his words are interrupted by the sound of hooves on stone and then a distinct barking sound.

Our last paladin has arrived.

Chapter Seven
Poisoned Saint

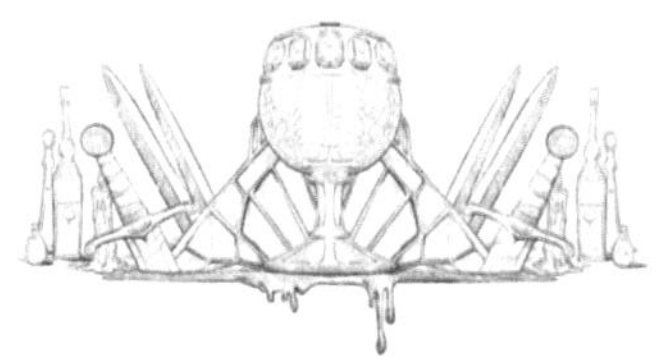

My breath catches at my first glimpse of our last compatriot. She rides in through the arch on the back of a dark bay, a brindled dog swirling around the bay's hooves, but I care not for either animal. All I see is the paladin.

She looks exactly like Marigold.

Well, she looks exactly like Marigold would look, if she were eight years older than when last I saw her, streaked in clay, and suffering from multiple injuries, some of which are infected. And if she wore rags, dented armor, and the worst excuse for a bear cloak I've ever seen.

I'm so stunned that I miss the greeting the Engineers give her, miss the furious silence of the High Saint who has been interrupted in his prayer, miss whatever they are saying about amulets.

It is as if my past has returned and placed a brand upon my heart. I am betrayed by surprise. It leaves a sore patch under my breastbone and a smarting in my eyes.

Lord of Sorrows, please take mine, I pray, as I have prayed a thousand times before, and unlike the rote prayers the others are so fond of, this one is only for me. It has been mine since I laid her body in the cold earth. Mine for so long that it is now a part of me.

I feel the prayer catching in my throat. Barbed in my unshed tears. I fight to release it — and with it, the breath I dare not hold much longer, lest I draw attention to myself. Some hurts are better kept to one's own soul.

The Vagabond Paladin — for that is what she undoubtedly is, in that cobbled-together armor — studies us with the kind of hardness that is all for show.

Hefertus shifts uncomfortably. I believe he thinks she is mad. I glance at the naked disgust and horror in the faces of the others. They feel the same way.

I don't share their reactions. I see through her daring ruse.

She has smeared mud across her chin and through her hair for this exact purpose. In the dried clay, I see the calculation of a razor-sharp mind. In the bold way she sits her horse, I see unrelenting courage. I see the eyes of Marigold when she pled with me to make it stop. I see my own empty hands, hands with no relief to offer.

With effort, I shake off the memories. They will claw at me again later. No need to indulge them now.

"Are you ill, Lady Paladin?" I ask her. I will heal her if she lets me.

But she lies to me, her voice as cold as the body of my former love. "I am well."

Am I the only one who hears the lie in her voice? Who sees the posturing beneath the front? Or am I the only one who cares?

I send a brief look to my brother and sister paladins. Perhaps the Seer knows. If she does, then she is not saying. The rest seem perplexed by this brash young paladin.

"Do you have the amulet?" Sir Sorken asks her as the dog trots over to Hefertus and snuffles his hand.

Hefertus mindlessly scratches him behind the ears, but when I make to do the same, the dog whines and shies away from me. I feel the frown tightening my face. I can't help it. Animals usually like me. They relax into my hands as I tease out their pains and aches. This one cannot seem to get away from me fast enough. His claws rattle against the bare stone.

I'm troubled by that. Not as troubled as I am by the Aspect of the Rejected God's paladin, but still troubled.

Why would the Rejected God send such a very young paladin? This one barely seems to be past squirehood. And this quest will require careful negotiation if the Cup is found. We will need to find a truce between ten different aspects — and one without bloodshed.

Perhaps the Rejected God does not see any chance that their aspect will succeed at this and could not spare a more experienced knight. Or perhaps he plays another game and the way she throws us onto the back foot is intentional.

Rejected Paladins are devilishly difficult to sort at the best of times, but they always surprise us. Sometimes it seems their renunciation of wealth is a renunciation of society as a whole. Sometimes they almost seem insolent in their rejection.

Each aspect that calls paladins works in a similar fashion. We embrace one aspect of the God and when we lean into that, he blesses us with power. But to access that power, we must forswear something, and if we slip, if we fall into what we abhor, then the blessing is gone, and with it, the power.

For instance, if this young paladin were to accept one of Hefertus's strings of pearls, having forsworn wealth as a Vagabond Paladin, she would lose her unique power — the ability to call on the God for help with open hands, just as she faces life with open hands ready to accept gifts, or accept their loss. Hers is a strange type of power. A power that renounces control.

That she comes to us wounded, swaying on her feet and streaked in blood, barely garners a second look from the rest of them. They expect her hollow poverty as they expect Hefertus's pearls and flowing locks. We are a collection of types and we fit them so strongly that you could set us in stained glass and use us to decorate a church and no one would blink.

"Here," they would say, "is the green-faced Poisoned Saint holding the cup with which he swallows our sorrows; here is the Prince Paladin, two fingers held up with the blessing he will speak over us; and here is the Beggar Knight, ragged and bloody, ready to take our evil and flee into the night with it."

The others do not give her a second look because she is exactly what they expect, thrust-out jaw and challenging stare included. After a first disgusted look, they hardly even care about the clay smeared in her hair. She was a missing puzzle piece. Now she is found. That is all that matters.

I do not feel the same way.

I sneak another look at her face and hope that no one notices me doing it. I don't want anyone getting ideas about why my interest tarries here. I'm tangled up with myriad thoughts and feelings slithering like a clump of snakes in the jar of my mind.

Part of me is upset about her obvious injuries. No mortal should contend with such pain. When she dismounts, she is favoring one side and one of her arms hangs lower than the other. The clay she has smeared over herself might distract the casual watcher, but my eyes see to the pain. Perhaps she has a broken or twisted rib. There's definitely infection in those gashes. Whoever bound them was either hurried or incompetent.

That would be enough to bother me, but the dog makes it worse. There's something wrong with the creature. When I look at it, it is well, and happy, and currently demanding affection from the blind Seer. She is trying to hide her shy smile at the attention, and that is all well and good, but the dog is a demon in canine form if I've ever seen one. It gives me a baleful glare and I return the sentiment. What manner of paladin rides with such a dog?

My heart is racing as it always does when I sense something that does not fit. There is something wrong about this Vagabond. Something on which I cannot place my gauntleted finger. Her beauty makes it worse. It stands in a rude contrast to her ragged filth.

My feelings of deep sorrow and tangled guilt at memories of Marigold muddy the waters further. Can I even trust my own observations when such a veil lies over them?

And under it all is something far more dangerous. Something I have not felt in a long time. Were I Hefertus, it would hardly signify. But I am a paladin of the Sorrowful God, called to heal others ... and called to celibacy. I should not feel the stirrings that I do.

"We'll go through the door tomorrow," the Majester General is saying, and I gather that he's been talking for a few minutes. "It's too late in the day to enter now. We'll camp for the night, have a friendly bout of swordplay to stretch the limbs and take one another's measure, and then tomorrow we go in together. No need to all spread out and get into trouble on our own."

"I am not here for games," the Beggar Knight says, and I think she'd say more but the High Saint interrupts her.

"You've ridden in while we were saying Terce. I'd like to finish."

She nods and bows as if to join him in prayer, but he's shaking his head. "We can't say prayers with your horse as part of the assembly."

"I'll guide her to the pickets." The words are out of my mouth before I realize I'm the one speaking. This is close enough to sin that I shuffle my feet and a bead of sweat forms along my hairline, but I am the only Poisoned Saint here, and the others do not notice.

"Very good. We will say the prayer without you, and you will join us in your hearts," the High Saint orders. Clearly, he is loath to wait even one more second.

It takes a solid effort not to smirk. I've always found pomp hilarious and the nerves I'm feeling at my slip are clawing down my tight control. I mask the rising smirk by making the holy sign, bent knuckle to forehead, heart, and sword arm.

"If you'll come with me, Lady," I murmur.

"Victoriana," she corrects me.

"Lady Paladin," I acknowledge, still refusing her name.

Hefertus's snort is very quiet, but not quiet enough to be spared by the High Saint, who shoots him a venomous look as he begins the chant of the second prayer. Hefertus joins him loudly in his clear baritone, a look of cherubic innocence on his face.

I lead Victoriana to the pickets. Her name is quite a mouthful and it doesn't suit the mud-streaked specter following me.

The dog comes with her. I could have done without his company. He springs forward to lope ahead of us. I keep one eye on him because I swear he looks as if he'd tear my throat out if he could. Quite the pair. Beauty and the Beast; Rose and Thorn.

"I think this is the only fresh water source," I tell her as we reach the pickets, grasping desperately for a safe source of conversation. "If you've a flask or skin to fill, now is the time."

She pauses, staring at me as if she wants to say something. I wait patiently for her words, but my eyes are busy. She looks very vulnerable under that thick clay. I can feel it almost as easily as I can feel the heat of the infection beginning in her wounds.

"Clay is not a good choice for infected wounds."

I shouldn't have spoken first, but the words rip out of me unbidden. Something inside me wants to protect her — and kill her dog — in equal measure. I shudder at that random thought.

Kill her dog? What a terrible impulse. What could have made me think that?

I force myself to look away and to turn to an old pillar, where the other paladins affixed the picket line. I run my hands over the worn carvings to where it is abruptly broken off. The head of the pillar lies a few feet away, coated in thick orange lichen.

She's replying to me. "I had little choice. My superiors bid me ride without pause or succor."

That brings my eyes up. She arrived here last. And has ridden without pause. I suppose I should not be surprised that an order known as "Beggar Knights" is stretched so thin, but still, I am.

"You're pausing now. Let me look at those wounds."

I shouldn't press her, but it's a matter of professional

integrity. How can I let another human walk around ailing when I have the ability to heal them?

Or at least, that's what I tell myself. In truth, I am as drawn to this woman as I am drawn to these ruins — illogically, instinctually, in a way I cannot properly describe.

Perhaps I should beg the Seer to pray for me that the God will tell her what my future holds. Stirring up such deep waters in me can only lead to tumult — as it did once before.

"No," she says, meeting my eyes defiantly. "I will bathe them here. I do not require the riches of your gift."

"Are you forsworn to healing then, too?" I press.

I don't know why I'm pushing her like this. Were she Sir Sorken or the High Saint, I'd gladly let the matter drop.

Annoyed, I fiddle with the pillar. Whatever was carved so thickly into the rock before is now worn down to only faint relief. The top portion narrows to a point and lichen grows in the grooves between the letters.

I frown. It looks very much like Ancient Indul, but that makes no sense. This monastery must be far more ancient than the Indul language.

"I'm not forsworn to healing. I just don't want it from you."

There's probably some deeper meaning to how she has emphasized "you" but I'm not paying attention anymore. I am tracing the lettering with my finger.

What's this one? The "au" sound? I think so. But it's been a very long time since I read Ancient Indul. I could use a priest right now. A scribing priest by preference. While we paladins are well educated in the holy scrolls, we also have to reach physical attainments for battle and war, and that prevents scholarly specialization.

A casual observer could be forgiven for thinking there is no war when the church rules all the world and installs and pulls down her kings. They'd be wrong. Wars abound as priest fights priest and paladin fights paladin. It's enough to make the heart weep.

I trace the letters and try to make the sounds in my mind. Pinnacle. Or mountain. Or rock? That's this first one. I think I was right guessing pinnacle.

"Are you listening to me, Poisoned Saint?" Her voice is faint in the background, but I'm trying to concentrate and she doesn't need me.

I hear her huff something and it almost sounds like a curse.

I turn back to the script. Pinnacle of something. Pain, perhaps?

"Look, you were warned. I'm not going to wait out whatever this is."

Yes, pain. Or aching? Pinnacle of Aching ... I know this one. Souls. Pinnacle of Aching Souls.

I think this next part is a date. And now, in smaller lettering, a note of some kind.

Woe to you, supplicant. Five woes. For the attainment of ... something. I can't decipher it. With a curse, I turn away and my eyes fall on her.

Blood rushes to my cheeks so that they sting.

Oh. That's what she was trying to tell me. That she was going to bathe here. I feel my cheeks go hot. She isn't indecent, but still, I am seeing feminine skin, a thing I've been avoiding since I joined the Poisoned Saints fifteen years ago and gave my squire vows.

Her skin is ripped and rent with slices, as if she recently fought a sword battle. They are inexpertly stitched. She prods at one with a finger while standing in the creek in just a pair of leather trousers and a corset-type garment that keeps her decent while letting her inspect her wounds. Already, she has washed off enough clay that I see the woman that was hidden beneath the grime. She is young. Twenty, perhaps? Twenty-one? And her small mouth frowns over her wounds as her long hair hangs in a sheet down her back, ready to be re-braided. She is both severe and terribly vulnerable.

My face is instantly hot. I go to great lengths to avoid situations such as this. Two weeks ago I waited a full six hours to refill my flasks because it was washing day for the nearby village and all the maidens would be ... well, just like this, I suppose. I'd spent the time healing an elderly man and then in prayer.

All of that effort, only to find myself here.

When she looks up and catches my gaze, I steel my jaw and gaze steadily back. I am annoyed that she's caught me failing, but I won't make it worse by pretending it's not happening.

"I tried to warn you," she says. "Celibate order, yes?"

"Yes," I grit out. "How long have you been a paladin?"

It's the first question that comes to mind. I ask because I don't want to talk about celibacy — or my very non-celibate thoughts — with a dripping woman standing in front of me. She is not a great beauty, but she is well-looking enough, and she radiates health and cleverness. Her sharp eyes seem to catch all the things I'm trying to keep wrapped inside.

"Ten days."

Her answer is like a wave crashing over me from a sudden swell of the sea. I am instantly sober again.

"Ten days? You must have been halfway here before you even said vows!"

I'm understandably shocked. This is not my aspect, but it offends the orderly paladin in me to see such haphazard planning.

"We were serving a remote village."

She prods again at an angry wound. Her stitches have popped along one side of it.

"Really, you should let me heal you." I feel physical discomfort watching her.

Her eyes shoot up and meet mine. "No."

I swallow down the annoyance I want to let loose. "Tell me, then, who is 'we'? I don't think you mean the dog."

She smirks as if I've told a joke. "Oh, he was there."

"And?"

"And what?" She says it so casually that I know she is dancing around something.

"And who else." I put steel in my words as I lean against the pillar I can't read.

Her dog trots out of the woods, turns its head to one side, and then barrels forward, stopping only when it is between her and me. The beginnings of a growl rumble deep within his throat.

"And a demon. He was troubling the village."

"Did he have someone in thrall who fought against you?" I ask, nodding at her wounds.

I don't expect an answer. I probably wouldn't give one, but she's young enough that she still thinks she has to answer when someone questions her.

"He did," she says gravely. There is a challenge in her eyes. "My paladin superior, Sir Branson."

"Blessed Saints." The curse tears from my throat like a growl.

I don't know what comes over me but I've left the pillar and I'm by her side in an instant, gripping her arm even as the dog snaps at my legs.

She orders it to stop. It's not listening to her, which makes sense, since it's not really her dog, right? It's her paladin superior's dog.

But I'm not looking at the dog, I'm looking all around us at the trees. God forfend she wasn't heard. We can only hope that Terce prayers have dragged on.

I saw a squire burned at the stake once for less than this. His screams were like tearing fabric. I thought my lungs would tear with him.

In a low voice, I tell her, "Whatever you do, do not confess this to the others."

"Confess what?" She lifts a brow in a challenge.

"That you have killed your paladin superior, taken up his mantle, his quest, and even his dog." My voice is growing rougher. I force out the words before it breaks. "That you're barely even out of squirehood and possibly not even called by the God."

She pales at my words. And then pain blossoms in my leg as her dog gives up on her and sinks his teeth into my thigh.

Chapter Eight
Vagabond Paladin

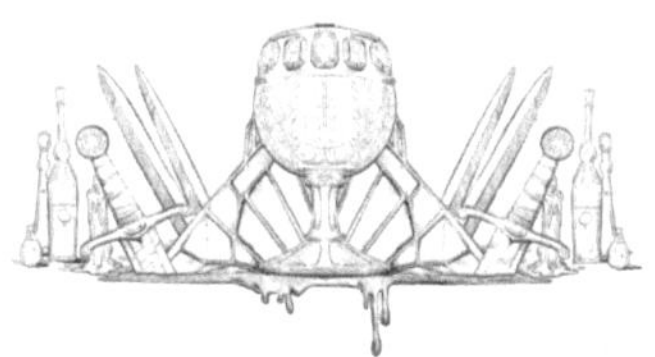

"Let him go!" I gasped, grabbing for Brindle's scruff and trying to rip him off of his victim.

The Poisoned Saint grunted, his breath coming in sharp gasps as one hand found the dog's head and the other fumbled at his belt. His eyes were wide and shocked.

God, if you have mercy, please keep my thoughts clouded from him. God, if you have mercy, please don't let my dog kill him.

I clenched my jaw. I had just ordered them to let him go and they'd vowed to obey me.

Surely you jest! The paladin knows what is happening here. We need to end him. Now. Go for his eyes! Go for his eyes!

He does not know, I assured him in my mind, hoping he could hear my thoughts. He only knows that I'm too young and that I killed Sir Branson. I can explain that to him. Unclamp your jaws!

My heart sped, making my fingers clumsy as they slid across Brindle's teeth and into his gums, trying to force his mouth open.

The paladin hissed, eyes clouding with pain. His hair fell in his face as he fought against Brindle, his brown eyes bright and wild. They caught mine for just a heartbeat and my breath caught, too. He was like an illumined page when he looked at me like that. All bright and glorious and noble. It stabbed at something deep in my chest that knew I was terribly unworthy of all of this.

Enough. There was no time right now for self-recriminations. I needed to get Brindle in hand. I gripped his neck skin harder, shaking it, hoping the doggy within the dog would listen.

"Brindle, please, please let go."

If the other paladins heard the girlish pleading in my voice, I'd lose any shred of respect I'd rode in with right there.

Brindle wasn't letting go.

"Saints and Angels!"

I cuffed him — hard in the skull. Wrong move. He didn't break his grip at all but a desperate gasping cry tore from the other paladin's lips. His face was paler. He gripped the pillar beside him with one hand, pressed his forehead into it, teeth clenched in a rictus of pain, his other hand prying at the dog's mouth right beside mine.

I turned to prayer. My last resort.

Merciful God in heaven, help me save this man!

I felt a whuff of something leave me. Was it only my breath? Only my breath, or a granting of the favor of the God?

I could not tell, but Brindle unclamped his jaw and the Poisoned Saint sagged in relief. I caught him as he stumbled, his face twisted in pain. It was more lined than before, which didn't detract from the thoughtful warmth of it. That warmth clashed badly with the purples and greens of his sickly coloring, but it was there, even as he huffed a laugh of disbelief.

"Brindle. Go stand by the horse," I barked, not bothering to disguise my fury.

He stared at me, licking blood from his teeth and then stretching with a baleful glare in his eye. Was it my imagination, or was one eye glowing red?

I thought Sir Branson said he could manage the demon. I thought the oath would bind him.

Hasn't anyone told you, little morsel? An oath is only as good as the one who swears it. Your knight tastes of plums and pain. You should take a taste of him yourself. Maybe you will, clinging to him as you do. I think I'll watch. How would that make you feel?

My cheeks felt hot and my head was swimming. I'd made a terrible mistake thinking that together Sir Branson and I could manage this demon.

You're right, you're right, you're right. Sir Branson sounded flustered. *I'll think of something.*

He'd always thought of something. When the road was cold with nowhere to sleep. When we ran out of bread and no one would offer a crust. When I got that infection in my leg and we couldn't find a healer ... he always thought of something.

And if I killed Brindle, he'd never think of something again. I'd lose him forever. I was starting to worry that I'd have to do it anyway.

Trouble yourself no more. The God will show us a way.

Brindle slunk over to the horses and plopped down at Halberd's feet with a stick in his bloody mouth. I let out a long, anxious exhale.

"Your dog bit me," the Poisoned Saint said at last, disbelieving.

I was still holding him up, I realized suddenly. It felt far too intimate for a man whose name I still did not know.

I ran my eyes up and down him quickly. The bite had pierced through leather breeches and torn a hole big enough that I could see the bruised and bloody mess and the gouges in his flesh. I grimaced and found his gaze.

His eyes really were warm. Even as he looked at me with distraught ... something ... they radiated an aghast humor. I couldn't read the "something" behind that. Sometimes it flashed like flickers of guilt in a tension around his eyes, but other times since I met him it was like the sting of cinnamon on the tongue. I had never encountered whatever that was before. I couldn't name it.

"Sir ... Sir, you have my humblest apologies," I gasped out. I held his tabard bunched in my fists as he grimaced and tried to put weight on his leg.

His face was very near mine, tight with pain, his lashes thick around his dark eyes, and I thought he had likely been pretty when he was younger, before wear and hardship sharpened his features.

"Adalbrand," he said tightly, his breath gusting out warm in the air between us as he huffed another laugh. "Sir Adalbrand."

"Is this truly funny, Sir Adalbrand?" I asked as he pulled away from me, swaying, letting out little hisses of pain from between his lips. He was about as heavy as I'd expected, given that he was a knight in half armor, but he was far leaner than Sir Branson had been.

Excuse you.

And his close proximity to me felt ... uncomfortable. But not entirely in a bad way.

I order you not to be attracted to this man. It will only embarrass us all.

You and the demon will be embarrassed? How terrible. I'm sure I'll do everything in my power to spare you.

Little morsel, tasty morsel.

Oh great. The other one was going to weigh in.

We read the inscription the sorrow-drinker was trying to parse out, tasty morsel. His Indul is rusty, I think. We can use what it said to secure a place here. If you want to do that instead of tasting sugared plums.

"There's something very wrong with your dog," the Poisoned Saint — Sir Adalbrand — choked out.

"I won't kill him," I said immediately, frowning. "He belonged to Sir Branson."

Sir Adalbrand held up his hands as if to ward off the thought. He was — I realized — treating me as if I were just as rabid as the dog might be. Just as likely to bite him. He couldn't seem to tear his eyes from my face, as if it would warn him before I leapt.

"I'm not asking you to kill the dog." He hesitated, like maybe he was asking that but wasn't sure if that was going too far. "But if you won't let me heal your injuries, then will you at least let me restitch your wounds and apply a poultice?"

My mouth fell open.

"I think maybe we should be worried about *your* injuries. The bite in particular."

"Oh, don't think for a moment that I can forget that." The look on his face was wry as he prodded at the area around his wound. "Saints and Angels. It hurts like a bear."

He gusted another laugh and I couldn't help that I warmed to that, could I? Something about humor in the face of tragedy had that effect on me.

Mmm, you never told me you could be lulled by honeyed words and dimples. I can make my words drip with sugar. They can go down sweet and sprout like mushrooms until their spores consume you whole. I can have dimples, too, if it helps.

The Poisoned Saint *did* have dimples. They were showing now as he twisted back and forth looking at his leg.

"You might want to inspect your dog's mouth. He seems to have dented some of the metal rings just here." He pointed to a leather strap that went around his thigh. A very nice thigh, even if it did have a chunk missing now. "The dog's mouth might be mangled."

I waved a hand, keeping my tone dry as the desert. "Never trouble yourself about him."

Excuse you.

I ignored whoever was offended.

Do you know what I read on that pillar, little luncheon?

I didn't know, and I didn't care. Was it not enough that he had bit a paladin?

Sir Adalbrand's mouth quirked in an ironic smile. "Then may I suggest that we both stitch and salve these wounds together? You'll owe me nothing. It will simply be the two of us being practical."

I paused. Because here's the thing about having nothing. You can never pay anyone back. The simple things they give away as if they are of little note, are treasures to you. What they take for granted, you are barred from. So, he might say that I wouldn't incur a debt by agreeing to take his help, but did he really mean it, or did he simply think I had something I could offer him later? I tried to be in no one's debt — for debts were not things I could pay. All they ever did was drive wedges between those who could have been friends.

"I'll owe you for the salve," I said carefully, trying to keep any eagerness out of my voice. A salve would be a wonderful thing. My wounds were not doing well. Even *I* knew that they were infected. "But I have a way to pay."

"Do you?" His smile deepened even though he still wasn't putting weight on his bitten leg as he limped over to the saddle-bags and rummaged around inside, his gaze shooting often to Brindle, who was playing innocent as he tore apart a stick and then shook it back and forth in mock play.

Adalbrand had a calm manner. I saw it in how the horses relaxed as he passed, as if he were a warm breeze blowing across their backs and taking with it the buzzing flies.

"I can tell you what is written on that pillar," I gambled.

The voice in my head cursed so loudly that it sent me rocking back on my heels.

And Sir Adalbrand's eyes shot up, his eyes narrowing as they settled on my face. "Can you, indeed?"

Well, now you've gone and done it, my girl. It's one thing to be a madwoman with a mad dog. It's another thing to admit you can read a dead language. There are maybe twenty scholars who can read that language. Most of them would need a reference to help with it.

The language couldn't be dead if he'd been studying it. It had looked like he'd been reading parts of it. He must have an idea of what it said. He'd just think I'd studied the same things.

Twenty. Scholars. Do you really think this paladin is one of them? Girl, I could barely tell the language was Indul. And I might not have mentioned it, but I was scholar-trained in my youth before I heard the Rejected God's call.

Branson was scholar-trained? He had certainly *not* mentioned it. He had ... not acted like it, either. I hadn't thought he'd cared about that kind of thing.

Well ... they're just so stuffy. Couldn't live like that. But here's the thing. The Poisoned Saints are amongst the most learned of all the Aspects of the God. No, scratch that. They are some of the most learned people under the sovereignty of the God.

Oops.

Yes, oops indeed. And now he will be wondering how you are performing this cute little trick. And what if he asks you to repeat it when the demon is not there?

I felt my cheeks heating, but Sir Adalbrand's eyes were still on me, clearly weighing me, even as he extracted a roll of bandage and a pot of salve from his bag.

Fine, Brindle said. *There's no getting out of it now. Might as well do this right. Tell him it's in Ancient Indul.*

I repeated his words.

"I worked that much out myself," the paladin said, watching me warily. "But my Ancient Indul is not up to standard. Not like yours, learned scholar."

His smile was teasing, but he sobered as he laid out the needles, thread, and salve across a cloth on a rock and began to shimmy out of his boots and trousers.

I looked away, face hot. I'd seen things in this service. The kinds of things I didn't like to talk about. Beggars frozen into snowbanks, the only difference between them and me a single blanket and the favor of the God. Women used terribly by men and barely saved by a whisper to us as we passed through a town. Children ... my brain stuttered over the children. It could not go there. Would not.

Through all that, what I hadn't seen much of was attractive men.

Look, I spent most of my time riding around with Sir Branson, righting small wrongs as often as possible, saying solemn prayers when he remembered them, and once in a while, going toe to toe against true evil. Good-looking men around my age were in short supply.

I'd met one or two — always married. I'd counted that a blessing. Our order was not a celibate order, but we did not engage in unmarried relationships. Those were forbidden. And who would marry a beggar other than another beggar?

I'd met a few other Vagabond Paladins, of course. Old bachelors, the lot of them. They'd liked me very much. Especially when I made them tea, toasted cheese on bread, and offered liniment for their aching feet. I didn't mind doing that. The God blesses generosity, and there's something satisfying about caring for someone everyone else overlooks. But I wouldn't have considered myself tempted in any way by the paladins of my order. Were there beautiful Vagabond Paladins drifting town to town in tattered cloaks with noble visages and flowing hair? Mayhap there were, and our paths had simply never crossed. Privately, I doubted it.

Or the old man knew better than to let you anywhere near them because when you're an old knight, having a girl around who has a nice smile and a handy way with a cup of tea isn't something to shrug at. I've seen it before. There are many kinds of selfishness, toothsome delight. Let me show you one that fits you. Let me introduce you to all the ways you can indulge before disaster catches up with you. I bet this knight would help tempt you to try a little selfishness.

I snapped my fingers at Brindle and he sat, whining slightly.

Oooh. Yes, you've shown me my place. He purred happily as if losing his agency was something he liked. *Now, shall I tell you what the pillar said?*

He'd better. Sir Adalbrand was cleaning his wounds and now

was a good time to fix my eyes on the rock and pretend I was reading it.

"It says," I began, waiting for the voice in my head to tell me.

There was a long pause, a snicker, and then finally an other-earthly voice spoke.

Tell your little toy soldier that the pillar says, "The Aching Monastery. Woe to you, supplicant. Five woes. For the attainment of Sainthood: Bring your dust, your blood, your inner pain. Draw them out each one and heights attain. Abandon now the bitter husk. Impale your weakness on its tusk."

I spoke the words, staring at the pillar as if I were reading them, but the sound of Adalbrand's silence drew my eyes back to his.

"Does it really say that?" he asked me. He was midway through stitching one of the gashes on his leg. The flesh around it was purple and pulpy from the force of Brindle's bite.

"I think so," I said carefully.

"It's ... the other paladins think this monastery might have been used for the creation of Saints."

"How does one create Saints?" I asked carefully. That sounded like something for the God to determine, not for man to orchestrate.

Precisely.

He lifted a single brow in an ironic look. "How, indeed?"

I thought about what the demon had read. "Perhaps they say it in this way to keep the fainthearted away?"

In my head, the voice laughed and kept on laughing, echoing through my thoughts. Madness would have been bad enough. I had someone else going mad inside my mind, and that was so much worse.

"Perhaps." Adalbrand was quiet for a long moment, his hands busy with the pull of thread through ruined flesh.

I was accustomed to horrors, but not accustomed to lingering so long over wounds. I felt my stomach flutter unhappily at the sight of what Brindle's mouth had done. If I could keep a demon under control, you'd think I could keep my own bile down.

Who says I'm under control.

"Talk to me while I work, Vagabond Paladin. Tell me about how you ascended to your rank."

I shivered at his commanding tone. I thought that if he ordered me to march with that voice, I would step straight into a blizzard and never look back. I glanced at his face. It was tight with pain, but his eyes were sharp when they focused on me. His dark hair was cropped short but sweat had formed around the brow of it, dampening his hair enough for a few small locks to fall over his forehead and across his temple. It made him seem younger, despite his situation.

"Did you hear the Call?" he pressed, eyes flicking up to mine from his work.

I shivered and wrapped my arms around myself, flinching at the burn in my own stitches. My work was not nearly as careful or proficient as his.

He stiffened slightly as he drew in a breath and let it out slowly. It made all his muscles flex. Even the ones in his neck.

"So. You didn't hear the call. Or you are uncertain."

My cheeks grew hot. I kept my eyes anywhere but his. "I knelt in vigil all night. Wounded. With the blood of my only friend in the world on my clothing. Is that not call enough?"

He grunted and then it morphed into a cynical gust of silent laughter.

"Perhaps." He shook his head and the shake held all the weariness of a man who'd seen as much or more than I had. "You're right. Is that not what faith is? A reaching into the darkness, conscious of the blood on your hands?"

"I don't know," I said, and for my trouble, I received another of those gusting laughs.

"And that solves the puzzle of why all your wounds are infected. They were not tended promptly. I watched a fellow paladin die that way, you know. It was a miserable death. At the end, he thought he saw his own mother gnawing on his bones."

This time when he glanced at me, his eyes were an open window to vast sadness.

I shivered. "I see what you're doing here, but if you love healing so much, why don't you heal yourself?"

He shot me a sidelong glance with a glimmer of a shared jest in his eyes. How was he so playful when he held such sorrow?

"You know I cannot turn my gift on myself, so why do you suggest it? Are you testing me, Lady Paladin?"

Did I not mention that? my former mentor asked me.

It seemed there were a lot of things he'd forgotten to mention.

I did my best to mask my lack of knowledge, flicking my eyes to his exposed leg. "Are you testing *me,* Sir Knight?"

I shouldn't have felt satisfied by his sudden flush, the bobbing of his throat, or the way his gaze couldn't dart away fast enough, but I did. And shame mixed with it when I heard the laughter of the demon in my head.

Plum. Sugared. Plum.

"Whatever you do," he said carefully, "do not tell the others what you have told me. Let it be our secret, me and you. A secret we take to the grave, hmm?"

"You must think me a fool." If my words held the sharpness of iron, well, my thoughts were equally sharp and terrified.

He paused, and whatever chagrin he felt was clearly set aside. He held my gaze with calm assurance.

"I think you're a woman pushed past exhaustion, threaded through with sorrow, and now responsible for a demon posing as a dog."

I sucked in a breath, afraid to so much as flinch. Had he discovered us?

He jests, snackling. And yet, don't you think it's funny that he sees I could be a demon and yet he doesn't slay me now? Were he a real man, he'd have lopped off Brindle's head already. Maybe I'll get to have two delectable treats. One that tastes of plum and cinnamon and another that tastes of ... what do you think your screams will taste of? Tart apple?

That echoing laughter was getting annoying.

And Sir Adalbrand was watching me, watching how my face had formed a still mask.

"You know all my secrets now," I said, breathlessly, hoping not to be caught in the lie.

"Truly? So few?" He teased, but his teasing had a note of sympathy under it.

"And you offer to heal me. I'd be in your debt and debt again. I don't like that accounting."

"Hmm." He'd finished his stitching and was smearing salve liberally over the wound. "That's fair, I suppose."

We were both silent for a long time and then he looked up at me and bit his lip — a shockingly vulnerable gesture for a man hard and lean with rippling muscle and lined from pain around eyes and mouth.

"A secret for a secret? Would that settle our debt?"

I couldn't have said why it was suddenly so hard to breathe. Maybe it was the infection affecting my mind.

Yes, we'll call it that.

I nodded wordlessly.

"I was raised the son of King Abrent von Menticure by his third concubine, Amaranda. They had a knighthood in mind for me, but I ran to the Aspect of the Sorrowful God when I was but fifteen and the Aspect took my vows. Sanctuary and service. They gave me one and received the other."

I nodded along. We both knew this was not the secret.

"I killed a girl. She was just fifteen."

The laughter echoing in my mind was like flames flickering up from the center of the earth.

Plums and cinnamon and sweet, sweet shame.

"A secret for a secret," I said, as if a debt had been paid between us.

He nodded, but there was a quaver in his nod, as if he were

reliving a memory he wished to forget. When his words came, they were rough.

"Now, let me heal you of your wounds. Secrets fester in the soul. I can do nothing for them. But I can heal the wounds festering in your flesh."

Accept his gift. Only the arrogant turn their backs on mercy.

With a long sigh, I opened my palm to him.

Chapter Nine
Poisoned Saint

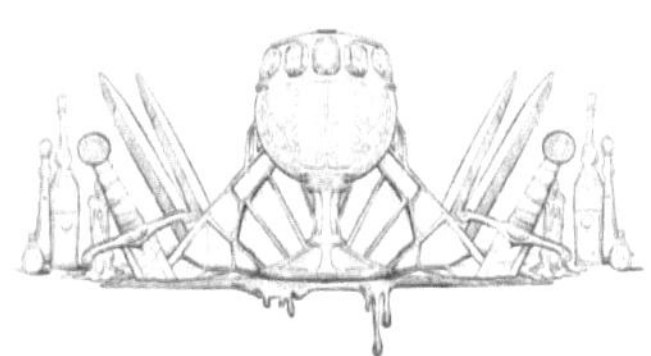

The thing about taking another's sorrows is that it makes you *them* for a moment. For what is more personal than pain? What is closer to the spine of the soul than the aches and agonies that wrack the body?

We are so intertwined in our flesh and spirit, heart and sinew, that there is truly no way to disentangle one from the other without destroying both. Unless, perhaps, that way is death — the eventual unraveling, like a pair of lovers breaking apart after passion. Inevitable, and yet unexpectedly wrenching.

I place a hand gently on her jaw — a terrible intimacy, I know. Unforgivable? Perhaps. Certainly unnecessary. I could touch her anywhere to take her pain. We could be fingertip to fingertip or palm to palm. Usually, I set a palm on a shoulder. But touching her shoulder feels like a bad idea, somehow. So, I cup her jaw, annoyed with myself when my fingertips choose to memorize the way the delicate bone is cradled under soft flesh.

I exhale out all thoughts of myself and my own pains, my own wants. I offer them up to the God.

Take them. And take her pains and infirmities. I will bear them in my flesh. I will bear them and hold them close until you will me to release them. I take them up willingly.

I feel the familiar rush.

The power of the God whipping through my heart is like a hot wind rushing into dark caverns. One quickening touch, and then, from the other direction, the ooze of molten turmoil rolling into me. I feel the slick of the infection that I'm taking, the sharp jagged edges of trauma, and the queasy feeling of bodily uncertainty. They settle over my bones as if the structure of my body has been gilded by these new sensations. And when, finally, I manage to take in a fresh inhale of the crisp forest air, I am breathing in every last scrap of her misery, and with it. I breathe her physicality in, too. All her scents, all her feelings, all that makes her *her* for just a heartbeat, is me, too.

I know her like I know myself. Know the sensation of living in her body, of her quick mind and sharp emotions. Know how it feels to be Victoriana for just one fraction of one second.

I wonder sometimes, in the quiet of the night, if the God feels this all the time. Does he dwell deep in our sorrows and joys every moment? Do I feel but a hair of it when I heal in his name? And if he feels all this at every moment ... what does that mean? Does he treasure each pearl of sensation, or are they just like the drops of a river falling over a great drop — momentary, sparkling, beautiful, and then erased in the blink of an eye when they crash back into the river, no more individual or precious than drops of water?

Don't forget me, I beg in my mind. *Don't let me be washed away.*

Is it faith that wrings the heart of a paladin and makes him certain he is worth keeping as an individual pearl, or is it the most sublime of arrogances?

When I exhale again, it is all gone, and what I feel is the twisting ache of new pain in my flesh, the wave of nausea from the infection I took, and the human warmth of skin under my fingertips. I snatch my hand back before it can curl around tantalizing flesh and tangle into silky hair.

I flex my fingers and step deliberately backward, in firm control of myself.

Lust is a choice. So is attraction. Well, not the first blush of it that sparkles like a diamond on the wave of the sea. But we need not look at a thing simply because it exists. We need not long for it. The heart can be directed, just like the thoughts and actions.

I do as I always do and carefully set aside every whisper of desire. They have no hold on me if I give them none. I allow warmth in my smile even as I withdraw all longing from my heart. The heart flows like a river and it goes where you channel it. I do not allow it to channel toward a woman who I know perfectly well I do not know at all. Any allure I feel is a combination of the false closeness of healing and the memories of another woman that I am painting onto this one. Forgery, all of it.

Only a fool would fall for a forgery.

"Thank you," she gasps and I harden my heart to the beauty of her voice.

"It is a gift of the God, not of me," I recite, grateful to lean on the formal words.

Her mouth quirks. "Then why do I see *you* favoring your left side in the same way that I favored mine?"

I straighten against the pain, unwilling to admit what has already been discovered.

She doesn't push the point, busying herself with dressing layers over her newly healed flesh and gathering her things.

I gather myself in a similar manner, pretending to be unnecessarily concerned over the wellbeing of the horses. They're all well and they snort at me in horsey annoyance at my fussing.

I cast a single glance at the pillar, still forcing distraction on myself. It confirms our suspicions. This monastery is a place for the creation of Saints. What shall I make of that? I don't like it, that's what I make of it. It doesn't feel right for people to try to manufacture what ought to be only a gift from the God. It feels like hubris to me.

She wouldn't have lied about what was said there ... would she? I glance quickly at her dog. It trots along ahead of us as we leave the horses by silent agreement. The dog's tongue lolls out cheerfully, as if it didn't just brutalize my flesh. I don't trust the creature. Not just because my leg burns with pain and makes me feel hot and flushed. Something dark lurks beneath that dog's short fur. I can't put my finger on what it is.

We return to the camp in silence. I know why I say nothing. Words right now would only make me slip. I don't look at the lady paladin long enough to determine why she is quiet, though. By now, I am well-practiced in the art of snuffing out attraction. The key is not to dwell. Not to spend time beyond the practical with whoever kindles interest in you. If I must, I will kneel in vigil in the cold, but I do not think it will come to that. The pain of the dog bite and the festering wounds that I took from her during healing are enough to quickly quell any rising tide.

I focus instead on the puzzle of a ruined monastery on the edge of the world.

It's cold here, but not as cold as I expected. The Rim must still be receding, bringing warmth as it rushes away. Already, the air is merely chilled rather than frigid, the sun a little brighter, the tide a little less grey.

What kind of place was this monastery? Usually, holy places have a sense of light to them, but I've never visited one abandoned for a thousand years. Can I expect the same from such a relic? Even so, something about it does not sit right within my heart. It goes beyond the cold. It goes beyond the strange group gathered here. It finds a place at the base of my spine and sits there, cold, hard, and ominous. What does this place want with my dust and my blood? Surely those are the God's alone.

We join the others as the sun leans to kiss the earth.

Hefertus has set up his pavilion. He nods briefly to it and I throw my gear under the silken shelter. Others may bring oiled canvas or wax-seamed leather. Hefertus mocks them all with his waxed silk, painted with cranes and a soft setting sun in a way that bleeds through on each side. It looks more fit to shelter ladies at a picnic than knights on a quest, but I agree with him that two are better than one in a pit of vipers.

And make no mistake, these others are our brothers, but they'd slay us if they thought we'd stepped off the path. They might even have orders to take us by surprise, though the amulets our betters agreed to distribute suggest they planned for us to work together at least in part. Mine is simply a stamp of the Cup of Tears. So are the others. The edges are even, no hidden code or key there.

Honestly, I'm at a loss as to why I am here at all. It's not a plague-ridden town or battlefield, and if this is an argument to be won by negotiation or by battle, I'm outclassed in both.

I don't watch the Beggar Paladin set up her things. I fix my eyes instead on the festivities. The Seer battles the Holy Inquisitor in a mock fight, and though she is blind and half-deaf, she is holding her own, predicting his strikes before they land and miraculously always just a hair out of reach.

He seems to be enjoying himself all the same. Inquisitors are known to prize sparring above almost all else beyond using their gifts to discern souls. They spar amongst themselves three times a day when they are at home. I wonder if the Seer has sparred in this decade. She seems to hardly know where she is.

I lose myself to the flow of their movements, disciplining my mind to watch and catalog how each of my peers fights. It is a good exercise in focus and an excellent way to keep my thoughts governed.

The Engineers decline to spar with the rest, but all the others take a turn at a bout. That's interesting, isn't it? They won't spar. They brought ... constructs ... to do their heavy lifting. It smacks of laziness. Even old knights should feel that twinge that wants to fight.

Hefertus does not surprise me. He's all smiles and charm, letting his reach and grace win for him. He beats the High Saint — who takes it poorly and masks his embarrassment with his helm and a sudden need for prayer.

I've always thought that the High Saints' helms are creepy. They encase the entire head in a steel cylinder with a flat top and only a cross in the face by which one might see or speak. The High Saint's prayers echo within it like a poorly tuned bell.

Hefertus, in turn, loses to the Hand of Justice. No surprise there. In fact, I'm not entirely sure Hefertus didn't throw the match. He's clever about politics and no one wants Kodelai Lei Shan Tora as an enemy or even a rival.

Sir Kodelai makes a show of removing his tabard, armor, outer coat, and jerkin, splashing icy water over his scar-laced chest and shoulders and preening under it before donning the jerkin only — unlaced and untucked. He makes an elaborate bow to his next opponent. It's hard to shed the shell of who you once were, and this one was a king.

His next challenger is the Penitent Paladin, and Kodelai wins in three strokes. No surprise there, either. Owalan Cantor — the Penitent — has deep, knowing eyes, and he sees everything, but his block is weak and his guard shaky in comparison to the master swordsman he faces.

Sir Kodelai has a very fast strike and a quick eye. I do not think I could best him. Though I will certainly try. I could beat the others who have fought, except for Hefertus. I wouldn't want to go up against my friend in anything other than a friendly game. That long reach and calculating mind are deadly.

The next match is on and even though I watch Sir Kodelai's every move, I don't even see the last strike that sends the Majester General to his knees in surrender, or the quick spin that brings a sigh of yielding from the Seer in the match after that.

"Give it a try if you can, Poison," Sir Kodelai says to me good-naturedly. He's barely even breathing hard.

I take to my feet, but the moment I do, he chops a hand through the air.

"My apologies, brother. I see you are bearing hurts not your own. Tomorrow. Give yourself a day to recover first." He's gracious in his dismissal, like a king granting a boon to a liege-sworn vassal. "There's no joy in beating the injured, right, Sir Beggar?"

I can't help it. My eyes shoot to the Vagabond Paladin at his words and I see her jaw clench in annoyance. Does the Hand of Justice use the pejorative intentionally? I don't know, and it seems that neither does she.

She watches him warily. I hold my breath until I see hers let out. Good. She's not going to take it as an insult. Yet.

With care for my leg, I settle back onto the stones and pull a strand of dried meat from my pack. Healing always makes me hungry.

"You are correct that I have been healed, Sir Kodelai," the Vagabond Paladin says carefully, her eyes following the former king a little too long and a little too boldly.

I want to curse. Maybe she's going to take issue with him after all. That would be terribly unwise. A man like Sir Kodelai will be prickly about his honor.

I clench my jaw and look from face to face. Hefertus shifts subtly in my direction. The Engineers pull together. Surprisingly, the Penitent draws near to the Seer. We're picking our allies in case things get violent.

And then her gaze rakes up and down him in a way that makes me uncomfortable and makes the Hand of Justice — who was once a king with a dozen wives — blush.

If she is still playing mad, then she is acting her part well. If she is not, then she is a fearsome thing, using every tool she has to throw off her opponent. I'm not entirely sure that I don't approve.

She braids her long hair as she watches him. It must have come undone during the dog attack. I hadn't even noticed it then. Now, every strand bewitches me and I must look away. I know it's not her intention. This is a matter of practicality if she wishes to fight without hair in her eyes. But the way her slender fingers flick through the strands brings back memories too sharp, too vivid, of another set of paler fingers weaving lighter hair.

"If you wish to spar, you can thank the Poisoned Saint for

taking my infirmities," she says lightly. "His sacrifice has left me free for such sport."

"So he is of some use," Sir Kodelai says, sending me a mirthful glance to take out the sting.

She is not willing to joke with him. Her brows knit together soberly.

"I am ready."

Her declaration is punctuated by the whoosh of her sword slicing through the air. A salute.

The Hand of Justice nods sharply. I cannot read why he is suddenly so stiff — unless he suffers from the same problem that I do. Perhaps he, too, killed a woman who looked shockingly like this one. Perhaps he, too, carries the guilt of that forever within the guarding cage of his ribs.

Or perhaps that is only me.

I ought to rip my gaze away from this fight as I did from the braid, but I don't. I am mesmerized by it. Caught. No more able to look away than the dancing snake can slip from the charmer.

Sir Kodelai is grace and elegance and a lifetime of experience. In contrast, his challenger is bold and sharp, her attack unrestrained, her defense undisciplined. But she is surprise and audacity and insouciant charm.

I hear my thoughts echoed in the stilted gasps and exhales of the others watching as their blades clash together and their feet dance across the rock.

"From the lips of babes, isn't it?" one of the Engineers says quietly, the loud sip he takes of his tea the only sound other than the slip of steel against steel and the harshness of exerted breath.

"You mix your metaphors worse than your tea," his fellow complains, but they are only background noise to me. "We should set Suture on her next time and see how she does. Shame to waste the chance to test out your theory."

I am memorizing the footwork, my own body responding to the movements as if I am trying to parse what I would do in Sir

Kodelai's place. I think I could beat her. Possibly. It would be a near thing, and that's somewhat concerning if I let myself dwell on it. Whatever there is between us is uncertain. She may be friend or foe even now. If she is foe, she would be worse to fight than Hefertus. He, at least, follows some kind of internal code. She is as untamed as the wind.

When she stumbles, I feel a twinge in my side.

She's quick to recover, and the way she follows, not with a sharp defense or even a flailing attack, but rather with a sharp spin that puts her inside Kodelai's reach, stuns us all. It's the *shick* of her knife drawing that makes us gasp, and then she has the tip of the knife pressed to his chin under his beard.

He laughs, utterly charmed.

"I think I like you, fledgling paladin," the former king says. He is not smiling. I am not sure Kodelai knows how to smile. But he is arresting in his demeanor. Admiration paints every line of him. I feel a pinch of something I hope is not jealousy. "I think we'll drink together now, unless someone else wants to take the girl's measure. Her benefactor, perhaps?"

He points at me.

I wave a hand as if it is nothing to me. As if my sword hand isn't twitching for a chance to take her measure toe to toe, body to body. Strength to strength. Every fiber of me wants to match against her — with her — *however* we fit together. And I will not allow that thought to go further.

I turn my back slowly, acting as though I find myself surprised to be in need of tea. I saunter over to the Engineers. As much as I loathe their grim creations, I crave their grounding presence now.

"Did you design your own armor?" I ask the nearest one. It hardly matters what response he gives. I know the God's Engineers. This question will earn me at least an hour of explanation. There is little that interests Engineers more than who made what, and few things that delight them more than speaking about their beloved armor.

I manage to keep them both talking, blessedly blocking out all else, until dusk when the High Saint calls for an evening song and we gather together around the fire and sing the Dirge of Ages. A fitting end to such a day.

From the moment I joined the Aspect of the Sorrowful God, this has been my favorite time. When I am within the walls of the order, we join the priests for their sunset song, and when I am in the field, it is observed wherever two or more of us are gathered together. It is the sound of home to me and a sacred sealing of the day — a gift to the God, though it is a poor one.

"Walk with me," the High Saint sings in an unbelievably angelic tongue.

He's a tenor. And a triumphant one. I find my eyebrows clawing up my forehead in my surprise. What in the God's name is he doing here? He could lead the choir in the Great Dome Cathedral with a voice like that.

When the others join in three-part harmony, beautiful though it is, it is almost a shame to mar his perfect melody.

"Walk with me, gentle spirit; Walk this compassion trail; Walk through trouble and tumult; Walk by my troubled wail; Walk with me, gentle spirit, and all along life's way; walk with me, noble master, and by my sorrows stay."

I lose myself in five verses of pleading with the God to attend us in sorrow, and as we're singing the last notes, the High Saint smiles and adds a piece I've never heard.

"Walk with me, gentle spirit; Walk this compassion trail; Walk with me in my great joy; Let my humble heart sail."

My mouth falls open. I don't mean to show my horror. But he's ruined the song. It's a dirge. It's meant to sing our sorrows to the God. He's brought joy into it? What is this travesty?

"I went ahead and added a small contribution," the High Saint says, pressing his palm to his chest in mock humility. "I just thought the song was too sad."

There are murmurs of happy agreement around the circle.

Agreement? They agree?

I look up, finally, from where I've been staring at the ground, and I meet the only set of eyes that seems as aghast as I am. The Vagabond Paladin looks ill. The one person I absolutely can't afford to be in harmony with is the only one who sees this as I do.

"It's a dirge," I say woodenly.

"Yes, it's really too bad. It should have a happy part," the High Saint says, and his saccharine smile matches his song.

I close my eyes so that I can try to stop imagining myself with my hands around his throat.

"Isn't it lovely?" he asks.

"It's meant to be bittersweet." My voice is controlled.

"Well, it was only bitter, but I've put the sweet in it. Supper?"

My eyes snap open.

He's offering me an open smile.

After insulting my Aspect of the God.

As if I won't spill his guts right here.

Get a hold of yourself, Adalbrand.

With all my discipline, I clench my jaw and turn, walking straight to Hefertus's tent and throwing myself into my bedroll. It's early. Too early to sleep, but not too early to lose myself in all the pain I took, and pretend that I'm not so annoyed by a paladin from another order that I want to see how purple I can make his face before I let him breathe again.

Do you think that's extreme?

Then you don't understand devotion. You don't understand what it's like to give your whole life to a love too great for one heart — to hold your tiny piece of it safe within, to protect it at all costs, to feed that flame with whatever shreds of hope or friendship you have.

If you don't understand it, then you don't understand paladins. And you don't understand me.

And you don't understand that sometimes we're angry at one thing because we're frustrated with another.

I fall asleep wanting to chew rocks.

I wake to what sounds like a muffled sob.

My eyes flick open, alert in an instant, but I freeze.

Hefertus's deep breathing from his bedroll on the other side of the tent is even. I see his large form faintly in the darkness. Light from the campfire still makes navigation almost possible despite the darkness. I slip from my blankets.

It's cold outside the tent. It was cold *inside* the tent, but our combined body heat was enough to keep things just slightly warmer than the air outside. I shiver in the cold, muscles tensing uncomfortably around wounds both real and magical.

The light of the banked fire is stronger here — a dull crimson glow like the inside of the womb.

I scan the semi-circle by its gleam. Beside our tent is the Majester General's thick canvas. It steams in the night air. He's inside, then.

To the other side of us is the door to nothing. A heap rolled in blankets lies against the door. I only know it's the Vagabond because her devil dog is sprawled half over her.

Past her is a filmy white tent that is half hammock, half shelter, like some monstrous cocoon. That can only be the Penitent Paladin. It moves as he turns in his sleep.

I glance up at the moon and reckon it to be midway through the night. It's shifted again. Moved just a fraction to reveal more land north and east of here.

A heavy leather tent is next, guarded by both golems. Their banked-ember eyes pierce the darkness, watching me like twin demons. I shiver again. I must think on how to keep them above ground. I would not like to be in an enclosed space with one of these hulking creations. I don't trust them.

The High Saint's tent is as plain as him. I try not to glare at it.

I skip to the black brocaded tent of the Hand of Justice. It is wonderfully made but worn. From within, snores like cutting birch logs emerge. Hefertus should be glad his only friend wasn't the renowned former king.

It's from the last tent that the crying sounds again. I hurry to the many-layered tent of the Seer. If she is ill or in pain, it is my duty to ease her troubles. And I would also be pleased to help. It bothers me how many ills she carries with her already. I would not see more added to her collection.

"Lady Paladin?" I whisper as I reach her tent. I feel a slight warmth coming from the entrance. She's in there. The door of the tent flutters like the edges of flayed flesh. "Are you unwell?"

A moan is the only reply.

I clench my jaw. She sounds like she's in pain, but the first thing you learn as a squire is that pushing your way into another paladin's tent is a great way to get a sword blade right to the throat.

"I'm coming into your tent to help," I murmur. "Please, do not kill me."

I think I hear a grunt, but I'm not sure. I take a deep breath and push my head into her tent.

My eyes are still adjusting to the darkness when a hand snakes out, seizes me by the throat, and I am launched backward through the door with a heap of paladin on top of me. She's wrapped in layers of rags so that I don't know where paladin ends and rags begin. I hit the ground hard, seeing stars, and then her face is right there, white eyes tinted coral in the firelight. She's lighter than I expected.

"I've looked and looked again," she says, her breath sawing out of her lungs. It stinks of fear. "At the end of every road is death."

"And such is true for all of us, sister," I whisper gently, trying to get a hold of her shoulders so I can ease her weight off my chest. My aching ribs feel like they might give. It's only a perception. I've taken the pain in the ribs but mine are actually undamaged. But perceptions can feel real.

"Every vision is the same no matter the decision. There is no path out." She bats her hands frantically at my chest. "How can I prevent it? How can I stop it?"

I try to soothe her. "All is in the hands of the God."

"You don't listen, boy." She grabs the front of my jerkin and shakes me. "It all ends in evil. It all ends in death. I see no way forward except through blood." Her eyes roll back in her head and her jaw clenches as she begins to shudder and shake, seizing right on top of me.

I manage to finally get a grip on her and spin her so that she's on her back.

My hands find her face and I try to take her pain, her misery — but whatever this is, it is not a thing I can take from her. I drop my hands, stymied, reciting a prayer in a frantic whisper.

When she finally stops shuddering and is still, I lift her and carry her back to her bed. Her breathing slows and evens and I think she is asleep, but I am deeply troubled. What has she seen that has left her in this state?

I can't go back to my bed. I wait outside the entrance of her tent, pull out the rosary my paladin superior gave me when I ascended, and say prayers as my fingers skim along the teeth that comprise the rosary beads.

"A Poisoned Saint must know two things, Adalbrand," he'd told me. "Prayer and body. Know the body so you may heal it. Know the prayers that you may know the one who heals. That's why I give you this string of teeth."

Now, as I feel them and pray, I wonder what manner of beads might be on the rosary for a Seer. If they pray by the beads, I've never seen it. Maybe they string visions together. Maybe hers have been stolen away.

When dawn paints the distant sea, I am drowsy and swaying. But I breathe a sigh of relief when I see the Seer come out of her tent. She is arrayed head to toe in armor, two swords swinging on her hips, a tabard of filmy fabric like the raiments of ghosts flutters over solid steel.

"Are you feeling well now, Lady Paladin?" I ask her.

She says nothing, but her pearly gaze finds my face somehow and she presses a shred of parchment into my palm.

She's already limping off when I read the ill-formed letters scrawled madly on the scrap.

I saw into the depths and he took my eyes, listened to the future and he took my ears, warned of the cataclysm and he took my tongue.

Chapter Ten
Vagabond Paladin

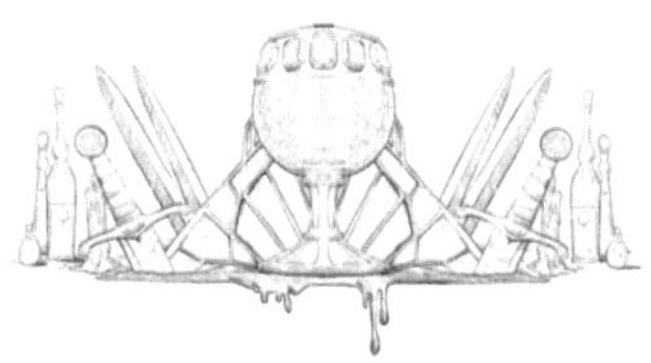

Today, we'll enter the monastery.

I slept poorly last night wrapped in my musky bearskin cloak, huddled against the door that was not a door as the demon and paladin fought within my mind. I did not pitch a tent. I wanted a wall at my back and I didn't trust any of the others out of my sight. Except maybe the healer. Maybe.

She's tempted by the dark horse. Did you feel her pulse quicken near him? I shall watch the sweet morsel fall from grace yet. It will be like the crackling on the edge of the pan. I savor the drama. It shall be my cup and sup.

As you will be mine.

Do they allow you to speak so, paladin? I'm appalled. I thought you had to at least pretend to goodness. Don't you all bathe in hyssop and launderer's soaps until your skin flakes from your muscles and the fun flakes from your bones?

At least we bathe, hound of hell. Your sulfur stench has filled my nostrils since the moment you arrived and I cannot discern if it comes from the brimstone of the hells, or if it is simply that your spectral intestines are ruled by wind.

If you are trying to insult me, your words need more teeth. But maybe you're too distraught as you watch your successor fall into a trap.

I huddled in my blankets, scowling, and clung to Brindle — the dog, not the spirits within him. He was my one true friend, though I wished I could rid him of parasites. He put a paw up on my arm and whuffed quietly. I scratched him behind his ears and frowned into the darkness.

I might have been young and I might have been "driven by passions as the water is driven by the course of the river," as the demon so aptly put it, but even *I* was not foolish enough to fall for a man sworn to celibacy. Even if he had eyes like sad pools of darkness.

Even if I could still feel his touch on my face.

You'd think the sparring afterward would have cleansed my palate. After all, there had been other fit, fine men fighting. My blood had been up and coursing through my veins with the joy of competing. My eyes had sparkled with the joy of it. That ought to have put him from my mind. It did not seem to have been enough.

Eventually, I blocked out my thoughts and the spirits' bickering well enough to fall asleep.

I woke to Brindle whining in my ear. He'd kept me warm through the night, the good doggy, and now he rolled over and presented his belly to be scratched. I obliged, but I gave him a long look. I still refused to kill him, but I recognized how terribly impractical this relationship was. A cunning woman would have killed the dog in the first moment. A smart one in the first hour. A practical one before the next day had passed.

I suppose I'd lost claim to being any of those by keeping him alive.

With a rueful smile, I leaned in close enough to smell his doggy breath and whispered, "So who's an almost good boy, then?"

I scratched him behind the ears and nearly leapt when a voice broke into my mind.

You're awake. Quick, little snack. Look at the door frame. Look! I swear a dog's eyes are not what they ought to be.

I tried not to sigh. These two were already wearing on me without ordering me like a slave.

Don't waste time sighing. You sigh like the bellows of a blacksmith's shop and look just as beguiling. Use your eyes.

I looked up. After the past week I'd had, it felt good to be able to lift my head without searing pain in my ribs. A stab of guilt shot through me. What I'd felt before was now taken by the Poisoned Saint.

He deserves none of your pity. Your pain feeds his power. Just as his beauty feeds your desire. That's selfishness, whatever pretty facade you try to paint over it.

No.

Trust me. As a denizen of hell, selfishness is my specialty. I am a master of it. An artist. An unparalleled practitioner.

The door was lit with soft pink light from the rising sun. Something had been carved into the frame. Letters — and if I had to guess, the same kinds of letters we'd seen at the other pillar. Ancient Indul.

Call it what you like. We always called it the Tongue.

As in the only tongue? Did they not have multiple languages when this monastery was in the world?

We had many languages, but this one was the common language. The one everyone knew on top of whatever language they were born to. The crass language. The Devil's speech.

He started to laugh as my finger traced them again. They were so worn that they were hard to feel, even standing out starkly in the dawn light and thick black shadows.

It says, "Confession Door. Speak your sins and gain entry." Oh, now this will be a lovely treat. What sins are housed in you, little delicacy? I can guess a few, I think. But it will be tastier to catch them as they slip between your lips.

Why would it want that? Sir Branson sounded worried. *That's not a very ... godly thing to want. Victoriana, I mislike this place. Perhaps you should ride off. Leave this to someone else.*

And risk censure by the aspect? When I'd only just become a paladin? They'd not just strip me of my title; they might strip me of my hands and send me begging in earnest without even the means to labor at something else.

Is confession not godly? It bares the soul. And it keeps the confessor under your power. What could be more religious than that, paladin? After all, isn't that how you have been whittling me down? By finding each vein and rooting it out?

To me, it sounded like a trick. Who would willingly speak aloud their sins in front of their rivals? And would saying them change them? Some things died in sunlight ... but others thrived when the sun shone full on them. Would whatever was in my heart and hands perish, or surge with renewed energy? And would I be able to tell which before I opened the door?

No, and that's the magic of it. It can take you where you want to go — into the Aching Monastery — but it has a price. Just like all of us do. And you must pay it.

I didn't have a price.

The laughter in my head told me that my watchers didn't believe me.

I ignored them and made ready, going to the creek to tend my horse, wash, and refill my water skins. If we were going into unfamiliar territory, I meant to be prepared. I didn't care if it was a monastery rather than a battlefield, nor did I care that I would be among fellow paladins who worshiped the God the same as I did. I had learned the cold lesson of the road — don't have it with you and it's lost forever.

Which is why you must be sure to keep me with you.

And who was that?

Does it matter? Just be sure the dog goes in along with you. And don't be first through the door.

Don't be first? Why not?

You'll want to brace yourself, sweetmeat. It's easier to do once you've seen one of these doors in action.

Wise council. Even if it came from the mouth of hell.

When I returned to the camp, I found the others assembled outside the door as the sun crept high enough to bathe the land in marigold rather than rose.

"You are late," the Majester General pronounced, each syllable distinct.

"No time was given." I frowned. No one else had their packs with them. The Poisoned Saint had a water skin slung across a shoulder and all the paladins I saw were armored and armed, but no one else was carrying a pack as I was. Were they so certain the way would be safe?

"We said first light," the older paladin said, judgment in his eyes. "And yet here you are at second light."

There's a second light?

Yes, the others can be quite fussy about it. Have I not mentioned it?

I wonder what they call the last light you see before your eyes shut forever. Is there a name for that, my foolish treats? I've given people that light before. It's my most common gift. Wait. There's also madness. I correct myself. It is my second most common gift.

Maybe they call it last light, Sir Branson suggested.

A bit too obvious, I would think. I'd prefer a name with more panache.

I ignored their byplay and made the sign of the God.

"My apologies, Majester General."

He grunted and turned to the others, his voice ringing like he was making an official announcement in the name of the church.

"We know this is the only door into the monastery. The High Saint confirms that he has explored every inch of the ground above, as does the Penitent Paladin. I, myself, confirmed their claims."

He drew a parchment from his tunic and unfurled it with a flourish.

"I've mapped the ground above. There are crumbled arches,

ruins, and pillars, but no doors except this door that seemingly leads nowhere, and yet it is our only path forward. All we who gather now bear the amulets of our aspects agreed upon. These declare that we are granted the right to travel within these premises. None other may follow or live under the aspects' curse. We claim the right of passage now, each in equal part, each a child of the God. Please confirm this, brothers and sisters."

Everyone made a show of drawing their amulet out and I held mine up, too. What fussy mummery. As if there were anyone else here to challenge our right to enter.

The Majester General inspected the amulets one at a time, and though I saw tics of annoyance in some faces, no one made to stop him. He was keeping notes, I saw. Making tiny ticks with a charcoal next to each name as if to confirm we each wore the symbol he'd already seen us wearing. Ridiculous. We all knew who we were and that we were the designates of our aspects. Did it really need to be confirmed?

When he was finished, he continued with his pageantry.

"I call upon you now, in the spirit of honesty and before the God, to swear that you are here in the name of your aspect and with appointed authority."

He paused, waiting for us all to chant, "We so confirm."

The Majester General smiled with the smug happiness of a man who has completed a slight and unnecessary task and now thinks he should be complimented for it.

"Shall we toss for the marching order to pass through the door?" He arranged himself beside the door, parchment and charcoal in hand. Clearly he'd be marking this, too.

Perhaps, when all this was done, he'd turn in his notes to his superiors like a squire learning to figure. I had a sudden mental image of him looking exactly the same, but half as tall, scurrying from master to master trying to show his work. It was hard not to snort.

You're such an irreverent thing. Had you any doubt as to why you ended up dead by your own hands after having been possessed by a demon — that's how I'll kill you, if you're confused — you could look back on thoughts like this, little snack.

Really? The demon thought humor was damnable? How very interesting.

I was about to respond when I felt a tug on my sleeve. The Seer was standing far too close, her pearly gaze just an inch from mine. I tried to flinch away but she seized my arm and drew her mouth close to my ear. The sound that came from it was like crackling leaves in the autumn. It was certainly not speech.

I shuddered. She could have been telling me my future step by step and I'd never know it when it was spoken in a tongue like that.

The Tongue, the voice in my head said smugly. *I told you it was on the door, sweetmeat. She's reading it to you. If she weren't so haggard, mayhap I'd try to occupy* her *mortal vessel.*

I didn't like having ancient warnings read in their original languages by people who were standing far too close. I tried to shuffle a step to the side to regain my composure, but the Seer followed me. Annoyed, I swallowed the words that tried to bubble up and kept my eyes focused forward.

The High Saint made a chopping gesture with his hand. "I claim the right to lead the way. I arrived here first, and so it is mine for the taking. Draw as you like for those who come after, but we will not draw for first."

The Prince Paladin opened his mouth, but then he looked to the Poisoned Saint, and when Adalbrand shook his head minutely, the Prince's mouth shut with a click.

Good, the voice in my head said. *Keep the dog close. Watch.*

Whoever had just given that advice was right. I may have been brave and determined to serve my order, but I had no need to present my back to these others. All of them watched one another with steely gazes and stone faces, and if a knife were to come at me, it would be planted directly into my back. Who knew what grudges these might bear to me — not personally, perhaps, but for the aspect I represented?

I had none of the information I needed about things at Saint Rauche's Citadel. For all I knew, the Vagabond Paladins had — at last — banded together and were now one, riding across every territory and stirring the people up to push higher than kings. Or perhaps they waged wars and allowed the wicked to flourish. How would I know? If any of it were true, I'd deserve the knife in the back these others might plant there. I had not thought before about how our aspect's wanderings left us vulnerable to a lack of information.

"Are there any objections to the High Saint leading the way?" the Majester General asked. And when no one spoke, he nodded to the man. "Then I grant him leave to enter the door first, and after him the Seer, and after her the Engineers, and after ..."

He rattled on, but my mind wandered as I traced the edges of the door. It was set in the empty courtyard. A door from nothing to nothing. How the others thought it would lead somewhere was beyond my understanding.

Faith. They have faith that something is here. I think that perhaps I wasn't very good at teaching you these large, demonstrative ways of having faith.

He'd taught me faith in important things, though. Faith when it really mattered. When you didn't know what else to do. When the food was gone or the child was gasping for breath.

That's the kind that counts. This kind ... well, it's not usually for us.

And was there something here behind the door?

So much more than you imagine, snackling. You're going to love this next part — or at least, I will.

The High Saint stepped forward, made the sigil of the God across his body, and then reached for the door handle.

The door did not open.

He tugged harder. Either it was wedged or locked.

Hefertus cleared his throat. "If I may."

He closed his eyes for a moment, and when they opened, they glowed with a faint light. He pressed his hand against the stone face of the door and even his large, tanned hand seemed fragile and temporary against that ancient rock.

"Blessings be upon this door."

The door swung inward and our breath caught in our throats, for it did not show the courtyard on the other side of the door, but rather steps that led down to a wide landing with a railing. From the center of the landing was an opening that must lead to more stairs, but from here it was hard to see much in the way of detail.

"And what would we have done if he wasn't here?" the Penitent Paladin whispered nervously to whoever was next to him.

What, indeed.

"Thank you, Prince Paladin," the High Saint said acerbically, and before anything more could be said, he stepped promptly forward and froze in the doorway.

He struggled for a moment like a fly in a spider's web, mouth opening and closing though no sound came forth.

I heard the Seer curse softly beside me, but I couldn't tear my eyes from the sight of the High Saint affixed in place, his movements growing fainter as his energy faded.

So. That was why the demon kept telling me not to be first.

Confess! He must confess! The demon in my mind crowed. *Or he will be trapped forever and time herself will slowly dissolve him in her wide mouth. I would not mind so much, except I think you'll leave before I get to watch his despair ferment to a proper vintage.*

I swallowed down a lump of bile, casting looks to either side to see if anyone else had noticed what was needed.

The Penitent Paladin began to pray aloud, using his beaded belt as a rosary. His prayers were fast and breathy, barely spoken so much as exhaled.

"He's trapped," the Majester General said, aghast. "What is the meaning of this? Prince Paladin? Did you do something wrong?"

The Prince Paladin simply raised a dark brow and shook his head.

It took me a full breath before I realized they all were thinking the same thing. They had not translated the words on the door. They had no idea what was required.

I spoke the words, clear and sharp so they would not be masked by the muffled cries of the High Saint or the prayers and oaths of the others.

"Confession Door. Speak your sins and gain entry."

"Say that twice, little sister." Sir Kodelai's eyes were narrowed when they meet mine, as if he were challenging me. He rubbed a jaw more chiseled than the rock itself and just as crisscrossed with scars. Kingship had not been kind to him. Paladincy did not seem to have been much kinder.

"It's a Confession Door," I said, holding my chin high and trying to look confident. The demon had better not have lied to me. "You must speak your sin or be trapped."

They call the devil the father of lies, you know. His children may not be fathers of lies but they are certainly sons. It would be good not to forget that, I think.

I agreed.

Even so, our demon captive seems to have this cat by the tail. If the paladin does not confess soon it may be too late.

"He needs to confess," I said, worrying my lip between my teeth. "A sin of some kind."

"How do you know that?" Sir Kodelai asked, stepping closer, hand on sword pommel, eyes locked on mine. Saints, he was touchy. Did he really think I had the power to trap a High Saint?

I swallow down the stab of fear that hooked under my breastplate — look, I'd fought him before, but he was powerful, and likely the others here would back his accusation, no matter how wild —as he took a second step forward. I made myself refuse to be intimidated, extending my gauntleted hand to point to the open door.

"It's written right there on the door frame." My voice hardly quavered.

That's right! Don't back down! They may be grand and rich, but in the end, we all die the same way.

"No one can read that," the Majester General said. "It's in an ancient script lost to us. What manner of devilry gives you mastery over it?"

He slipped a step toward me, too. And now fear truly danced down the fibers of my frame, for what answer could I give? My knowledge *did* come from devilry in its purest form.

Yes, my sweetmeat, yes, my precious little tidbit. It's my gift to you. As is their suspicion. As is the way knowledge begins to corrupt your delicate soul.

I sent a quick glance around me. I shouldn't. It showed fear, and you should never show fear when surrounded by enemies, but I needed to assess the danger.

I can assess for you. One paladin stuck in a trap for the unwary — I did tell you not to be first. Two paladins accusatory. One paladin sympathetic. One paladin ironic. Delightful, all.

Who was sympathetic? I saw not a single look of support in the faces surrounding me.

Who do you think? I could feel his wink in my mind.

Brindle edged to my side, a silent shadow slinking in like a thief carrying goods to be fenced. He slid his furry side along my greave and then gave a very impressive doggy yawn, as if none of this was of any concern to him.

It really isn't. If the faithful kill you, little treat, I'll gobble your soul up as you're dying and then I'll hop to the next meal. I'll be sorry to have missed the show, though. And your incompetence. It's hard to find a truly pathetic person, and they really make the best objects of comedy. I'll be laughing over you for years to come.

I gritted my teeth but just in time, a throat cleared from behind me.

"Whatever are they teaching you boys in the monasteries these days?" It was the younger Engineer — Sir Coriand. "I suppose you can be forgiven, Kodelai. You came to the church late in life, so your tongue is rigidly stuck in the common language, but Roivolard, I thought better of you."

The Holy Engineer clucked his tongue and the Majester General — Roivolard, I supposed — went beet red.

"Don't be so harsh, Coriand," the other Engineer said, hitching his sword belt in a way that only accentuated his barrel belly. "You can't expect blustering generals to pick up the finer points of language."

"Are you saying she's telling ... you can't mean she's telling the truth?" the Majester General asked warily, looking from the Engineers, to me, to the High Saint — Joran Rue — stuck in the doorway. Sir Joran seemed ... faded ... somehow. As if whatever was on the other side of the door had sipped out his coloring.

"Well, I differ slightly on the translation. I'd read it as, 'The door of the confessor by which sins are spoken and entry made.' What do you think, old boy?" Sir Sorken said, sidling up to the door and peering into where the High Saint was stuck. "Care to confess a sin and see if it loosens up? I'd think any sin would do, but you'd better pick the biggest and best or it might think you're trying to cheat."

There was a muffled sound from the door.

"What's that?" Sir Sorken was almost boisterously loud. "Bellow it out, my lad. Let the whole place hear you."

"Pride." The High Saint's beautiful tenor was leeched of beauty now. It rasped like a stringed instrument in the hands of a novice.

And as if by magic — for, of course, that was what it was — he was released.

He stumbled forward and then spun to look at us, eyes wide in his plain face and hands trembling.

"You should have warned me," he said between heavy breaths, his head swiveling to me. "You should have told me what was coming. I should have ... I should have..."

He sat heavily down on the floor, head in his hands, and this time it was I who took a wobbling step forward. Was he ill? He didn't look right.

Well, he confessed pride. I'd say it's safe to bet that the toll taken was his confidence.

Toll?

But was it taken temporarily or forever? That's the question. And oh, I cannot wait to hear the answer. Little confection, I hope you're thinking about what you'll say. Whatever it is, I shall use it to consume you. As will the door. As will any who hears it cross your rosy lips.

I licked those rosy lips, uncertain what to say or what to do.

I didn't have to decide immediately. The Seer pushed past me and through the door, whispering something that sounded like crackling leaves. Whatever she said was born away by the wind, and whatever price she paid was invisible.

The Penitent Paladin went next. He carried no bag, but he drew his sword, ready despite seeing what had happened to his two peers on the other side of the door.

"Does it make you pay both ways?" he muttered, but no one could answer.

His confession took me by surprise.

"I am a great swordsman," he said as he entered. "And I take comfort in the thought."

I don't know what I expected, but when his sword clattered to the ground, I yelped like everyone else. Beside me, Brindle barked once, sharply.

The Penitent Paladin's right hand was gone. Vanished. Where once it had been, there was now only a grotesque stump.

He paled, staring at the hand that was no longer there.

"I swear I can feel it yet. As if it is not gone at all."

His voice was a ghost. Or perhaps it was the blood rushing through my head making me feel as though I could hear nothing else.

Why would he lose a hand when the High Saint had only had to sit down?

To each man the penalty equal to the crime.

Then what would happen to Brindle when he went through

with me?

What indeed?

Mayhap he should stay outside.

The double snort in my mind told me that neither spirit was willing to be left out.

The Seer picked up Sir Owalan's sword and offered it to him. They tottered side by side, watching us, their backs to the adventure ahead, like two souls marooned together on a vast land.

"Will you go next then, Engineer?" The Majester General asked Sir Coriand. He seemed to be trying to get control back over what was rapidly deteriorating.

The Engineers laughed together as if they could read each other's thoughts.

"Oh, I don't think so, my lad," Sir Coriand said, a good-natured smile on his lips. "I think we'll let you all tromp around in there first. We'll keep the tea on out here and you can tell us all about it."

"You don't think you should represent your order within the monastery?"

"We're representing them perfectly out here," Sir Sorken said with an ironic quirk to his mouth. "There's not an Engineer alive who would pay that price lightly."

"Our hands are important," Sir Coriand agreed, and — Saints help me — I do not know how he managed to find another cup of tea, but he was sipping it, using his sword to poke around in the dirt at the base of the door as he drank. "What do you think they constructed this door out of, Sorken? Seems a waste of blessing-imbued copper."

"And yet there it is looking terribly copper-like," his fellow paladin said, taking the tea from his fellow so that he could sip it himself.

I watched them, fascinated, as ghost ribbons of steam swirled up around them and the marigold light flashed hard and unforgiving off the blades of the swords they were so sorely abusing.

"We could lend you one of the golems, if you like," Sir

Coriand said, looking up suddenly. "Yes, I think that might be best."

"Apologies, brother."

It was the first time I'd heard the Poisoned Saint speak all morning. He was poised beside the Prince Paladin. They were friends, I thought. They'd certainly shared a tent, which the demon had found funny and told ribald jokes about no matter how much I tried to shut him up.

Still jealous? he purred to me. *So am I. He's a pretty one, your sickly paladin. As pretty as that golden giant, in his own dark way.*

"Apologies, but I will not be going down into the depths with your construct."

"Stay up here with us then," Sir Sorken said, uncaring. His baritone seemed deeper than normal and when he sipped, his thick, gnarled lips looked like moving tree roots. "We've plenty of tea to go around."

There was iron in the Poisoned Saint's tone. "With respect, I think the golems stay with you."

Sir Sorken paused, blade dug half into the earth, his brows lifting like he'd just found something almost as curious as what he was studying. He peered at Sir Adalbrand for a long moment.

"Interesting. You certainly nurse a healthy bias, don't you? Will you be going down then, Sir Adalbrand?"

The Poisoned Paladin coughed, and I almost thought — for only a sliver of a second — that he glanced at me out of the corner of his eye before he swaggered forward and through the door. Whatever he muttered was lost as he passed through to the other side and clasped the High Saint on the shoulder. And if his eyes glittered a bit more when he looked at me through the frame, who was I to judge? I did not know what had been taken from him.

"Blessed Saints," his friend cursed before laughing, and then abruptly diving through the door as if he were diving into the sea. He landed on his shoulder, tucked, rolled, and popped up to his feet. When he straightened he laughed again, the picture of health and boyish pleasure.

But only for a moment.

The Seer screamed, and then the Prince Paladin was on the floor, writhing and shuddering, and the demon in my head laughed and laughed until he was hushed by Sir Branson.

"Lord have mercy, Lord have mercy," the Majester General gasped his prayer, clinging to the parchment as his hands trembled. He was twisted around, blocking most of the view of the other side as he watched those who had already crossed the barrier.

Over everything else, we all heard Adalbrand praying, his words panicked as battle shouts, his eyes on his patient, then on us, then back again. He had laid hands on Hefertus, and though I thought he was healing him, he was also jerking and spasming with his patient as the healing took. Beside him, the Seer's breath sawed so loud and uneven that I feared she might fall, too.

Sir Kodelai sucked in air through his teeth beside me as the Majester General's prayers all ran together.

I heard a pop and glanced over to where a white-faced Sir Coriand had broken the handle off his cup. His hands shook a little until the golem beside him leaned down and took the pottery, like a mother might take shards of glass from a toddler.

"Thank you," he said quietly, patting the golem on the arm.

For its part, the golem ducked his head in acknowledgment, and by the time my eyes were back on the tableau, both Sir Hefertus and Sir Adalbrand were sitting on the stony floor, arms wrapped around one another for support.

Think carefully of what you will confess. It must be great enough that you can accept a punishment for it, but small enough that it doesn't kill us.

Us?

I'm coming with you. I doubt the door can tell the difference between dog and demon. Or paladin. It will likely see me as an extension of you.

How charming. Also, did that mean that the Prince Paladin had confessed to too small a thing?

Likely. What else would make the door so angry?

It's a door. It doesn't get angry.

That's what you think.

I was so lost in thought that I did not see the Inquisitor or the Hand of Justice cross through the door.

When I looked up again, it was just the Majester General and me left to go through. On the other side, the Inquisitor had already begun to descend the stairs and only the crown of his white head was still visible.

"Well?" the Majester General barked as though he thought I was one of his recruits.

"Well, yourself," I said, rearranging my stance from ready to casual. I didn't take orders well. It was basically a precept for Vagabonds.

They don't understand that we're blown by the wind and the will of the God. We aren't subject to their schedules or rules.

The Majester scowled. "It's just the two of us out here. You can cease with your displaying. It makes you look like a barnyard rooster, so pleased with the arrangement of his feathers that he does not see the chop."

I looked insolently at him and then flicked my gaze to the Engineers.

"Just the two of us?" I pressed. "Do Engineers suddenly cease to count?"

Stop antagonizing him, sweetmeat.

The snickering of the Holy Engineers was echoed by the snickering of the demon in my mind.

"The Majester only sees people who listen to his orders," Sir Sorken whisper-yelled to me.

"Then I suppose there's no one left for him to see here at all." I combed fingers through my hair, feigning ease.

The Majester huffed, spun, and with parchment still in hand, strode straight into the door with the word, "Gluttony" spoken so loudly that it seemed to echo off every rock and wall.

Ugh.

He twisted as he stepped through — shifting before my eyes from a strong, straight-backed man to a crooked-spined shadow of himself.

I took a hesitant step forward.

"You don't have to go through the door," Sir Sorken said, leaning back on his golem — was this one Cleft or Suture? I couldn't quite remember.

You do. You must.

Whoever was speaking in my mind now sounded panicked.

For duty.

For honor.

For Sainthood.

Wow. That was a lot of ambition pouring out of one dog. I gave him a long look. I should leave him here. But what if the demon leapt from the dog to Sir Sorken or Sir Coriand? I'd killed one paladin when I couldn't oust the infestation. Did I have the heart to murder a second time?

You must. If the hellion leaps again, you must be quick. You must be sure. I wish I could banish him myself.

I sighed.

"Come on, Brindle," I said unhappily. Unlike the others, I shouldered the bag containing my worldly possessions, grabbed the dog by his scruff, and strode to the door, stopped right before it, shook myself, and then entered.

"Doubt," I whispered as I stepped through.

Because wasn't that the worst of it? Worse than the murder of my mentor, worse than the envy I felt when I saw the riches of others, worse than everything, so much *worse* was the worry that gnawed at me day and night that all of this was for nothing. That the God was merely invented by men to explain natural phenomena. That those claiming to be his servants were deluded. And that I was likely mad.

My worst sin. Confessed now.

I heard a curse in my mind.

I told you not to pick the worst one. What does it take to beat sense into this girl?

If I knew, it's not something I'd let slip, fiend. I'm on her side. Always.

The price was too high.

The price was too high.

I felt terror sweep into my heart like a winged creature, knurled and inky, streaking from the shadows straight into my heart. It clawed up my throat and beat against my vocal cords, begging me to scream.

Doubt? It asked me. *I shall take thy doubt and multiply it. I shall shatter thy mind with uncertainty and use the shards to pin thee to the floor, flay thy flesh from thy bones, and open thee wide until there is nothing left that thou'st know but pain.*

The punishment was too great. It was too great. I couldn't do it. I whirled, looking back to the door, every shred of me wanting to dart back to the ruins on the other side. The glowing eyes of Sir Sorken's golem glittered as if it knew. They taunted me, called to me, mocked me.

Enough. Pull yourself together. My squire was bold as a lion and brash as a bear. My squire was insouciant as a squirrel stealing your last bread.

The breath sawed in my lungs and I forced myself to spin back and release Brindle from my grip.

So you doubt. Who doesn't?

Well, paladins don't.

We've both crossed the path of death. Doubt is letting go of what you know. Faith is seizing hold of what you will know. You're halfway there. Hold on.

I appreciated Sir Branson's confidence as much as I loathed the demon's laughter, but his laughter rang once more in my mind as I finally saw clearly into the hall and the place we'd paid so steep a price to enter. This was no monastery. Or at least, it wasn't like any I'd ever seen.

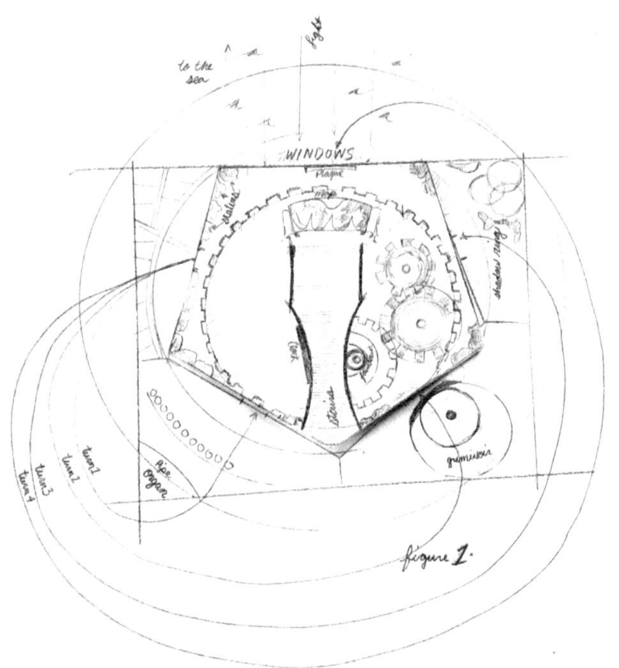

to the sea
light
WINDOWS
Plaque
Clock
Stairs
turn1
turn2
turn3
turn4
Pipe organ

figure 1.

Chapter Eleven
Poisoned Saint

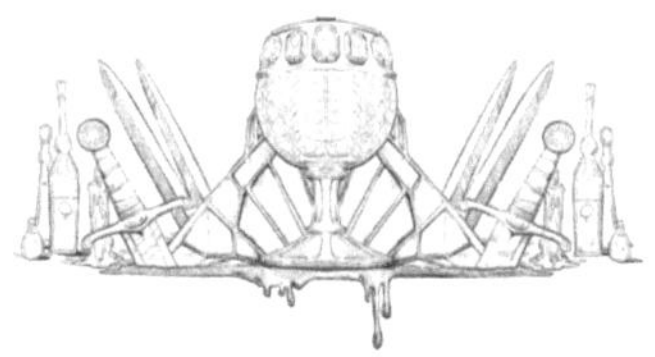

I take a long breath and force my vision to clear. Hefertus's massive arm curls around my shoulder in an unlikely vulnerability. I can smell the rare spices he anoints himself with every morning. Frankincense and something else.

The spasms I took from Hefertus leave my hands trembling and my limbs weak, but the curse I took when I went through the door is worse. It burns in my veins and runs through my mind, opening all the locks, throwing all the bolts, swinging wide every door — not a physical mark, but a mark all the same.

Without meaning to, I have invited something inside that should have been kept out. An enemy has breached my walls and I lifted the portcullis with my own hands. It leaves me with an oily feeling of dread and a terrible inability to govern my own thoughts. All my tight control falls suddenly slack.

I don't know what penalty the others took, beyond Hefertus. I've taken half his penalty, and I can feel it clearly enough. His was a simple punishment, though not an easy one. Death — even a quick one — is not easy.

Now, answer me this. What sort of door to a monastery demands so high a toll? Is it to purge the soul of sin? Or is it to hide something beyond this door?

I rather think it might be the latter. I do not trust this place.

I have read of attempts to make people holy by force. They never end well. Not for those being made or those doing the making. I have the creeping feeling that this may be one of those places. I have no desire to be made or unmade by it.

I force myself out of my own thoughts. The floor beneath me is polished rock— light but shot through with dark veins. I focus on the strength of it beneath my feet, remove Hefertus's arm from my shoulder, and pull myself to my feet.

When the Majester General steps through the door, he has a tic in the corner of his eye and is masking something at his left side. He looks ten years older. I open my hands to offer healing but he waves them roughly away. He wants nothing I might offer him. Well and good. I'm not sure I have strength left to give.

"I propose we do this systematically. I shall lead the search," he barks. I see in him an echo of my own determination not to bend to the toll of this place.

He doesn't bother waiting for the Vagabond Paladin. It seems the others are willing to disrespect her without thought. I wonder what it's like to live your whole life like that — as an afterthought. Is it freeing, or painful ... or both?

The Majester has his parchment out and ready, charcoal poised over it, but he's too late with his commands and his authority has been shaken off already, like a light dusting of snow on a crisp morning. I'm the only one waiting with him and it's not for him that I wait.

"This will be madness," he mutters, pushing past me to rush after the others as if he can chivvy them back under his wing.

I wish him well with that, though I smirk at his back. After all, what is a general without his army?

My father had generals. They were not his, but they pretended to be and he pretended with them. I recall them distinctly. They did not make lists. They did not try to manage those who did not salute them. They lazed about like fat cats, eating, drinking, and then studying a map for an hour, ordering the deaths of thousands, and going off for a nap. This Majester is as much a general as I am a Saint.

I draw in a deep breath, forget the Majester, and instead, try to look as if I am not waiting as I study my surroundings. This monastery — or the foundation of one, I suppose — has all the welcome of an open tomb, and while the door back remains open, who knows how exacting the price to return might be? It would be best for all if we did what we came to do and then left without returning. One trip. One risk.

My eyes flick over the stark polished stone. The faint light that seeps through the door is all the light in this place but it is enough to see dimly. It may seem bare, but where there is one trap there will be others.

The snuffle of a dog makes me turn, and there's the brindled hound and his mistress. Through the door behind them, the world looks as if I am peering through water. I faintly see the gleam of a golem eye and then nothing but ripples and shadows.

The Vagabond Paladin carries all her worldly possessions in a sack over her shoulder, her hair wild and falling from the braid she wove to crown her head. She has cleaned it since yesterday. I barely swallow down the desire that swells up within me at the sight of that mass of clean hair. I've always had a fondness for long, tumbling locks but this is beyond the usual temptation.

It's my payment. I felt it the moment I went through the door and confessed my inability to keep my heart's longing to myself, and now here it is laughing at me as it twists my heart and body against my best interests.

"Lust," I told the door, and the ability to control it is what has been stripped from me.

And now, when I should be looking away, instead, I let my eyes feast. Now, when I should be moving away, my feet are rooted in place. Now, when I should keep my tongue silent and my thoughts on pure things, my tongue speaks in greeting and my thoughts tangle round and round, feeding me a steady stream of possibilities.

If I had any sense, I'd run faster than the Majester General to escape this woman.

Be still, I warn myself. Be wary.

But wariness is a citizen of another land.

"Walk with me?" my traitor tongue asks on my behalf.

"That might be best," the Vagabond says, gripping her tattered sack in an arm so laced with feminine muscle that I see little glimmers of it under her wristguard and the threadbare fabric that swaths her shoulder.

Unbidden, my mind reminds me of what an arm like that would feel like slipping through the caressing grip of my palm and fingers. I bite my lip so hard that it bleeds, and that is enough to put my mind back on the task.

I have counseled others on how to remain steadfast. Surely, my temptation is no worse than theirs have been. I remember one brother dolefully telling me he had been assigned as an advisor to the Princess Surina, who had already killed five lovers and still had more lined up merely on the rumor of her charms and great beauty.

"Just don't think of it," I had told him. "Discipline your mind."

I wonder if he found that advice as impossible as I do now.

"There will be other traps," I say calmly, beginning my descent. The bite in my leg twinges with every step. "We must be vigilant."

The dog slides by me, nose close to the steps. I breathe in his wet-dog scent with gratitude. It's hard to be too taken up with love when you're smelling wet dog and feeling the pain of his bite in your flesh.

"Of course," she says.

Her eyes are everywhere, noting our surroundings, keeping track of things. If you travel from place to place all your life you must be good at that — quick judgments, lightning assessments. She's a good choice for an ally. Or so I try to convince myself.

"With two of us, perhaps one can help free the other."

I know that I mock myself with such weak arguments. Were I truly in need of a partner, I could have asked Hefertus to stay with me.

We descend into the darkness through a precisely cut cavern. The ceiling and walls — hewn from white rock any church would envy — are thickly embossed with cunning images of animals, beasts, and angels with five tongues. I find that troubling. Why five tongues? Why not two — or one?

This is not like any monastery I've ever seen. But then, again, this is ancient. Perhaps ancient monks did not yet embrace the clean lines of the holy. Perhaps they found holiness in the wild and untamed things.

A few steps down and the ceiling vanishes upward, the stairs widen to three times their expanse, and a hall opens up below us. My tongue cleaves to the roof of my mouth.

Even within Saint Rauche's Citadel, I have not seen grandeur to this scale. Nor will I, I think.

We'll be walking a hundred more stairs to descend to the shining floor below. And when we do, we'll be in a room bathed in white light from several dozen long, narrow windows, cut like massive arrow slits in the rock on one side of the hall. Between them, at the very center, is a larger triptych window of stained glass. It is tall and narrow, too, and sections are missing, shattered on the ground like fallen leaves in autumn. I can almost make out what the depicted scene the window once bore might have been, but the missing pieces make it too difficult to be definitive. Through the windows — both the slit windows and the triptych — I can easily see the sea as she reflects the face of the sun back to him. She is a dark pewter laced with my favorite color — rich marigold, like my Marigold's eyes.

The same color spills across the floor below, where someone has taken the time to intricately lay a mosaic of rock shards into what I can tell is a map, and yet, it looks like no map of ours, nor any I studied from ages past. It's breathtaking in the loving detail paid to every nuance of land and sea. Even the scrollwork around it is a work of art.

"Look!" I hear Sir Kodelai call from twenty stairs below. "I can see Cantora on that map. She sank beneath the sea a thousand years ago with her great ships and their purple dyes."

"And are those the Sephorus Islands?" I hear another paladin reply. "Before the mouth of the God opened and spewed out fire upon them?"

Strangest of all is how the artist has laid out the circle of the earth, dividing it out as if he had unraveled the peel of an orange and tried to reassemble it flat, rather than simply portraying the disk of the known earth.

I trace the edges of the mosaic with my gaze and follow them to the edges of the room, where white marble statues line the walls. They are so large that at first, I think there are cupboards carved in their bases, surrounded by sculpted roses. I realize, after a heartbeat, that they are doors to other rooms. Doors for men — but the nearest one is smaller than the foot of the statue towering over it. The roses clustered around it are large enough for me to curl up inside one and sleep like a honeybee.

I inspect the nearest statue — carved from white marble laced with gold veins. I'm not sure we could replicate it today, so intricate is the detail, so large is the scale. It depicts a bearded, half-naked man. A sword hangs from his scabbard; another is buried in his chest. Flowering vines twist up his legs. A chain wraps around his knees, binding them together, and each link of it is carved separately and interwoven. How long would that chain alone have taken to craft? A pair of wings fold tightly against his back and his mouth is an open cavern, his head tilted back unnaturally as if his jaw were broken. The whole of his head is levered up and back so that he looks as if he is swallowing a terrible brew. I feel my own lip curling in sympathy. The artist's attention to detail only makes the result resonate that much more in the heart. The statue's hands are lifted upward, each finger sculpted in loving detail to show the strain it takes for him to hold up the edge of the ceiling. I feel it, too.

I can barely snatch my eyes away to look at the next statue but when I do, he looks just like his fellow — if his fellow were dressed exactly like me. Beardless, like me. Haunted expression like —

"Like you," the Vagabond Paladin breathes, breaking into my thoughts.

I look back at the first man. Mayhap if my angle were different, I would see Hefertus in the set of that jaw.

"And there's me," she says, her voice like the sound of someone who has just discovered they've been sealed into a jar of wriggling maggots.

I follow her pointed finger and there is her doppelganger. Her stone hair is tangled all around her in taunting deshabille, a single gauntlet and pauldron on one arm her only armor. The rest of her is hidden beneath artfully draped rags. There are butterflies in her hair and on her wrists, and her gauntleted hand grips the hilt of a sword that has been buried straight through her shapely thigh.

I feel my face grow hot as sunrise, as if — fool that I am — I think a marble statue formed thousands of years ago is somehow a representation of the flesh and blood woman beside me.

Oh, the payment the door took is hard indeed. I would have chosen differently.

I look back at my own semblance. I see now that his open mouth is full of something. It gushes down his chin and falls in cloying strands as far as his belt.

Were I a weaker man, I would flee this place right now. And, perhaps, I would return to my aspect and my story would simply be of how I saw terrors and left others to die. Or we might be at war with whichever aspect found the cup. Or, perhaps, I might be called mad.

Instead, I swallow and take another step, nearly colliding with the cursed dog, who looks almost as if he is laughing at me, though I know full well that dogs do not laugh. The bite wound in my thigh twinges in a reminder not to get too close to this one.

He is no jester but a deadly threat. I almost think I see a red gleam in one of his eyes — a trick of the light, no doubt.

"Is ..." The Beggar Paladin pauses to clear her throat. "Did it move, just now?"

I glance backward at her and regret it immediately. Her face is lit with the marigold of the sea and with equal parts horror and wonder. She has a little of the divine about her — enough of it that, were I not a holy paladin, I might be tempted to worship at her altar instead.

I have to clear my throat, too, but for other reasons. Even then, the end of my sentence takes a higher note than I'd meant it to.

"Did what move?"

"The demon trapped on the ceiling," she says. And I follow her hand to where it grips the hilt of her sword and then follow her eyes up, up, up. "Did it move?"

On the ceiling of the great hall is a strange relief sculpture, but unlike the pure white of the ones below, this one is part gild and part jet black. The gilding follows the edges of what looks like a cutout of leaves and flowers, vines and branches, and scroll-work edged with rats and sharks, trumpets and daggers. But between the cutouts and under all that gilding is a mass of glossy black. I would have thought it was lacquer meant to enhance the gold. But my eye has trouble following its surface. It seems to twist beneath my eye as if my gaze is oil, slipping off the hidden form.

It is from this dark relief sculpture that I feel the pull I felt before. Something sings a single note to my heart, bids it come, bids it die. I feel the pull worse than hunger, worse than thirst.

And it is at the very peak of that culminating desire that I see the twitch.

Something in the inky darkness — something gleaming with just the barest edge of marigold — *something* has moved.

I feel my muscles go rigid and my bones nearly leap from my flesh when she sets a hand on my arm.

"Let's go below," she says in a tone slick with caution. "Look no more at the monster."

My voice leaves me sounding hollow. "Monster? Is that what it is?"

"I hardly know. But I know evil. To look is to see. To see is to understand. To understand is to become. And to become is everything. Do not become evil, Sir Saint."

Chapter Twelve
Vagabond Paladin

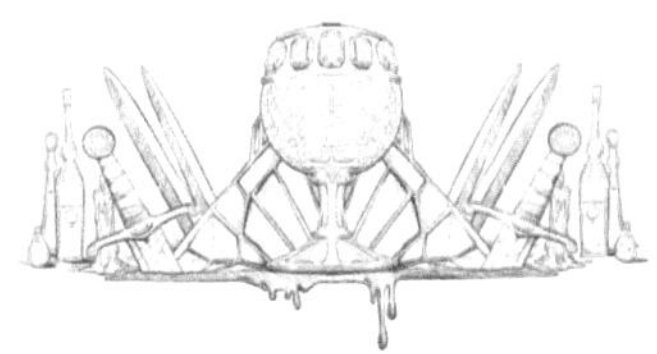

B*y the five bones. By the Saint's cowl. By the —*

I felt the demon rip the voice from Sir Branson and take it himself.

Ignore it, snackling. It's not your concern. Keep going.

But it was a demon. Most certainly. I had no doubt. And neither did my companions, based on their reactions. I should cast it out. I should not flee.

I adore your arrogance that you think you could cast out a demon someone else trapped thousands of years ago. Ages have passed. The world has turned. This place was buried and revealed and in all that time this trap has held ... and you will open it? You adorable child. You sweet summer lamb. You will disassemble the cage? You will remove the bait?

Bait?

What would you name it? This is not a prison made to hold demons. There's a special name for that place, if you'll recall. The denizen you just saw is the minnow slid onto the hook. It waits for a much bigger fish.

But what would a *living demon* be bait for?

More demons? Perhaps these monks were set on the destruction of evil forces?

Whoever was counseling me now seemed very uncertain about his suggestion.

And I was just as wary. I bit my lip until I almost tasted blood. Fear coursed ragged and sharp through my veins. It was my payment for entering this place, I knew it. For I had not been this terrified when my own, dear Sir Branson tried to kill me, nor when I was forced to slay him, nor when his face was torn off by his dog.

Fear is a useful weapon when one must be careful not to slip into a roaring river, but it is a terrible thing when there is no clear danger and one must watch every shadow for what might be the threat.

I peered upward again. I didn't like the look of these massive statues. I didn't like that they looked like *us*. How could they have been made in our image when they were created thousands of years ago?

There are great forces at work here. Don't you feel them? Or are you too thick? Too human?

Quiet, fiend.

Quiet yourself, sweetmeat. You need me down here. Need me more than you ever needed the old paladin. He's nothing now but an echo of a conscience that isn't serving you. Lean now on me. You'll need it if you're going to lead this pasty cohort to victory.

I swallowed and followed Adalbrand down the stairs. He was acting strangely, seeming to want to be near me and distant from me both at once, and he still limped from where Brindle had bitten a chunk out of his leg.

Worth it.

I was worried he might be an unstable ally.

I stole a glance at him. His shoulders were slumped and face was pale from healing the others. Interesting that none of them stayed behind to make sure he was capable of continuing. Was it possible that Poisoned Saints were as overlooked as Vagabond Paladins?

It's not quite the same. The things that blind the average person to our worth are not quite the same as what makes them squirrelly around the Poisoned Saints. With us, they are blind — they see only surface things and since our surface is grimy, they do not see the gold beneath it, just as they cannot see the rot beneath a lacquered surface. In the case of the poor Poisoned Saints, no one likes the reminder that they bear for us what we cannot bear ourselves. It makes the soul squirm a little. Guilt is handled easiest when banished deep underground.

Amen to that, the demon agreed. *I never have dealings with guilt. He cheats you every time.*

The demon spoke as if guilt were a person.

Of course he is. He wears a strange hat and has too many eyes for his face.

I shivered. This place was not the right setting for stories that made the spine crawl.

Perhaps Adalbrand's strangeness, then, was only his reaction to this beautiful but haunting place. Or perhaps he was likewise possessed by a slightly indulgent demon who would rip his throat out if it could.

I swallowed the hysterical laugh that tried to crawl up my throat and rested a hand on Brindle's head.

He smelled incredibly doggy for an animal that was really only one-third dog. I leaned into the scent, trying to remember what was real and physical in a world stained through with spirits. I did not want this monastery to get under my skin any more than it was and already it was creeping under it like an army of ants on a quest to raid my heart. What kind of monks would have been in a place like this?

Can't you feel the power here? Even a thousand years later it pulses through me like life blood.

The power made me itch worse than pepperleaf.

What if it can make you a Saint? What if it made the other Saints you know and adore?

I wasn't sure how I felt about that. Was it possible that some of the statues in the churches I had visited were of mortals who came to this very place and sat underneath that glossy black demon, and somehow were refined into something brighter and more holy? And if they were, who was I to say that this was wrong or threatening? A good paladin would want it, wouldn't she? No matter the discomfort. No matter the price.

Say your catechism, my dear. I always find that helps.

I didn't think it was going to help this time.

The demon started to laugh.

It's a good suggestion, even if it was made by a fiend, Sir Branson said wryly. *Is that how you begin, demon? Do you take the unsuspecting slowly, first with good advice and then gradually with a souring of it?*

I shivered. I would not be taken by a demon. Not now. Not ever. I glanced up at the ceiling again, horribly conscious that now there were two demons in the room, and I — a hunter of demons — seemed unequal to the task of destroying either of them.

I want to be very clear, Sir Branson told me. *The demon in your head is not a toy. He is not tame. You must not grow used to him.*

Oooh, what's this now? Treachery?

We were nearly to the bottom of the stairs and the other paladins were all staring at words etched below the triptych window. Someone had thought they were important enough to carve them as tall as my hand into the stone and then inlay them with bronze. As one, the others turned to look up at me.

Good thing I'd brought the dog. Apparently, I'd be working translation duty for the duration of this foray. I reached down and laid a hand on Brindle's head. He looked up at me with those liquid puppy eyes.

"Who's a good doggy, then?" I whispered to him.

Isn't he warming to the heart? You know as well as I do that you could never kill him, snackling.

The demon laughed in my mind.

I glanced over my shoulder and saw Sir Adalbrand looking up at the broken window with a wen between his brows. Did he see something there that I did not?

Read the words, demon. And let's see what it takes to be made a Saint.

The laughter grew louder but the demon complied.

"Our hearts spoke out our hopes
And our souls bore the cost
The man and the spirit
and all that was lost.
Bold together we race
where no others have trod.
For we are more than men,
We have become ... Saints."

So, these people really did think they could become Saints. Those privileged few chosen by the God to do great works upon the earth or sit in his council after death. What devoted worshipper wouldn't crave that? Surely, no paladin would back down from such a challenge.

I glanced around at the eight paladins with me — each representing a different way of viewing the same god. Were these people Saint material?

"What does it say, Beggar?" The Majester General asked me. Charming. He should double as a jailkeeper with a face like that.

I kept my own face blank and even as I repeated the demon's translation, trying to judge the reactions of those listening. And if it was strange that a demon was rattling off the recipe to be made a Saint, no one noticed. And if it was odd that every eye seemed to light and every back grow straighter, well, no one mentioned that either. But I was keeping mental notes.

"So, this really is a place where Sainthood can be found," Sir Kodelai said with a reverent sigh. No one could fault him for his holy ambition. "It's been four generations since a Saint was named. Is it possible that we needed a place like this to finally achieve holy perfection before the face of the God?"

"If we find the Cup, perhaps," the High Saint said in a quelling tone. By the glimmer in his eye, I thought he found it a personal affront that someone else would consider themselves to be worthy of Sainthood when he was standing right there — practically an inch from their noses — being the most austerely holy of them all. "Let us pause and pray."

I wasn't interested in listening to more of their chatter and I didn't want to spend a moment more lingering here than I had to — not even in prayer. There was an itch between my shoulder blades that wouldn't go away, and the manner in which the paladins all paused to kneel together around the broken triptych made my skin crawl.

The sea breeze drifted in through the panes of the triptych in sharp, cold gusts. The original window had depicted two characters, one pale in whites and blues, the other formed of dusky dark crimsons and flaring golds. Flowers in varying states of bloom were scattered across the bottoms of their individual panes. Someone had taken considerable efforts to depict each in their own window and then the pair of them tangled together in the larger middle windowpane. Just enough of the windows had been lost that both individual windows were missing the creatures' faces and whatever had been in their hands.

The dark creature seemed to stand in a sea of water and the light creature in a sea of fire. These seas were depicted in the colors of the other. But in the center, there was no sea, just two beings — man, beast, devil, or angel, who could say — tangled together in what could have been an embrace, a mutual death, or a terrifying battle. Whichever it was, one thing was very strange. One of the two characters — and it was impossible to tell which one — was holding a trident, and each of the three tips was streaked in red.

I didn't want to be near that window, though I could not have said why. That it was placed directly over the rhyme I'd recited for the others only made my stomach flip more. It was possible these monks merely had a theology that involved unfamiliar symbols and that my reaction was mere prejudice.

Unlikely. You've never been very prejudiced, my girl, except against the rich.

On the whole, I was inclined to agree with Sir Branson. Something was wrong here. If this place truly created Saints, then perhaps it weeded out unworthy candidates by showing them that window and then tossing anyone who didn't see how problematic it was.

I would be the first to confess I hadn't seen the great places of the earth's kingdoms, despite my wide and varied travels, but among those I had seen, there'd always been a clear theme. Good was depicted as slaying evil. Had this been a knight with his foot on a devil's neck and that trident stuck in its back, I would have been happy to kneel in prayer before it. It deeply troubled me that the others didn't see the wrongness of a stalemate.

One of them added a happy verse to the song.

Yes, that was my first clue that the High Saint was not as high as he claimed to be.

The voice in my head snickered.

I adore your judgmental heart, little snackling. Don't ever change it. It brings you closer and closer to me. Let's go see what other paladins we can break, shall we?

Do you ever trip on your own certainty, Hxyaltrytchus?

No, but the tail can be problematic.

And now my cheeks were heating at being complimented by a demon for what was surely a sin. Tonight, I'd need to mortify my flesh to make penance. Perhaps I'd spend another night without the tent.

Or you could pass on the tea the Engineers make. That would be a fitting punishment for a judging heart.

The God forfend. That punishment was a bit steep.

For the first time since this began, I thought the laughter in my head might be Sir Branson's.

I broke off from the others, hoping that in their reverence they wouldn't notice me shuddering as I slipped away, and headed down the bank of windows at speed toward the towering feet of the statue that looked too much like our Prince Paladin. Brindle loped beside me. Even given his possessed state, it felt better to have him with me.

It is better. You'd miss us if we left. Who would teach you to look past the surface?

I already did that well enough.

Yes, but not like I do. I can show you the infected heart of a man and tell you how he will rot.

What a delight.

And then I can offer recipes for rotted heart.

The light spilling from the stone-encased windows was unnerving — it seemed too bright and the sun still too low for all that had happened so far. But perhaps, if I searched steadily and carefully, I could complete the search in one day and I wouldn't have to pass through that eerie door again. I hadn't liked confessing my core sin. Saying it aloud felt too much like cementing it into reality. And what if I had to add another sin to the list tomorrow? What if I was struck dead for greed, as I was fairly certain Hefertus nearly had been?

You have all your things. You could camp in here. Wasn't that your original intention? The horse will be fine. He's beside a stream, and I'm sure the Engineers won't be so heartless as to not check on the animals.

That *had* been my original plan. I glanced up above me at the gleaming black form barely visible from the marble floor. I wasn't sure, anymore, that I could sleep in here. In fact, I was hardly certain that I could sleep *above,* knowing there was a demon trapped just below me.

And yet you sleep every night with one cuddled next to you. Ironic.

Brindle, oblivious to our conversation, trotted ahead, sniffing everything, from the mosaic map on the floor for a world that didn't exist, to the feet of the statues. I hoped he didn't feel the need to scent mark them.

It must be nice to be as oblivious as the other aspects were about demons but unfortunately, that made them poor backup if I were to try to cast the one above out.

You can't. Not unless you open the trap. And if you do, then he'll be loose first. You can't remove him on your own. You need backup.

Once, when Sir Branson lived, we were rustled from where we were sleeping in a barn loft as a man with a red nose and redder eyes pled with us to join others of our aspect in his village.

"They say they can't do it alone," he'd told us, nearly tearing the edge of his jerkin as he wrung it back and forth between nervous hands. "Please come."

We'd gone, grim and miserable, to help. It had taken two paladins, a squire, and a night of prayer, though fortunately we'd managed to dislodge the demon the easy way — without violence. Had we not been near to help, Sir Fransisci might have had to try a more brutal method — or failed entirely. I hadn't thought of that night in decades. It had been ... troubling.

"I thought you'd agreed that two were better than one," a deep voice said, ripping me from the memory as the Poisoned Saint caught up with me.

Three is better than one. But four is entertaining. Dance for us, pretty knight. Bare your vices so we can laugh.

When I glanced at him, his eyes were scanning the room around us, catching on details and then discarding them as if he were looking for danger. It was not easy to rule anything out quickly in this place. Everything was carved or sculpted or decorated, so ornate, and breathtakingly intricate, and all of it carved in white stone. I couldn't help but wonder what the rooms aboveground might have been like. Could they have matched this grandeur? You could host a ball in this main room at the bottom of the stairs and the beauty of the hall would outshine any guests.

Sir Adalbrand's hand rode on his sword pommel, ready to draw at a moment's notice. When his eyes finally caught mine, they glittered with suspicion, matching the shining cup embroidered on his tabard. It was the only bright thing on his person. His cloak and tabard were black and his chainmail was rubbed with something to blacken it, too. He looked out of place in this spotless white realm.

"Not one of the faithful?" I asked him, looking over my shoulder a second time, this time not at a demon but at those who were far more devout than I could be with my tenuous hold on faith, the God have mercy on me. Whatever power they felt seeping through the air and into their souls when they prayed eluded me, left me empty and dry.

"You're a puzzle, Lady Paladin," Sir Adalbrand said with a small smile as he matched his pace to mine. He kept a wide berth from Brindle. That bite must still pain him.

A puzzle he wants to solve. Snicker.

Did the demon just say "snicker"?

The demon's teasing might have made my tone sterner than usual. "I don't see how I can puzzle you. I say what I mean and mean what I say."

He might be pretty to look at and gentle with those hands, but right now Adalbrand was an unwelcome distraction. I had a quest to complete, a demon waiting to drop on me from above, another ready to tear my throat out in the night the moment my paladin superior slipped, and a bad case of terror still lingering from passing through the door. It made every shadow seem exaggerated and every item feel threatening. Even the strange map on the floor made my skin crawl.

My heightened fear kept telling me that this was no monastery but an elaborate gate to hell, and that could not be true.

I did not need distractions on top of everything else.

"And you don't stay for prayers," he said softly, but his soft tone had a blade buried in it, ready to slide out and strike if he did not care for my answer.

Interesting.

I met his eyes then. The last orange in the morning light made their brown depths cinnamon. I could almost taste the spice on my tongue.

So can I, the demon purred.

"You didn't stay for prayers either," I said equally softly.

He licked his lips, considering. He was weighing something. Measuring his words with care.

"Didn't your parents teach you to pray? Or were you born untamable?"

If I did not know better, I'd think he was beguiling me. His expression was subtle, barely playing in the fine lines around his mouth.

I hesitated. But what would the truth hurt? Especially now, when the secrets I had to keep were so much more dire than the ones about my past.

"My parents were good and devout, but they died at the hands of fever, one after another over the course of two nights."

He looked stricken, and paused, laying a hand on my arm.

"You have my sympathy. Did you come to the Rejected God after that?"

I pressed my lips firmly together. I was not telling him this for sympathy and I didn't need his condolences. Or his touch. What I needed was to satisfy his curiosity enough that he would leave me to my work.

"My parents were peddlers and laypeople for the Aspect of the Rejected God. Already on the road. Already devout. It did not seem too great a leap to seek out Sir Branson and beg him to make me squire after they passed. I had met him two weeks prior when our paths crossed and I knew him to be a paladin respected by my parents."

"How old were you?" His habit of tilting his head when he listened to me was in full force. This was no idle conversation. He was interrogating me. Though why he did that now remained to be seen.

"Eleven years."

"And he took you as squire?" He sounded surprised.

"Why would he not?" I couldn't quite keep the prickle from my voice. Why would he doubt me on this?

The dog seemed to cough. It was circling a massive broken

clock nestled against the staircase.

Or rather, a clock that seemed broken, because the hands did not move and the time looked like nothing familiar to me. It had four hands and all four pointed up, and on the face of the clock there was a cup engraved. Which could mean anything. It didn't have to be the Cup of Tears. It could be a clock that timed tea breaks. Who would know?

The clock's round face was supported by carved hands. There must have been a hundred of them, each the size of a real hand and intricately carved from white marble and then polished until they gleamed. They wove in and out and around one another so that no two were posed the same way.

The ticks around the clock were not labeled with numerals or letters and I didn't bother counting them beyond checking that the clock base didn't open.

Sir Adalbrand continued to press his conversation. "You were too old for great book learning and too young to be of physical help. A burden from the moment he took you on."

The dog coughed again and Adalbrand frowned at it.

Rude to call you a burden. Rude.

I felt my face flush. I had never thought of things like that. I'd always thought that Sir Branson was moderate in every way, neither too generous nor too stingy, not too holy nor too profane, not too indulgent nor too disciplined. Just a man.

I accept this eulogy with gratitude. Blessings on you.

And yet Adalbrand made a good case for him being more than that.

"He must have been a good paladin. Worthy. Honorable," Sir Adalbrand said gently. The hand on my arm drifted to cup my elbow, as if he were trying to lend an old woman support.

I turned to him, eyes narrowing, and shook his hand off. If he wanted to touch me, he should get my permission.

I agree. Too much flattery is never wise. Why so many flowery words for a man he never met? Why all this touching? From a Poisoned Saint, no less.

I was already agitated and this conversation was making it worse.

"And I killed him?" I hissed, turning my body so that if he drew on me I'd be ready in my defense. "Is that what you've come to bring to mind? Will you make a demand now before you agree to keep my secret?"

Cough.

I glanced over my shoulder again, but the others were all still praying, some kneeling, some at parade rest, others with hands lifted upward. I didn't need to fear what the paladins might hear or see.

"No," Adalbrand whispered back in a tone fit for the halls of a library. Something I could not read flickered across his expression. "That's not what ..."

"Thank you for your interest," I said coldly, turning sharply to the first door we'd come to and striding through. I didn't care where it went so long as it was not where Adalbrand could blackmail me.

It led to a hall with a smooth marble floor and white paneling on the walls that was carved to look as if it were woven. Someone had fitted the wall panels with candle recesses and in each one was a cup or a goblet or a tumbler. Each was individual in material, shape, and size. Inconvenient. How would we find one cup among many?

Wait for me! The blasted knight is in the way.

I should stay to study the cups — though surely the Cup of Tears would not just be one among many, would it? But the terror that had gripped me when I stepped through the door descended twice as strongly now that I was away from Brindle and Adalbrand. It took hold of my heart and squeezed. It bid me flee whatever was chasing me, and all my years of tight self-control unwound at once.

I hurried up the hall to where it branched, took the branch to the right, and opened the first door I saw. I had no more reason to choose it than any other. Unreasoned panic alone drove my steps.

I stopped in my tracks the moment I entered the first room. I had expected a room of study or hall of prayer. I'd expected books, perhaps, or lines of pews. This, however, was someone's personal room. And that someone was wealthy, indulgent, and appeared to have left in a hurry. So preserved was the room, it looked as if the owner had just leapt up for a moment, planning to return to the unmade bed, and it gave me the terrible feeling that he was watching me over my shoulder.

Something grabbed me by the pauldrons, shaking a gasp from me, spun me hard and to the left, and pinned me, face-first, against the wood paneling.

My heart hammered in my chest, breath coming in sharp gasps. It couldn't ... there couldn't be someone living here, could there be? After all this time? Of course not, it was unbelievable, but I couldn't shake the feeling.

The wall smelled of mildew and dust and rotting books. But it was nothing compared to the panic I felt at having my chest pressed hard to the wood by a force between my shoulder blades. My right cheek was flattened against the wall and I could not turn.

A door slammed. My dog barked. My heart choked me with fear.

My attacker had been smart enough to pin my sword hand. I fought against the vise-grip on my gauntlet, unable to shake him loose or even see who it was who had pinned me. Behind the door, Brindle's growls were deep and demanding.

What's he doing to you? Are you dead?

He! Which he?

My breath sawed in my lungs. All I could see in my mind was the looming shape of the black demon unfurling from the ceiling and sliding down the wall to rip out my windpipe. A scream rose in my throat.

"I wouldn't scream." The voice was right in my ear, quiet, growling, but laced with something dangerous. I thought I felt the warmth of lips against the shell of my ear.

Adalbrand, of course.

I let my exhale out slowly.

"What are you doing?"

Look, I've wanted to be pinned to a wall by an attractive man in armor for about as long as I've fantasized about men, but I thought that — ideally — we'd be married and he'd be interested in having fun, not growling threats in my ear.

I couldn't fault the actual person who pinned me. He lived up to the standard of my dreams just fine. The Poisoned Saint was attractive enough to be distracting, but it was pretty clear from how he slammed my hand against the wall when I tried a twist escape that he wasn't doing this for fun. Well, not *that* kind of fun. He might be one of those who enjoyed cruelty to others, and if he was, he could march *right* off.

"I heard you when you went through the door, even if no one else did," he whispered. "I heard you confess to doubt. That isn't the confession of a paladin."

"Isn't it?" I asked through gritted teeth while trying to aim a kick backward. "What is the confession of a paladin? Murder? In a moment, Brindle will come through the door and then you'll have two of us to face at once."

"Just like Sir Branson did before you stole his cloak and sword?" His whisper became a growl and the brush of his lip stung as the bristle of unshaven face scraped against my ear. "I don't know what you are, but you are no Vagabond Paladin."

I held on to my dignity. I wouldn't plead or demand.

"Who are you to judge? The book says, 'For each judgment wrought, to each a dole given.' If you're judging me, then you'll be judged the same way."

"I welcome it." His breath was hot. I tried again to shake his grip and flinched when he slammed me back against the wall with twice the force he had used before. Pain made my breath spasm and my vision darken. "May the God judge me indeed, for you are no Vagabond Paladin. The Vagabond forswears wealth so that the generous God might provide. The Vagabond asks for a blessing in faith and receives it in a way that no other paladin is given —

straight from the heart of the God, in acknowledgment of her physical deprivations. The Vagabond lives a life soaked through with faith, and by your account, so did your lay parents, and so did your mentor."

"If you have a point to make, make it."

I kicked out at "make it" and tried to land a blow to his vulnerable knee, but he must have dodged. It was only meant as a distraction as my off-hand went for the dagger in my belt. He was faster than me and just as cunning. He pinned my off-hand with a knee, not once lessening the pressure on my back and other hand. I had to clench my jaw to keep from crying out as his steel greave dug into the small bones of my hand.

"When you confessed to doubt, you confirmed my fears." He was no longer whispering but his voice was breathy. "That you are no paladin, but a pretender. That you should not be here at all."

Again, that stab of fear sliced through me from gullet to brain. He knew the edge of my secret. That I was unworthy. That I should not be here.

You should. You must.

"Tell me you deserve to be here," he breathed into my ear and I shivered.

"I do not," I confessed.

Saints and Angels, girl. You deserve it if any of them do. Who cares who is "worthy"? In the end, it's always the one willing to get dirty and do the job.

"Tell me you are the best your Aspect had to offer," he pressed.

"I cannot."

How do you know? You met so few of us!

"Tell me, then, if you can, whose authority rests on your shoulders." The steel in his voice he'd been masking with gentleness slid out now. He was readying himself to fight me and kill me. I could feel it. "Tell me what gives you the right to stand with the rest."

"The authority of the God," I breathed and a prayer slipped

from my lips unbidden. "Bless me, Rejected God, for I am rejected even as you so often are."

My prayer might have been feeble. It might have been a dashed-together thing compelled more by desperation than true faith, but I supposed it was also enough, because the Poisoned Saint leapt suddenly backward, and by the time I turned to face him, his jaw had dropped and he was watching me with trembling hands and eyes wide as an owl's.

"Well. Well, now." He ran a hand through his hair, his eyes wild and vulnerable, breath huffing out between statements. "That was unexpected."

"What was unexpected?" I asked, shuddering with relief, drawing in a long breath, and rolling my neck from side to side. I was ready. The second he leapt for me again, my sword would be up and I'd run him through.

My knees were bent, stance ready, sword on my hilt.

Don't draw yet. I saw something strange through that door ...

I didn't draw.

But I wanted to. My breathing was heavy. Fingers itching.

Across from me, Adalbrand licked his lips. "I've only heard the voice of the God once before. When he called me."

Once before what?

He glanced upward, reverently, looking to the heavens, but all I could think of was that there was a huge, bulbous demon between him and the God. Perhaps even now it laughed at him.

I trembled despite myself, and blood was thick on my breath. How dare he confront me like that? How dare he pin me to the wall like an enemy? If he wanted a fair fight, I would give it to him. Right now. Right here.

"You know," I said, acidly, "it was unexpected for me, too. Maybe it was too much to ask for a warm reception from my fellow paladins, but an actual attack? Accusations? Threats? What a delight."

Yes! Get him, snackling!

His face paled.

I raised a single eyebrow.

His eyes were locked on me as if I were some kind of miracle that had been revealed to him.

"You took my secret, freely offered to you, and used it against me," I said, quiet steel in every word.

Behind the door, Brindle growled, but I wasn't ready to deal with him yet. One animal at a time.

That's right, snackling. Eat his gizzard. Grind his heart between your knuckles!

I ignored the voice in my head.

"You used violence to demand answers."

The Poisoned Saint swallowed and made the sign of the penitent. Knuckles to forehead, then nose, then heart. "How shall I beg your forgiveness, Lady Paladin?"

Make him do more than beg. Make him pay for his failing.

They were all fools.

"Are you unable to see that I could use violence on you, too?" I kept my voice low. Threats are delivered best when they are delivered quietly. "I could come up on *you* from behind. I could slam *you* against a wall. Perhaps I don't have your strength, but I have my cunning."

He watched me like you might watch a raging bull who has paused to size you up. Which seemed terribly unfair, since he was the one who had just attacked me.

"An eye for an eye," he muttered, so quietly that I barely caught it. His face flushed hard when he spoke again. "I had no right to manhandle you."

"No. You did not."

"I had no right to use your secrets against you."

"No."

"But I had to know."

I lifted an eyebrow. Did he, now?

"Are you likewise afflicted with a punishment from the door?" I asked him as fear spiked hot within me. "Something that twists your mind?"

He nodded and looked away with an expression I'd seen many times before. It was the expression of a survivor realizing they had to deal with the hand they'd been dealt and couldn't go back to how things had been before. He'd made this mess — mind afflicted or not. Now he must deal with his creation.

He squared his shoulders and turned back to me suddenly. I expected another apology or — perhaps — a justification. People tended to do that when they were particularly embarrassed.

"I will give you another secret of mine," he said instead. And it was my turn to be surprised enough that my hand fell from my hilt.

"And what? That will make us even?" I felt amusement tickling the corners of my mouth.

"Yes," he agreed, so fervently that the word sounded like a vow. "I will give you my secret and then I will kneel before you and if you wish to take my head, then that is your right. Perhaps death will be better than the shame I feel now."

"Hold just a moment, there's no need to run around headless."

I threw a hand up but already he was kneeling. He drew his sword from a kneeling stance and I stumbled backward defensively, only for him to slide it roughly across the stone. It spun away until it hit an ancient rug and stopped.

"Your sin is doubt? Mine is lust," he told me, his eyes wide and palms held up as if making an offering. "I told you I killed a girl. I did not lie. I got her with child and watched as her family abandoned her and mine refused to lend aid. She died giving birth to a stillborn daughter. I came too late to do more than watch her die before my eyes in a frozen, filthy hovel. I killed her as surely as if I'd done it myself. Killed her with my appetites. Killed her with my thoughtless taking. I left that day and swore myself to the Aspect. But we both know that makes up for nothing. It remits no guilt. No life I could live could make up for two innocents robbed of theirs. That's my secret. Do with it what you will. Both my secret and my life are in your hands."

Chapter Thirteen
Poisoned Saint

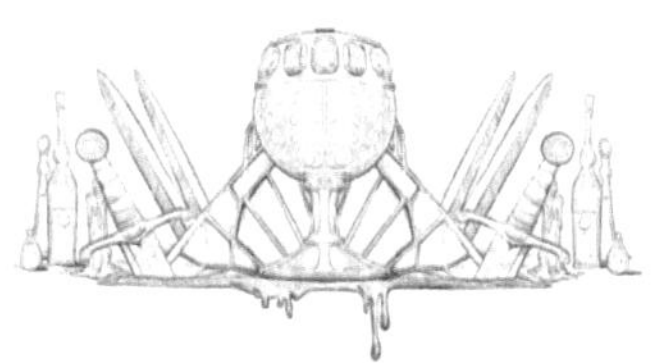

She stares at me, stunned into silence. As she should be. I have just confessed to the grimmest of crimes — a selfish act and abandonment that led to death. I am as guilty as any convicted criminal and I know it in my bones.

What I have not told her — what I dare not tell her — is how like my Marigold she is with that solemn expression and that look of skeptical doubt in her eyes.

"She is mine," the God had said directly into my mind when I questioned her.

Said it with a searing light that still fills me.

Said it like the ringing of heaven's bells.

If she kills me now, I'm not sure I'll feel it. I will still be soaring on the vibrant emotion of the echo of that voice. It cut me deep, cut me hard. And yet, at the same time, it warmed me as nothing else ever has. Not the embrace of another. Not the burn of ambition or the warmth of compassion. It warms me to the marrow and burns away all else.

I didn't think I would ever hear the voice of the God again. I still can't believe it happened. It's a miracle more wondrous than what Hefertus weaves. And it is for *her.* She who is untested, untried, so unlike the rest of us that I wondered how she could even be a paladin at all.

And why did I care so strongly about that?

It pains me to recount the last few minutes. The surge of longing in my heart at the sight of her compelled me to follow. She'd been leaning forward as she strode through the monastery, her pointed nose leading the way as if she were an arrow loosed from a bow, bent on ransacking this entire place in search of the Cup. How could I not flare at the sight of that?

Then that surge turned to a burn. It heightened my sense of this woman and bid me notice her every flinch and movement. I joined her without thinking about it.

And then came the realization of what I was doing, the shame of it, the need to justify myself. It suggested to me that she might be fraudulent, that perhaps I was mistaking myself for a guilty man who was making a fool of himself when it was *she* who was guilty of duping us all. It's so easy to blame another for a guilt that is your own. Easy to deflect your folly onto another.

That deflection propelled me into the need to act and I was acting before I knew what had come over me. Before I questioned it — as I should have. I have not been so foolhardy since I was a boy.

My cheeks burn with shame. And so they should.

I can see how the door has twisted both my thoughts and desires.

But I also know that it can only twist what is already there. Nothing can manufacture these things in me. If I have desire rolling through me like a tide, that is no excuse to single one person out. It's no reason to demand they meet some sort of arbitrary standard. If I have suspicions, that's no reason to make violent demands. And if I have shame, that is not the fault of another, it is the fault of the flaw, the fissure within my own soul.

I swallow hard. I am a mess. Where I would usually be compassionate and kind, patient and accepting, I have let myself become twisted. No, that language is too passive. I was all the ugly things that passion can be — possessive where no possession is warranted, demanding where I had no right to demand, violent in my pursuit of my own wants.

Shame burns through my chest and makes my belly churn.

She rolls her eyes at me. Such a slight gesture. I cling to the way it trivializes what has come before. It promises a chance at reconciliation.

"I'm not going to kill you." Her words are like dawn after a night of illness. "And I don't think you're a murderer just because you were part of a dreadful tragedy. Get up."

Her eyes are old in her young face.

"A dreadful tragedy?" I whisper. How she can dismiss my crime so readily? "I left her to suffer on her own."

"And how old were you at the time?"

I feel my cheeks grow hotter. My youth does not dismiss what happened then, just as my ... whatever this is now ... does not dismiss what I did a moment ago. If anything, it makes it worse. I indulged myself so thoughtlessly while other boys were busy riding horses and shooting bows. Had I stayed with them and done that, a life would have been spared.

"I was fifteen," I say quietly.

"A child," she says.

"Not a child at all. Not once a child was fathered by me. A poor excuse for a man who let those who depended on him perish."

She sighs and to my horror, she wanders over to the nearest bookshelf — there are ten separate bookcases, each gilded along the edges of the shelves — and runs her finger along the spines of the books. Dust is thick on these tomes, but they do not crumble as I expected.

"Oh, you're one of those."

"One of what?" I am loathe to take to my feet again before she's rendered judgment, but it seems like she might not bother to do even that. Behind the door, her dog gives up growling and lets out a pitiful whine.

"One of those fools who think that everything in the world depends on them and all the failures in it are their fault." She turns to look at me a little coyly. "Am I right?"

I stiffen and clench my jaw. "I take my responsibilities seriously. I am accountable for my actions. Both in the past, and in the present. I wronged you with my accusations."

She says nothing to that, and I have to turn awkwardly to keep her in my line of sight while maintaining my kneeling posture as she rounds the room.

She reads the spines of the books and tilts her head to the side as she regards a bed and a tufted chair, both finer than anything that existed in my father's house. With the air of a practiced thief, she checks behind each book and turns the bedding and cushions. She sifts through trinkets on the sideboard and side tables. Her fingers dance over music boxes set with leaping goldfish, fans painted with peacocks, a bedframe thick with intricately carved songbirds.

"You would think a thousand years would have turned all this to dust."

"There is clearly a miracle at work here," I agree, my eyes trawling over the fine golden and crimson brocades. "What we call magic."

She tilts her head to the side as if she's listening to someone other than me and then marches over to the desk and begins to take out each drawer and examine it. The desk is a thing to behold — its legs are slender and delicate, but they wrap around in a way that the eye can't quite follow until they become four lovely maidens holding up bullfrogs larger than their heads, who, in turn, hold up the desktop. The drawers of the desk are full of parchment and bound books — more things that ought to be dust. She rummages through them with a disregard that makes me flinch. Midway through, she pauses and gives me a very long look, her gaze resting pointedly on my knees as if to draw attention to how I am still kneeling.

For one so young, she is very exacting. It is almost humorous

— her blasé attitude about my crimes, combined with her fierce judgment of my penitence.

I give her an abashed smile. She is trying. I am difficult and irrational as I fight my internal battles but still, she is trying with me.

She scoffs lightly, but there is a ghost of a smile around her lips, too. Perhaps, young as she is, she is experienced enough to see that I am trying to fix the mess I've made of this.

"You go from penitent to charming far too easily, Sir Paladin."

"What would you have me do, Lady? Here I am, on my knees before you."

"I am not your God to take your confession," she says lightly as she examines a strange bronze sphere placed on the desk.

It sits in a bracket fitted to a stand that lets her spin it on an axis. She moves it, tentatively at first and then with more force, watching it spin with a puzzled expression before she stops it and peers carefully at the surface. I wonder why she is so fixed on this one oddity when the room is spilling over with so many.

Beneath her frosty exterior, I see to her heart where doubt still rages, where fear still makes her eyes dart toward any sound, where tight intelligence is making sense —somehow — of whatever is etched onto that sphere.

"You are my fellow paladin. You can accept my apology on behalf of the God," I say. I don't know if I mean my apology to her or my apology for everything.

"I could have killed you. Intentionally or by accident," she says carefully. "Why did you attack me? What if I'd spun and hit you before you pinned me, before I knew who you were?"

I wonder if she'd still have that haunted look if she could hear the God as clearly as I just did — if he told her what he told me, that she belongs to him. What a marvel *that* is. I am not certain that I belong to anyone or ever will. Surely, I am the God's, too, but he has made no such clear claim of me.

"Do you think you could have?" I ask, curious. "Killed me? If the fight had been fair?"

She levels a steel stare at me. “Care to try again?”

I gust a laugh. I can’t help it. The ridiculousness of all of this is too much.

“I do not. But I will confess one more thing to you.”

“Please, no more confessions.” The look she shoots me is far, far too old for her face. She runs her fingers over the etching of the sphere and turns it slowly.

“My confession is only that this place gives me the shivers,” I say carefully, watching her to gauge her reaction. I think I see a glimmer of forgiveness there.

She looks up, eyes dancing in a way that squeezes my heart — though whether that’s my actual heart or a result of the effects of this place … well, I can’t tell. I dare not trust my own judgment right now. I’m compromised.

She is deliberate in her answer, though still teasing. “Are you telling me that you don’t enjoy being bottled up in a rabbit warren a thousand years old, the whole of which is watched over by an imprisoned, sleeping demon suspended from the ceiling like a chandelier?”

“How do you know it’s sleeping?” I’m impressed. She’s very young and it was well hidden. It took me almost to the bottom of the stairs to realize it was up there dreaming whatever dreams fiends find.

“I’m a Vagabond Paladin, Poisoned Saint. Wherever demons sleep, their nightmares are full of me.” It is her turn to look chagrined when she says, “I would have liked to cast it out.”

I tilt my head to the side. “Don’t you have that ability? Is that not your specialty?”

She snorts. “Could you heal an entire army at once?”

I consider.

“But there are nine of us down here. Surely, together …”

My words trail off and she smirks again.

“How much do you think your friend Hefertus knows about the casting out of demons? Or the puffed-up Majester?”

"Hefertus could probably order the world to rid itself of the creature and it would be gone," I say easily.

"And with it, whatever is left of his mind."

I incline my head. She's right, of course.

There's a ghost of a smile and a dare in her eyes when she speaks again. "I hope you're planning to get off your knees because I have something to show you."

I hesitate, gust a tiny, rueful scoff — directed at myself, of course — and this time my smile is bashful. "I'm afraid I can't get up yet."

"Until I forgive you?" Her eyes twinkle. "Consider it done."

"It's not that." Although forgiveness ... I didn't expect it, and it's sweet as overripe raspberries.

"Until I promise to keep your secret?" Her tone is wry, almost mocking. "If impregnating a young woman amounts to murder, then likely we should see more men dangling from hempen ropes."

"It bothers me that you trivialize my sorrow." I'm sad to lose our teasing, but on this, I must be firm.

Has she had much dealing with men like me? Or with anyone who was not possessed or desperately looking for help with someone who was? She followed a knight around begging for scraps from her childhood. I should not expect her to see the world as most do.

"It bothers me that you are so prideful that you're still on your knees," she shoots back. "Fine. I will keep your secret. I'll do better, if you like. We can search for this cup together."

"Together?" I am wary. This is ... better than I hoped for. I think. It's certainly more than I expected. It's forgiveness and a ghost of second chances — to protect rather than harm, to help rather than hurt. I'll take it. I'll do what I failed to do before and keep those dancing eyes from glassing over with the varnish of death.

"Together," she confirms, offering me a hand and pulling me to my feet.

"Your word on that?" I can't help myself. I always have to press for certainty. It's as much a part of how I'm constructed as my sinews and bones.

"Do you want some kind of oath, Adalbrand?"

I like how she says my name with one eyebrow lifted. I like how she seems utterly unaffected by me. Usually. I draw women like flies to a half-eaten pie and I must remind them often that I am sworn to the God — a fact, I have noted, that only seems to make them more ardent in their declarations of what they would do if only they could. I don't begrudge them that. It's nice to be considered desirable, even if they do rather try my vows.

I answer carefully. "An oath would be appreciated."

She laughs and it startles me. She blows like the sea wind, hot and mellow, then cold and sharp, with barely a hint of the change before it rushes over you.

The dog whines on the other side of the door a second time and she stares at me, biting her lower lip on one side as she looks me up and down. I don't think I've felt so judged since I was a new squire under uniform inspection.

"Will you help me cast out the demon if we are given the chance?" she asks, as if this is the sticking point — as if every paladin here wouldn't lend her aid with that.

"Of course."

I go ahead and look right back. She's given me license now that she's doing it to me. The wear and tatters on her clothing only serve to highlight the flawlessness of her black hair. That scar above her eyebrow and the other on her chin do the same for the perfect swoop of her cheekbones. She is contradictions. Doubtful but certain, marred but incomparable. And I must school my heart to stop cataloging them all.

"Fine, then we will make an oath." She leans a hip against the desk, arms crossed over her chest. My gaze snags on the posture. She looks amused by me and for the first time since I arrived in this place, I feel a glimmer of light. Humor, in my opinion, is the buoyancy the heart needs to go on. "Tell me what you want to swear."

From the other side of the door, the dog barks.

"Are you going to let him in?" I ask, smiling with her as if we are sharing a joke instead of forging something more akin to a peace treaty or maybe — just maybe — a friendship.

"Not until we're done this."

Well, I don't want to be bitten again, so that's fine with me. I've never met a paladin before who let a dog trail them. Perhaps there are certain rules or proprieties. Maybe I'm meant to overlook the mild mauling.

"I'll swear to work hand in hand with you until the cup is found and returned to the church," I offer. "That I will guard your back and join counsel with you in this and in all else. And that, if we have the chance, we will cast out that demon."

"A dangerous oath," she says and her eyes are still dancing, still teasing, still drawing me in.

They don't look quite so much like Marigold's anymore. Marigold's never had that edge. The edge that tells me she might be cleverer than me, brighter and faster and stronger. I find it only draws me in worse, trapping me like a fly in a spider's web.

"What if we never find the cup?"

"Would you like to add conditions for if we fail?" I offer.

"I never factor in failure," she says, and her grin grows and then freezes, as if she realizes she's admitted something that makes her look bad. She rallies, but her new smile is a bit weaker. "Let's have a little confidence. Let's assume we will find the Cup and return it."

And I know better than to make an oath like that. I really do. If there's no Cup of Tears here, this will bind us together for life. And then what will we do? Serve side by side like a tortoise and a wolf yoked together? I don't even know which of us would be tortoise and which the wolf.

She smiles and shows her teeth.

Fine. She's clearly the wolf.

I wrench my gauntlet off and offer my palm, and when she takes it in her warm one, I have to swallow. Her clasp is firm and certain.

"May it be and ever be," she vows to me, and I return her vow with my own.

"My sword is yours and my honor until we succeed."

When I let go of her hand, she leans over the sphere and points. "I think you're going to be glad that you teamed up with me, Poisoned Saint. I might have found something interesting here."

Chapter Fourteen
Vagabond Paladin

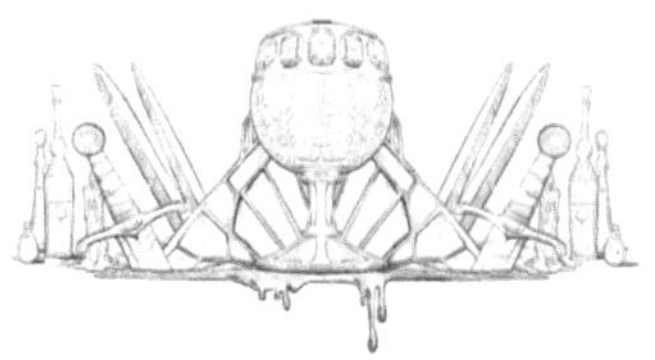

The door into this terrible place had scrambled us like eggs before they were cooked. Fear and doubt laced through every inkling I had, twisting up my good judgment, and making me suspicious and fretful in a way I usually wasn't. That quick attack from Adalbrand had left me so rattled that it took me a complete turn around the room "searching for the cup" before I was calm enough to deal with him head-on. I hoped he hadn't noticed. I hoped I'd looked as if I was in possession of myself and not quivering with nerves like an un-blooded girl who'd never faced a demon.

He'd sworn to me at the end of it — or with me, I suppose. What a mad, warrantless thing to decide to do. Had Brindle been on this side of the door, I think he might have bit me.

You really did ruin her, didn't you, you moldering old armor suit. Here she could have been the one wheeling through this world pinning pretty knights to walls and cutting throats but no, you filled her with catechisms and prayers and empty hands.

He had. Thank the Merciful God.

I think this Adalbrand is sincere. He means to keep his word to you. This kind usually does. They don't thrash out at others. They eat themselves from within.

Except for when they were thrashing out at me, apparently.

I rather think that's unusual for him. It's completely unlike you to be anything but bold, for instance, and I feel your bowels trembling like jelly.

Rude.

Though, if I were frank with myself, I could admit that a second set of eyes would be useful in helping me calibrate back toward a more objective view of things — even if those eyes were equally off-kilter.

You already have two more sets of eyes, little morsel. What need have you of a third? I see past the veil of skin to where each heart festers.

Somehow, the perspective of a demented spirit wasn't quite the same as another living, breathing human. Call me any name you like, but I'd stand by that.

You just like that he's living and breathing. Are you sure you're not the one twisted by the sin of craving another? Doubt is so passé. Give me something thick and meaty like lust to work with.

Was Sir Branson hearing this?

Well, the knight did admit to lust, my girl. And that's a real concern. The problem with lust is that it is treating people like objects. When he admits he has that problem, he's admitting that he's willing to treat you like you aren't even a person.

Just treat him the same way — like a snack. Good for one sweet taste and then gone.

I swallowed hard.

"What have you found?" Adalbrand asked, slipping to my side so smoothly that he could be the haunting spirit and startling me out of my internal conversation.

"Look at the sphere," I said aloud, tracing the edge of one of the etchings. "See this ragged edge? Doesn't that look like the coastline of the Grayling Sea? There's the distinctive rabbit-foot shape."

Adalbrand grunted, leaning in closer. I tried very hard not to be overly aware of how he filled the space, how his masculine scent was stronger since our brief encounter.

If he hadn't taken me by surprise, he'd never have gotten the better of me. He was quick but I could be quicker.

Taking you by surprise is *getting the better of you. I'm going to enjoy watching you wreck your ship on this rock. He's going to leave you hollow and gasping and broken.*

"It does look like the Grayling Sea but surely it's a coincidence."

"Follow the edge of it. Here's where it would disappear under the receding ice wall, if this were a map."

"But who would put a map on a sphere?" He traced the edge with his finger, still bare from when we shook hands and made that oath.

If you don't find the Cup of Tears, the pair of you will now be bound together, charging this way and that like knights errant. Best to find it. And fast.

Have I mentioned that it's hard to have a conversation when the people in your head won't be silent?

I forced myself to do it anyway. "Did you note the strange map mosaic on the floor as we descended the stairs?"

"Mmm," he agreed. "It was difficult to see details, though, unless you stood high enough and looked down. Up close, it looked only like the rock shards that comprised it. I don't see the connection."

"Don't you?" I asked, enjoying myself enough to raise an eyebrow. I liked teasing him. I hadn't teased anyone in a long time. I remember my father loved to tease — to pull my little braids and pretend to steal my treats. "A paladin of a scholarly aspect like you?"

The poisoned look he shot me fit his title perfectly. It brought my smirk to the surface.

"Capture it in your mind's eye, Sir Paladin. Wasn't it a strange shape?"

He nodded, eyes distant and staring at a tapestry on the wall as he agreed. "Like the peel of a fruit flattened on a table."

"Yes," I said, "as if someone was trying to make a sphere flat."

His frown when his gaze found mine was thoughtful. He spun the sphere on its axis, finger tracing what would be a coastline if it were a map.

"But it's not a map of our world, is it?"

"Part of it could be."

I rummaged around on the desk, looking. Bound books were piled with parchment and quills. A bottle of ink had been left open and dried up. I still couldn't believe all this had been preserved for so long and could still be handled without collapsing into dust.

I opened one of the bound books. It was full of sketches and diagrams and scrawled handwriting in the Indul language. I could recognize it, even if I couldn't read it without the dog.

"Someone stuck a bit of glass in the sphere just here," Adalbrand said, and I looked up to note where it was on the sphere. "I wonder if that's significant."

"Maybe it was the location of a capital city. Or a cathedral of note." I bit the end of my finger and glared at the diagrams. They didn't show a cup, that was for certain. They seemed like engineering schematics. Maybe if I brought this book to the Engineers they'd have an idea of what it was for.

If it's not for your precious cup then why bother? Keep the book to yourself.

Poor advice. Knowledge was always worth pursuing.

Is it, though? Remember that boy in Minsca? The one who tried his grandmother's recipe for summoning demons? The one who made it work the way she never did?

I shuddered, remembering the carnage in that little town.

He had knowledge. Worth it, do you think?

Fine. Branson had a point. I was still going to ask, though. I shut the book hard enough that dust puffed up from the pages.

"Do you think, Sir Adalbrand," I asked carefully, "that they thought the earth was a ball?"

He scoffed and then paused. "But how would they account for the ice walls?"

I pointed to the top and bottom of the sphere. "These islands are raised and flat. Could that be their representation of ice walls?"

He frowned and leaned in closer. "But they had to know it wasn't true. When the walls shifted and revealed more of the earth, where would they put it on the ball?"

I shrugged. It was only a guess.

"And how would they account for the moon reflecting the surface of our land perfectly?"

I shook my head again. I didn't know, but the more I looked at the sphere, the more I was sure that was exactly what they were trying to depict. That it was a map so strange and foreign as to seem almost primitive.

"Do they think, then, that they are not under the heavenly rule of the God?" He was so horrified that he flinched back, hand drifting to his scabbard, only to realize it was still empty. He huffed and went to retrieve his sword as I pushed the drawers closed.

When he returned, he leaned in, and then with the air of someone a little embarrassed of himself, he pushed his fingernail precisely on the small glass bead.

The sphere opened with a snick.

Inside was a pewter cup that would have fit in my palm perfectly.

"There are a lot of cups in this place," I said carefully.

He swallowed, turning it over in his hands. "How will we know which is the right one?"

You'll know.

I shook my head, huffing a laugh. "Maybe one of the others knows. Or maybe we'll simply have to take them all back with us."

Trust me. You will know.

Adalbrand smiled as he tossed the cup up and caught it again. "I don't think that this is it."

"Why not?"

He pointed to the body of the cup. "Because it doesn't look like the pictures."

He felt in a pocket and produced a piece of parchment and showed it to me. The Poisoned Saints, it would seem, were more helpful with exact instructions than the Aspect of the Rejected God had been. His parchment showed a cup with a wide base and embedded with cabochon gems. The walls of the cup were etched with something — but the sketch was unclear on the details. The cup he was holding had no gems.

"This is someone's dirty secret," he said grimly. "A family heirloom, perhaps? Hidden in that sphere?"

I nodded. That made sense.

"Any other secret compartments that you care to open?" I asked him, but he shook his head. I was still wary of him despite his vow. A man who took you violently by surprise once might do it again. A little teasing and friendliness might lead to a partnership eventually, but we were not there yet.

"On to the next room then, shall we?"

He kept hold of the cup even though he knew it wasn't the right one. Interesting.

We tried three more rooms, this time with Brindle dogging our steps. Two we checked separately, the last we checked together.

Each room we searched was more elaborate than the last, decadent in a way I wouldn't have credited to a monastery. There were none of the plain, stark outfittings of our houses of prayer. These were laden with treasures more suitable to the apartments of a king. Had I the desire, I could fill my pockets to the brim with curiosities and live a life of luxury. I would do exactly that, were I not sworn to abstain from riches.

The room I'd checked on my own had a cage in it large

enough to hold the bed. I counted five avian skulls and assorted bones inside. No cup.

All these rooms seemed to have been abandoned with haste. Clothing was flung everywhere, blankets tangled, cushions disarranged. I searched systematically, looking for anything that might be the cup or a clue for finding it. I found three more books just like the first, though in different handwriting, as if four people were working toward the same goal — the same invention. I kept them with me, interested to try to see what manner of project had inspired all four of these people at once. Perhaps it was a clock like the one in the main room. Or some other wonder of art and craft.

I did not find another cup in the rooms, and by the time we went back to the halls, someone had removed all the cups from their alcoves in the wall.

Brindle kept his eye on Adalbrand, snuffling his way from room to room with doggy enthusiasm. I kept a close watch on him. I was worried that in the low light of this place, his eyes might glow their hell-and-heaven brightness and betray us. These rooms were lit with clever windows, narrow but effective, cut into the rock on one side and out to the sea, and then cut from room to room. The depth of rock and narrowness of the slivers would make spying difficult, but they let in enough light to search the rooms without lantern or torch.

It was not until the third room that we found a clue.

There was a tapestry on the wall. At the very top of the tapestry, the cup from Adalbrand's sketch was carefully embroidered, complete with the blue cabochon gems on the walls and something that looked like eyes all around them. Beneath it was a dark building ringed with reaching branches. It was picked out in an outline beside the sea, and that wouldn't have been enough to tip us off, but the building extended down beneath the earth to where a long staircase ended with a clock on one side and a fountain on the other, and beneath it all were gears.

"I think the cup must be here somewhere," Adalbrand said

from beside the desk. He held up a single sheet of parchment. Someone had scrawled across the bottom, but at the top was a very accurate depiction of the Cup of Tears. It looked much like Adalbrand's sketch, but the eyes sketched around the gemstones were clearer.

He passed the parchment to me. "Can you read it?"

Beside us, Brindle yawned, apparently bored beyond belief even as the demon inside him sprang to attention.

"It says Aching Cup," I replied after Brindle translated.

"That's close enough to Cup of Tears. It could be that your translation is not precise. And the rest?"

These little poems are so delicious. I can almost taste the fear worming through them. Let me read it for you.

It worried me that he liked this so much.

This most holy of cups,
This most painful of drinks,
It cuts down to the quick,
It does more than one thinks.
Do you reach for the heavens?
Do you clutch at the air?
One deep drink of this pain brew,
And your heart will be there.
For what's gone can't be brought back,
What's once lost can't be found,
But one dash of this brew,
And you'll find yourself crowned.

I spoke the words for Adalbrand and then asked, "What does the symbol under the poem mean?"

"It's an old one." He sounded wistful. "It's a symbol for a Saint. The crown with the blade stabbed through it."

"I haven't seen it before. Do you want to be a Saint, Sir Adalbrand?"

"You heard the poem. What's gone can't be brought back. I can no more be a Saint than I can be a tiger." I liked how his smile always had an edge of sorrow to it.

"Do you want to be a tiger?" I teased.

He looked up from the parchment and considered me for a long breath. He wasn't playing anymore. He wasn't twinkling.

"Do *you* want to be a Saint, Lady Paladin?"

Before I could reply, the door crashed open and the Majester General strode in, startling us both. He was carrying his pen and parchment, and over one shoulder he held a crimson sack that clanked with every step. I realized by the second step that the sack had been his tabard and by the third I was stifling a smile. Now I knew who had been collecting all the cups.

His comportment screamed "command" in a way that would make anyone with a hint of duty in their heart straighten and salute. Obviously, I slouched more at the mere sight of him.

Beside me, Adalbrand's spine went stiff and his chin rose.

I barely kept in a snicker. Someone had a tendency toward people pleasing and conformity, it would seem. You'd never catch me doing that.

"Anything interesting to report here?" the Majester barked.

He glared at his parchment like he was annoyed not to have an aide to jot these things down for him, and the look he gave me suggested he was considering changing that. I set my hand on Brindle's head. The Majester's gaze followed the motion and I saw the moment he registered that any assistance from me would be accompanied by dog drool. He shook his head minutely.

"If you're asking whether the residents had some odd items, then I'd say yes, and we did find a poem, a tapestry with a depiction that I'm pretty sure is the cup, and this pewter vessel," Adalbrand said with a stiff formality that seemed wrong in his mouth after all the confessions he'd poured out from the very same lips, "but if you're asking if we found the cup, then the answer is no. And yes, we've been thorough."

"How many rooms have you searched and did you mark them?" The Majester gently extracted the pewter cup from Adalbrand's hand, turning it this way and that with narrowed eyes before adding it to his sack. He took the parchment, skimming over the drawing and poem. He did not ask for a translation.

"Mark them?" Adalbrand sounded surprised.

"Can I borrow your back, Beggar?" the Majester asked me.

"Excuse me?"

Beside me, the dog snickered. Out loud. I would swear on it before a confessional priest.

He looks just like a rooster I possessed once, sweetmeat. It strutted around like it owned the place before *I took it over, and you wouldn't guess what it did after.*

Did it claw someone's eyes out and eat their soul?

Good guess. Have you played this game before, my sweet dumpling?

No one but me noticed the laughter or the distracting byplay.

The Majester General waved parchment and pen. "I need a surface to write on."

I blinked. "Well, you *could* use my back but there's a des —"

I didn't get a chance to even say "desk" before he spun around me, settled the parchment against my backplate, and began to scribble.

I glared at the perfectly serviceable desk. Its owner had been a great lover of the arts and had fitted it with a pen holder sculpted from golden marble in the shape of a reclining woman wrapped in a boa constrictor. The constrictor had five heads and the woman had five hands, and she had a place for a pen in the center of each of her five palms. She looked profane, indeed, but her desk was still a better place to write than my back.

"Is that a map?" Adalbrand asked from somewhere behind me. It sounded like he was suppressing a laugh.

Great. I was the butt of everyone's humor here. Could no one take a grave in the ground full of dead people's possessions and a great rotting demon seriously? No? It was just me?

I huffed a sigh. I liked maps. I would like to see this one. And I didn't like being a desk.

"It won't be a thorough search without one," the Majester

said, pride in every word. "Can you point out which rooms you searched so I might mark them?"

"We searched here and here together and split off to search here and here. We saw no one else. But it looks as if you have a tick on almost every room so far. What's this?"

"A fountain. It's on the other side of the stairs from the clock. Handy if we're here for long. The Penitent declared it fit for drinking and the High Saint blessed it. There was no cup in it, though. We'll have to start looking for hidden chambers, perhaps," the Majester said. "Or a key to unlock the other door."

"Other door?" I repeated, but my words were eclipsed by Adalbrand's.

"Wait, is this the shape of a pentagon with one triangular section off to one side?"

"It is." The Majester General's voice warmed. I imagined he was probably well-liked among his aspect. There were almost no Beggar Paladins as genial and gracious as he was, and he was generous with information and comradery.

Rude. I've always been very generous. I spent an entire day once cataloging all the cheeses I've ever tried for your educational use. In the order in which I ranked them, no less.

So generous.

"And look, all these cells that are clearly people's personal chambers are located in this triangular section outside the thick main wall of the pentagon. I measured it at the windows and it's nearly a pace thick of pure stone. Imagine the work it took to carve this wonder. And those statues!"

"Did you think they looked a lot like us?" I asked, staring at the fireplace opposite us, annoyed.

Brindle trotted over to it, spun three times, and then collapsed into a doggy heap, his tongue hanging out of his mouth as if he were laughing at me. Sure, dog. Live it up. Laugh at my expense. It's not like I'm the one who feeds you or anything.

I like it when you're annoyed. You think better then. Put your mind to the task of that map, sweet morsel. What did that glass bead mark?

"The statues?" The Majester seemed surprised. "Well, I expected the monks here to be human, didn't you?"

"No, I mean specifically like *us*. There's one, I swear, that is the Prince Paladin's exact doppelganger. Right down to that firm jawline and straight nose."

"Well, he does rather have the kind of face that ought to be immortalized," the Majester General said absentmindedly. "Likely he's not the first man to look so godly that an artist was inspired by it."

The dog started snickering in my head again. I gave it a black look.

"So, this corridor you went down opposite to the clock," he said, tapping something on the map in a way that sent vibrations through my backplate, "goes through a door at the exact center of that side of the pentagon and then proceeds into this triangle-shaped section full of smaller rooms. There's one more area in this section of the pentagon that has a locked door." He tapped my backplate hard as he noted it. "And then these two sections appear to have no door at all. But perhaps one is hidden. This one is carved all over in bas-relief and a keyhole could easily be hidden in the design. And this one appears to have a large glass section with only darkness behind it, so possibly there's a hidden entrance there, too. The last section is windows, of course, cut into the rock face and looking out to the sea. I wouldn't expect more than meets the eye there."

"You think there are triangular sections behind each of the other walls?" Adalbrand asked.

I could hear the Majester's smug smile in his voice. "It's what I'd do if I were building this place, and I've learned that in battle it's best to assume your opponent is at least as clever as you are."

"Are we in a battle I don't know about?" I asked the air in front of me.

"A battle to find the cup," the Majester said testily. "And our opponent is those who hid it — long dead now. I'll take the cup you found, if you don't mind. I'm collecting them all so we can test them together tonight. It will be a completely fair and above-board investigation, I assure you."

"Of course," Adalbrand murmured.

"Would you have noticed a key when you were searching?" the Majester asked.

"If it looked like a key, then yes," Adalbrand said. "We saw a map. Of the world. On a sphere."

The Majester barely skipped a beat. "The Holy Inquisitor claims he read about that once. That there was a time that man believed the earth was a ball." He sounded testy. "Before you tell me all the reasons that's nonsense, please know I've already heard a rant from the High Saint and am not in the mood for another. Unless this round ball unlocks one of the doors in this place, I'm simply not interested in it."

"Well there was an interesting — " Adalbrand began, but the door to the room crashed open.

I spun, drawing my sword in a single motion. I vaguely heard the curses of the Majester General, whose parchment had fluttered to the floor when I moved, vaguely noticed that Adalbrand — the fool — had automatically moved between me and the door without even drawing his blade.

Brindle barked.

Once.

Sharply.

But it was only Sir Owalan. Out of breath. White-lipped. Blood streaked down his dove-grey tabard. He opened his mouth to speak, turned, vomited, and then tried again.

"The Seer is dead."

Chapter Fifteen
Poisoned Saint

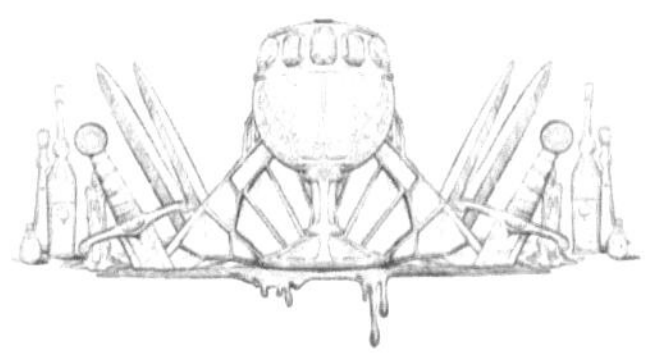

She told me that there was no way out. She told me the way forward was through blood. I just hadn't realized her vision was so immediate — that it meant *here, today.*

"Saints and Angels."

I look up in time to catch the sardonic look on the young Vagabond's face.

"Are you sure?" I gasp, forcing my gaze back to an unsteady Sir Owalan.

He nods roughly, holding the doorjamb in a trembling fist.

"Where?" I grit out.

The Majester has retrieved his map, but the Vagabond has not put her sword away. Good. We must have been attacked. Or a trap was sprung. Or something.

"The lock," Owalan says.

His face is turning green again. I could try to ease his suffering but perhaps the Seer has a chance. I've been there before when someone was pronounced dead too soon and, together with my brothers, I brought them back.

I don't know which of us moves first, me or the dog. I'm running past the Penitent Paladin before I even catch the benediction he murmurs as he makes the holy sign from forehead to sword arm.

My hands are sweating and my brow furrowed as I pick up speed down the corridor and out into the main room. The statues loom high over me and the sunlight streaming through the windows has turned from the gold of dawn and sped right through to the swell of afternoon. The granite blossoms around their feet mock me.

I'm but a gnat in this towering vault of a room, small as a mote of dust tumbling through the light beams. My legs take forever to cross all that white marble and each footfall echoes loudly through the hall.

My lips are already murmuring the prayers that come before healing.

God grant me strength to take pain from another. God grant me your power to heal. God preserve us. God have mercy. God have mercy.

I haven't even reached the third "God have mercy" and then I see them — clustered around a heap on the ground.

Hefertus is pale, his face set like flint. I have seen him at the scene of a tragedy before. This is his way.

Beside him, the High Saint is in a crouch over the Seer. He clutches at his hair, his mouth wide and drawn in a look of horror. His eyes find us first and he flinches backward, falls to his bottom, crab-walking. His hand finds his sword hilt.

I'm already frowning before the Inquisitor sets a hand on the shoulder of the Hand of Justice — also crouched over the body. The Hand looks over his shoulder and his eyes narrow when he sees me. He stands in one fluid motion and draws his sword.

It's only then that I realize they think I'm a threat.

Beside me, the dog barks.

I throw up my hands, trying to turn my headlong run into a skidding halt.

"I want to heal her," I gasp out, but Kodelai Lei Shan Tora is already closing the distance between us, his sword held in high attack posture.

Unfurling beside him like a sleek white flag, the Holy Inquisitor spools out, his sword liquid and flowing as it leaves the sheathe and falls into low attack posture in his off-hand.

They aren't waiting for an explanation. They're ready to kill me. Fury is etched into their features.

In response, fear claws up my throat like a sleeping wolf woken before it is ready. It makes my mouth dry and my hand unsteady.

I force control back over myself, letting the growl rip from my throat as I finally skid to a halt, and gather enough focus to draw my sword.

I'm still in the act when a blur of tatters and dread-black hair slips past me like an ill wind and leaps in front of me.

Sparks fly and the air splits with the sound of steel on steel. I feel the vibration through my feet as the Vagabond Paladin bashes Sir Kodelai's blade to the side and forces him backward with a daring backhand. It leaves her open for an attack, but both of the others are too stunned to seize the opportunity.

Sir Kodelai takes a defensive step backward, surprise etching his mature face. Already my dervish savior is spinning to her left, her sword held in a crosswise defensive stance, hands high, blade sweeping down and back to protect her spin.

Her dog intimidates the Inquisitor, rushing in low and harsh-throated for a feint at his pale boots.

I don't think Sir Kodelai planned on killing a woman today. I don't think he knows what to do now that he's faced with the possibility.

The Inquisitor is faster than his compatriot — even missing his usual sword hand — and unlike the Hand of Justice, he was expecting his opponent. He ignores the snapping dog, likely trusting the protection of his high boots, and takes a step-and-twist to escape her reach, spinning neatly into a perfect full defensive posture. Perhaps he is ambidextrous.

I realize — too late, what is wrong with me? — that I'm just standing there. I am stunned by the beauty of the black viper of a woman flowing before me. With defiant boldness, she holds back a pair of blades that had been bent on my blood just a breath before.

My surprise is no excuse.

Abruptly, I force out words. "Halt! You spend heartbeats where she might still live."

"Still live?" The High Saint's laugh is high-pitched and barely clinging to sanity. "Can people still live without their heads?"

"And hands?" Hefertus asks dryly. He's very still, watching all of us, but not moving for his sword or anything else.

It's only then that I snatch a glimpse of the poor Seer.

I've witnessed many deaths — most by illness, disaster, accident, or war. These are the times that healers are sent for. I will not now enumerate the many deaths I have witnessed. Suffice it to say this is the most grisly of all — including the poor man I tended who had been mauled by a bear.

The Seer is sprawled on her back, centered in a mural of blood. Her clothes — loose and many-layered — look like crushed flower petals. The layers overpower her in death in a way they never did in life. One of her hands clutches a knife. The other hand is clenched in a fist. It is ten feet to her left, just under the lock of a door. An arc of spattered red links it to the rest like the string of a marionette.

Her head has been placed on her belly. I don't mean that she is curved forward. Oh, no. She is flat on her back and someone has placed her head on her belly like a ham on a platter for a Christmas feast. A trail of blood paints a whorl from where her head was wrenched off, up and around her slumped shoulders, and then across her limp garments to where it has been placed, as if someone had broken her by accident but was so tidy that they thought the head ought to be kept with the body.

If that was the case, then why not the hand, too?

The others are right.

I can do nothing for her now.

And the knowledge that I failed her last night is a bitter pill to swallow. Had I realized what she meant … had I realized what she was warning of … I would never have come down into this place.

"H … Hold," I stutter, hand still held up while the other makes the benediction and then runs across the toothy prayer beads strung at my belt.

God have mercy. God have mercy. Lord have mercy. God have mercy.

The prayer is more a panic response than anything else.

There is one more clash of sword on sword as the Vagabond's defense encounters the attack of the Inquisitor, circles it, and then with the force of her greater muscle, breaks hard, cracking the hilt from his hand and sending the sword skittering across the marble.

Her dog is barking wildly, the kind of ripping full-throated barks that make sane men keep a wide berth.

Hardly a moment has passed. The High Saint is still scrambling to his feet. Hefertus reaches down to casually help him.

The Majester and Sir Owalan's footsteps are slow behind me.

The dog leaps forward and, with reflexes like lightning, the Vagabond Paladin intercepts his leap. He was leaping for Sir Kodelai's throat, of course. Why would he leap anywhere else?

Her off-hand snakes out, grabs the scruff of his neck, and with a lunge-and-spin she slams him to the ground and then stills, still twisted and half-bent, wheezing in a long breath as her gaze flicks from paladin to paladin.

Her dog is utterly unaffected by such a violent reproof. He crouches low, growls still rolling through him in gentle waves.

We are all still as we watch one another.

Still with that kind of quiet that comes right before death.

"Nine of us came down," Sir Kodelai says grimly.

He has not sheathed his sword. It remains ready, just outside the reach of the Vagabond Paladin. She has certainly saved my life. The others — on edge already — thought my desperate charge to save the Seer was an attack. I would have been skew-

"Enough of this," Sir Kodelai says grimly. His sword is still bared, tip inches from the Vagabond Saint, who is holding her growling dog back. "I will perform the judgment tonight, by the grace of the God. We will return for the body for a proper burial when all is in readiness."

Hefertus grimaces at that and he's not alone. I see dour lines on the Inquisitor's face and feel them on my own.

"Any who defies this order shows himself guilty," the Hand of Justice says.

Convenient.

I don't think he noticed Sir Owalan slip around him. People miss Owalan. He has a constant attitude of trying to disappear into the walls. But he's kneeling now over the severed hand. He's picking it up. He's prying the fingers apart. He's finding a key.

A strange key.

The head of the key is an exact color and shape match for the stones in the map mosaic that represent land.

If I were a betting man — which I'm not, for the God alone spins fate — I would guess that it marks the exact same spot on the map that the glass bead on the sphere does.

Owalan meets my eyes and then silently slips it in the folds of his tabard.

Interesting.

"None of you is to be alone," Sir Kodelai says severely. "We will exit this place together. Now. In silence."

The High Saint is still praying in fervent desperation.

"IN. SILENCE."

I can hear the snap of the High Saint's jaws closing.

"You will lead, Vagabond Paladin."

I clench my jaw. If I know one thing about my new partner, it's that she takes orders poorly.

The order hangs in the air for a full minute. And then Lady Paladin Victoriana rolls her neck and takes to her feet in all her slender glory. Her hand slips from her dog's neck and his growl rumbles low and burred in his throat, but when she spins on her heel, he turns with her, and when she starts to stride away, he falls into step just a pace in front of her. She looks over her shoulder, a puzzled expression on her face, as if the corpse is a set of figures she can't quite balance.

But she does as she's bid.

"Prince Paladin," Sir Kodelai says.

With a shrug and a wink for me, Hefertus follows her.

"High Saint."

Interestingly enough, no one questions him. No one refuses. No one so much as speaks.

Until it is Kodelai left alone with me and the dead Seer. I offer her one more look.

"Walk beside me, Poisoned Saint," the Hand of Justice says. "We two will watch each other, that all may be above reproach."

Why did he choose me when it could have been the Majester General? Or the High Saint? Both of those Aspects are known for more rule-abiding ways than we Poisoned Ones.

I shrug and fall into step beside him, walking with a trick I've learned that lets my cloak flow behind me like I'm a hero in a story. I can see it catch Sir Kodelai's eye and the curious wen in his forehead tells me it's done what it needs to do. It's caught him off guard.

"Tell me, Poisoned Saint. Tell me, death dealer. Where were you in all of this?"

"I followed the Vagabond Paladin when she split off from the rest," I said easily. "I was with her."

"The whole time?"

"We were separated checking two different rooms at one point."

"How long was that for?"

"Perhaps five minutes," I say calmly. "Maybe a little longer. There was a tank in the room I searched that had been full of fish. It took me some time to search through their bones."

He nods in thought. "Then you are not beyond reproach."

"An interesting way to think of it."

"And you visited the Seer last night. You slept outside her tent. I beheld it when I woke during second sleep."

I shrug noncommittally.

"What did she say to you?"

"That she saw a vision. And there was no way out."

The Hand of Justice looks over his shoulder. "That certainly seems true for her."

And with that, we make our way to the stairs in silence and we follow the rest up the long march of steps. Behind us, through the arrow-slit windows and the broken triptych, the sun is low and red in the sky, as angry as the Hand of Justice, angry as the God himself must be to see his servant slain so.

And I find that it haunts me that this place is down in the earth instead of reaching for the sky, that it holds a demon instead of an angel, that it draws sin to the front of my character, rather than virtue, and that in just a few hours' time it has slain the best of us.

And I find that I am afraid.

And So It Complicates ...

CHAPTER SIXTEEN
VAGABOND PALADIN

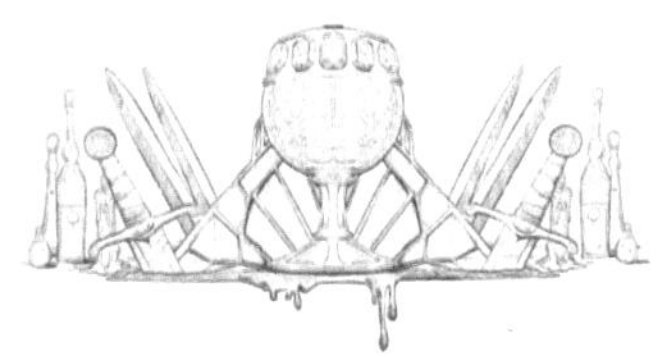

Oooh, this is where things get exciting, little sweetmeat. Tell me, tell me, little morsel, tell me, little bite, who do you think ate the Seer in front of a locked door in a house she should never have visited?

I glanced upward at the demon still locked above us. It wasn't him, was it?

If it was, then you've no defense. Look at him crouched there, ready to devour, ready to eat. But no, he could not reach down to possess her. He's truly trapped. Don't you see the mechanism?

I could not see the mechanism, but I trusted him that it was there. I could tell the demon was stuck. I couldn't explain why, only that I'd known from the moment I'd recognized it existed, just as I'd known I could not remove it on my own.

I'd always thought demons could not be physically trapped. That they had to dwell within the body of something else to manifest themselves. The ones we saw always did. Except for that one time we found a demon possessing a creek.

Well, a creek is a living thing in its own way, dear girl. Imagine what it would be like to be a creek. The places you'd go! The people and animals you'd meet!

The demon seemed annoyed by that line of thought. *Forget demons and creeks. Think about your Seer friend. Who do you think killed her, high and mighty one?*

If her head hadn't been placed on her chest, I would have thought she'd died of madness. She certainly seemed close to it.

You should have had her read your fates while you had the chance, morsel. One of your band of upright little knights is a murderer. But which? Which? The pretty one whose eyes melt for you? His statue of a friend? The pinched ascetic? The querulous son of order?

I still didn't think it was a person who had killed her. We were all paladins. Above reproach. And besides, that monastery was haunted — by a demon at the very least, but I was sure the rest of them must have felt how it called to us, how it made demands. Plus, there was that blasphemy of a door. Perhaps some spirit manifested itself and killed the Seer. Perhaps the demon above was no longer dreaming. Perhaps whatever it was flew out the keyhole and into her heart.

And cut off her head?

Perhaps.

And her hand? And made a pretty picture in her blood? You're grasping. You're hoping. It makes you deliciously vulnerable. Will you be next?

No.

What a pity.

Perhaps I should leave.

Perhaps, my girl. Perhaps.

Sir Branson seemed troubled. But why?

We were not an aspect that usually meddled in politics. We didn't stay in one place. We were the wind that blew as it chose or as the God directed. We were no more likely to remain than the castle a child builds out of dust on the edge of the road. Of course I would melt away and it would be as if I never was. If not today, then tomorrow or the next day. It was both the beauty and horror of our aspect. To be fed every day on adventure and new hope, and every day to discard all that went before for a taste of the novel. Blessing and curse in equal measure, but mine, all mine.

And it is beautiful and worthy. But it is the demon that concerns me. Were it to become free, it would become our responsibility. Our dread task. It hovers there over the heads of all who enter that house.

Then we should cast it out right now. Recruit the others. Use our abilities together to dislodge it. I glanced upward and shivered. Brindle peered up with me.

Try.

I focused my mind and lifted my heart to the God and felt ... nothing. Not even the slight tug I had felt in the past when I had prayed beside Sir Branson.

Mayhap it was because Sir Adalbrand was right and I was no true paladin.

I think not.

Mayhap I needed to sit and pray for a full seven-day under this roof.

That I doubt, also. I felt along your prayer as you lifted it to the God and it confirmed as I suspected. You cannot remove this demon. Not on your own and not while it is behind the mechanism. If the mechanism were opened and it were set free, then yes, you could try, but ...

But I'd be on my own, without any other members of my aspect. With the demon possessing no physical body, I could only turn to hours or even days of prayer, during which I would be completely vulnerable.

Or...

Or it would possess either me or some other who strayed too close.

The demon in my head began to laugh.

Elegant, if I do say so myself.

I was caught, wasn't I? Free the creature and I could fling it from this earth, but if I failed, it would escape, bringing death and destruction with it. Don't free it, and it would remain here forever, ready to break free and entrap someone else.

I don't even see how to free it. But we must be ready if it slips out.

Ready for what?

Ready to die with honor, trying to do the impossible.

That sounded like my destiny, certainly. I was forever being served up the impossible.

The laughter in my head — nasty and cruel — built to a crescendo and echoed on and on, making the inside of my mind loud even while the outside was silent as we ascended the stairs together.

I think everyone else was thinking the same thing — not about the demon, but about how this murder made no sense. I didn't think any of the others were close to the Seer, but I felt ill at her death, and I was certain the rest did, too. I glanced over my shoulder every so often to see them trailing behind me in a line, and when I finally reached the top of the staircase, the muscles in my legs aching and my breath coming just a touch faster than I'd like, I paused.

Oh yes. The door.

The laughter in my head spooled out like a coil of rope about to be woven into a noose.

Would it take something more from me if I stepped through it again?

Will it take your restraint? Please let it take that! Please. I'd love to see you unraveled, little knightling.

Facing it left me with cold, slimy dread. I did not want a second dose of terror.

Courage now. Take courage. We dare not abandon that — or hope — or we perish. Step forward now, I'm here with you. I'll walk through with you. You will not be alone.

Never alone, the demon cackled.

I didn't dare wait to think it through a second time. I held Sir

Branson's words close and stepped. I confessed nothing, hoping it would not be necessary on the way back.

My gamble paid off.

I found myself on the other side of the dread door, panting, discomfited, but whole. The terror that had sloshed around inside me all day was gone now. Vanishing as easily as it had come.

I drew in a breath, perhaps my first full breath of the day, and it was only then that respite hit me and I had to lean down and brace myself with my hands on my thighs, taking in great gulps of joy so powerful it felt like agony.

I was alive.

I was alive.

God have mercy. Lord have mercy. I was alive.

I'd been under a demon's hanging body all day. I'd sifted through a place so cursed it was practically a tomb, with no promise I'd ever get out again. I'd been attacked, sworn to, and attacked again.

But I'd held my own. I'd survived.

I drew in a second huge breath, bracing myself, and straightened.

I was not going back.

In the morning, I would pack up and leave.

The Vagabond Paladins would simply have to live without their cup. The relief tore through me just as the cool of evening air hit my lungs and I was — for a moment — euphoric. I didn't have to go back. They couldn't make me. I could just stay up here in the sweet air of the world.

Around me, dusk was settling in grey velvet like a warm coverlet. Above, the moon and stars swelled with light. Out past the crumbling ruin, the sea muttered. And I was free.

No! No, no, no, that's no fun at all, little treat.

Brindle bumped his skull against my leg. I leaned down to rub the skin behind his ears and press my forehead to the silky fur there.

Do as you must, my girl. It never hurts to buck the aspect now and then. Remind them that we're beggars, not kings. Harder to steer. Harder to push. Harder to grind down because we're already on the bottom.

I opened my eyes.

The tableau of two Engineers sprawled before a fire sipping tea was no surprise. They watched me owlishly as if I were a bard performing. Perhaps they'd been at it all day. Perhaps they'd drunk the stream dry with all their tea brewing. The thought made me feel so light I nearly laughed.

Brindle padded away toward the woods to take care of doggy business and I took a step forward, my feet light underneath me.

Something grabbed me around my neck so suddenly that I couldn't scream, couldn't so much as speak. I reached up, scrabbling against a tight grip on my throat and an iron forearm, fighting down the sudden surge of energy that filled me with strength but clouded my mind.

"What are you doing?" someone ground out from behind me. The Prince Paladin, I thought. He sounded horrified.

I couldn't breathe. I thrashed against my restraint.

The Engineers stood up, their faces appalled in the flickering flames.

My eyesight was charring around the edges.

My attacker spun me to face him. He put a second hand to my throat and shook, and I had to grab his forearms with my hands so I could move with the shaking rather than be moved by it. It took some of the whip and snap out of what he was doing but did nothing for how his thumbs dug into my windpipe.

I struck out with a foot and connected with a greave. Struck a second time, higher, and felt him flinch at the strength of the blow.

"That was a demon down there," the High Saint said, sounding almost hysterical as he shifted to keep his feet. "A *demon,* and you didn't stop it, didn't cast it out. That's your job. It's your only job."

Little black flecks danced in front of my eyes. I kicked a third time, this time aiming higher, but he twisted and my blow landed to the side.

Focus, Victoriana. There'd be a weakness somewhere. But my thoughts were coming from too far away. I couldn't quite seem to grasp them.

There was a sudden scream as my vision darkened completely, and the pressure was gone. I fell to the ground, huffing, cradling my neck in both hands, scrambling to get my feet under me and get into a fighting stance. A low rumble sounded from over me. It went on and on.

"Well, of course it bit you," the Prince Paladin said from far away. "You attacked its paladin. You're a fool, Joran Rue."

"Emotions seem to be running just a little high, hmm?" one of the Engineers said, as if stating the obvious would sort out the problem.

But whatever else they were saying was lost as the blood roared in my ears and breath sawed in my lungs. I pawed for my sword hilt, found it, and drew, sinking into a defensive stance. My neck and throat hurt badly. Every breath felt like fire as I willed tears not to come.

It's fine to cry. An honest emotion.

Not here. Not now.

I was the only woman here. And this was the second time one of them thought that gave them license to attack me. I didn't dare show weakness now.

Saints and Angels, but my throat hurt.

Brindle made a doggy huff, pacing back and forth in front of my wavering blade. I drew in a breath, narrowed my eyes, and forced my blade to steadiness.

"Try that again now that I have my sword," I croaked out, sounding more frog than paladin. "Try again now, High Saint."

Sir Kodelai stepped through the door into the chaos of lifted voices. On either side of him, the Inquisitor and the Penitent were staring at me and the High Saint as if the pair of us were possessed.

"It's her fault," the High Saint was saying, pointing at me, face flushed in the firelight. "She could have prevented it if she'd done her job."

In front of me, Brindle's growl went on and on.

"We're all upset," the Majester said. "But we should take refuge in prayer, not in attacking one another. This is madness. This can only end in more needless death."

In lower tones, I heard the Inquisitor explaining to the Engineers what had happened below. His sword hand was restored. He kept flexing it like he couldn't believe the blessing of it. The same relief was in the posture of the Majester and Sir Owalan, like they could breathe again after being squeezed too hard.

I don't think they're going to fight us.

I took in a long, painful breath and let my guard ease.

Sir Kodelai cleared his throat. He looked majestic, even now in the middle of chaos — perhaps even more so in the middle of chaos, for he was the firm rock within the waves.

"I am the Hand of Justice," he said coolly. "Appointed by the God. There will be no vigilante justice here, so restrain yourself, Aspect of the Holy God."

The High Saint ducked his head, his words cutting off abruptly.

"Good," the Hand said. "Sheathe your sword, Vagabond."

With a frown, I obeyed. I wasn't prepared to fight them all, anyway. Especially now that the Inquisitor had his sword hand back. He'd been deadly with his off-hand down below. I wouldn't like to fight him now. He'd been holding back when we sparred last night.

"You are not children," Sir Kodelai went on, running a hand over his oiled beard. "You are paladins. A child of the God was killed in this place and together we will find justice. I will spend the night in private prayer on this matter. I will beseech the God on our behalf, praying in front of the door through the night.

Until this matter is settled, no one shall go in and out the door or leave this camp. Are we agreed?"

It was while he was still speaking that Sir Adalbrand stepped through and almost collided with the Hand of Justice. He was breathing hard but the look of utter relief he wore made me swallow hard.

Relief softened all those hard lines of his face for a moment, and seeing him here filled me with an instant sense of solace. Here was someone who wasn't going to kill me out of hand. That was all it was. Comradery. Safety. There was nothing else there, just reprieve. It was a reasonable thing to feel.

If you say so.

He ran a hand over his jaw and then his eyes caught mine and narrowed, as if searching for something. His gaze cleared for a moment, but it still ranged over my drawn sword, defensive posture, and the dog pacing back and forth before me.

"But surely we already know what happened," the High Saint said bitterly. "There was a demon in there, and the girl did not cast him out." He pointed at me, finger quivering in the firelight. In all the chaos, the sun had finally sunk the rest of the way, leaving us in darkness. "The Seer died and the girl is responsible. The blood of the Aspect of the All-Knowing God is on her hands and hers alone."

"The girl?" Adalbrand asked, and his voice snapped like a whip, making Sir Kodelai startle. I wouldn't have expected the big man to be capable of it. "We are all holy knights of the God. And while the Vagabonds choose to wander and fight demons, they're no more bound to it than you're bound to debate theology and heresy in every keep and hold. If you wanted the demon cast out, you could have done it yourself."

"There was no way to remove the monster," the High Saint said, looking more worried about Adalbrand's words than for my sword. That was humbling. "I did pray it would go. I'm not the one the God grants strange requests."

This time his petulance encompassed both me and Hefertus.

Hefertus laughed and drew his belt knife to pick at a tooth with the edge of the blade. It was dramatic. I adored it. I should have thought of that. He flicked the end of the knife and leveled a long look at the High Saint.

"I thought it was fine where it was, Sir Joran. My good sense told me it wasn't going anywhere."

The High Saint laughed at that, a touch hysterically.

"I don't think it killed the Seer," Hefertus said, sounding bored. "It was stuck up there. Trapped. I studied its cage with care and saw no way out."

"It's a demon. It can leap. To any open vessel."

Hefertus rolled his shoulders. "*Open* vessel? Is that what you are, High Saint?"

"Enough," Sir Kodelai said, emerging from his tent. I hadn't even seen him go in, but he was carrying a wooden box out with him. He unfurled a small prayer mat, forcing Adalbrand to move out of the way, and then laid the box on it and slowly began to remove his armor piece by piece. "I will entreat the God. In the morning, we'll go together into the monastery and we'll dress the Seer's body and enact the God's justice."

And after that, I would leave.

"That's good enough for me!" The High Saint said loudly, as if we were all waiting for his stamp of approval. Ha. "The God is satisfied. We shall set all other arguments aside!" He shot me a glare at that, as if it were I and not he who had throttled the other. "Let us gather around Sir Kodelai to pray, brothers ... and sister."

I blinked at him. Was he in earnest?

He coughed awkwardly, and when he met my eye and saw the rage there, he swallowed. I held his gaze for a long moment. My throat still hurt. He'd hurt it out of panic and shame. I was not sure I could forgive that.

Excellent! Feed your anger.

Annoyed that I must be contrary to a demon, I sheathed my sword and whistled to Brindle to call off his pacing.

Very well. I would give grace for now. But I would not forget.

When I looked up, Adalbrand was watching me, but I could not meet his eye. Where he had been peaceable, I had drawn my sword. Where he had been collected and reasonable, I had heard only the roar of blood in my ears. I was ashamed that I was exposed for him to see.

"Gather," the High Saint called. "Let us gather."

I resented being ordered around by a man who had just choked me, but I couldn't help the warmth in my heart as we gathered around Sir Kodelai. These community moments were always rough on me. A tiny taste of a "could-have-been" that I would never possess, except for in these few fleeting minutes. Community of any kind was not a thing granted my aspect.

Sir Owalan set a hand on Sir Kodelai's shoulder — bare of pauldrons now, but still broad and hard under his jerkin. Beside him, the High Saint limped over to set a grim hand on Sir Kodelai's other shoulder and one on Sir Owalan's shoulder.

I didn't know what the others saw at moments like this one. But I know what I saw. I saw a faint glow and a warmth like the air over a boiling kettle.

It made me softer toward the idea of forgiveness ... or at least tolerance.

I saw it grow when the Inquisitor bowed his head and stepped up to place the splayed fingers he'd newly received back from the grave across the back of the High Saint's hand. With his other hand, he beckoned the Majester over and wrapped an arm around the older general's shoulders.

The Majester's head was bent, but he made room when Hefertus pulled in beside him, wrapping his huge arms over the High Saint's and across the Majester's shoulders. He placed his other hand over Sir Kodelai's clasped hands, breaking the silence as he murmured.

"The God grant us an ear."

The two engineers had moved in silently. They clapped their

ered on that very sword had she not stepped quickly to the forefront.

Sir Kodelai is not amused. He studies her with a curled lip.

"Eight of us remain."

He pauses and looks at us one by one.

"One of us is a killer."

"Nine," Hefertus corrects him. "Nine of us remain. There's a dog." My friend flicks his long, golden hair behind his shoulder, points lazily to the dog, and then gets to work tying his hair into a knot on top of his head. I've served with Hefertus before. This is his version of rattling his sword in the scabbard. He wants everyone to know he's ready for a fight.

"Fine," Kodelai says, his sneer deepening. "Eight and one animal. A beast which nearly skewered himself on my blade seconds ago."

"Or ripped your throat out," Hefertus adds.

The Hand of Justice shoots him a look so full of poison it could taint an entire city's water supply. He refuses to note the correction.

"I will discover who did this and bring them to justice. Tonight."

"We should search her body," the Majester General suggests from behind me. He is out of breath. I think he's had people to run for him for so long that doing it for himself is a novel development. "Perhaps she found the cup. Or the key."

It is at this moment that the High Saint hits the ground again — so hard that I flinch. He could shatter his kneecaps this way. His forehead hits next and my heart speeds so hard it stutters painfully. Is he dying, too?

But no.

Prayers tumble from his lips, hard and fast, and so thick that word runs into word. Perhaps it is panic. Or guilt. Or reverence. Whatever the motive, he can hardly kill us from there. I put him out of my mind.

"Is anyone else hurt?" I ask, and find my voice is hoarse.

hands over Hefertus and Sir Sorken reached out and wrapped a meaty hand over my pauldron, drawing me into the group. He didn't even look at me. And that was the thing with praying over someone. We were one in that moment. Differences set aside. No need to ostracize or jockey. No place for grudges.

Even extremely warranted ones.

Like the one I had.

The light was so bright now that it felt blinding to me. I glanced over my shoulder at Brindle and hoped he'd stay put. He yawned.

I will stay right here.

Good enough.

It still felt awkward when Sir Adalbrand found his place between me and the High Saint. He didn't look at me. Didn't touch me. His hand was on top of the High Saint's and his other reached over and clasped Hefertus's forearm, his wrist brace barely brushed mine, and yet I felt his nearness like one feels a fire near. It was impossible to ignore.

We said the benediction together, in unison. And for those moments that our lips moved as one and our bodies were joined by touch and intention — for those moments — I felt like I was a part of something bigger, greater, deeper than I was on my own. For those moments, I felt more like a paladin than I had since I kept vigil. It bound me to these others, knit us to each other in hope and faith.

And when the words were spoken, the God entreated, our duty — but also our gift — imparted, we broke apart. The gaze of the High Saint grazed mine and for a moment there was a ghost of a smile on his lips, as if all had been forgotten.

I did not find forgiveness so accessible.

"We made stew," Sir Sorken said, enunciating the word "stew" like he was making a grand announcement. "I hope you like mushrooms. The ruin is full of them and Cleft has a surprisingly deft touch."

We ate mushroom stew and drank tea in a strange attitude — a kind of mix of gentle grief over the Seer combined with an almost jubilant relief — the kind you feel when the end of a difficult job is finally over and you can rest.

The High Saint whispered a quiet word to Adalbrand, and when he went to get his bowl of stew, his limp was gone and Adalbrand's was worse. I couldn't have explained why that rubbed me the wrong way. Perhaps it was unreasonable to expect the paladin sworn to me to keep his healing from the one who hurt me so.

Particularly unreasonable since you intend to abandon him in the morning.

Ouch.

The Majester explained what had happened down below to the Engineers with the air of one giving a military report.

"Bad circumstance," Sir Coriand said. "Very sad. We should sort through the Seer's things. Send anything personal on to her family."

"Did she have a family?" the Majester asked.

Everyone shrugged.

I felt my throat carefully and tried not to look at the others. No weakness. No give. If they saw me so much as flinch, another of them might take a swipe at me.

"Everyone has a family," Sir Coriand said. "Originally."

I tried hard not to think of mine.

"What's it like down there?" Sir Coriand asked. "A proper monastery?"

The Majester produced his map and we all pored over it.

"Strange architecture," Sir Sorken had said. "More like a house of learning than a house of faith."

"More like a house of sin," the High Saint said acerbically.

"Do you really think so?" Sir Coriand asked. There was a note to his voice that made it hard to tell if he were serious or teasing. "I was in a house of sin once. It didn't quite have this architecture."

The High Saint sighed as if unwilling to concede that he could be wrong.

"And the cup?" Sir Sorken asked. "Any sign of it?"

The Majester produced his sack and dumped it out beside the fire. With a grunt, Hefertus began to line the cups up from tallest to shortest.

"Interesting," Sir Sorken said, studying them grimly, though what he saw, I couldn't have guessed. To me, they just looked like cups. None of them more or less likely to be a prized Cup of Tears. None of them had the cabochon blue gems. But did the cup really have that, or was it mere fancy? How accurate were records a thousand years old?

I didn't really care anymore anyway. After we buried the Seer, I would be gone. Another leaf drifting on the winds.

Oh dear. This is one of the things I neglected to tell you.

"Will you go down again tomorrow?" Sir Coriand asked gently.

He was treating us like ... survivors, I realized. The same kind tones, the same interest in trivial things to keep us occupied. The same nonjudgmental way of asking without prying. I'd done this myself. Young as I was, it still made people trust me, listen to me, tell me things. It felt unnerving to have someone using it on me. Sir Branson had never done that. He'd always left me to make my own judgments and find my own comfort.

"We all must," the High Saint said grimly. I saw him flicking through the beads of his rosary as if on instinct. "For the Seer."

Yes, that's the part I forgot to mention. Once Sir Kodelai began his ceremonial prayers and beseechings, well ... you can't leave before he passes judgment. It's a law of a sort.

If I broke it, would they take away the paladincy?

Yes.

It may still be worth it.

They'd also torture you to death. Slowly.

That would not be worth it. Fine, so I'd wait for the Seer to be buried and also for the judgment to be made. He'd said he'd do them both at once. Mayhap it wouldn't take very long.

The High Saint looked up, his face a mix of grim concern and smugness he couldn't quite hide.

"You Engineers will have to come, too. Do not fear. You get back what you have to give to the door when you come back up again."

"Are you certain of that?" Sir Coriand asked lightly.

"The Inquisitor has his hand back," the High Saint said, pointing at the hand with which the Inquisitor was holding his bowl of stew.

We all stared at it grimly.

"And will you offer up the same sin again, I wonder?" Sir Sorken asked.

"What?"

"You confessed to pride on the way in. Will you choose a different sin next time?"

"I hadn't ... I hadn't thought."

The High Saint's eyes met mine and I looked away. I didn't want to see into his soul. I didn't like the look of shame in his eyes. I wanted to go back to the moment where we were all in unity praying over Sir Kodelai.

"I need to get water," I murmured. My voice was rough from being choked, but I couldn't help that. I stood, gathering up my dishes.

"What did you lose when you went through?" Sir Sorken pressed as I left the fire.

"My confidence." The High Saint sounded agitated.

"So it stands to reason that if you want to keep your confidence, then you should offer something else. Greed, perhaps."

"That's no sin of mine."

If they landed on an accurate sin, I was too far away to hear it.

I made my way to the stream, checked on Halberd and cared for him, washed my dishes, and was refilling my water skin when I heard the drift of voices.

It was only then — for some reason — that I remembered my promise.

In the chaos of having to defend myself, in the relief of returning to the land above, in the pain of my bruised throat, I'd forgotten it entirely. It stung as I remembered my words to Sir Adalbrand. Words that meant I couldn't just abandon him.

Oh, I forgot, too. Sir Branson sounded ashamed of himself.

The demon only laughed.

I had promised Sir Adalbrand that I would work hand in hand with him until the cup was found and returned to the church.

I couldn't just get up and go. Not now.

Saints bless it. What my curse lacked in originality, it made up for in sincerity.

The mere thought of returning to that place under the ground made my skin crawl and my stomach try to worm its way out of my mouth. I had not wanted to go back for Sir Kodelai's judgment. I certainly didn't want to go back for any longer than that.

Perhaps I could convince him that we could keep our vow without going back down there.

I wish you the God's blessing with that.

Thank you, Sir Branson.

The demon's laughter told me I'd guessed wrong again.

The voices grew louder and now I could distinguish words.

" ... with us."

"Cramped enough in there already," Hefertus complained.

"You saw how the High Saint was looking at her. And the first victim was a woman. It stands to reason that if her killer strikes again, he might go after the other woman here."

That was Adalbrand. He sounded thoughtful, though why he was worried about me was a bit of a puzzle. I'd held my own down in that monastery. Against two opponents at once.

The man is a knight. Will you truly deny him the right of chivalry?

I glanced over to Brindle, who looked up from lapping water innocently.

Perhaps you feel like you need to prove yourself, but you really don't. That's a desire that can only lead to trouble. People who need to prove how independent or strong they are ... well, my girl, those are the weakest people in the room.

"I find it strange that you think whatever killed the Seer might harm the Beggar. Whatever killed her, I would guess it was most likely due to her insight. So what did she know that we don't?" Hefertus's voice grew nearer.

"The future."

"Ha. Yes. But what else?"

Adalbrand shrugged, but he looked thoughtful. I'd pay my last coin to know what he was thinking.

It's copper. I doubt he'd take it.

"I should also remind you that it's unseemly for you to invite a lady into your tent," Hefertus said, but now it sounded like he was teasing. "People will talk."

"I'm sure you can manage to chaperone."

"Oh, it's not you that I'm worried about, my friend. A hot-blooded woman like that? Who knows what she might do in the darkness."

"I wouldn't get too excited, Hefertus. If I had to guess, I'd say she will likely sleep, or failing that, she may plant a dagger in one of our throats. As yours is by far the prettier, I will pray for your sake that it remains whole."

Hefertus was still laughing when they turned the corner around the ruined masonry and saw me there, squatting over the stream, filling my water skins, likely looking as wild as a creature of the forest.

The hitch in Adalbrand's breath told me I *did* look like a threat. Good. These two shouldn't underestimate me. I had two knives. That was enough to put one in each of their throats.

I pushed back my long hair and stood. It had escaped from its braid again. It did that a lot. I was fond of it, though, and I would not cut it. It hid my face nicely when I didn't want to answer questions and it kept my neck warm in the winter.

Adalbrand's eyes met mine as I straightened and I froze, searching in them for any glimmer of all his angst from below. He seemed lighter. I wondered if he felt as guilty about that as I did. A woman was dead. What right had I to feel relief?

He smiled warmly. "We have room in our tent for one more if you'd like to share the watch, Lady Paladin. If there really is something prowling about, perhaps there is safety in numbers."

"The dog sleeps with me," I said awkwardly. I could have sworn I heard his snicker as Hefertus rolled his eyes and squatted down to fill his own water skin.

Adalbrand swallowed and looked grim for a moment before giving a sharp nod.

"Spare us, Poisoned," Hefertus said in a way that sounded like a curse.

Adalbrand spread his hands out. "You wanted to be safe. What's more safe than a killer canine to guard you?"

"Not having a killer canine," the blond paladin complained. "Look, Lady, I'll tell you this once, that dog is trouble."

I nodded. There was really no animal more troublesome.

"He'll probably bite someone."

Adalbrand grimaced. Maybe he was feeling that bite all over again.

"He might get you in such a deep hole that you never dig out again."

I sighed. "All that is true and more, Sir Hefertus. Do you want me in your tent or don't you?"

"I don't," Hefertus said, kicking at a stone. He pointed at Adalbrand. "But he does, and I suppose that will have to be enough. Just be sure to put your bedroll between us, Bran. I don't much care to be killed in my sleep — from that without or that within."

Hefertus leaned a shoulder against a chunk of rubble that had once been a low wall and watched his friend through slitted eyes, clearly weighing and measuring.

"I'll have a moment with her, if you'll allow it, Hefertus," Adalbrand said.

I held back a tiny shiver. The intensity of his cinnamon eyes was enough to burn a parchment. When he leveled that look at me, I could hardly tell whether he was furious or simply intent.

"Poison yourself with her if you wish, my old friend," Hefertus said, snorting. "But be wary. She acquitted herself well down below."

He left us and Adalbrand drew near — not touching me, never touching me, but close enough that I could feel the warmth of his breath on my chilled skin. He looked paler than he had before. Was that from drinking in the High Saint's pain?

"I know not what was forged between us in the bones of the earth, Lady Paladin, but I feel it still. It goes beyond the vow we made. As if a line has been drawn between your fist and my heart."

"It's not of my making," I said steadily. He was so ... sure. His very certainty was shown in how he moved and how he spoke. Like he already knew the whole story of our lives and was reading it again simply for his own enjoyment.

The light in his eye — fierce though it was — made me want to melt for him.

Celibate, remember? There won't be melting.

Yes. Good. Excellent reminder.

Realizing I'd been leaning toward him, I straightened and forced my face to a flinty expression.

"You've bound me just as handily, Sir Adalbrand. I can no more leave this place than I can fly. Even if it makes me shudder to think of going down below for a second day."

"I won't hold you to that," he said, and now his fierceness had a hint of pain — a lion with a thorn in the paw. He ran a hand through his hair.

Lions are still lions, and this one will shred you like grass.

"I made vows to you," I said simply. "We are bound together because of that."

He bowed his head. The faint light of the moon shone off his armor despite its blackening.

"And we are also bound because we are friends — if you'll allow it," I said, softening my words, and when he looked up at me the softness in his gaze was too much. Like a burst of fire through the belly.

I took a step back.

Seriously, he should think about swearing to our ranks. Hell's forces are always recruiting and this knight knows how to tempt.

"My friendship is the least of all I offer to you," he said through a thick throat.

"I think it will do well enough."

"I made vows to you, too." I didn't know what he was trying to tell me. I could feel him hinting at something deeper than his words but when I tried to grasp it, my hands came back with nothing. "I have the faith to honor them."

I smiled slightly. "I wish I had your faith."

His answer was so soft that I barely heard it. "You have more than faith. You have blessing."

Which was how I found myself turning in early under the covering of a crane-painted silk tent. I was given a space on the far side of the tent from Hefertus and Brindle was kind enough to lie at my feet.

"If the dog moves, I stab him," Hefertus groused from my left. Even with Adalbrand between us, he was still unhappy.

"I'm pretty sure that if you move, you'll crush us all, and then he'll have to attack, so it's a coin toss really," I said dryly.

And if Adalbrand's muffled chuckles were balm to my soul, who would deny me? Below, in the monastery, it had been hell. Could we not enjoy a single night of reprieve?

Enjoy it at your peril.

It was hardly excessive. After all, I had the edge of a ruin as a pillow and Hefertus smelled of horse.

Admit it, sweetmeat, you like it just fine.

I fell asleep trying to ignore both a demon and the loud chanted prayers from the man kneeling in vigil before the monastery door. But before I drifted off, I thought I caught the edge of another prayer muttered low in a soft tenor as teeth clacked together on a string.

Chapter Seventeen
Poisoned Saint

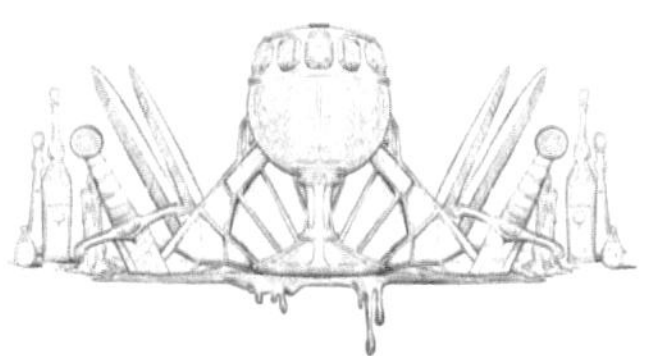

I wake for the first time ever to a pair of eyes looking right into mine. They are large and brown as good earth and deep as my forever guilt, and for the first time in years, I forget to say my prayers upon waking.

I look and look and it almost hurts that she doesn't look away, that she doesn't so much as blink, just stares into my eyes with the same intensity that she does everything — like someone has lit her on fire and she's trying to live an entire life before she's consumed.

I don't want to go down beneath the earth again. I don't want to seek the cup. I don't even want to see the Seer buried — as much as it shames me to admit those thoughts.

That door ruined me yesterday and it will ruin me again. How can I protect the innocent, defend righteousness, and take the pain of the suffering, when my heart and mind are not right? I cannot. It steals my honor. It unmans me.

I do not want to go.

But I also do not want her to go without me. I can imagine her crouching in the darkness, looking up at that terrible statue that matches her. I can imagine it coming to life and picking her up and putting her into its gaping mouth, and something inside me rejects that like it rejects the yawning, grasping darkness of a life without faith. I cannot. I will not.

I blink and it's gone and she's biting her lip as she looks at me. She whispers and I shiver lightly at the intimacy of it.

"We're bound to go down there, aren't we? There's no way out."

I nod, but my mouth is dry and I don't know how to reply to her. I hear her words, but I also hear the words of another girl.

"The baby's dead, isn't she? And I am dying with her," Marigold had said to me all those years ago.

And my heart twists because I couldn't save the other girl and I have a terrible feeling that I can't save this one. I say those terrible, damning words that I've said once before.

"I'll be here with you," I say with my stupid thick tongue and poisoned lips. "You won't have to do it alone."

She huffs a laugh. "I'm always alone. I always have to do everything for myself. Alone."

A smile plays on the edge of my lips. I feel something of a fool lying here in my bedroll next to a stranger and whispering with her rather than strapping on my armor and steeling myself for the day like a proper knight ought to.

"Is this why you're so fierce? Because you must always be alone?"

"You think me fierce?" She seems taken with the idea. She has a freckle on the end of her nose. What a strange thing to note.

"It's your best quality," I admit.

She shakes herself and sits up in her roll of blankets. Her tangled hair is everywhere, dark as the waves of the angry sea. She tames it so deftly that it's already transforming into a woven snake while I am still sitting up and finding my boots.

Hefertus is gone, his bedroll left in disarray as it always is. He's scattered some kind of jewelry over the top of it as if it took him time to decide on what decorations to wear. I wonder what the Vagabond thinks of that — she who is forsworn against wealth. It's nearly as wildly inappropriate to have that wealth of gold and gemstones in her tent as it is to have her wealth of femininity in mine.

I steal an unwarranted glance at the curve of her hip. A wealth of femininity indeed.

I am reminded of why my order calls no women. The most dove-plain among them hide a secret — that their words are life and their caresses more valuable than all of Hefertus's gold. Just waking to the deep eyes of one of their kind has snared my heart and strung it up like that demon suspended in the ceiling. I may never slip free of this trap.

"I'll give you your privacy," I tell her with a half smile. It's rueful, for I know I am a fool, but as kind as I can make it for all my failings are no fault of hers.

"Maybe I don't want privacy," she says, shrugging her surcoat over her jerkin in a way that makes my mouth a little drier. She's dressed in more layers than a southern nun and yet the addition of just one more tantalizes me. "Maybe if I'm going on an adventure, I want a companion."

"Didn't you always have a companion? Weren't you with Sir Branson?"

The lines in her face grow deeper. I'm taken by surprise and a little guilty. Fool. She only just buried her friend and you must rub salt in the wound?

"That was different. The pair of us were a unit," she says, looking at her dog rather than at me.

I make a mistake then.

"We could be a unit," I tell her, like I'm not damaged and ruined. Like I'm not so pickled in guilt I could be served alongside ham. Like I won't ruin her with me.

She hums as if considering my offer. "Are you going to turn insane on me again inside the monastery?"

Now it is my turn to look away and swallow.

"I beg your forgiveness, Lady. I am deeply flawed. Something terrible lurks in the depths of my heart and sometimes I'm not sure if it's me."

I keep my eyes averted as I finish dressing in my own kit, yanking and pulling at straps with more force and vigor than necessary.

I expect her to scold me or chastise me. She does neither. When I look up, her eyes are full of a knowing she can't possibly have at her age.

"I am riddled with flaws also, Sir Knight. As are we all. I would still like a companion on my adventure."

"And who would you choose?" I keep my tone teasing, trying to stay away from heavy things. I note she offered me no forgiveness for my foolishness before. "Who would you choose to take with you on this grand adventure? A butler, perhaps, all the better to help you find a cup?"

I work at the remaining straps of my armor, this time with less vigor. I dress lightly. I do not need more than the basics. After all, we are going down into a terrible, broken monastery, not out onto a battlefield. More armor is just more work to lug up the stairs when we are through.

The lady paladin seems to agree. She sticks to a breastplate with no backplate, keeps her gauntlets and pauldrons, but tosses aside all else. She checks her sword belt twice.

"I'm missing a knife," she says, her face lined as she frowns. "I could have sworn I had two on this belt when I went to sleep."

"Maybe Hefertus borrowed it to shave."

"How is he so light on his feet? I did not even hear him awaken and look at the mess he made! He could not have done that silently."

Beside her, her dog pants, a doggy smile on its devil face. I'm not fooled. I know perfectly well it will bite me with no provocation.

I give it a long, dark look. Don't cross me, dog. I have too much human blood on my hands to worry much about dog blood.

"Hefertus is a mystery," I allow. "And he's never one to shy from adventure."

"Neither am I," she says resolutely. "And I suppose today will be another adventure. I'll skip the butler and take you with me, I think."

I could get drunk on this kind of courage, this kind of carefree boldness that tells me she drags few ghosts behind her. She's light and free as a bird of the sky. I adore it. I want to be it. Or be close to it. I will take either one.

"Tell me about this adventure," I say, indulging her as I roll up my blankets and tie my things into my pack. It's overly cautious to bring it down the stairs with me, but yesterday we left the Engineers up top. Today, we will have no one to come after us if something goes awry. I want to be ready.

"It's the story of a brave paladin," she says, shooting me a mischievous look. I think she doesn't realize how much her eyes twinkle even when she's trying to be serious, never mind when she is joking. That's worth more than any relic.

"Does this paladin have a dog?"

Her smile is the dawn. "She does, in fact."

"And a hapless companion who will make terrible mistakes and require rescuing?"

"Oh, you've heard this story? Well, don't spoil the ending."

We're both on our feet now. Equipped. Packed.

And I do something even stupider than all else that has gone before. I know better. The mad thing that ran through me yesterday and opened all my locked doors is gone now. I have full possession of myself. My mind is my own. I, therefore, have no excuse this time. But I still step close enough that I can speak more intimately. I let myself soak up the warmth of her in the air. I let myself look once more into those brown eyes and I do not guard my heart as I look into hers.

"I do not know the ending yet, Lady Paladin. And I am not eager to bring this story to the end."

And she must be as foolish as me, because she swallows, looks at my heart right back, and says, "Maybe we won't have to."

Surely she must realize that I would already walk across the flat circle of the earth's face on just the chance that my story with her would not be over yet. The idea that we share something — even if it's only a story — stirs up fancies in me that I've long suppressed. I can imagine myself on the road with her. I could kindle a fire while she huddled in a blanket and I would catch her first morning smile. I could check the hooves of her horse while she inspected the tack. I could throw sticks for that terrible dog.

I swallow roughly, grateful for reprieve when she rips her eyes away and leaves the tent.

I learned long ago to stop dreaming of things I can never have. I am too washed with guilt to be worthy of even the hope of them. But she makes me dream forbidden dreams.

I take a moment to compose myself and whisper Lauds. I follow them with a prayer of my own.

Sorrowful God, make me strong and accurate. Ready me for what comes next.

My usual prayer seems weak before the task ahead. It will have to be enough.

I leave the tent and join the others.

I am not the only one who has prepared himself. Around the circle of the ruins, the others carry their various bundles and packs. Hefertus has tied his hair back as though he expects trouble. The Majester is carrying a helm and the Inquisitor has tied a strip of cloth across his brow. Even the High Saint is freshly scrubbed and looking wary. He whispers frantically into the ear of Sir Kodelai, eyes darting in every direction, gestures emphatic.

"Brothers." Sir Kodelai interrupts the High Saint to speak to us from where he stands by the gate. "Listen now to the will of the God."

I always wonder about fellow clerics and paladins who claim to know the will of the God. Do they really speak for him? It feels like a risky thing to claim if they don't. And the satisfaction in Sir Kodelai's eye tells me he likes this. He *is* this. It's harder to trust someone who is enjoying the power so much.

By all accounts, Sir Kodelai is the most upstanding, most

honorable living paladin. He has served the Aspect of the Vengeful God in the most exemplary manner since renouncing his land and crown and giving himself to his Aspect. But this gleam in his eye — this is new to me. This is worrying. I seal my lips shut and try to watch everyone at once.

The early morning breeze ruffles hair and nips cheeks pink. Eyes are bright, feet restless. I sense nothing else — no malice or subterfuge. There's anxiety rolling off the High Saint, but there's always a little of that with him.

If there is a threat near, I do not see it.

Sir Kodelai's voice booms through my observations. "We will go down together into the monastery again. We will gather up the Seer to be laid to rest. And I will speak to you of guilt and justice."

He's carrying his wood case. The one with his incense and other accoutrements of the Vengeful Aspect.

"Please set down your worldly goods. They will not aid us today."

"Unless we're locked in there," Hefertus says. "Then we'll be glad we have tools and food."

"The door will not lock," Sir Kodelai says. "See? I have removed it from the hinges."

So he has. Interesting. It does not prove his argument.

"You all know that in matters of justice, you must yield to me. Please put down your packs."

We are none of us excited to obey his orders, but we do. The consequences, should we ignore him, are too grave.

"We discuss life and death today. And a murder most grim," he says, and his beautiful face has an expression of reverence. He's dressed in finery, I realize. A nice black velvet coat is under his tabard. He's dressed his hair and oiled his beard. This is sacred to him. And it must, then, be sacred to us. "Who here can never say they have committed murder, whether in the name of the God or otherwise?"

I meet the High Saint's eye by accident. It's burning with holy reverence as he nods. Nothing wakes a High Saint up like reminding them that we are all sinners in the hands of the Merciful God. It's like wine to them and they'll drink it to the dregs.

"So it is and always is," he intones gravely.

Sir Kodelai shoots him a quelling look and it's hard not to laugh at how the piety of the one has ruined the performance of the other's piety.

"Which is why I bid you each to confess that sin as we enter the door today," he says firmly, cutting off discussion.

I feel a chill of unease. That's an odd request. It feels almost unreasonable, and yet I cannot think of an argument for why I should confess one sin and not another. Nor can I think of an argument for why we must all confess as he bids us. If he's thought of a reason, he doesn't share it with us.

"You want each of us to leave our possessions here and follow you into the monastery, confessing at the door that we are murderers and the lowest of worms?" The High Saint looks like he might start worshipping Sir Kodelai if he isn't reined in.

It takes all my self-control not to roll my eyes. When I accidentally catch a glimpse of the Beggar Paladin, she's making a face like she bit into something sour. I catch Sir Owalan watching her and biting his lip with amusement. You grow inured to this nonsense over time ... but it takes time, and the Vagabond hasn't had that time yet. Her reaction — and how adeptly it mirrors my own, though I disguise it — is like a breath of fresh air after being in a sick house.

Sir Kodelai claps Sir Joran on the shoulder. "Actually, High Saint, I was hoping *you* would lead the way and I will bring up the rear, bearing in mind that all gathered here are under my authority."

He gives us all a grim look to remind us that if we so much as flinch from his outrageous demands, we'll be flayed alive in public — wonderful stuff — and then he turns back to the High Saint, who wastes no time in intoning his next words.

"Let us pray. Glorious God, from each of us our bounty, to

each of us our need, may the Lord of Heaven render that on which our spirits feed."

There is a ragged "amen" from the group, though this time I accidentally catch Hefertus's eye roll. The prayer is a mealtime prayer. About as fitting for this occasion as breaking out an aged wine and popping the cork might be.

"Well, lead on then, Saint," one of the Engineers says, taking a noisy slurp of tea. I wonder idly if he can smuggle in his kettle. It will be a difficult day for the Engineers without the steady stream of tea they ingest. "Go confess to murder like a good knight."

The High Saint gives him a black look, but he spins sharply on his heel as if he expects to be inspected — by Sir Kodelai, no doubt — and plunges into the door with the heartrending cry of "I confess, I am a murderer!"

I taste iron as I bite into my lip, certain the door will suck the life out of him for that, but to my surprise, he strides through, looks around, and then keeps going as if nothing has happened.

The Majester follows, hot on his heels. He has kept his parchment and pens, though he leaves his pack and extra weapons behind. His face is lined and grim as he states, "Murder," and strides through the door. Just like the High Saint, nothing seems to happen.

I catch the Vagabond's eye. Does she see this?

She shrugs.

Hefertus goes next, a calculating look on his face, and I know what he's planning before he tries it. He says nothing as he steps through, only bending when he's caught, frozen mid-stride by the door. When he finally confesses "murder" it sounds like a curse.

"No dawdling behind this time, Beggar Knight," the Hand of the God says pointedly, and the Vagabond's cheeks are stained bright when she strides stiffly to the door.

Her dog growls at Sir Kodelai as she steps through. She has kept a thick bearskin cloak by means of wearing it, and who knows what she's tucked beneath it. She was a flurry of arranging and sifting through her pack before her name was called. I suspect she's stashed all kinds of things on her person. Survivors and beggars are like that. They keep what they can and will be as devious as necessary to keep it close. Those who don't, die fast enough to convince the rest.

I step through quickly after her, and I hate that I feel nothing when I confess I am a murderer — or rather, nothing more than the normal pang of terrible shame that I always feel when I admit to myself or to others that my failures killed a girl still not in adulthood and the poor pale babe she bore. They're both on my mind when I almost collide with the scowling Vagabond Paladin.

"Some of us," she says pointedly, "have far too much power. And some of us enjoy it too much."

I purposefully misunderstand her, hoping I can cool her temper before the Hand of the God arrives.

"If you mean me, Lady Paladin, then let me confess I am entirely powerless before your charms."

She laughs, a low snicker-y laugh like she doesn't believe me, but she relaxes, which was my aim in teasing her.

"Lead on, sir jokester, and I hope we deal with the poor Seer and find the cup quickly. I have the most terrible feeling of visiting my own grave when I come here, and I should like to note that it's a far grander and far more terrifying grave than I ever expected."

I could not say why I smile at that, or why I hurry down the stairs so quickly, but I'm not alone. We are all silent as we descend the endless stairs to the vault below. Just as before, the absolute scale of the place makes it feel sacred, intimidating, holy. We are like red ants trailing in a line through a cathedral too small to fully comprehend the glory around us.

Light bathes the white hall in ivory laced with the colors of the triptych, and for a moment I am transported to the Aspect of the Holy God's church in Saint Rauche's Citadel. I can almost hear the chanting echoing through the nave as I did when I visited there last.

By the time we reach the mosaic floor — in silence, I might add — those following us are nearly on our heels.

The last ones to have entered other than Sir Kodelai are the Engineers, and I note with a certain degree of approval — despite my general condemnation — that they have found a way to subvert Sir Kodelai's orders by bringing their golems. The golems carry all their belongings — including, I would like to note, a kettle still steaming and bubbling.

There will be tea. It cannot be stopped any more than the sunrise.

"You can hardly expect us to agree to come down here for your ceremony and leave the golems up there unsupervised, and if they're coming anyway, then they should carry for us," Sir Sorken is saying. "We've both done as you wished — our hands are empty and we've confessed to murder."

He says "murder" in an overly dramatic way of which I fully approve. After all, none of us should have been asked to do this. This entire act is a violation. The Aspect of the Vengeful God is making enemies here.

They leave the golems at the foot of the stairs and we walk the rest of the way in silence. Though this monastery is pristine and bathed with morning light in a way that makes the carved flowers blush and limns the hummingbirds carved alongside them, we are going to a scene of a terrible tragedy.

The others duck their heads under the importance of this act, or scuttle quickly, eyes forward. Not my Vagabond though. Her eyes are upward and narrowed, first taking in the demon — still caged, I might add; if he killed the Seer, then he did it from there — and then inspecting each of the faces of the mighty statues that tower above us. They are graceful and fluid in their frozen agony. They make something in my chest seize and choke.

I look away to where our shadows shoot out in front of us, since we stride with our backs to the arrow-slit windows. The shadows seem darker somehow, as if stretching out to reach for the black violence ahead. My imagination is so over-alert, it almost makes me think I see something twitch within mine.

I'm almost grateful when — eventually — we reach the poor Seer. Time has not lessened the horror of her corpse. Her face is grey, eyes like river stones dried along the banks, hair a matted tangle. The blood in her head has spread across the chest of her clothing, leaving it tarry and ruined.

Sir Kodelai's voice is rough when he speaks.

"Arrange yourselves in a circle around the Seer."

We do as he says, but I am uneasy. There's an edge to the Hand's voice that wasn't there before.

"I will investigate the death of your servant, oh Lord," he intones. "I will investigate in the presence of those here."

He rounds the body within our circle and I frown. This doesn't seem right somehow. This feels like some sort of horrible show, and not an investigation.

Sir Kodelai pauses dramatically. "What is this?"

He reaches down and from under the edge of the Seer's spread garments, he brings out a belt knife, chipped and well-used, about the size of my hand.

"To whom does this belong?" he asks, holding it up between a finger and a thumb. He looks from the wounds on the Seer and then back to the knife and then back to us and there's a look on his face that makes my stomach flip.

I have seen that look once before.

Oh no.

There was a man in a village I came across. His mother-in-law begged me to go into his house, for her daughter was there, dying of a fever. She and her child both. The village blacksmith had already died of the same fever, so deadly it was. I hurried to the cottage and I found the man of the house there, seated on the steps, taking his ease with a pipe in his hand.

"Your wife," I'd gasped. "Your child. I'm here to heal them. I'm of the Aspect of the Sorrowful God."

"I heard the blacksmith died," he replied, coyly, flipping a knife in his hand as if to bar my path, eyes not meeting mine, mouth twisted in irony.

"Last night," I told him grimly. "So let me past, that I might save thy family. I can heal all but death."

"What are the odds?" the man had said, and he said it with that exact look on his face. "What are the odds that he and my wife and child are the only ones with this fever?"

That exact look.

I won't detail what he'd already done with the knife in his hand. Nor will I tell you what I did to him once I'd seen how the inside of his cottage was more red than brown and fit for nothing but the flame. Suffice it to say that when I confessed to the door that I was a murderer, it was not only for Marigold's sake.

"It belongs to me," the Vagabond Knight enunciates quietly from beside me. "I noticed it was missing this morning."

And my blood runs cold as something clicks in my mind and I realize why we are here in this circle. And why the paladin has asked us to carry nothing down with us. It is going to take all of us to carry *two* corpses up so many steps.

"Wait," I say, throwing up a hand. I hardly know what I shall say, only that this must be stopped before it fully begins. "Wait. We are here in a place full of wonders and demons. Let us not forget there may be things happening beyond the ordinary."

Sir Kodelai pauses in front of me. He is, possibly, attempting to appear compassionate, but he can't quite seem to arrange his features the right way, stumbling into condescension instead of compassion.

"You are a healer, Poisoned One. You take our pain and sorrows, you stain your own heart with them. And don't you think that twists your judgment? Don't you think it inclines your ear to those who do not deserve either your mercy or the mercy of the God?"

"I do not," I say firmly, though there is some truth to his claim. I certainly feel more for those I have healed. That tiny thread never completely snaps.

My mind is racing underneath it all. We are all bound here by tradition and law. We can't just walk away. And yet this isn't right. I was with the Vagabond almost the entire time we were beneath the earth, and I would have seen murder in her eyes if she'd killed while we were apart.

"There are no dog prints in the blood," I say, finding a piece of objective evidence at last.

"Dogs can be tied," Sir Kodelai says, and across the circle, the High Saint is nodding soberly and the Majester is frowning. Sir Kodelai is garnering their support. Successfully.

Sir Owalan shifts uncomfortably. He sends little glances behind him at the unopened door. Maybe he, too, wonders what might have come through the keyhole.

"You haven't considered this long enough, brother," I say, shooting a glance at the Vagabond Paladin. She's said nothing. Why would she say nothing?

She is frowning, looking at the knife in his hand like one might look at a tool that has just broken while you're using it. She's too new. She must not realize what's happening here. It's that very innocence that pierces my heart.

"I have considered all night," Sir Kodelai says slowly, with a kind of finality. "I have *prayed* all night."

"And did the God speak to you?" I ask, desperately.

"Adalbrand." Hefertus's warning is low and urgent.

He's friend enough to me not to want me to wreck my life upon the rocks. I glance to where he stands, shifting uncomfortably, scratching his beard with one hand and twisting his triple strings of pearls with the other. He's added a string of black pearls to the mix. He's not even looking at me. His eyes are fixed on the falcons carved and set in a shape of guarding over the locked door, as if they might come to life and attack him.

"I am the Hand of the God in this matter," Sir Kodelai says in a low voice. "And all present are under my hammer."

I look around the circle, but no one is looking at me. They will let this play out. My blood roars loud in my ears. A wise man would let this drop. Who am I to interfere with the judgment of the God? All evidence speaks against me. The girl herself has shown herself capable of murder.

And yet.

I have healed her. I have felt her soul.

This was not her.

There was a Poisoned Saint caught in treason when I was a squire, and a Hand of the God was sent for. The Hand prayed seven days in the halls of our aspect and then declared that he had word from the God. We were roused from our beds in the second hour, yawning and confused. My paladin superior had held my shoulder tightly and whispered in my ear.

"Do nothing, Adalbrand. Say nothing. Close thine eyes if thou must."

And then the Hand had said, "This is the Vengeance of the God."

He drank from a small ceremonial cup as his power went out from him. It tangled around the accused paladin's throat and the man fell to the ground, writhing, and died there on the frosty cobbles before us all.

I look back and forth between Sir Kodelai and the wide-eyed Beggar Paladin. And in my mind's eye, I see her writhing on the white marble ground, magic tangled around her throat, and I know that this is one thing I will not stand by and witness.

It is not compassion that guides me now. It is not kindness, though a kindly or compassionate man would feel the same. It's not even this sprouting interest — delicate and new though it is — that is already bending my heart in her direction. It's honor that bids me speak. Chivalry that refuses to allow injustice.

"Stand before my judgment, Vagabond Saint," the Hand of the God says, and just like that, power arcs out from him like soft, wafting white smoke. It reaches out in tendrils and wraps around the Vagabond, sweeping her off her feet, drawing her forward, and then forcing her to her knees before him.

My hands clench but I don't move yet. Think, Adalbrand, think!

Victoriana's spine straightens. There is no fear in her eyes. But there wouldn't be. Not from her. And yet her chin trembles vulnerably. Her eyes are wide even if they are bold.

Her dog leaps forward, snapping, and the same gossamer, smoke-like tendrils wrap him up, too, but they do not bring him to his knees. Instead, they stretch and pull, lifting him to hang over our heads, ineffective, held by a single back paw. His snarls rip through the air, punctuating the emotions swirling in the faces around me.

We're all tense and there's a taste in the air of blood, thicker and brighter than the taste that already lingers from the actual blood spatters around us. I have a creeping sensation up my spine, a feeling I can't explain that tells me this beautiful temple adores the bloodlust in this circle. It feeds on it as ravens feed on the corpses of the fallen. And like instruments tuned to a single note, some of the paladins ring with that taste. Anticipation is foremost in their expressions. They want this. They feel it is right and good. One of the Engineers taps his chin with a single finger.

This is madness. I must speak even if my argument is not fully formed.

The words tear from my throat as quickly as I can disgorge them.

"I throw down a preemptive challenge, Aspect of the Vengeful God."

Across the circle from me, Hefertus rolls his eyes.

Chapter Eighteen
Vagabond Paladin

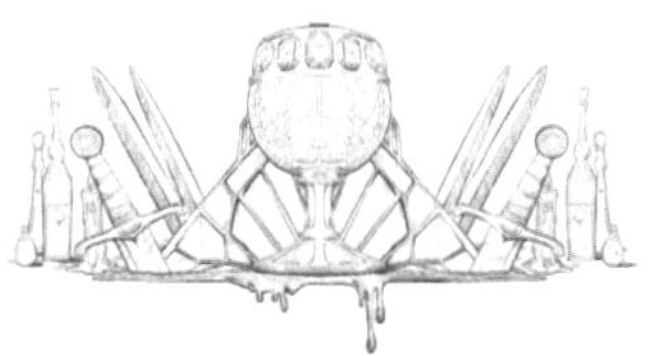

The dog cursed in my brain so intensely that one curse rolled over another. I gritted my teeth against the mental maelstrom, shifting my weight from knee to knee. All my senses prickled, demanding my attention, insisting a blow was coming quickly, that they could feel the rush of the air, smell the sweat of the attacker. I shook myself free from the onslaught and forced my brain to focus. There was no attack yet, though even if there was, what could I do about it? I couldn't even draw my sword properly from this position.

How could Sir Kodelai think I was guilty of such a grisly crime on the scant evidence of a knife found here? Was I to have sawn off her head with my belt knife? Not that I couldn't, exactly. I'd seen pigs butchered with a knife no longer than my palm and I could only assume people were the same. But I had never engaged in such mad butchery, nor would I, God forfend. Besides, what motive could I possibly have to kill the Seer? I did not know the woman.

And now what? I wasn't even sure what happened next. I'd never seen a Hand of Justice perform his duties before.

Adalbrand preemptively challenged. For you. *What have you done to this man?* Sir Branson sounded panicked, and it infected me, making my heart race. I didn't even know what that meant. *No one does that. Not many men would give their lives for an innocent person — never mind one who might be guilty.*

But I *wasn't* guilty. This was all a misunderstanding. They had to realize that.

They don't. They don't realize and they won't until you're dead. His panic was spiraling, making his voice higher and higher.

But I was a paladin. A servant of the God!

Remember when I told you that I hadn't quite had time to tell you everything? I might have forgotten about this part.

No, he'd told me. I knew about the right to challenge. If someone thought Sir Kodelai had judged wrong, they could challenge him. But only *after* he'd carried out justice.

I was going to die no matter what and for no reason.

Unless it's done preemptively. Sir Branson cursed, seemed to shatter apart in my mind, and then gathered himself again. *Saints and Angels! Adalbrand must really believe you're innocent, my girl.*

His voice trembled a second time and was blotted out by more cursing before it returned as my two specters fought for control of the dog. When he resurfaced, he was yelling, as if trying to drown out the demon.

To preemptively challenge like that means that he will share your fate. If he is wrong and you killed the Seer, he'll die with you.

This was all out of control. My heart was in my throat, pulse racing like I was in the heat of battle. The last time I felt like this, a band of highwaymen had set on us in the night while we slept, taking even Brindle unaware. I'd woken to fishy-breathed laughter in my face, the stark white light of the moon, and a sticky blade at my throat. I remembered thinking that they could have at least kept the blade clean.

We'd survived that. With cool heads and decisive action.

I could survive this, too. I took a long, measured breath and refused to join the tenants in my head in their loss of control even though the grey smoke choked and pulled at my throat like a noose and the scent of it — a cloying bergamot — made my stomach twist.

I scanned the faces surrounding me, my heart bobbing a little — like a child's toy boat pushed under the water and then popping up again. I saw no challenge in anyone else's expression. Hefertus, Sir Owalan, and the Inquisitor looked worried. The High Saint and the Majester looked eager. The Engineers watched with riveted gazes, as if they were being taught a new technique.

They agreed with Sir Kodelai, then. They thought I was guilty. Or they didn't care. And they would punish another innocent person along with me. They stood around the broken body of the Seer as though surveying a breakfast table and deciding what they would eat first.

"Any judgment I bear must be born alone," I said firmly, loudly enough to carry. Let them chew on that. I could go to my death bravely. I was no craven. "It's mine alone to prove I am innocent or accept my fate."

This is madness, sweetmeat. Bravery means nothing when your sweet, hot blood is flowing over the crisp white marble. You'll not be able to snatch it back again. Once spilled, twice regretted, as we say in the depths.

"The challenge has been offered. It is not for you to speak to it, Beggar," Sir Kodelai said with a chopping motion of his hand.

He was every inch the king he had once been, tall, straight, noble of brow and jaw, beautiful and finely dressed, and superior to me in every way. He would not be out of place right now in a throne room or before an assembly of bishops. He held himself even now with grave dignity, his face a mask of duty.

I had never liked kings. They were too blind to see they were no greater than beggars, no more secure, no more inured to the whimsy of fate allowed by the sovereignty of the God.

Speaking of which.

Rejected God, I beg your aid. Deliver me from evil and false accusation.

There. A respectful prayer. I may not be truly called by the God, but I could honor him with the proper sort of request — not reaching above myself, not asking for anything it wasn't in his nature already to grant. If I died with this prayer in my heart, I'd hold no shame walking through the bright gates of heaven.

If the God planned to honor my prayer, he didn't do it immediately. I had not thought he would. I was not the beautiful golden-haired type who was instantly rescued by princelings and the God to be spared and lauded.

I twisted, trying to see better as Sir Adalbrand stepped forward. The man worried me.

He was as calm as always, a slightly wry smile ghosting around the edges of his mouth. He flicked a single, assessing glance at me but he looked away almost immediately before he could even see my violent denial of his fool sacrifice. Other than the flutter of his pulse in his throat, there was no outward sign of nerves in how he moved or how he held himself. Was he truly that confident in me?

Chivalry. I told you it ruled this man. It's a beautiful thing to behold.

I didn't think so. This wasn't because I was a woman. This was something else.

Fine, then it is attraction. He's besotted with you.

It was more than that. It was something deeper. I knew the man well enough by now to recognize he was self-controlled.

Usually. But remember when we were down here before, how his tight control was blown away by the winds of this place like seeds from a dandelion? He's not to be trusted, sweetmeat.

Yes, I'd definitely trust a devil's judgment on that over the paladin currently trying to save my skin.

It's toothsome skin.

Adalbrand looked at the Seer as he stepped up to join Sir Kodelai. Just one glance, but his nostrils flared when he passed her, as if he hated that her corpse was being used for show instead of being respectfully carried away. The tiny dimple in his chin grew deeper when he clenched his jaw with determination. When he ripped his eyes back, I saw in their depths the edges of pain and bitterness. He was calm and immovable as a rock on the outside while a well of guilt and ripping sadness tormented him on the inside.

And I wanted both. I wanted to be near the calm and I wanted to assuage the guilt. But I'd never forgive myself if both ended here with me. I'd walk the halls of heaven as guilty as he trod the ground of the earth.

"I won't allow it," I said, my words garbled by how dry my mouth suddenly had become.

"And what will you do to prevent matters from progressing, Beggar?" Sir Kodelai asked as he flicked open the bottom of his wooden case. It had telescoping legs. He shook it and gravity lowered them, so that all he had to do was twist a knob on each one and his box was now a very small table. "Will you murder me, too?"

"I'm not a murderer," I gasped. But I knew it was a lie. I had killed Sir Branson. My best friend in this world.

Killed is a relative term. I'm still mostly alive. Although I do miss my tea.

"We are all murderers here, or we would not have come through the door," Sir Kodelai said gravely. "Or have you not yet realized what this place is for?"

"Is it not a monastery?" I asked as he drew his ceremonial cups from their velvet-lined slots, drew out the vial of blessed holy water, and then set them up very precisely on his small table.

"It was a monastery in the parts that were above the earth," he said, meeting my gaze with his glacial one for but a moment before unstoppering his vial and pouring out a mouthful into each pewter cup with a measured eye. They were carved all over with skeletons, and each of the skeletons covered its eyes with ragged phalanges. "That part has long passed away, as I am certain you noticed. I took my time yesterday while the rest of you were busy with your treasure hunt. I studied this place with care — as I told Sir Coriand last night when he asked me — and I ferreted out the purpose of this great vault below. It does not store records, to the sorrow of the Engineers, nor does it store a cache of weaponry for the Majester, or a storehouse of holy relics for the High Saint, but rather, this vault is a carefully wrought tool. It will indeed make you a Saint by drawing out your sins one by one, feeding them into that trapped demon in the ceiling, and washing what's left of the sinner until he is either clean or dead."

"No man can be clean by his own effort," the High Saint intoned.

"Indeed," Sir Kodelai said, still looking at me. "Which is why — I suspect — so many have died in the attempt. I was once a king. I sent men to their deaths. And then I became a judge of all the world, and I send more men to their deaths than ever before. I rend and tear. I strip and expose. But their blood is not on my hands. Their blood is on their own hands. I am only the vehicle that makes them clean and offers them up to the God."

I shivered. He sounded wrong. Insane. Dangerous. The Aspect of the God I knew was violent against evil but he comforted the victims of it. I did not know this murderous God of Sir Kodelai.

"Shall we make you a Saint, Beggar?"

"No," I whispered, shuddering.

"And what about your valiant benefactor?" he asked, looking over at Sir Adalbrand. "Shall we make him a Saint?"

"No," I pled.

"Are you going to stop playing with your food, Kodelai Lei Shan Tora?" Adalbrand asked coolly. He'd adopted a casual stance and again, I was impressed by his nerve. His eyes were sharp and his jaw tight, as if he were even now calculating and calculating again and coming up with options for how to fix this situation. I wished I could appear so in control of my own actions and destiny. I felt as out of control as a ship on a stormy sea.

"I am gracing the murderess with a lesson. It is a sign of my mercy. I have forsworn all power." The smile barely flickering around the edges of his mouth suggested a lie there. "But not in this *one* matter, in the taking of the God's vengeance. For, in that, I am his Hand."

"Why are there only two cups?" I asked as the bonds around me tightened.

And at that, Kodelai's smile deepened and the look in his eye sent spikes of fear through me.

"One is for me — the mortal judge. The other is for the challenger. We will both drink a draught of holy water. Nothing else. There is no poison in the cup or the water. There is no magic here. No curses set ahead of time or blessings asked. We drink down the attention of the God and turn his eye to our case. We beg his eye upon us. When we are finished, the God himself will judge. He who is right will be spared, and if it is Sir Adalbrand, then you, too, shall live, Beggar. And if it is me, then you shall die."

There was a satisfied exhale from the circle. I ground my teeth at the sound of it. So, they found it fitting, did they? They thought I was getting what I deserved? I would not forget this.

"You don't need to do this, Aspect of the Vengeful God. None of us will like this outcome." I was not given to threats, and this was not a threat. Just a statement of the facts. I didn't kill the Seer.

"Until this is decided, you will not speak."

He flicked a hand and the ghostly bonds surrounding me sprouted another woolen thread. It spun up around my throat and then threaded through my lips, cinching tightly like a gag.

I dug in hard on my training to clamp down on the panic clawing up my throat. The worst enemy was the one you could not see or feel. It snatched the last control I had, ripping it away.

You've put yourself entirely into their hands! You should have fought!

And what? Renounced my paladincy and my life?

And not died!

"Shall we drink then, honored paladin?" Sir Adalbrand asked, his voice cutting through that of my accuser.

"Choose your cup." Sir Kodelai's words rang like a funeral bell.

Adalbrand reached for the closest one and then Kodelai reached for the remaining vessel.

They lifted them and Adalbrand examined his, tilting it around so he could look at every side and edge, peering into it, and then looking at the bottom.

I felt a bead of sweat forming on my brow. One could hardly blame me for it. They were about to drink to my health — or lack of it.

I'll admit to some curiosity. I've never been present for a judgment like this and certainly never one preemptively challenged. I've heard so many rumors but I could hardly credit most of them. It will be fascinating to finally see ...

Oh yes, wildly exciting to offer my life for a scrap of knowledge.

But you know you are not guilty.

But did the God know that? Was it even he who judged or was there really poison in that cup?

Maybe they'll poison your saint after all.

Look, it's not easy to be blasé in the face of possible death. Especially not when one is trussed up like a feast-day goat. And particularly not when the God failed to show up the first time you asked. Just like he had failed to come in his glory to call me to the paladincy. I was not his favored worshipper.

Adalbrand finished examining the cup and cleared his throat. Sir Kodelai laughed.

"It's not a trick. It's not a ruse. This is how the God will judge."

There was a shuffling sound. The others were — unconsciously — leaning in closer. The High Saint, so terrified yesterday by the corpse of the Seer, leaned so far forward now that he had stepped in the edge of her puddle of blood. I swallowed down my gorge at the sight of it. He hardly seemed to notice. Was this the penalty then, for confessing murder to the door? Were we inured to horror, fascinated by death, coldhearted in the face of pain?

You don't seem to be.

Adalbrand took in a long breath.

"Do you wish to take back your challenge?" Sir Kodelai asked gently. "There is still time. Two need not die today." He gestured toward me, though his eyes did not meet mine. He already saw me as disposable. "She's clearly guilty. That crow of a woman. That mongrel of a paladin." His voice was so kind I almost missed how deeply he was insulting me. "Their whole aspect is as valuable as leaves in the autumn. They tumble in the wind, they drift from place to place. They bring nothing but portents with them and leave nothing behind them. They beg and borrow and never repay. What have they ever built? Where are they when they're needed? They cannot stick in one place. They're a blemish on the name of holy paladin. If they cast out a demon, perhaps that is of some utility, but who is to say they've even done that? It's only their own lips that confirm it. And this one is younger than she should be. I do not believe she is a paladin at all. See how her sword is too large for her, though she wields it well? See how she does not offer prayers unless compelled, how she scowls when we sing, how she drew on me — *me* — when I challenged you? These are the things revealed to me last night as I knelt in prayer. We have among us an imposter. We have among us a doppelganger. She is not who she says she is, and even if she were, it is her knife that I found here, and surely she is most likely to have killed the Seer."

I like this one. I'll possess him next if I get the chance. This is a heart that can be twisted as you so stubbornly refuse to be, little treat. Imagine what I could set loose in the name of the God if I held the reins of this man?

Was he sure the man wasn't already possessed?

Oh, it doesn't take the demonic to make a heart glory in evil ... but it helps.

"Why would she want to kill our sister paladin?" Adalbrand asked calmly. He didn't even seem upset; he spun the cup between his fingers as if toying with it. His eyes were no longer on the cup, though. They flicked from paladin to paladin, weighing, assessing.

"She saw how you went into the Seer's tent that first night. We all did. And then she went into your tent after the Seer was killed. She has designs on you, paladin. You're a well set-up man. I'm sure you've had offers before."

See? I keep telling you ...

The cup stopped moving. Adalbrand's voice was like chipped ice.

"We're a celibate order, Hand. Do you accuse me of breaking my vows?"

Sir Kodelai smirked. "Has anyone told her that? Jealousy is a powerful motivator."

"The Vagabond and I had only just met when the Seer was killed. How quickly do you think she formed this supposed attachment? How quickly do you think I succumbed, first to the elderly Seer and then to this young paladin? These are vile claims."

"Who else had a motive? None of us. It was only her. Of course she wants you. She's a beggar. A woman destitute. And you fed her on kindness. You feed her still."

He's only half-wrong. Oh, my sweet treat, my delicious morsel, he has the truth half-right, like a man grasps the tail of an adder.

At this exact moment, the gag felt enormously unfair. I would have liked the chance to defend myself.

"So your accusation is that she is a woman, and therefore she is weak where the rest of us are not?" Adalbrand asked, returning his cup to the slow swirl as if he had not a care in the world. "And therefore she must be a murderess? It seems rather arbitrary."

"We've all confessed to murder," Hefertus muttered from the sidelines. "Maybe you should be accusing all of us."

He was ignored.

"I had a concubine much the same as this callow girl when I

was a king," Sir Kodelai said with a condescending glance at those watching. His gaze perused them, weighing, and finally landing on me before he said, "In fact, I had several."

I shuddered. Lord forfend I was ever alone with this man. I did not trust him. I did not believe — now that I had watched him in action — that he had ever been called by the God at all. Perhaps he really did poison those cups to prove he was right. Perhaps he did any number of terrible things.

"Your taste in companionship is truly singular," Adalbrand said dryly. "That being said, throwing her sex in her face is hardly enough to prove her a murderess. Nor is a stolen knife. Anyone could take her knife in the night and plant it here. We did not guard against each other."

"It was used to kill the Seer."

"Can you be so sure? Should you not examine all our blades and knives?"

Sir Kodelai's lips thinned and he slammed his cup on the top of his wooden box-turned-table.

"Last night I knelt in vigil under the moon and the sky and the gaze of the God and I came away with an answer. It is not for you to tell me how to serve the God. It is not for you to judge. That is my right."

Adalbrand cleared his throat and Sir Kodelai's eyes burned with the insolence of it.

"I thought it was the God who judged. The God who demanded vengeance. Are you not merely his Hand?"

Sir Kodelai's mouth twisted, but he made a quick shake of the head as if trying to control a flapping line of temper, and then he managed to bark, "Yes." He drew in a long breath through his flared nostrils and tried again. "I am the Hand of the God and he will judge today. I give to him this contest between us."

Adalbrand lifted his cup. "It's still not too late, Sir Kodelai. No one needs to die here today."

"I think someone does," Sir Kodelai said grimly.

He snatched up his cup, shot back the water, and smacked it down so hard on the case that the whole thing shuddered.

With a shrug, Adalbrand lifted his cup, too.

"The will of the God," he said grimly, and then he drank it down and delicately set his cup next to Sir Kodelai's.

For a long moment, nothing happened.

We remained still in holy silence in this white hall of pale stone and crystalline light, we tiny few in the great echoing vault. For one delicate moment, everything hung in the balance.

Sir Adalbrand moved first, leaning heavily onto the folding table with one hand. A leg cracked, split, and the whole structure collapsed with a clatter, one of the cups rolling and bouncing to careen off my knee and over to a wall. The other landed perfectly on its base, spinning round and round with a rattle before it finally wobbled to stillness.

My heart seized in my chest. Oh no.

Adalbrand reeled, caught himself, turned, and was violently ill to one side, and then wiped his mouth with the back of his sleeve, his breath heaving.

"I'm sorry," he said while the cups were still spinning, his face green, his eyes wide. "By the God, I am sorry."

My head spun. My heart hammered. Was this it, then? Was I to die, too? Was he dying on my behalf?

Sir Kodelai hadn't moved. Not even a hair. He collapsed so suddenly it was like watching someone step on rotten ice in spring. One moment he was upright. The next he was a heap of bones and dust with his helmet and armor tumbling wildly in every direction, clanging against each other like garish wind chimes.

So the rumors were *true.*

The bonds let go of me without warning and I caught myself with one hand, gasping for breath at the same moment that Brindle smacked the mosaic floor with a doggy squeal.

I forced myself to my feet on shaky legs.

"The God forfend," the High Saint gasped, clawing at his hair. "What has he done? What have *we* done?"

We all gasped in a breath at once, sharing looks of mutual surprise and horror, but before we could let it out there was a loud *click* and the ground beneath us shuddered.

"I may have made a mistake just now," Sir Owalan whispered, and then the floor beneath us began to move.

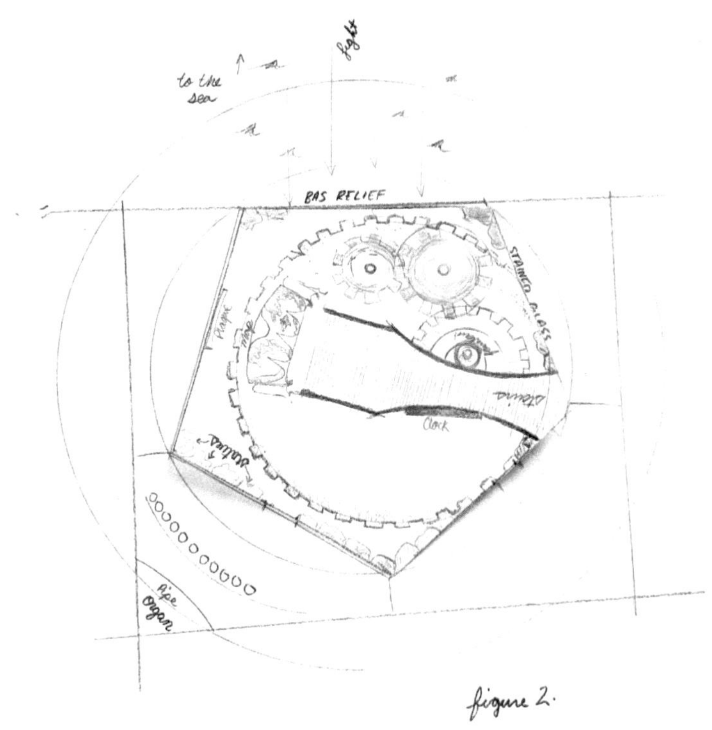

to the sea
light
BAS RELIEF
STAINED GLASS
stairs
Clock
statues
pipe organ

figure 2.

Chapter Nineteen
Poisoned Saint

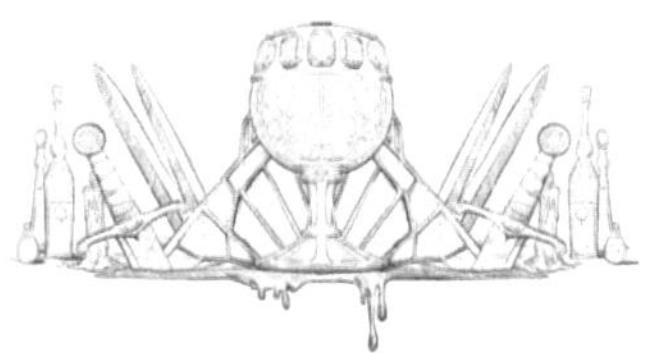

My hands are still shaking from my role in this horrific pantomime when the floor beneath us begins to shake and then, to my horror, to move. It turns ponderously, the motion forcing all of us to focus more on keeping our balance than anything else. I sink into a half crouch, trying to look everywhere at once to find the source of the movement. An earthquake? A judgment of the God for the travesty of that mock trial and execution?

Little rippling growls tear from the brindled dog's mouth, but they're muted under the sound of grinding and a slight squeal. Something is moving that has not moved in a very long time.

"Imagine the size of the gears!" Sir Sorken exclaims to Sir Coriand over the sound. "I told you those weren't just decorative."

"But wouldn't you need to put the axle straight through? If it were merely balanced on top, the torque at just one end would break the whole structure." Sir Coriand's voice is hard to make out in the din.

"Clearly not," Sir Sorken yells back, wonder on his face as he looks upward. "Though from the sound of it, it could use a solid greasing!"

I follow his gaze to see that even the patterned metal grate on the ceiling where the demon is held is twisting as the room we are in spins. After what feels like an hour later, though it could only have been a few heartbeats, the room begins to grow darker and I swivel again to look behind us, to where the windows that had let in the bright light before are now sliding to face ragged stone and strips of corridor leading to the rooms we explored yesterday. In their place, a cutout bas-relief — that used to be the wall to the right of the windows when going down the stairs — is taking its place. The cutouts are small, too small for a person to go through, though sea birds could certainly try. And the light that shines between them illuminates a carved scene of a man grappling with a five-headed serpent. By some odd coincidence, the wind whistles through the holes in just such a way that it makes a hollow tune of sorts, though an irregular, broken, chimeric one.

I steal a glance at the Majester, who is staring at the broken windows covering yesterday's corridor. If he failed to gather all the cups from those rooms yesterday, he certainly never shall.

I startle when the Vagabond throws off her fur robe, dislodging a waterskin and a leather-bound book she had stuffed inside its folds. Of course. I knew she hid something there. She startles me by taking off like a shot toward the staircase. She barely seems burdened at all by the armor she wears. She could win a footrace in the deserts of Haroun where I was raised.

Behind me, Hefertus curses and runs after her, the brindled dog hot on his heels. He'll have a time and a half catching her.

I turn to look at Sir Owalan, standing there with his mouth forming an "O" and his hand still on the key inserted in the lock.

He waits until the room finishes turning and comes to a juddering stop before whispering.

"I just wanted to see what it would do. I was curious."

"So were we all," Sir Sorken says approvingly. "Well then, my lad. Open it up. Let's see what all this fuss is about!"

"Shouldn't we bury the bodies first?" I ask, dismayed. They're walking right through this scene of murder like children trampling a prized flower garden.

"Oh, just shuffle them off to the side somewhere," Sir Sorken says, his ugly face blank when he glances over at the dismembered Seer and the dust and bones of Sir Kodelai.

Perhaps I should have confessed to anger. It wells up in me now, bubbling to the surface.

"Put them on one of those beds, maybe. A good resting place, hmm?" he says, as if to mitigate his disregard.

"Oh, he can't do that," Sir Coriand says distractedly as they open the door. It swings out to show another door of lacework, and at the center of it is an ivory carved plaque that shows a sun going over the plane of the earth. It marks the sun at the left edge with three lines, the sun halfway to peak with five lines, the sun at peak with one line, the sun descending to the right with two lines, and the sun dancing along the far end with four lines.

Sir Coriand shakes the lacework. "It's latched and I don't really see the mechanism to open it."

"I think it would open if the room turned again." Sir Sorken is just as taken as his fellow Engineer, pushing his ruddy cheek hard against the lace as he tries to peer in and up at the mechanism. "Look, just there."

"Oh yes, of course," Sir Coriand says happily before turning back to us and saying, "But you can't put the bodies on the beds. Now that everything has turned, the hall that led to that wing leads somewhere else."

"Where else?" Sorken sounds distracted.

"To wherever we thought this door led. Until we solve this puzzle, at least. It is obviously instructions to turn the room again. What a lovely marvel of engineering this is. Well worth the trip to see it, all casualties of course excepted. Can you see what lies through the lattice, Sorken?"

Sir Sorken grunts. "Hall's too long. Could be hell herself for all we know."

"It's a puzzle?" the Majester asks, scratching feverishly on his parchment.

"Do keep up, Majester General," Sir Coriand says. "It's times of day, isn't it? But the numbers must mean some kind of order, though why it starts at noon and hops all around, I wouldn't know. Probably worth noting, though. Good thing you brought pen and ink. The real question is, will that fountain still work? If that still splashes water up after the whole monastery has been swiveled, that would be a real wonder, don't you think, Sorken?"

"I prefer my wonders less opaque," the other Engineer complains, "but yes, I'd consider it nigh on impossible."

"Yes, rather," Sir Coriand says, giggling like a schoolboy.

"Are you saying that the room I opened is down there now? Across from the clock?" Sir Owalan asks, eyes wide, pointing a trembling finger back toward the clock and the entrance that used to lead to the dormitories.

"I thought we were very clear," Sir Sorken says. Which clarifies nothing for the Penitent. "If you're confused you should consult the Majester's map."

"He means yes." I am annoyed and it shows in my shortness. "But before you go running off, help me with our fallen."

I still feel sick over Kodelai's death. The most respected and well-known member of the Hand of Justice and he died at my challenge. I feel responsible. Just as I feel responsible for letting the Seer's warning go unheeded. Two deaths, and they're both ultimately at my feet.

Sir Owalan pauses. And so do the others, looking from me, to the fallen, and back again.

"They look well reposed as they lie," the High Saint says tentatively. "And there's really nowhere to put them."

"Or any way to wash after touching them," Sir Owalan agrees.

I feel my mouth fall open, but before I can reply, the High Saint says, "Let us pray."

We're swept up in the rote prayer for the fallen, spoken in concert over the bodies. It takes long minutes. Minutes where I'm bound in place, wondering if Hefertus and Victoriana are at the top of the steps. If they've found we can still leave this vault. If they've left without us. I look up, but from this angle, I can see nothing but the demon looking down on me. I dare not break tradition, or spit on these poor fallen souls, but I ache to move, to answer the questions plaguing me.

When, at last, the High Saint speaks the final words and we all intone, "Amen," the slap of feet on marble has grown loud. We watch as the Vagabond and the Prince return, both out of breath, both sprinting back to us.

"The door," Hefertus bursts out while they are still quite a way off. "The door is shut."

The dog reaches us first, his expression so intent that my heart seizes for a moment, sure he is about to attack. Instead, he slows and circles both us and the dead, sniffing around the perimeter. If he disturbs the bodies then I will have no choice. He will join them in death. I hope the Vagabond realizes that and prevents it from needing to occur. I shoot a glance at her, hoping she reads my warning, but she mistakes it for a question.

"The door is still open but it doesn't matter. It leads now to a solid rock wall." Victoriana's eyes are hard with what I take to be fear. "We're trapped in here."

Now my heart really seizes and I fight a sudden dizzy spell as I realize what she's saying. No food with us. No water if the fountain has ceased. No tools to carve our way out, and even if there were tools ... how would we do it? The door was never a proper door to begin with. It was always a miracle. We don't even know how far beneath the earth this place is.

Sir Coriand looks over his shoulder, abandoning his study of the plaque for a moment. "Is the fountain still running?"

"The ... my apologies ... what?" Hefertus asks, looking at the other man like he is mad.

We are all staring at Sir Coriand together. Does he not understand? We are trapped in this underground grave like bugs under a bucket. There is no way out. We are dead men and women already and we know it.

"Yes," the Vagabond says carefully. She's a little white around the lips. "There's still water pouring through it."

"Well, that's alright then," Sir Coriand says.

"Indeed," Sir Sorken echoes heartily.

"I don't see how." The Majester sounds wary. He's speaking the way you speak to madmen.

"Oh, well if the engineers who built this place figured out how to keep the water running even after the whole room turned — and trust me, that's a feat — then they planned for another way out. We'll find it eventually."

"Like we found the cup?" the Inquisitor asks snidely, his hand resting on the pommel of his sword. His jab fails to find its mark.

"We'll probably find that, too."

"And how will we find any of these things," Sir Owalan scoffs, as if he is not the one who had locked us all into this mausoleum. "We can't even get out of this place!"

"Well," Sir Coriand says, looking slightly surprised, as if he's been asked by a child how he knew a goat was a goat. "I'd advise checking in places we haven't yet looked. Like that door you opened."

We all look at each other, but Sir Owalan is the first to break. He bolts away from the charnel hall we're in and dashes down the mosaic floor, one lone figure dwarfed to insect-like size under the ponderous white statues now charcoal in the fainter light coming through the carved holes of the bas-relief wall.

"Has it occurred to anyone else that this place was built at far too large a scale?"

The Inquisitor says so little that I turn to look at him, wondering if he means something deeper by that, but he says nothing more, simply looking up at the demon in the ceiling, a thoughtful expression gracing his face. It's only when I notice that his long white hair is swirling a little that I realize there's a slight breeze still drifting into the monastery from the holes in the carved bas-relief.

"Too large a scale for *what?*" Sir Coriand asks, as if he's looking over blueprints instead of stuck in a trap.

The Majester and the High Saint take one look at one another and then hurry after Sir Owalan. That's probably for the best. None of us should be alone down here.

Hefertus turns to me, panting. "Things have gone very badly, brother."

I nod as I shoot a glance at the Vagabond. Her braid is slightly askew and her cheeks flushed from running, mouth screwed up into a worried knot. She nods back at me, once, sharply, acknowledging the situation. She doesn't seem too rattled from her ordeal earlier — or this one now. Perhaps I am the only one who finds this so unsettling.

"I think we should stick together," she says. "Whatever killed the Seer is not me, and it's still out there."

"You don't think it was a human?" Hefertus asks her. "One of us?"

"Do you?"

He runs a hand over his tidy beard. "I don't know. I'm not certain of anything now. I'm glad I wore all my pearls, though. If I'm going to die, I'd like to be buried with them."

"That's really all they're good for in the end," the lady paladin says with a wry smile.

"You don't think they bring out my eyes?"

The Prince Paladins lose their common sense first. Who thinks of pearls when they are trapped in a ruin?

"I'd still like to see to the dead," I say quietly. The other two nod, looking around, but there's nowhere to put them.

"You'll need a broom and a shovel if you want to move the Hand," Hefertus says grimly, and I could swear the dog's bark of response sounds just like a laugh. "I don't know what to do for them, Adalbrand. We are too poorly equipped."

"We could drape my cloak over the Seer," the Vagabond suggests.

I shake my head. With all of our supplies gone, we must make use of what we have. All of it.

"I think I have the pattern memorized." Sir Coriand sounds pleased. "Once we figure out how to solve it, we can spin the room again."

"Perhaps you could wait before you open any more locked doors," Hefertus says.

"And if you have a lantern in those packs your golems brought, that would not go amiss," the Inquisitor agrees. His eyes are haunted and I wonder what he sees in this place. Does he see it as I do? A prison and a grave? Or as Sir Owalan, the High Saint, and the Majester do — a challenge given them by the God?

"We did have a lantern, I think," Sir Sorken says. "And I think we'd all do a little better with a cup of tea. Let's go find the golems, hmm?"

As we make our way toward the stairs, Sir Coriand shows us the gears hidden in the mosaic pattern of the tile. The one we're walking over is larger than the bases of some towers. "You are all certain you didn't notice the gears from the stairs?" he asks, looking at us as if we are all terribly dull.

"I was more focused on the demon in the ceiling," the Vagabond says.

She's screwed her face up into a brave look. I wonder if she doubts whether she will survive this. Doubt, after all, is her flaw. Is that the result of the death of her mentor shaking her belief or has she always been on the edge, believing but not believing, driven by doubts like a ship before the wind? I'd like to know.

"What demon?"

"The one hanging over us like a thundercloud waiting to break." She points at the ceiling and the Engineers exchange a look I can't quite decipher.

"Tea. Promptly," Sir Sorken says.

As we hurry past, my eyes drift down the new hallway. It's like the other — long, with inset shelves, but that's all I can see at a glance. It hardly matters. I'm sure I'll end up walking through it eventually.

"I want to thank you, Sir Adalbrand," Victoriana says out of nowhere. She's so close her shoulder brushes mine and for a moment that's all I can feel. I hadn't noticed her joining me.

I turn to look at her and just like always, her wide brown eyes make my heart stutter for a moment. What a gift it would be to be an innocent man and be free to lose myself in those eyes. To try to win their smile. As it is, I am gentle in how I respond, careful to neither demand what is not mine, nor offer what I do not have.

"No thanks are needed, Lady Paladin."

"You saved my life." Her voice is full of things she does not say. It is thick and heavy like crystalized honey.

"You were innocent." I try to strain the longing from my voice. I do not know if I succeed. "Anyone would do the same."

She snorts a laugh and the tension of the moment evaporates in a shared wry smile.

"I think perhaps you failed to notice, Sir Knight, but no one else did the same. In fact, I was quite certain they would have lapped up my blood like dogs when Sir Kodelai was finished with me."

"I don't like blood," Hefertus says from behind us. "Never had a taste for it."

When I turn to look at him, he lifts a brow at me, his eyes all judgment. My cheeks heat. He's right, of course. I have no business talking to the Vagabond. I am only making things worse. By the time I school my face to neutrality, she has turned to the Engineers.

"I kept these books," she is saying, trying to get Sir Coriand's attention. "We found them in the rooms but I forgot about them when the Seer died."

"Are those what you were smuggling under that horrific excuse for a cloak?"

"They're all variations of the same thing, I think, but your Ancient Indul is much better than mine," she soldiers on. "There are diagrams."

"Diagrams?"

That has his attention. He snatches the books as we reach the golems.

"Tea, I think, Cleft," Sir Sorken says as Sir Coriand spreads the books out and begins to study them side by side. They both crouch over the find like crows over a day-old kill.

"They *are* the same! Look, these people were all creating something. But what? And the way they arrive there is entirely different. Do you think it's the same thing that they're making?" Sir Coriand is entranced.

"The sketches are very similar if they aren't," Victoriana says. "See this one compared to that one. And what is this word? Is it not 'Saints' as we see on the plaque just there?"

She points to the plaque at the bottom of the stairs. Sir Coriand looks at her quizzically. He's as taken with her as I am, I think. I can admit my weakness there. As old as he is, and as distracted, still he would be a better fit for her than this broken paladin is.

I watch the golems suspiciously as they carefully draw wooden cups from the bags they are holding and then put leaves in them with huge, clunky fingers.

Cleft — less horrible, as he is made of stone — pours the still-steaming water into the cups to brew tea.

Has so little time passed that the water is still hot? Can that really be? I glance where the windows used to be and I feel, suddenly, as though I am being crushed in a vise, as though I am trapped in rock, locked in a cage. I can't quite catch a breath.

Hefertus is chuckling over something Sir Sorken said. The Inquisitor is examining the lanterns suspiciously, taking tea absentmindedly from the hulking golem. The eyes of both golems burn and burn as if they, too, are imprisoned within stone. And for a moment the world swims. I catch the Vagabond's eye and the corner of her lip turns up conspiratorially, and my breath catches. And I am well again for a moment.

Lord have mercy. God have mercy.

I exhale the prayer and draw in a long breath, accepting the tiny wooden cup from the massive rock hand that offers it to me. When I look up into that eye, it flickers. What big hands you have, Cleft. You could crush the life out of me with them. And yet here you are, handing me tea.

"Cunning little cups, aren't they?" Sir Sorken says, looking up at me as if he sensed my thoughts. "I had Cleft carve them for you yesterday when you were down here."

I am drinking tea made by what is either a trapped soul or a soulless abomination in a cup that *he* carved. I feel ill.

"Drink your tea, Sorrowful Saint," Sir Sorken says to me, a note of mockery in his voice. "Stop fretting about a morality you built all by yourself."

Just that one jab hits me in the wrong spot. It stirs up my anxiety at being sealed in a tomb, my longing for what is not mine to have, my ethical dilemma at working with one who does not share my convictions, and my concern that the God is not listening when I call. I'm about to snap at him but once again we are arrested by the sound of feet slapping down the corridor.

It's Sir Owalan. His eyes are wide and he's sprinting, his filmy robes fluttering around him like the wings of a moth. Carefully, I set my tea down.

"You have to come," Sir Owalan calls when he's close enough for his voice to travel. "All of you! Now!"

"We're drinking tea, my boy," Sir Sorken says in his naturally booming voice.

"It's important," Sir Owalan gasps.

"Has someone died?" I'm instantly tense. My hand is on my pommel before I realize it.

Owalan shakes his head, puffing for air.

"Tea is important," Sir Sorken says firmly. "Shall I have the golems pour you a cup? I think you could use it, hmm?"

"No tea," Sir Owalan gasps. "We might have found the Cup of Tears. But we need all of you if we are to attain to it."

Chapter Twenty
Vagabond Paladin

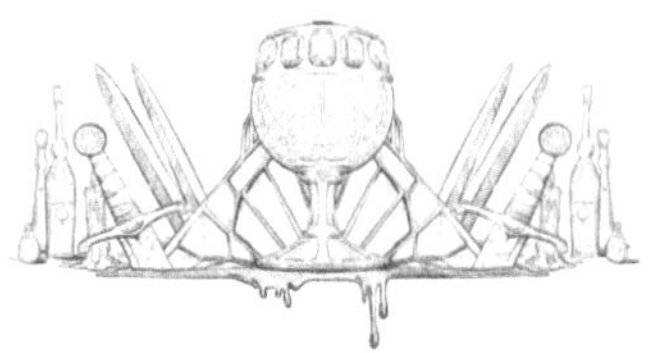

N*ow things will grow interesting, tiny trapped treat.*

The demon had been crowing since we discovered we were all trapped. The idea that we were sealed inside what seemed to him to be a huge stew pot delighted him and made him even more unbearable than he already was. I felt far more conflicted. Was it deeply troubling to be trapped in what might be my grave? Look, I was too young not to feel distress. Whatever made the aging Engineers so casual about it wasn't in my blood. But I was also too distracted to take it as seriously as I ought.

Adalbrand stood up for me back there. He chose to take my penalty with me.

I had known I wasn't guilty. But even so ... what if the God had judged me? What if he'd taken that moment to judge me for Sir Branson's death or the demon's continued life?

Am I making you fall from grace just by existing? Now that's a sizzling thought!

What if Adalbrand had died with me because of my secret? Because of my crimes?

I shot a glance at him. Again. My eyes kept finding him like lodestones to iron.

Mine, too. By the ages, he's a pretty one. It's the eyes, I think. I adore a salty sorrow.

He'd taken my side. He'd stood with me. I'd only had one friend who'd ever done that and he had been slain by my own hand.

All is well and all will be well, and even my death will be well. Stop fretting so much on it. I'm perfectly content here in Brindle. He was always a good doggy.

I had thought that I was driven only by freedom and the wind and the hope that perhaps faith would find me. It turned out I was driven by something else. A deep, roiling need to belong to someone. To be their ally or friend or kin. It bit down deep and branched out wide, a tree growing a hundred years in a single gasp.

My gaze snapped back to him a second time. When his gaze met mine, it crinkled warmly around the eyes. Warmth. Friendship.

One day when I was about thirteen, I wandered too far and slipped into a stream in spring. Soaked and lost, it had been hours before I found Sir Branson again. I was cold right through and the fire that day had been like the face of the God.

This warmth is just like that.

I stumble my way through a brittle thanks. It's not enough. Can anything be enough for someone willing to stand by me? I drag my attention immediately to the Engineers, afraid he will see all I'm hiding. That I want his nearness like I want the fire.

That's how romance always goes. Either you find a kindred spirit or you find someone who needs saving.

And am I his kindred spirit, then? I hate my traitor heart and how it leaps with hope.

You're the one who needs saving.

I force myself from the thought and force myself to talk to the Engineers about the journals instead.

A desire like mine for Adalbrand feels like selfishness. I'd rather go back to familiar territory. I've been rejected by these other paladins just like my Aspect always must be. Not surprising and certainly not threatening.

They tried to kill you. They tried to eat your bones and sup on your pain. And you call them holy? You call them brothers? Why are you not gibbering in a corner or bathed in their blood?

Revenge was the God's own possession and it was not mine to execute. I must be wary. I must be wise. But fear could make your bones age before their time. It could cloud the mind and pause the hands and still the breath, and I dared not allow any of that. Besides, you could not ask people to be other than what they were. There was no point to that.

I was on a ship once. A ship of exploration sent out to find the rim of the ice along the sea or possibly a new continent. The ship was mired in doldrums and there was no way out and the fun I had with the men on the sea keeps me warmer at night than the fires of hell.

Really? I was trapped under the ground with a bunch of so-called "holy paladins" who had just tried to holy their way into killing me, and he figured the best way to deal with that was to tell me stories of misery and death? Wonderful.

I already told you I'd just as happily possess one of them.

I gritted my jaw.

I kept hold of the last man and with all our strength we rowed for shore, and when — after a very long time — we made it off the ever-rolling sea, he'd found he had such a taste for the dead that I —

Enough. *Enough.* Perhaps I couldn't cast him out, but I could make his existence miserable if he did not cease.

How would you do that?

I'd recite the catechism in my mind from dawn to dusk, as I'm sure the High Saint did already.

I felt the demon shiver. Good.

Look, I'm not saying our situation trapped in a breathtakingly gorgeous dungeon wasn't terrifying, but I was already in a terrifying situation and I had been since the beggar attacked Sir Branson. Living hour to hour with a bound demon who might just pick his lock and escape was not for those who couldn't handle their stomachs twisting and their nerves getting a little frayed around the edges.

Now that I had also been singled out and rejected — albeit passively — by most of my brethren, I was in an even more precarious situation.

The causes of these worries were not going away anytime soon. Did my hands shake? I'd simply have to let them keep me sober and focused. Did my belly roll? Not a problem. There was nothing to eat here anyway.

"Look at this diagram here," Sir Coriand was saying, but my mind was not on the books.

My eyes dragged back to Sir Adalbrand again. He wouldn't let this descend into hell.

We shared a tight look and I felt myself leaning toward him, as if the lodestone were growing stronger. Does fear amplify everything? It certainly seemed to be amplifying it in me. I could only hope it didn't cloud my judgment.

Hope, unfortunately, was not really my strongest attribute.

Hope in the God, dear girl, and calm yourself. Like unraveling a demon, you must take this one step at a time.

Good advice.

Deliver me from evil, I prayed. *Deliver* us *from evil.*

I almost — almost — thought I felt an echo of something in my heart, like a song one remembers but can't quite recall.

And then Sir Owalan was there.

"The Cup is attainable. Hurry!" He squirmed as he waited for us and I hoped he was right.

Mayhap, once we found it — if we could escape this place — there would be no need to linger. We'd all be free of our orders. I could be rid of those who sought my death and they could be rid of me.

Adalbrand's hands moved over his straps and buckles as if checking and rechecking as we gulped down what remained of our tea and gathered our things with brisk efficiency.

With my eyes drifting constantly to him, I was too aware of the graceful way his fingers moved as he eased his sword in and out of the scabbard, checking the draw.

“Ready, Lady Paladin?” he murmured to me. He seemed tense; the lines in his face were deeper than I’d seen them before.

I left the books where they sat. No need to carry them around, and the golems could watch over them. One of the golems — Suture — was collecting the wooden cups with the air of a stingy innkeeper.

“I think we should be careful not to split our forces,” Adalbrand said in his lovely, rumbly voice.

I glanced at him, and this time when I smiled, his rueful smile joined mine. It softened him and made him warm and I wanted to uncurl before that warmth and let all my secrets flow free.

So all it takes is pretty smiles and dimples to soften you? I could have offered those instead of terror.

I gritted my teeth. If the demon had nothing useful to contribute, he could go stick his opinions somewhere else. If there was terror to be found down here, it would be me. I would unleash it on anything that came after us.

Growing a spine, are we? A little late for that, I think.

“Agreed,” I said firmly to Sir Adalbrand as we joined the others in following the impatient Sir Owalan. “We should stay together.”

“Well, what’s all the fuss about then?” Sir Sorken’s booming voice asked from the front of the group.

“We went into the room and it’s magnificent,” Owalan said as he led us. He moved like a dog, dancing first forward and then back, impatient that we only moved at a quick walk when he wanted to run. “Whoever built this place had an eye for beauty, don’t you think? And for punishment? It makes me more penitent. More certain that I must bow and receive what lashes are given.”

These Penitents turned my stomach every time. I didn’t like their approach to the God. It was the opposite of mine. People think the Prince Paladins are the opposite of the Beggars, for they have wealth where we have none. But I think sometimes they are the closest to us in attitude, for both our Aspects look to the God with open hands and both practice a faith that has no actions, only uses us as conduits for the work of the God.

The Penitents, on the other hand, think their self-mutilation will reward them, that pain brings blessing, and that the God only listens to one with mortified flesh. This deprivation — though it looked like my poverty on the surface — was not at all the same. It was far more like the High Saints with their attention to every detail of liturgy.

I didn't trust Sir Owalan. Or his putting keys into locks without talking about it first and possibly trapping us all in here to die. Or how he clearly had taken that key from the Seer's hand, more intent on seeing what was behind that door than on keeping me from being executed for a sin I didn't commit.

"How nice for you," Sir Sorken said placatingly, and beside me Adalbrand snorted under his breath. He scratched the side of his face though there was only a shadow of hair there, his eyes roaming ahead of us, more impatient than the rest of him.

I rested a hand on Brindle's head as we reached the door. Was he coming in or staying out?

And miss you making a fool of yourself over a man sworn to reject affection? I'd never turn my nose up at that kind of entertainment.

I'd glimpsed the hall into the new room on our way past, but it curved in such a way that I'd seen no more than the smooth white stone walls and empty insets where the other hall had cups.

"Was this place raided in the past?" Hefertus asked as we entered the hall in a cluster. The man was ridiculously unflustered for someone in a trap. Did he think he could wish his way out of it?

Perhaps. And perhaps you could, too.

Prayers weren't wishes, though sometimes they felt the same.

"Can we hurry and forget the empty shelves?" Owalan asked, agitated.

"Perhaps one of us should wait with the golems," the Inquisitor suggested when he was still just outside of the door. He stood with his body turned back the way we came, the picture of reluctance. Until he'd spoken, I'd forgotten he was there. Some people disappear into the background, but he seemed to disappear into the foreground — there, but forgotten. With his flamboyant flag of long white hair and his black fitted clothing adorned with silver, you'd think he'd be more noticeable.

I could see his point. The last time we walked through a door as a group, it had gone poorly. Why do it twice? It made sense to leave someone to watch our backs. Almost superstitiously, I looked up at the ceiling. Was it just me, or did the demon seem to be breathing?

Sir Owalan shook his head vehemently. "We need everyone. You'll see when we get there. I can't explain."

"I need you to explain," the Inquisitor said quietly. His fingers danced up and down the hilt of his sword. "Or I won't be going anywhere."

Sir Owalan's dark eyebrows met in the middle. "Some things must be seen with your own eyes, Inquisitor. Stop questioning and believe."

What a ridiculous thing to say. Worse, he trotted off down the hall the moment he was done speaking and no one could ask for further clarification.

"The golems are by the stairs," Sir Coriand said with an assured smile. "I'm sure they'll keep an eye on things."

Which was no comfort at all. Did they have the ability to think for themselves?

I should hope not.

Or the ability to rescue us from this room if we became trapped?

The laughter echoing in my head was all I needed to hear from the demon.

There's no turning back now. Hold your faith fast and ignore the demon. I'll keep him in check.

The Inquisitor cursed under his breath, but after one longing look backward, he joined us in the hall. Before we reached the end of the hall, we found words carved into the stone of the floor. They seemed like a continuation of the verse from the plaque in the main room.

"Can you read it?" Adalbrand asked me, but before I could answer, Sir Coriand read the verse aloud.

Choose now holy vessel,
Be careful, be clear,
For the bones of others,
Will root out your fear.
Wash your cup with sorrow,
Bathe your vessel with blood,
But choose your gift wisely,
Be it fire or mud."

"That does seem to indicate there will be a cup somewhere," Sir Sorken said. He had his hands jammed into his belt and was looking around with a vaguely curious expression. Could I get away with that? I loved how it made him look like he didn't care.

Sir Adalbrand snorted at that and then walked deliberately over the words like they didn't daunt him at all. His chin was held high, eyes watchful. He had a way of walking that made him look like a hero striding through a tale. He could choose to use it or not, I'd noticed. Right now, he was employing it in full measure. I swept into his wake as we turned the final curve and spilled out into the vault beyond.

And what a vault it was. It rivaled the main hall we'd just left.

The ceiling soared up into the rock and it must have been drilled through from the top, for pinpricks of light shot down from the ceiling — so many of them that they lit the room so that the white stone was bathed all over with the soft light of the world above.

If I had thought that the statues in the main room were

impressive, the ones filling this cavern were teaching me that I had dreamed too small. Lining the circular room and looming high up the walls were statues of Saints. Saints standing and sitting and praying and dying, mouths open as if about to break out into a heavenly chorus. They were carved in intimate detail and by the hand of a master — no, it had to be many, many masters to have worked so many.

Or the demon-possessed.

What?

I'm just saying that we have skills.

I doubted that. Everyone knew that the God had given to men the right to create art. The devil and his minions could only subvert what was already made.

And what would you call taking over another's hands and will? Not subversion? Would you like to try it, then?

The figures were angelic.

Breathtaking.

The light from above bathed them in a soft glow so that every apple-cheeked curve almost seemed to blush and the dip of every throat became a well of secret shadow. The faces I saw were smitten with rapture — almost to the point of pain, necks and arms stretched in flowing lines of sinew and muscle as they reached to the heavens. Clothing was optional, included only where the folds and translucent waves could best highlight the figures underneath. But weapons were in plentiful supply, and like the statues in the main room, some were brandished, some were carried in sheathes or belts, and some were buried in thighs and biceps and chests.

Do you like them, pretty snack? Shall we make you into one?

I could barely take in the sheer decadence of this much human talent stored up in one tiny hidden corner of the great rolling earth. It snatched my breath like a clawing wind. It ought to be in a cathedral somewhere that men may marvel at it.

And yet, I recognize none of them, my girl. Are they so old that I can't see a single one that I know? Who is that with the tri-forked beard? What maiden swoons there in the arms of that warrior and why do his limbs almost appear as tentacles?

Mayhap Sir Branson was simply as poorly educated as I was.

The demon laughed long in my mind.

They're ours. All ours!

Who were his?

Tell me, my girl, if these are Saints, then why does this dashing one holding the sword seem to be wearing nothing but a tabard, and why does he look so lasciviously upon the maiden in the crown? Better yet, solve this riddle — why does her crown look so very like a pair of antlers?

What was he saying?

I told you! They're ours. They belong to my twisted kingdom and they shall drive you mad!

Hefertus burst forward. "There are keys! It's an organ." He looked over his shoulder at Adalbrand, his eyes boyish with excitement. "Come look at this, brother! I would wager no one has played these pipes in a thousand years."

I hadn't even noticed the ivory keys at the far end of the room. I'd seen keys just like that once before on the great pipe organ in Saint Rauche's Citadel. They came in layers.

"Hefertus played when he was in training. He was said to be gifted," Adalbrand said from beside me. When I glanced at him, he looked amused, but the amusement was painted over a troubled energy. His eyes darted from Saint to Saint as if he could not place any of them either.

"Look," Sir Coriand sounded breathless. "Their mouths are the pipes. Imagine the hands of a master here. What would Master Harkumenus's Fifth Choral sound like played on that instrument?"

"Forget the music," Sir Sorken said in a happy rumble. "Imagine the craftsmanship. To carve each one perfectly on the outside and *also* on the inside so it can sing the note? I thought the fountain was a marvel."

"This is truly a miracle," Sir Coriand agreed.

"I don't like this," Sir Adalbrand muttered. He seemed to be moving his body at an angle, as if to shield me with himself. I didn't think he even realized he was doing it.

This man is honor carved right through. Let's see how honor deals with this next thing, hmm, sweetmeat? Let's see how you manage with your vulnerable soft flesh. This is going to be so delightful that it almost makes up for being trapped within a canine cage.

Did he know something I did not?

Within the ring of hundreds of ivory figures piled one upon another was a smaller ring. And now my heart truly stopped — or at least stuttered. Because these statues were familiar. Once again, they were us.

They stood — towering over the humans they reflected — on swaying lacework platforms. Those platforms hung from chains in the roof — chains constructed of something that looked like ivory stone, but stone would fracture under so much tension.

I scanned them, tension running up my spine. Everything within me screamed at me to run.

There was the Seer, missing her head. It sat at her stone feet with one of her hands. And there was the Hand of the God — not depicted as a pile of dust as one might think, but rather hanging from a carven noose, his neck plainly broken. Each of the statues extended one hand and held it out flat, facing upward — except the dead, whose hands had turned to face the floor. Leading up to each one was a stairway of lacy white stonework and bones that looked human. These stairs swayed with the platforms, like ships upon the high seas, and between the statues there were more chains hanging like the long moss that flows from the branches of trees in the deep south. They tinkled lightly against one another whenever they swayed too far.

I glanced behind me to the door, gripping my sword tightly.

Too late to run, oh, it's much, much too late. Look!

I looked.

On the ground, and lining both sides of the path on which we trod, reaching as far back as the feet of the steps to the pipe organ, washing up in shoals that nudged the ankles and knees of the Saints, were cups. Tall and thin, squat and wide, stemmed, fluted, belled, cabochon, carven, enameled, bejeweled or plain as a farmer's water ladle, they lay waiting.

Upon his platform, the Majester raised a cabochon cup and then slotted it into the hand of his statue. It fit with a click. And suddenly the poem made sense.

"Choose a vessel," it had said. Easy enough.

Is it, though?

"Be careful," it had said. Not as easy.

Caution laughs at you, little treat. She whispers in my ear and we giggle together.

I was being mocked by my own dog.

"Who's a good boy, then?" I whispered grimly.

Brindle's tail thumped against my leg.

Still not me.

"But which one is the cup?" the Inquisitor asked, aghast. Not too bright, our Inquisitor.

In the distance, Hefertus sat down at the instrument. I hadn't even noticed the stone lace bench that was fitted beneath the six rows of keys. They seemed like too many for one man to play.

Unless that man had six arms. I spy with my diabolical eye someone with six arms.

I wasn't in the mood to play games.

I'm always in the mood, but my toys never last long. It's such a shame. Maybe when you are weak, you'll let me in and I'll play with you, little morsel. Maybe you'd like to be a Saint after all.

"The cups fit in the hands," Sir Owalan called from where he stood beneath a towering version of himself, a cup in one hand hovering over the hand of his statue. "Watch."

He set the cup onto the palm of his doppelganger. Even from afar I could hear the *snick* when he twisted it and it seated, and then — in a way that defied sense — his statue seemed to glow. It was faint, so faint it could be my imagination, but I didn't think so.

"I think it will show us which one is the cup," he said, smiling. "But it needs all of us."

The High Saint had placed his cup, too, though now he sat at the feet of his statue, bent double in prayer.

That was three. There were six more that could be placed. The Engineers' statues were depicted together, and their hands were joined with a place for two cups there.

"We ought to consider this with care," I said at the same moment that the Inquisitor called out.

"How did you choose out of so many?"

Good luck reining them in, my girl. They're already caught. Flies drawn to blood. They can't be called back now.

But I already could see that the High Saint and the Majester had chosen cups like the one Adalbrand had shown me, short and squat with cabochon gems. They were not taking any risks.

"Choose wisely. We might not get another chance!" the Penitent called down. "We all need to make our guess and then see what happens."

"I'm surprised you didn't guess for us, my dear boy," Sir Coriand called up, but there was an edge to his words.

"The icon only accepts the cup from your own hand," the High Saint said, finally straightening from his prayers. His face was lit with holy ecstasy. "This is how we know this is from the God. It is tuned to each of us as only a creator could tune it."

I like the proud most of all. They are always certain they cannot fall into my snare and then, trapped, they taste the saltiest.

"The instructions did indicate to be careful and clear," Sir Sorken said in that way of his that carried across the huge booming room. "I think it best to heed them, hmmm?"

"There were instructions?" the Majester asked, at the same time that a whooshing sound went through the room.

From beside me, Sir Coriand sighed far more loudly than required.

The game is now run by the moths, the demon said from inside my head. *How long will it take before all singe their wings in the flame? I hope it's soon. I'll drink their despair. I'll bathe in their loathing and I'll laugh when your heart breaks for their foolishness.*

"Sit," I said firmly. "Stay."

The dog Brindle chose to obey.

"How will you choose?" the Inquisitor called to Hefertus across the wide gallery, his forehead wrinkling in cautious concern.

Hefertus called back as he shifted, hands hovering over two keyboards. "Easy. I'll choose the most lovely."

"But ..." The Inquisitor looked at the rest of us, and this was the most human I'd seen him. His lips moved a few times before he finally pushed the words out. "But that is farcical. Surely, you will use a better method. Or you'll ask the God to make your hand choose the correct one."

"I like the pretty one," Hefertus called, and then his hands fell to the keys. From the mouths of the Saints came a ghastly moan that was half music and half agony, and with a creaking snap, something fell behind us.

I spun. Behind us, on either side of the door from the hallway, were a pair of winged figures with swords in their hands. The sound we heard was the sound of their lifted sword arms descending. They hit the floor so hard that the room rocked and a fine sparkle of dust spat upward. Their swords, which had dangled precariously over the doorway before, were jammed across it now, and I did not think any of us could wriggle through the gaps left behind excepting perhaps Brindle.

Hefertus, unconcerned, played on. And now the mouths played hollow, breathy notes, with a yearning melancholy that wrung my heart. He perched before the great instrument, hands spidered out and shoulders rolling with every stanza he played. The light from above seemed to shiver as if the whole room breathed in the music and awoke to it. And whether it was the air forced through the ancient pipes and rippling out the mouths of the Saint statues, or whether it was some great power raining down blessing or curse upon us, dust motes spun into the air and twinkled over everything like the birth of stars.

"I think we should be looking for the real cup," the Inquisitor said, breaking the spell.

You could bargain with me and I'd tell you which is the true cup.

But that was a trick. None of these cups was the real one. Obviously.

Or all of them are.

It amounted to the same thing.

Or you put your cups on there and you have to drink from them and you all burn up like Sir Whatever-His-Name-That-Will-Not-Be-Remembered, and won't that be fun.

My heart was in my throat, choking me, strangling me. It wasn't the challenge. What was picking a cup? It wasn't being locked in, though I was. It was realizing my hand was forced, that I had no option but to play out this pantomime. That I was just a piece on a board played by hands not mine. Every shred of me fought against that, clawing up my throat and biting through my skin.

I could not accept it.

I was mistress of my own destiny and I always had been, with nothing but the road before me and the horizon behind, hands empty, heart full. The idea that I could be shuffled and prodded into a cattle chute for slaughter made my blood feel too thick and the world around me swim.

Sometimes there are no choices.

But there had to be. There had to be a choice.

The Engineers had moved farther into the room and the Inquisitor bounded after them, searching side to side like a hunting dog ferreting out the scent of the cup.

I was spinning, my mind frantic, heart in my throat.

Something gripped my arm suddenly and I was wrenched into the burning cinnamon gaze of Adalbrand. His face was hard, strength radiating from the bones of it, and I remembered, as I sometimes did around him, that he had a decade of experience that I did not have. And it showed now in his measured look. He also had the hard strength of a man given to daily training since childhood. Though I was strong and capable, too, I could feel his greater strength in how he held me.

"Fly to your rock, little bird," he whispered to me, so quietly no one else would hear.

I clung to the feeling of his hand on my arm. I clung to how strong and real it was.

"How," I gasped.

"Find your faith. Build your nest high in the rock and fly."

His voice was barely louder than his breath. He made a self-deprecating moue with his mouth before leaning in closer.

"It's what I tell myself. It's what I think when the world seems to overwhelm me."

He was giving me a talisman then, something of his held up against the darkness.

He had grabbed my non-sword-arm. He held it still, my sword hovering between us like a wall that could not hold in the tide. And all my wanting for warmth and closeness flared up hot and tight, washing over me even as his sad eyes burned.

The music swelled, strange and strangling, like the Saints were being choked to death as they gasped out Hefertus's tortured song.

"We have no choice now, Lady Paladin," Adalbrand said gently, and I realized that the way he was standing blocked me from the view of the others, kept this weakness to just the two of us. My heart swelled with the kindness of that. "We are in this. You and me both. We dance to the tune or we die under the rock."

"Both?" I asked.

"Both." His tone was very certain and his eyes burned with something.

Devotion. They burn with devotion. I have seen it before. But toward you or toward the God?

"Fly up to the rock, little bird. Let the God protect your heart. And let me guard the rest."

He looked sharply to the side for a moment, as if checking again that we would not be heard, and then leaned in closer, making a kind of a shelter over me out of all that muscle and knightly strength. I could feel the warmth of his flesh radiating out to me.

"I feel it, too," he confessed. "Something is not right and we are trapped, but what else can we do?"

"We can always fight," I snapped, but I was snapping at myself, at my own limitations.

"We can die," he said gently. "Or we can play our part in this."

"I can't seem to make myself submit to a force I cannot see." I couldn't quite keep the wobble out of my voice.

He shook his head. "You're courage and fire. I've watched you."

"In physical things. But I cannot grasp faith and I do not like uncertainty. How can I be brave when there is no path under my feet?"

He swallowed, and for a heartbeat, the aching look he gave me was so full of untold words, so full of bridled passion, that it shot something hot and wanting through me.

"If you have no faith then let me be your faith for now. Walk on me as your path. I promised myself to you until this quest is completed. Take my strength now as your own."

This felt like more than what he'd promised before.

This is indeed more. He offers not just chivalry, not just alliance. I think, perhaps, my girl, that he offers you his heart.

I didn't dare believe that.

"And what would that make me, if I fought with borrowed strength?" I asked wryly.

"A holy warrior," Adalbrand said softly. "Like me. Like all of us, empty on our own, filled only by the light of the God."

Adalbrand's hand gripped my arm tighter and something in me melted.

"I'll borrow your faith, Sir Paladin."

He nodded and his smile grew until it was almost painful.

"So we choose cups and we place them," I said grimly. "And we let whatever trap this is spring on us."

"Trust I will stand with you in arms, whatever grief on us descends. Have I not stood for you so far?"

"I don't need to be coddled," I said. One last attempt at dignity.

"I'm not coddling you." His voice was rough and pleading. "Is it impossible to believe that I want to defend you? That while I know I cannot have you, I want you all the same?"

I swallowed. That was ... exactly how I felt and it was forbidden. He could not have it and I could not take it.

"Let me give you what I can in place of all that I cannot."

I nodded hesitantly, but at his sad smile, I drew myself upward and stepped slightly to the side, sliding from his grip. He let me go, but I felt how his body turned to angle toward me as I moved past, how he inhaled sharply when I was close as if he wished to memorize the scent of me, how he trailed after me as I searched through the cups like a swan trails after its mate.

What had I done to this man?

What have you done, you minx?

What had I done to myself?

You're broken. A paladin with no faith. A woman who will not take a man held out to her on a golden platter. A holy one who will not end the life of a dog to destroy a demon. Broken souls are my favorite kind.

Just for that, I chose a broken cup. And when I lifted it, Adalbrand lifted an eyebrow, but he said nothing to me, merely snapping up a black, narrow tumbler of his own. The piece he chose was carved all over with owls and ravens. Mine was unadorned except for a fat scar that ran the length of it. It would not hold water well with such a crack. I did not care.

A throat cleared and I looked up to see that the others were already in their places. Even Hefertus. The music had stopped sometime during our whispered conference and I had not noticed.

"If you're about done defying both your aspects," Sir Sorken said grimly, "I think you'll find your places on the ends. And then we shall see which of us is right and which of us is dead, hmm?"

Chapter Twenty-One
Poisoned Saint

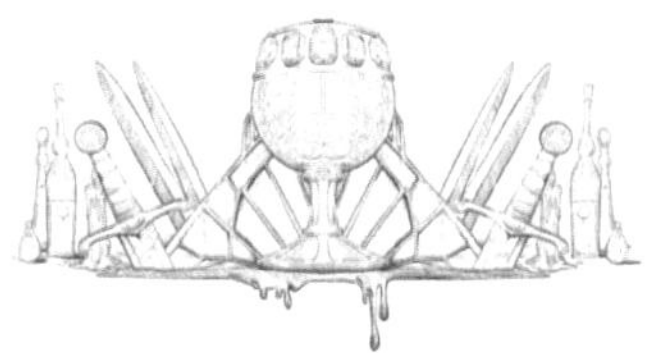

I'm still caught in the swirl of emotion that comes from being near her. I have never felt this. Not with Marigold, who I thought was the love of my life, not side by side with the women I have served with, not even in dreaming desires for the other women I've known in pieces and scraps. I cannot justify this — not even to myself. It is not that I healed her and wore her soul for a moment, though I have no doubt it was rooted first in that. It is not that her eyes have haunting similarities to a woman I once loved, though that has not helped. It is not her dauntless courage conjoined with stunting doubt — but it is partly that.

The strangeness of how she is a single-edged sword, sharp on one side and yielding on the other, is an intoxicating brew — an exact mixing of all I love best in another human. There's also a sense that she sees beyond the surface, as if she can claw the world away as one draws back a drape and see what lies beyond it. I see it in her eyes when she squints at the statues of the Saints and then draws back. I see it in how she watches her dog with a tilted head and how her eyes narrow when they encounter the Penitent. I want to be near the woman who scowls at false holiness and sees the value in small things. I want to guard the tiny innocence she still burns like a stub of candle at her core while outside she is hard as flint and twice as sharp.

I puff out a long breath. She's nervous about this offering of cups, though it seems a small thing. Even if we must try every one upon these pedestals, it will only be tedious, not dangerous. But I would be a fool to discount her wariness. What does she see that I do not?

I choose a cup of ravens and owls for their eyes, so like hers, which can see to worlds beyond, and I cross to the far side of the room from her. The statues that are akin to our forms and faces — and do not think for a moment that does not make my skin crawl as if it were lined with grubs — are in a rough semi-circle and the Vagabond's image is directly across from mine, both anchoring the ends.

I look up into staring, empty eyes just like mine. Whatever artistry depicted me here — be it glorious or depraved — has read me well. The white stone forms lines of sorrow, and the set of the shoulders is tight with determined pain. That's me in every line. That's my worried brow, my lips curled into the edge of a smile, my scar on the tip of my chin. A nick I received in some scuffle before I was even a man, never mind a squire. I can't help the ironic smile that curls my lips. I never thought to see myself set in stone. I'm no Saint nor king. My father would scorn it on sight.

I set my feet on the steps and try not to flinch when I see they are woven of human bones. Those are two femurs my foot steps on. This next step is jaw bones and scapula. I stop looking after that, looking up, instead, at the great image before me. It's not a Saint — because it is me.

It's a terrible perversion to have an image of me set up like it is a Saint, though. This troubles me deeply. My stomach roils with it and my chest seizes. I have the most overwhelming urge to smash it, to tear it down. It seems too close to an idol, too near to a sacrilege.

I am no Saint, despite my moniker. I am only a man of flesh and blood, seamed through with darkness and light. I am only a humble knight before the great God. I hope he will forgive this blasphemy, as it is not of my making.

I think, perhaps, that I see why the Beggar Knight is so reluctant to play her part in this. I am, too.

God have mercy.

I set my cup into the hand. There's a place there for it, a ring carved into the stone, and at a glance, I can see varying rings with varying patterns set into the hand. They look like the tumblers of a lock at different depths. The cup I selected goes down four layers in and it mates up neatly with the tumbler there. A twist, and it clicks in place, stuck now and secure.

"Are you sure this will determine which cup is the real one?" The Inquisitor sounds like a cornered animal, surrounded by men with sticks. "Because that doesn't feel right, Penitent. I sense something else here ... something very different."

"Why else would there be so many cups?" Sir Owalan sounds very confident. "How else would we decide on which to use?"

"Use for what?" The Inquisitor shifts back and forth like the ground he's standing on is burning hot. He can read the spirits. It's his aspect's dispensation. Does he sense something now he is not putting a voice to?

"There were slots in the clock in that main room, I noted," Sir Sorken says. "Slots for cups, I wager. Did the rest of you notice it? No?"

"We could return home with all of them," the Majester suggests. "Let our bishops sort one from another."

"Could we? How grand." Hefertus's words are almost a drawl. "If you wouldn't mind lighting the way, Majester, and showing me the path out, I'll be happy to follow. Though I'm not sure my stallion can support the weight of hundreds of cups, I'll certainly give it a try if it means being free of this place."

The Majester's voice snaps like a flag. "Obviously, I don't know the way yet, Prince Paladin. Your mockery is not welcome."

Hefertus is right. It would take an army to carry all these cups from this place.

I look across the room and see the Vagabond Knight hesitating over her cup. I can't make out her features well from here, but she looks to the sky as I bid her. Perhaps, in her heart, she flies up in faith and entrusts herself to her God. The idea that I could spark faith in another snatches my breath for a moment. It's a dear thing. Precious.

I must pluck my gaze away from her to quell the emotions rising up. Here, as in the other vault, we are tiny, living, breathing, messy, colorful dots in a massive white vault that reaches so high up that I cannot clearly see the roof. The statuary towers over me in layers of figures, white with dove-soft shadows and muted edges. If this place were in St. Rauche's Citadel, it would be honored by the soft chanting of monks and the burning of rare incense, and pilgrims would come from all across the face of the earth for a single hour of blessing in such a place. Instead, it is shut away from the world, preserved, standing ready.

I wonder if I can find a favorite depiction of a Saint in those clustered on the wall nearby. I focus, finally, on their faces and my heart freezes.

The Saints are familiar in how they are depicted with graceful limbs and distant expressions, carved with symbolic weaponry and the flowing clothing of the righteous.

But these are not *my* Saints. Nor any that I recognize from ancient texts — and I have read so, so many texts.

As the light twists around them, my stomach twists, and I have a terrible feeling that they are no one's Saints at all.

That one is posed like Our Lady of Kindness. But it is not her, for that Saint certainly did not have a forked tongue, nor did she wink one eye in derision.

The one just there looks like the Hunter King, with his bow and stags. But the Hunter King never had human victims bound to the back of his stag, their wide eyes helpless and naked forms trussed so tightly that the chiseled ropes bite into their flesh.

My lips fall open and I bite back a gasp.

This is all wrong.

And I didn't see it until now. I was too entranced with Victoriana to see what she saw. I raise a hand, about to try to stop her — but with a sigh I can hear from even this far away, she clicks her cup into place.

It's too late.

We all freeze, tense with readiness. My gaze flicks across the other paladins, but no one has moved. We're waiting for something to happen. Maybe for a cup to glow or for the rejected cups to melt away.

There is nothing. Silence reigns.

It feels eerily like the moment before Sir Kodelai died.

The Majester laughs a little nervously, and his laugh bounces back at him from every wall and up into the cobwebbed ceiling.

And then a whisper bursts from the mouths of the not-Saints. It's half sigh, half song, and just at the very edge of hearing it carries words. Words I cannot understand, though I feel as if I know what they say. They are telling us it has begun. They are telling us we are accursed.

A subtle shudder runs up my spine and an echo in my unconscious mind whispers, *run.*

Sir Coriand is yelling at us — a translation, perhaps?

"Give us your rival's blood and your rival's pain, but choose with care or you'll see no gain. For the cup you desire, the cup you'll receive, in sacrifice, you'll learn to believe."

Trite, but threatening.

For the first time since we arrived, I think that perhaps this is no monastery. This is no ancient place of worship. At least, not to the God. And whatever pretender made this place is powerful and terrible and he wishes to make us powerful and terrible, though we are but motes of dust in this yawning mouth of a monastery.

I want none of it.

It's the Majester who moves first, shouting as he half claws his way up the arm of his image. He starts chanting and I feel his blessing settle over us — the one only Majesters can give. A blessing for a whole group.

He's given us acute awareness, and with it, I see what he has seen, and my gaze snaps straight to Victoriana. She draws her sword with easy fluidity, raising it grimly as I draw my own, but she's so far away. Too far away. As if someone planned, knowing we were partnered together, to force us apart.

The statue on the wall behind her is a man with a long beard and a holy expression, hands clasped before him in prayer. He shudders, lifts his face, lifts an arm, and then — as my skin crawls up my back — he draws his sword, steps forward, and leaps. The statues on both sides leap with him. Their weapons flicker as they move so quickly, stone legs launching them forward. They are larger than life — giants made of white stone and whatever wild magic has brought them to life.

The Saints on the walls have come alive.

Some of them, at least.

I think the ones with pipe organ mouths remain fixed to the walls, but it's hard to tell in the sudden maelstrom of white marble bodies, carved to perfect human form, white marble weapons braced in marbled hands. They stalk toward us from every side, some slow and ponderous, others moving quickly, dashing across the cups, crushing and shattering and destroying as they race.

If this is a race to find the true cup, it's almost certainly over with half the cups crushed. Somehow, I don't think it was ever that.

The dog barks sharply — twice, and then no more — as he leaps between towering white bodies, darting towards his mistress.

When the Engineers curse and begin to haul on the chains holding their platform, I realize that they've seen what I failed to see — that the chains are part of a ratcheting pulley mechanism, and as they fly through the old men's hands, the platform begins to ascend above the fray.

Should I do the same?

Before I decide, it's already too late.

A whoosh of air rushes past me and I move, led by instinct

and sudden battle fever. I whirl, duck, and pop up just in time to avoid a blindfolded Saint who tries to harvest me with his great marble scythe. His blank eyes drive a spike of terror straight into my spine. How do you reason with mindless antagonism? How do you fight stone with steel? I don't want to break my sword, but it's all the weapon I have. There's no time for qualms. He's already moving again in the space of an exhale, slicing toward my head. It's a game of leap and dodge now and I will either be quick or I will be dead.

Hefertus curses in the background, and it worries me enormously that his curses seem to be quieter the longer they spin out. I hope he's not already overrun. I'm not sure I can get to him in time to back him up. He was midway around the circle when this began.

I need to *see*.

In a feat I haven't tried since my squire days, I concentrate all my efforts and leap up onto the cupped hand of my stone image. Letting my momentum carry me, I launch from there to the shoulder of the blindfolded statue with the scythe, dodge a stone arrow that narrowly misses my shoulder — how does it even shoot? — and then pivot from the shoulder, spinning through the air to land on the back of a stone tiger ridden by a Saint who seems to think one carefully draped cloth is all the clothing he needs to wear while he tames the beast.

"The poem, my children," Sir Coriand calls down to us. "Blood and sorrows. The cup needs blood and sorrows."

Easy to say from up there. Down here, we're fighting for our lives. There will be blood — oh yes, and sorrows plenty — but there won't be much riddle-solving.

It's not easy to keep your balance on a stone tiger sculpted at one and three-quarters real size while its rider reaches a massive stone hand back and tries to throttle you. I do it anyway, fighting to hold on as I keep out of the reach of his grip. At least his arms are subject to the normal rules of anatomy.

I turn a blow from a stone sword streaking toward me from

my left. There's so much power behind it that even turning it sends quivers up my arm, but the force breaks the stone blade, and that blank-faced Saint with a ram's curling horns upon his tousled head must attack the second time with no weapon but a stub. Unfortunately, it's just as deadly broken and even harder to defend against.

When your enemies are stone and half again as large as you are, all the rules you've learned fighting men must be thrown aside.

My heart is racing with the intensity of the moment, every muscle straining with what I demand. Part of me loves this — the exertion, the pushing myself to the edge — but the rest is just gasps of thought between near misses and a barrage of sensation I must translate and makes sense of before I miss the one thing that kills me.

I leap from the tiger, trusting years of experience to help me land. I almost twist an ankle, but I roll at the last minute over a clinking, shifting floor of crumpled and broken cups.

By now I've lost all sense of the battle as a whole. I'm just one man weaving out of the way of a Maiden-Saint as she tries to skewer me with her trident, her fishy face implacable right down to the gills in her neck.

I'm running with high knees over the multiple arms of a tentacled stone creature — no, wait, this is the bottom half of one of the so-called Saints. No Saint of our faith has ever reached rippling arms toward the innocent, scowling through a seven-braided beard.

I don't have time to shudder. This is the madness of nightmares and curses. This is the power of the dark realm beneath the earth where those damned by the God play out their wickedness.

The sound of this battle is almost creepier than our emotionless attackers. It feels all wrong. There is the occasional cry from one of the others, but mostly all I hear is the grind and smash of stone on stone or stone on steel. There are no screams or curses, no desperate exhales or wheezing gasps. It's not human. It's not like any battlefield I've ever been on. Does it make it more or less horrible not to slip in blood and over corpses? More or less horrible not to see flashes of humanity in the faces you cleave in twain?

A man with shells in his long flowing beard and a crown on his head bears down on me with a club fashioned to look like shells but made — of course — of marble. I try to dodge his attack, but my spin is caught short by the movement of a female Saint, face swathed in carved scarves. She tries to grasp me, stone fingers raking across my side, and I'm forced back with a grunt of pain into the path of the shell club.

It glances off my sword arm, sending me gasping, but long training takes hold and I channel my pain into awareness. I need higher ground.

I slip through a gap made by two statues — the shortest of them is still a head taller than me and my metal blade is notching and chipping as I turn strikes. I feel the damage as if it is damage to my own body. If this sword fails me, I have no backup here. Everything was left above thanks to Sir Kodelai, may the God shelter his soul.

I'm slowed by the injuries I've taken already and my arm screams with every movement.

Through the gap, I spin and leap again, attaining the platform where my avatar swings. There are too many of them on the ground. I need to get up high if I want to see what's happening.

I sheathe my sword, kicking a grasping stone hand away while ducking under another, and haul the chains through the pulleys with a desperation born of pain and weariness.

As my platform wobbles upward, the pipe organ begins to play again — a hollow, spooky sound that makes me think of walking among the dead at night after a battle. The stanzas tumble over each other, keening and crying. I know this song. I've heard it once before and it has haunted me in sighs and snatches ever since.

The chain won't budge, jamming in my hands like a choked wheel.

I spin.

A stone Saint hangs off the side, making my platform rock wildly. I snatch up my sword seconds before it rattles off the side. I barely have it in hand before the Saint rushes me. He's hooded and reverent, eyes downturned, features smooth of emotion, but he claws at me with a stone hook, aiming for my shoulder. I duck under his strike, twist my body roughly to the right so that I lead with my left shoulder, and with all my weight I slam into him.

Pain splinters through that shoulder — it's as if I fell from a sharp slope and crashed into rock ... which of course is what I've done. It's enough, though. It knocks him backward and he slips — stone on stone — and falls from the platform without a cry.

The organ cries for him, soaring now in a melody too bittersweet for this world.

Someone screams from below. A masculine cry of torment. Every call is one of us. I don't dare ignore any of them when I'm the only one who can save a life.

I'll deal with it in a moment.

I need to solve my riddle first and look over the battlefield — even if that battlefield is more akin to a church sanctuary than a muddy strip of land.

My arm throbs as I hurry to my owl cup. I think I know what I must do. I slit my left thumb on one of the notches in my sword blade and flick a drop into the cup before I spit into it.

I'm my own adversary, so this is my blood. And I'm made of sorrow from bones to skin. I can put any part of myself in that vessel. What I give to it now shows what I think of this madness.

Go ahead, revile me. I care not.

My cup gives off a slight glow. I'm not sure if I'm relieved or annoyed that my efforts have accomplished the task. I'm not enchanted by the puzzle, or the battle, or the trickery that brought me here. I feel like a goat tied in the middle of a cage of lions — offering, tribute, sacrifice. I'll gore them all before I agree to go easily down their throats.

I spin and scan for the scream. The Engineers are so high up that I can only see their grim faces looking over the edges of their platform. Not them.

Sir Sorken is shouting to someone below. The Penitent, I think. At least he's being helpful.

I follow his gaze and see Sir Owalan stab his belt knife entirely through his forearm. His back arches and his mouth opens in a pained rictus.

I've never liked Penitents. They're always pulling stunts like this, forever acting dramatically to draw the attention of the God.

His arms reach up as if in prayer and my heart is stuck in my chest. I almost forgot they could do that — that the God gives them blessing in proportion to their self-inflicted wounds. My mouth twists involuntarily. I wish they could keep it to themselves and I wouldn't have to remember. Either way, this isn't an injury I need to concern myself with. The Penitent can fend for himself with that.

One of the statues tries to hit him, but the blow glances off the Penitent as if it is a feather smacking into him rather than stone. Though Sir Owalan is clearly in agony, sweat breaking out across his brow and blood flowing from his wound, a second attack also fails to injure him. He is immune to any assault other than his own.

No need to worry about him. He's crazy but not in danger. His madness protects him.

Hefertus's platform is empty.

My heart stutters for a moment and then I see his cup is glowing. He's solved his puzzle already.

I find him at the organ, playing that melancholy song, golden head down, arms spidered out, lost in his anguished melody.

Though the Saint statues attack from every side, their blows miraculously miss both him and the organ. I sense the power of the God at work there.

Behind him, the floor is cracked, all the vessels crushed to dust, and around the pipe organ there are bits of stonework battered to nothing. I watch as one of the Saints pulls down his stone cowl and throws a hammer at Hefertus.

It whips toward him end over end. I grunt, feeling the blow before it hits my friend. It slams into his skull.

No.

It doesn't.

It falls to the ground right behind him as if it hit a stone wall where his head is.

A chunk of stone flies up from the floor where the hammer rebounds.

The Prince Paladin can clearly take care of himself. Or the God can. Or something.

I find the Majester next. He's looking at Hefertus. His hands are up. I see one make a flinging motion and then one of the Saints flings a discus at my friend.

Wait.

He's controlling that statue. And he's attacking my friend with it. I feel my mouth form a firm line. Interesting how challenges bring out the heart of people. If it was he who screamed; I don't have time for his pain.

I hear a shout from below — higher pitched, feminine. My heart is in my throat as I spin.

Victoriana.

She's not on her platform and her cup isn't glowing. She either hasn't figured out the puzzle or she's not her own adversary and therefore can't use her own blood. She should take her dog's blood. There's an adversary if I've ever seen one.

I scan through the bodies and find her standing over her fallen dog. He's lying at her feet in a clump of fur and blood as she spins and bats at the statues, her braid an inky whip around her, her sword an extension of her arm.

I knew that creature would get her in trouble; I just thought it would be the perpetrator, not the victim.

What's she doing halfway to the Inquisitor's platform?

Oh.

He's fallen, pinned under a broken statue. It's in three pieces and the Inquisitor is under one of them. I do not know if he lives. It seems his qualms about this place were justified.

Saints and Angels. He must be the source of the original scream, and she's trying to get to him.

Of course she is. She has more honor than anyone else here — and I include Hefertus in that, because my dear friend would rather play music as everyone around him dies than lift a hand to help.

I need to get to her.

Even as I think that, I see the High Saint cutting through the chaos, a statue clearing space before him and another keeping the rest of them off his back. Both these Saints he controls are slow and lumbering. How are they doing that? He doesn't have the Majester's way with command, but he's figured out a rudimentary system.

I don't have time to discover what has given them power over the denizens of this place. Perhaps they merely asked and were granted their requests.

I need to move.

Something catches the edge of my peripheral vision and my breath is jagged in my chest as my gaze is torn back to the movement.

The Vagabond spins out of the grasp of one adversary, kicking up a foot and pivoting in the tidiest spin attack I think I've seen. She executes it perfectly, fearlessly. Her quick strike hits the flat of a stone sword and it shatters. I haven't seen her in real action before. Apparently, she was holding back in the friendly bout up top.

This Vagabond Paladin could hold her own against any fighter in the capital. I'm not entirely sure *I* could win if we turned on each other. *This* Vagabond is a fearsome thing indeed.

I'm impressed. I don't mean to be, but I am.

Her second blow knocks the stone teeth out of a lion. It leaps forward, rearing up on hind legs from where a female Saint with many braids flicks out a stone whip in one hand and holds the lion with the other.

The Vagabond doesn't hesitate. She spins under the lion and bashes it in the side of the head with both the hilt of her sword and her gauntleted hand. On her way past, she kicks up onto the lion's haunch, spins into a double-footed kick, and both her hands wrap around her sword hilt. The stone whip catches her across the pauldron but she grits her teeth and lands her kick, knocking the Saint's stone head off her shoulders.

She's bold and powerful, skilled and agile.

But she's only one woman.

More enemies closing in on every side and she won't leave the dog. She circles it, batting back the enemy one at a time. She can't hold on like that.

Grimly, I grab my second chain and tug hard, releasing the ratchet and sending my platform careening downward. Hopefully, there's no one beneath me. I can't stop this descent and I won't.

I know one thing — whether we find the cup or not, whether we find a way out or not — I will not be whole if the Vagabond dies. I may never be whole again.

I crash to the ground and hear a cracking sound as the stone shard breaks away and shatters. Pain rips through my shins. I ignore it.

A sword is in front of my eyes before the dust settles, thrusting downward toward me. I use the Vagabond's clever idea and hit it on the flat. It shatters in the most satisfying way, but I have no time to enjoy the victory.

I pivot, leap over an enemy, and almost crash into the Penitent, my heart in my throat.

He spins, looks at me wild-eyed without comprehension, and then spins away again, a whirlwind of movement and violence, kicking and lunging through the white, perfectly formed stone bodies surrounding us.

I feel like a child among murderous adults. They dwarf me, unfeeling, unknowing, bent on my destruction.

I try to do what the Majester has done and command them with my mind.

Move! I roar with all my thoughts, but nothing happens. Whatever trick is at play for him and for the High Saint has sidestepped me. I don't have time to figure it out when these statues threaten everything.

I clamber over the body of a fallen stone Saint — I think she was a virgin sacrifice or something. Her pinched waist is the perfect place to plant my boot between the swell of her hip and the sweep of her rib cage.

I'm pushing up and over her cold stone flesh when I see the Majester raise his sword over his head and bring it down in both hands, tip pointed at a place between his feet. It's not until it lands that I see what he is striking.

It's the throat of the Inquisitor, pinned under the stone.

What has he done? I swallow down bile.

This is murder, pure and simple. No true paladin would commit such an unholy act.

My guttural roar of fury bubbles up at the same moment that the Majester is kicked from behind. He stumbles forward, spins, sword up, and then throws himself at his attacker — the Vagabond Paladin.

Of course.

She's crying — tears streaming down her face — but her lips are clenched together and her eyes are narrowed in rage. Her strikes are fast and sure.

Her sword hits his in the familiar ring of steel on steel, striking at the exact moment that a crescendo peaks in the passionate music Hefertus is spinning from his haunted instrument. Perhaps he is finding his cadence in the rhythm of our deaths. There's something poetic about having my last moments set to the melody of a friend's tears.

The Majester's blade slides down the Vagabond's, locking them in a clinch for a half second, but it's long enough for the High Saint to suddenly be there.

"Majester. Beggar. Don't move."

The High Saint's voice is calm and precise but loud enough that I can hear it even as I sidestep a fresh attack from a female Saint with a light veil drawn round her head and hanging down to her knees. The fabric of the Saint's veil is carved to be translucent so that the swells of her cheeks and her wicked smile are easy to make out while she still appears veiled. It's artful. And terrifying. And not holy at all.

I breathe out as the combatants freeze in place. Good. They will listen to reason.

It's only when the High Saint slides in, slips a cup under the Beggar's eye, swipes a tear, then flicks a knife across her cheek and takes her blood with it that I realize he has used his boon from the God against them.

"Go in peace," he intones, making the sign of the God self-righteously. At least he didn't kill her for it. I should be thankful for that, right? Count my blessings? I am counting only how I might get revenge, a cut for a cut, a wound for a wound.

These fools are using their God-given gifts most flagrantly and someone must call them to account.

The High Saint whirls away, prize in hand. I taste the violation of Victoriana's person like rotted meat in my mouth. There will be war between the High Saint and me. I shall press him until he comes to her on his knees. Until he stands vigil for three nights in prayerful repentance. Until ...

Swords clash again between the Majester and the Vagabond, released suddenly from the High Saint's grip.

This is the High Saint's gift, exercised now in a harsh way. If he keeps his sacraments perfectly — and we all know he has — he may ask a request of any other follower of the God and they must give it. In this case, standing still in the middle of a fight while he raids the Vagabond's tears and blood. But this is an abuse of the power bestowed on him. A blasphemy.

The God will judge.

I hope.

I channel my anger into forcing the veiled maiden back. I lose track of the Majester and the Vagabond as I push forward, noticing, out of the corner of my eye, how the Penitent is taking blood from the fallen Inquisitor. The milky paladin must have spilled tears as he lay there, crushed, for they are raided — most indecently.

I feel a pull, dragging me toward him. Perhaps it is not too late to save him? But if I divert my path, it may be too late for Victoriana.

I've always hated prioritizing those who need my aid. I hate it now.

"I'll have your tears, girl," the Majester is saying grimly as I finally break free from the attack of the veiled maiden. "It won't hurt you, so why deny me?"

"I'm not your adversary!"

"Then what would you call this dance?"

I can't see them.

The statues of the Saints are too thick for me to catch a glimpse as I try to push past a robed Saint waving a censer. He thrusts it at my face and it's all I can do to dance back from the lunge.

I split his censer with my sword, spin a second Saint statue over my shoulders in a move I haven't had to use in battle since the Sixth Plague War, and then aim a careful blow at the delicate ankle of the trident-bearing Saint just in front of me.

He tumbles to the ground in a heap and I leap onto his shoulders just in time to see the Vagabond on her knees, straddling the dog, sword held in both hands as she blocks a blow from the Majester with all her strength.

She's bleeding freely from one side and for a moment I'm

shocked that the Majester has managed to bring her to her knees … until I see that her head is caught in the pale marble hands of a statue. The curving female Saint looks past me as she holds the Vagabond in place, a look of empty nothing in her eyes. Beside her, a second empty-eyed statue makes a grab for the paladin's off-hand, catches her forearm, and levers it backward. She cries out in pain.

And that is too much for me.

I fling myself forward, uncaring of the blows aimed at me.

One takes me hard on the left scapula, barely deflected by my breastplate. I stumble, but move with the blow, forcing myself forward despite the flaring pain in that side.

Another knocks my right hip. Not enough to stop me. I've battered my way through worse.

I see the Majester raise his sword in what is clearly meant to be a killing blow, but I ram my blade through him before he can bring his sword down, right beneath the heart.

And now I've committed murder, too. Not my first. Never my last.

He stumbles.

I feel the tremor in my grip, through the sword, as his quaking flesh makes my blade shiver and buck. His collapse pulls the blade down with him, but it also drags down the statues he was maneuvering. I snatch my sword free before it can be further harmed.

My heart stutters in my chest as my lungs heave with effort. I swallow down bile. I hate killing. Hate wounding. I'm not sure which I've done now. Not sure.

I think I've killed him, but there isn't time to check.

With a shuddering breath, I step back from his body and toward the Vagabond.

Shock paints her face with long lines. Her hair is spread and tangled around her neck and shoulders as if she's been dragged down into a river and strangled by weeds. She's forced her statue attackers away and is breathing as hard as I am.

"Are you mortally wounded?" I gasp out.

"You killed for me." Her words are sharp, disbelieving. She looks every inch the warrior queen despite an arm that hangs at her side.

For just one sparkling moment in the middle of horror, it is just we two, looking at each other. Something sparks hot and fierce between us and it's more than brotherhood or common cause. It's something that shoots deep and hard through me and it's never coming out again.

"I'll heal you," I gasp, struggling up to my feet. "I'll heal you both."

I'm surprised when she half shakes her head — is that denial or refusal? Will she not take my gift?

The strains of the organ turn to a sad, sweeping strain.

"The blood!" Sir Sorken yells down. "This isn't over. Get the Beggar some blood for her cup or you'll be crushed!"

I look up and see the statues moving past the ones that fell with the Majester. They have all turned toward us. With their targets winnowed down to two, we'll be fighting all of them at once.

Before I can say a word, they break into a run toward us.

I growl in my throat and grab the Vagabond by the arm to guide her. She screams when I force her to her feet, but her teeth are gritted and her eyes are all determination. A broken arm, I think.

"The dog," she gasps.

"We'll come back for the dog," I tell her. "After."

I push her ahead of me with my off-hand. Hers falls uselessly at her side — a compound fracture, then, if I'm any judge.

I feel jagged inside, but the Engineer is right. We must get the blood and tears in the cup and we must do it now, or we'll be clobbered again.

I glance behind us, guarding our backs as I hustle the Vagabond to her platform.

Over my shoulder, I see the Penitent at the Majester's cup.

saws in my lungs. Victoriana lets out a vulnerable, trembling exhale that melts me straight to the core. Hefertus's organ lets out a last gasp and all is still.

"Well," Sir Sorken calls out in his usual cheerful tone. "I suppose that's done it, then."

Chapter Twenty-Two
Vagabond Paladin

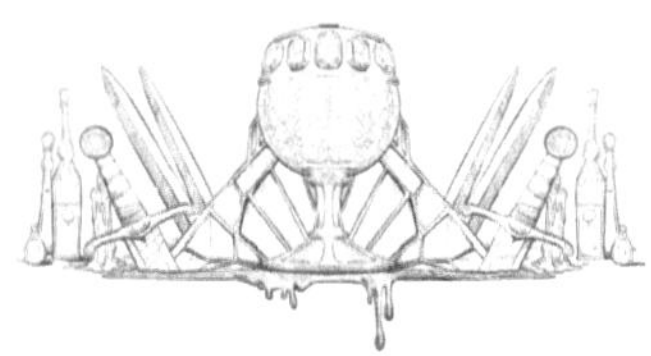

"I have to see to the Majester," Adalbrand gasped out. "I ... my desire for revenge is a slap in the face of the God."

"You can't possibly mean that," I said stupidly. Of course he meant it. Of course it was true. It just didn't feel true when I'd seen the Majester murder the Inquisitor with my own eyes. The pale-haired warrior had done nothing to him. Worse, he'd been trapped under the statue's rubble, unable to defend himself. A more ignominious deed could hardly be designed.

Pain was etched across Adalbrand's face.

"We forgive. It's who we are." He swallowed roughly. "Or at least it's who we should be." He looked down, seeing something I didn't. "It's who we should be," he repeated, as if convincing himself, and then he looked me over with a critical squint. "I'll be back for your arm. You're safe here, yes?"

He reached for me as if he would cup my face, winced, and then spun with a muttered curse and was gone, hurtling down the steps from this terrible platform and into the wreckage below.

I gathered in a long breath.

Well then. That was very Adalbrand of him. Very chivalrous knight. I gave his back a long, dry look. And what about me? Was my lack of chivalry an offense to the God? I hoped not. I would not offend the one who had given me a second chance.

I also wasn't about to go haring off to the rescue of Sir Sword-in-the-Throat.

Pain still radiated hot and jagged from my broken arm. If Adalbrand couldn't heal it, I'd need to set it. It felt wrong in every way. I'd had worse but I knew this kind of pain was more than a warning. If I didn't tend the arm properly I'd lose it ... or worse.

I was about to follow him, but a scraping sound arrested me, long and terrible like the wail of a dying soul. The fallen statues slowly stood.

Great. Just really excellent. I swallowed down a lump in my throat and jutted out my chin.

I could fight them again. I could. But I'd rather not. Already they'd scored their claws through the flesh of my soul. And this arm would be a problem.

I was still bracing myself for a second attack when they began to recede toward the walls with excruciating slowness. I let out a puff of breath.

No more fighting today, then. Good.

What had been a beautiful room of wonders was a smashed, bloody mess. That the urgency of the attack was over did not take away the bitter sting of the treacheries committed here. We'd turned on each other. We'd killed.

And for what.

I turned to the worst of it. Brindle.

Broken on the ground. He'd be defenseless against even slowly retreating statues.

I leapt from the platform, misjudging the height slightly, and stumbled awkwardly when I hit the ground. Bursts of black clouded out my vision as the raw ends of my broken bone jarred against each other. My sword was still drawn. There was no blood on it. *I'd* destroyed only statues, thank you. Not like that God-forsaken Majester.

Saints and Angels, was Adalbrand really going to fuss over him?

I should have sheathed the sword before leaping, but I wasn't thinking straight. I sheathed it now before I started to run.

I'd missed whatever had taken Brindle out in the fight. Something had hit him hard — the flat of a stone blade, I'd thought — and sent him careening through the air to smash into the floor. There had been blood and he'd wobbled, and then his pelvis had collapsed under him and those … those … those demon-loving, unethical, rotten-hearted, *selfish* paladins had tried to kill him.

They'd wanted blood. They hadn't cared whose it was. Even a dog's. I wasn't sure I could forgive them the way Adalbrand could.

Even if I had mixed feelings about the dog-knight-demon.

I didn't think they should have Brindle's blood and I didn't think they should have my grace.

I'd been the one who had gone to all that trouble to save his life at the river, and I'd been the one who had to cart around an excess demon that I was not fond of and have it live in my head, have it give me an ongoing commentary about the ways it would like to kill me, feel its icky black soul brushing up against mine. Gah. These other people hadn't earned the right to draw Brindle's blood. That was *my* right if it was anyone's — and I was choosing not to exercise it, so they should stay out of the matter.

Besides. He had those trusting doggy eyes.

I ran between the receding statues — they weren't violent anymore, but they *were* still mindless, and they could easily scrape over the dead. Parts of them that had been knocked off were floating up into the air, repairing themselves. I shuddered. I did *not* feel the power of the God in this magic. And if it was not his work, then whose was it?

There were gaps between the pieces and fissures across the faces. If the magic could bring them back together, would it also repair them after we left this place? How many times had it done this before? And did the scholars who wrote about this monastery *know*?

For it was obvious now that this place was not erected to serve the God. This was no house of holiness.

We'd all of us been deceived.

And I could feel that deception trickling through my blood and reaching its clawing hands up into my hot, rage-filled brain.

When all this was done, I was going to hunt down the head of our aspect and we were going to have a talk about paladins going where demons feared to tread. Or something like that. And then he was going to ... well, actually it was hard to say what he'd do. Apologize, maybe? Discipline me? Ask if I had a coin to spare?

I snorted at the ridiculousness of it.

I made it to Brindle just in time to tug him out from the path of a moving statue. I was out of breath and turned around, unable to sort out my jumble of emotions, my hands trembling as they pulled a heavy dog by the loose skin at the back of his neck. My nose was filled with him — wet fur, the tang of blood, something that smelled just a little of smoke.

Please don't be dead, Brindle. Please don't be dead.

I shouldn't even care. I had almost killed him myself back at the river.

But I did care. The thought that he might be gone gripped me like a hand gripped a rope on a ledge.

He was breathing. I could smell his doggy breath, and when I yanked a gauntlet off, I could feel it very faintly against my fingers. Alive, then. My chest seized sharply.

Of the demon and of Sir Branson there was no sign. So. Where were they?

I looked upward, swallowing, fool that I was. As if I'd be able to see the demon if he fled his coop. He wasn't the black blob caught in the ceiling; he would simply jump to another person.

The Majester, perhaps. That might explain a lot. I shot the other paladin a long look. Adalbrand knelt over him, head bowed in prayer.

I would have bet my own life that Adalbrand could have repaired the Inquisitor. The man hadn't been even close to death. He was merely trapped, both his arms and pelvis stuck under the weight of a fallen statue. And a man didn't have to be dead for you to take his blood. After all, the High Saint had easily taken mine.

Maybe I should work on finding the forgiveness Adalbrand gave away like a flower offers up pollen, but I wasn't sure I had it in me to be like him.

My glance at the Majester's fallen form turned to a glare. Was there a demon in there? Come out, come out, little demon. Show yourself and let's end this.

"Here now," Sir Sorken called down. He and the other Engineer were lowering their platform at a leisurely speed. I understood them, I thought. They were practical men. They wanted no part in battle or murder. They'd help where it cost them nothing, but they'd stand back if there would be a price. "Are you certain you want to spend yourself for the Majester General, Poisoned Saint?"

"The God forgives and the God condemns," Adalbrand called up grimly. "I meant to stop him, not to kill him."

"He did kill the Inquisitor though, yes? A terrible blemish on all of our names. He has made us complicit in a crime most foul," Sir Sorken said, his voice booming down to Adalbrand, who was turning a gasping, choking Majester onto his back. Blood ran from the Majester's mouth, staining his beard. "Perhaps best to leave things alone. This may be the judgment of the God after all."

Adalbrand frowned. "I don't want this blood on my conscience, too."

Sir Sorken shrugged as he descended, looking like an overly practical angel. "Heal him if you wish, but you might have to kill him again. In my experience, people don't really make mistakes, they just show you their intentions. He'll be at the Vagabond's throat a second time, given half a chance. A strange choice for a target." His eyes speared me for a moment before returning to the dying Majester. "You'd think he'd realize she isn't the weakest here, but the Majesters have always been more interested in groups than individuals. Perhaps he struggles to separate the two."

"Whatever you do, stop quarreling, and let's get down," Sir Coriand complained. "I want a fresh cup of tea and a bit of a think. If we have a fallen paladin in our midst then we'll report him to his aspect when we get back above, as is proper. No point fussing about it now."

"Agreed."

Adalbrand ignored them, crouching over the Majester and placing his fingers on the other man's forehead. He closed his eyes, healing the man, no doubt.

If Sir Branson was here, he'd say it was chivalry. I swallowed a lump in my throat at the thought. Had I lost my old mentor? Lost him forever now? The thought left me strangely bereft.

Adalbrand's shoulders slumped, head fell forward, and then he collapsed beside the other man, face-first into the dust.

My heart froze and I felt ill as I scrambled to my feet, ignoring the piercing pain in my arm. But before I could move, there was a loud curse and then Hefertus was there, lifting Adalbrand.

"You always overdo it. I tried to tell you that it's too much. You don't need to take *everyone's* pain. He could have died and we would have lost nothing. The Engineers even warned you."

The Engineers were warning no one now. Their heads were bent together over their cup.

"What have I done?" a rough voice asked. And then, as my eyes widened, the Majester sat up, brushed himself off as if he hadn't just *been dying,* and said, "I killed him. I killed him. But I was only doing what was required of me, wasn't I, Engineers?" He shot a panicked look at Adalbrand. "And then you killed me."

"A life for a life." Hefertus's voice was bored as he took a flask from his side and lifted it to Adalbrand's lips. The Poisoned Saint sputtered, coughed, and then pushed away from his friend looking dazed but conscious again.

The Majester spoke like one sentenced to death. "There were rules. We all had to follow them."

"Some followed more cleverly than others," Sir Sorken remarked, looking up only long enough to be sure we'd heard him before he returned to the cup.

"We beat the trial and it meant nothing," Sir Owalan said despairingly, limping over to us and running a hand over his face. It was the first he'd spoken and he looked gutted. Clearly, his priorities rested in one place alone. "One of us fell from grace. One of us is dead. And none of these is the Cup of Tears. Must we do all that over and over until we find it?" His gaze swept the room. "And what if it is one of the broken vessels?"

Nearly all the remaining vessels were battered or broken. They were in shards or crumpled messes in shoals across the ground, forming long furrows where the statues had scraped their way back to the walls. If I thought our salvation lay among them, I'd give up now. We could not fight this battle a hundred more times and live — time alone would make that impossible and we'd die of thirst on the first day if not at the hands of marble statues.

I snorted.

The "Saints," or whatever they were, looked down on us innocently, as if they'd be the first to question whether anything had happened at all.

"Who? Us?" they seemed to say.

"Fallen from grace?" The Majester's voice was hollow. He patted his chest, fingers streaking through the blood smear there as if he couldn't believe a sword had plunged through him and been removed. "I've broken the commandment. I've drawn steel on the innocent and taken blood without cause."

My Brindle remained silent. I was so unused to having my thoughts clear of the influence of others that I hardly knew what to do with myself. I expected a snide comment or a victorious laugh. Instead, there was only my own voice asking me, *Can he really be so good an actor? Does anyone believe he did not mean murder?*

"It's not one of the broken vessels," Sir Sorken said. Not like a comforter, but like a man breaking news to a king. He straightened. "And it's also not the vessels we chose — but those are not useless."

"No, indeed, and you'd best hold on to yours," Sir Coriand agreed, removing their cup from its holder. It continued to glow faintly in a way that made my eyes cross, as if they couldn't quite agree it was happening at all.

Sir Coriand had a look in his eyes I couldn't parse. It looked a bit like hunger, but that couldn't be right. After all, the Engineers were the only ones who had been entirely out of the fight. Except for Sir Hefertus, I supposed. But he was meant to be bereft of common sense. It was what his aspect forswore. They had clearly done it deliberately.

"The cups are one part of the solution, but an important part. Or at least they should be."

"Solution?" Sir Owalan complained, but I wasn't looking at him. "Speak plainly."

My eyes trailed to Adalbrand. He squared his shoulders, rolled his neck, and then, with obvious pain writ large across his features, he made his way to the Inquisitor.

I lifted Brindle's head onto my lap. No voices. Not one.

Worry bit around my edges, tugging and terrorizing me. I hadn't stopped to think of what would happen if the dog died by something other than my hand. It seemed a terrible thing to have neglected now that I was there.

Perhaps I should have quizzed Sir Branson on the things he had failed to teach me. Perhaps I should have worked harder to oust the demon.

I ground my teeth together, annoyed with myself for these failings.

The Majester muttered from where he stood, "There's murder in my heart. Black doings. Terrors unknown."

Look, he kind of sounded demon-possessed, if I was honest. It was unnerving. And yet, I sensed no demon there.

"The solution we are searching for is the riddle of this monastery," Sir Coriand said. "We're in a trap. Or perhaps I should say a giant puzzle box. It's terribly clever, really. I wish I had the funds to build one myself, but it would take a king's ransom and access to the arcane, I would think."

"And a lifetime to build," Sir Sorken added.

"And a lifetime to build."

"And slave labor. Or prisoners. Or supplicants, I suppose, were they dedicated enough."

"Or monks," Sir Coriand suggested gently.

"The ones who are bent just a little. You know. Twisted. Off. Not right." Sir Sorken was nodding.

"And about a hundred or a hundred and fifty years, obviously," Sir Coriand said absently. "Which we don't really have, unless you've solved the puzzle of age, my friend."

"I'm working on it. No progress as of yet."

Sir Coriand paused, realized we were all listening, and cleared his throat. "But building a replica is neither here nor there. For now, suffice it to say, we won't be getting out of this one until it's solved. And it's wickedly clever. Puzzles within puzzles and all that. If there weren't so many tragic ... incidentals ... it would be quite a lark, really."

"He means deaths," Sorken clarified.

"Yes, that. The solution for this room required every living person in the room to participate. Interesting that it didn't need the dog, don't you think? But I suppose the dog didn't sign up for this. Maybe consent is required."

"I consented to nothing," the High Saint said with a barb in his tone. I shot him an angry scowl. I hadn't forgotten what he'd taken. And I hadn't consented to *that.*

"Well, the door did try to keep us out. I think that perhaps entry is consent. Except where the dog is concerned, at least. He came with the girl. It wasn't his choice. And we had to work together as a group. It couldn't be solved separately one at a time.

It stands to reason that the rest of the riddles will be like that, too."

"Surely there cannot be more." Sir Owalan sounded aghast. "This would test the patience of a true Saint." He paused. "Or is that how it creates Saints? Through tests that stretch us to the edges?"

"Which is your goal?" Sir Coriand asked with a faint smile. "To be a Saint or to find the cup? I think — perhaps — that the puzzle box offers both to you."

"Please, Brindle," I whispered. "Please be well."

I needed him back, if only to have an intelligent conversation.

I cleared my throat. "I'm not certain anymore that this place makes Saints. I think it's trying to kill us."

"Well, it's certainly being creative about it," Sir Coriand said tolerantly. "Well? Cup or Saint?"

"I want the cup," the Penitent said at the same time that the High Saint spoke. "I want to be a Saint."

Sir Coriand laughed. "Well, at least you won't kill each other if you want different things."

And just like that, every eye turned to Adalbrand.

He sighed, his head bent over the Inquisitor. When he looked up, his face was lined and tired.

"I can do nothing for him. His soul has fled."

"Oh, Merciful God, have mercy, have mercy," the Majester moaned.

The wicked part of me wondered if the God had as little mercy to spare as I did. Perhaps he'd flick the Majester's request away as one flicks away a gnat.

It would serve him right.

The look in Adalbrand's eyes was murderous, and I thought that perhaps the Majester owed Hefertus a great debt, because the looming paladin had followed his friend and right now it was only his meaty palm that held the Poisoned Saint back from lunging at the Majester. Adalbrand may have healed him, but it seemed he still struggled to forgive. A part of me felt very satisfied with that.

"I can't remember why I did it," the Majester said uneasily. "There was some voice telling me it was right." I felt a chill at that. "Blood was required. And with him broken beneath the masonry, it was a mercy. No one wants to live with their legs and pelvis crushed to powder. That's what the voice said."

"I could have healed that," Adalbrand gritted out between clenched teeth.

"No one can heal what the God has wrought," the High Saint said, making the holy sign. "Come with me, Majester, and I will hear your confession and grant you reprieve as I may. We shall take this matter to the God where it belongs."

"I ... I ... yes." The Majester looked shaken.

He was already turning his back on Adalbrand, led by the High Saint, who seemed unconcerned by the other man's flushed face or white knuckles.

Annoyance bubbled up in me. First, the High Saint had taken my blood and tears by trickery. Now, he ignored the Poisoned Saint and condoned the murder of the Inquisitor. I hated him for his arrogance. I hated him worse for the insult he dealt to my friend.

Good luck to them getting help the next time they needed it. Now that I knew what they did to the defenseless, you wouldn't see me offering any.

"Bring your cups," Sir Coriand commanded. "If we went to this trouble to earn them, we shouldn't leave them here. I think I saw slots for them in the base of the clock."

I turned my eyes back to Brindle. I didn't care about the Cup of Tears. Not anymore. Losing Sir Branson now in finality hurt more than I'd expected it to. *And* I was worried about the demon. *And* I was so angry that I wasn't sure I could hold all that anger inside my one measly heart.

I bit my lip hard and held on to my dog. I tried not to see how weak his breathing was, tried not to cry at how soft and furry and vulnerable he looked like this, and I tried not to think about what it would mean if Sir Branson was really gone after everything we'd been through.

Or worse … if Adalbrand offered to heal Brindle.

He'd told me he'd been one with me when he healed me, hadn't he? He'd known me inside and out at that moment. What would that mean if he touched Brindle? Would he know what I'd allowed in the dog?

Fear spiked hard, and when something touched my shoulder, my eyes shot open and I jumped, my sword arm reaching for my hilt.

"Easy. Easy now."

Adalbrand squatted in front of me, hands held up like I was a dangerous animal. Beside him, his friend Hefertus squatted, too, one eyebrow lifted, one finger tracing his pearls mindlessly.

"You've been through a lot," Adalbrand said carefully. He was drawn and pale again. And why not? He'd nearly taken death from the Majester — who I saw out of the corner of my eye striding jauntily to the door as if he owed no man anything. There was a paladin I could stab in his sleep. No regrets.

"If you're thinking of murdering the Majester," Hefertus said in an undertone, his eyes finding mine and locking on, "I have prior claim. He attempted to kill me while I did nothing more violent than play a heartbreaking tune."

"I *was* thinking that," I admitted, as the heels of the Engineers vanished. There was no one left but us three. Four. I wouldn't give up on Brindle yet.

Adalbrand ran a tired hand over his face. "I just healed the man and now my friends are fighting over who will try to kill him again."

"I did try to warn you not to, brother," Hefertus said, smirking at me as if sharing a joke. "Some men were born needing to die. Your heart is too soft to see it. The Vagabond sees, though. You can't live destitute without knowing who people are at the core. What they'll forgive in the rich is never overlooked in the poor, and what's praised in the stable is often persecuted in the outliers, right, Beggar?"

"Yes," I agreed fiercely.

Adalbrand looked back and forth between the two of us. "Must I remind you that the God forgives us as we forgive others? Must I remind you that we are commanded not to let hate and anger seethe within us?"

I should have felt chagrined. I knew that. He knew that. I did not feel at all as I should.

Hefertus merely laughed. "Preach all you like, Poisoned Saint. But give us some credit. The God demands forgiveness, yes, but he also demands wisdom, and it would be supreme folly to forget what we saw today."

"I can heal your arm," Adalbrand told me gently, ignoring Hefertus, who snickered at what he clearly considered a win. "I know it's broken. You favor it still. Show me."

I tried to remove my gauntlet and flinched.

"Set the dog down and —"

"No." My denial was too fast and I knew it.

He raised his calming hand again and he kept his voice carefully neutral.

"I will remove your gauntlet for you."

So I sat with a heavy doggy on my lap as a beautiful, disheveled knight gently drew a metal glove from my hand and checked my knuckles one by one with the smooth pads of his fingers while an even prettier knight looked on and snickered. This was possibly the most storybook-like moment of my life. And it was drenched all through with pain and blood and awkwardness.

"Your hand is unbroken," Adalbrand said almost sternly, as if rebuking us both for our unforgiving hearts and silent innuendo. "Let us see to the arm."

My sleeve would not move without me hissing in pain, and eventually, it had to be cut.

"You can have one of mine to replace it when we get up top,"

Hefertus said easily. “I have a silk blouse the color of a blooming lilac that would look very fine on you indeed.”

Adalbrand shot him a poisonous look that I might have liked. It did not slow his work. He cut my sleeve slowly, inch by inch, with his knife. His eyes flicked up to mine every few seconds as he worked, one hand cradling my arm at the elbow, the other cutting my sleeve. His expression was open and sure. And I found I wanted to give myself over to him entirely — let him tell me what to do, who to fear, who to forgive. Surely he could do a better job of it than I.

“I should charge for admission,” Hefertus snorted from the sidelines. I blushed hot and looked away. “I could bottle this angst and sell it to elderly kings to use in their harem.”

“Don’t talk to me about elderly kings,” Adalbrand said with an edge to his voice.

“I always forget your father was one until you get prickly about it. Your loyalty is so very unearned, my friend.”

“Loyalty is a gift, not a reward.”

“From you it surely is.” Hefertus paused. “Not to put too fine a point on things, but we need to talk. I think we must do it now while the others are out there fitting cups into clocks. Which means the pair of you must put your — whatever you are doing with one another — to the side so that we can deal with the business at hand.”

My cheeks heated, but he was not looking at me and neither was Adalbrand. Adalbrand had the corner of his tongue stuck out of his mouth as he carefully cut my sleeve and Hefertus swallowed hard, his eyes on the dead Inquisitor. I bet that if we checked, the poor man would still be warm.

“They killed him in cold blood and they turned on me and on the Beggar.” I didn’t care that Hefertus used the slur for me. I didn’t think he noticed when it happened. “Lines are being drawn.”

“I think it was panic, mostly,” Adalbrand said, wincing as he peeled back my sleeve and finally got a proper look at the place where my bone stuck through the flesh of my arm. I hissed and bit off a whine when he tried to touch the skin close by.

The Poisoned Saint's eyes met mine, sharing the wince. He was so pale.

"I don't think you should heal this," I said, forcing firmness into my voice. "You've already taken too much from the Majester. Just ..." I felt a bit ill to say it when relief was an option and my voice stung in my throat. "Just set it if you can and wrap it. I can endure it."

If I breathed a little thinly after that, can you blame me?

He looked from me to the dog, his face twisting with indecision.

"Not Brindle," I said quietly.

"Definitely not Brindle," Hefertus agreed dryly. "I swear to the God, Adalbrand, you take the martyr role too seriously. Do what the girl says and bind her arm, and when you have the strength to sit upright, you can heal her. That won't be until morning at the earliest, and we both know it. The second you're safe, you'll collapse. Which is why we need to speak *now*. We've been working together loosely. We slept in one tent without killing each other. Can we speak words to this? Can we put our honor to an alliance until we get out of this cursed den?"

Adalbrand said nothing. His hand hovered over Brindle and fear seized my heart. I grabbed his wrist with my good hand and his eyes snapped up to meet mine. I've never been much of a secret keeper and I was afraid he was seeing my last secret laid bare in my eyes — but fearing something and letting it happen were two different things.

"Not the dog."

He looked at me for a long moment and I winced internally at the expression in his eyes. He was weighing what it meant that I didn't want healing for my dog. Yes, Adalbrand, I'm a mystery. Can you live with that?

He drew his hand back and cold washed over me. I could feel that with it, he was withdrawing some of the trust he'd given me, and that hurt. Even if he was right. Even if there was absolutely no way I could give in on this point.

It was one thing to overlook that I'd killed my mentor when he was possessed by a demon. It was entirely something else to reveal that I had *not* killed the dog the demon leapt into. He would judge me. And knowing Adalbrand, he would carry out his judgment with grim determination.

"Alliance?" Hefertus asked again, an edge of warning in his voice.

"Have I ever denied you, old friend?" Adalbrand asked, but his eyes were still on me, frowning.

"And you, Vagabond?" Hefertus asked me.

I glanced at him, surprised. He was only the second person to ever ask this, and the first was staring at me like I might shape-shift into a snake if he looked away.

"I welcome such a union," I said gravely.

Hefertus nodded. "The others will form their own alliances. The High Saint and the Majester will work together. The Engineers will stay a pair. The Penitent will have to land somewhere. Do you think the Majester killed the Seer, too?"

"What?" I asked, genuinely surprised. That was a strange leap of thought.

"She had the key in her hand, didn't she? The one Sir Owalan took when he thought no one was looking and then slotted into that lock the next morning. The Majester might have been after that. Or he might have just wanted to eliminate the competition. Like he did with the Inquisitor. I don't believe his pretense at repentance."

Adalbrand grunted, unwilling to commit.

Hefertus snorted. "You're too trusting, Adalbrand. Someone knew what this place was. Someone who killed the Seer before she could stop us from being sealed in here. Someone who knew she had the key."

"Wasn't she going to use the key?" I asked. "She was right there by the door."

"Unless she took it from the one who *was* going to use it," Hefertus suggested. "Perhaps she saw it in a vision. Perhaps she was trying to stop it from coming true."

"Perhaps this is all speculation," Adalbrand said firmly. "And Victoriana still has a very bad fracture."

There was a shuffling sound and we all turned to see Sir Owalan coming into the room from the hall. The broken cups crunched under his feet like shells upon a stretch of beach.

"I came to get your cups," he said, eyes tight. "You don't mind, do you? Only, there are slots in the clock for them."

"Do as you must," Adalbrand said, returning to my arm. He was swaying slightly.

"You shouldn't heal me," I reminded him. "Not now when you're so weak. Wait until tomorrow when you've had time to rest."

The arm hurt — like a burning rat was chewing right through my bone — but I could live with it until tomorrow.

"We should set it at least, just in case."

I don't know if you've had your arm set by two fretful paladins just strides away from a corpse. It was not my finest hour. I had to bite down hard on the hood of my cloak to keep from screaming as they levered the bone back into place through the tear in my flesh. By the time they were done, I was trembling, fighting tears hard, and yet spilling them silently anyway. I felt both freezing cold and sweaty.

"We need to talk about this place," I gasped as the pain still made me shudder.

"Later," Adalbrand suggested. His eyes were thick with sorrow and winced every time they strayed to my arm. I missed the lighthearted man I'd met days ago.

"Now," I insisted, panting. "This is no holy monastery to the God. Or to any God, I think."

"There is no God but the one God and the Saints are his servants," Hefertus quoted immediately, crossing himself.

"Yes, that," I agreed. "And this place is not his."

"Then whose is it?" Hefertus asked, his somber paladin eyes deep with worry.

"A place of demons," Adalbrand said in a low voice. "A place of evil."

We nodded with him.

"And we're trapped in it," I said, forcing my shuddering voice to be firm, but my teeth betrayed me. They clattered together as my body dealt with the quick doctoring done to it.

Adalbrand was gentle, but his hands were winding my torn sleeve around my arm as a makeshift bandage and the way it made the bone rub on itself forced my eyes to smart and my brain to spin.

"We have a plan," Hefertus reminded us. "We can watch each others' backs. But what about the rest. The puzzles? The cup? If the monastery is not what it seems ... are they what they seem?"

I shrugged and immediately regretted it.

"And if we are not becoming Saints, then what are we becoming?"

"Devils," Adalbrand said, and it sounded like a curse.

"No," Hefertus said, chopping his hand through the air. "Not me. Not you. Not the Beggar. And we'll do what we can to hold the rest back from the brink."

"How?" Adalbrand asked him, meeting his eyes. "We have to play through. There's no turning back now."

"There's always a choice," I said dully. "Even if it's an impossible one."

"We don't know it's impossible yet," Hefertus said, quickly changing the subject. "We should carry her dog out with us. She won't be able to carry him."

Adalbrand's eyes lingered on Brindle for a moment and he looked like he wanted to say more, but in the end, he merely nodded. After all, what more was there to say?

They had to take three trips.

One for Brindle. One for the dead Inquisitor. And then

finally one for me. For some reason, my legs didn't want to hold me properly and I needed to lean on someone to walk.

"Shock," Adalbrand said calmly. "It happens to everyone. There's no shame in it."

But it felt shameful when he'd taken a chest wound from the Majester and was still on his feet. He wasn't the one who was struggling to keep his head clear enough to stand.

"We'll sleep — both of us — and in the morning I'll heal you, too," he said, and I thought the offer was as much to comfort himself as to comfort me.

I nodded grimly but I didn't say much. I was starting to realize the inevitable truth that if Brindle didn't pull through on his own, Adalbrand would certainly heal him. And when he did, he would know our secret. And what then? Would he think I planned this trap? Would he — like the High Saint — blame me for the loose demon in the ceiling and whisper in the ears of others until they came to slay me for my sins?

Chapter Twenty-Three

Vagabond Paladin

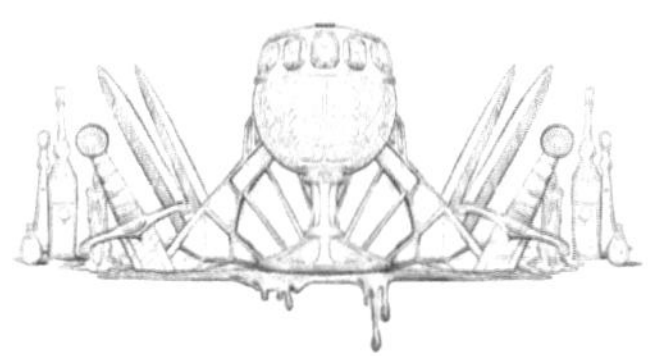

By the time we reached the main room, I was so spun up with nerves that I hardly noticed that the others were gathered around the great clock until Sir Owalan slotted the last cup — mine, as things would have it — into place. How they could act as if nothing had happened, as if what had just occurred hadn't revealed traitors and murderers, as if this were just another puzzle, mystified me. How could they not see the imposing threat of this clock made of hands? How could they seem so serene when Adalbrand and Hefertus had carried the dead Inquisitor right past them to lay beside the others?

The Majester had his head close to Sir Sorken's, worried lines in his forehead as he whispered violently to the other man. He was rumpled and bloodstained and losing all the majesty he'd carried before. I no longer saw anything but a shabby excuse for a knight. As always, Sir Sorken looked slightly bored. His wiry curls and generally disheveled appearance were unaffected. I doubted the end of the world would shake him.

With a click, Sir Owalan twisted his cup in place, his eyes brimming with ambition. Fool. Could he not see that his precious cup was not worth all of our lives or the stains we were rubbing into our souls?

The room lit up with a warm glow and the *tick* of a clock.

"But what do the hands mean?" Sir Coriand asked in awe. "Are they hours, or days, or years?"

A second *tick* rang through the room and Hefertus growled, "It had better not be years."

It was sunset on the other side of the bas-relief carving, shining through to the left of the stairs. As we settled on the floor around the stairway, which was now facing darkened windows, black against the wall that had been a corridor into the living quarters, the evening breeze caught at the cutouts whistling a dull note a little too close to the sound of the pipe organ for my liking. I shivered, flinched, and then shivered again.

"I think they plan to solve that sun and moon puzzle tonight," Adalbrand said as he lowered himself to the floor. He was trying to sound confident and at ease, but he'd flopped a little too much as he landed, and when I sank to the ground with him, he turned to face me. "I need sleep. Now. Can't hold on much longer. Hefertus knows."

"Do I ever," Hefertus said lazily. He'd guided us to the spot where he'd lain Brindle and now he produced my fur cloak. He was taking his role as the nursemaid of our newfound alliance very seriously. "We'll take turns resting. You two first. I'll wake one of you for the next shift. Sleep back-to-back. We don't want more surprises."

That was how I found myself huddled under the fur cloak, my arm on fire and my back pleasantly warm as Adalbrand breathed heavily at my back. He was lost to sleep the moment he lay down.

"Hefertus?" I whispered as my own eyelids fluttered.

"I'm here," he growled. "I've got your backs."

"Can you watch my dog?"

"Don't plan to take my eyes off the cursed thing."

That was the best I could ask for. I let my eyelids flutter closed and fell into the rhythm of Adalbrand's breath. The pain was jagged and sharp in my arm, my fevered forehead cold and clammy, and yet, I slept.

Pain made sleep fitful, and when I woke, I heard murmured voices in the darkness, only to fall back to sleep, awake, asleep, awake again. By the third time it happened, I could not tell if I was still sleeping and dreaming fevered dreams or actually listening to two men murmur together.

"The heart wants what the heart wants," Hefertus was murmuring.

"The heart can be told to go to hell." Adalbrand, I thought. His voice was still thick with exhaustion and my back was cold.

"A cruel fate, that. I would not wish it on your heart."

"Sometimes I would."

The next time I woke it was still dark. I woke to breath in my face. There was something about how it hitched that told me he was awake.

"Adalbrand?" I whispered, hardly louder than a breath.

"I'm here." His voice was just as faint. I heard how labored his breath was. He was paying the price of pain he took from the Majester. "Hold on."

"You forgave the Majester. You saw what he did and you healed him anyway."

He said nothing and his quiet compelled me to speak, though my brain was hot and wild with pain and possibly infection.

"You're a mystery, Poisoned Saint. Why do you refuse to believe you can be forgiven when you forgive everyone else?"

His wry snort was so faint I barely caught it at all beyond a soft gust against my cheek.

"You tell me, Vagabond. You have so much courage that you wade into danger without a thought. If you have so much faith in the future, why can you not have faith in the God?"

We lay there in silence under the tent of my bearskin cloak for a long time. And whether he was wounded by my question or taking his time to think — as I was — about the truth laced all through it, I did not know. I knew only that he had caught me and cut me with his precise words, and I could not shake the two sides of myself that could be both brave and cowardly all in one.

When I woke a third time, I thought I was dreaming. Hands gripped my waist and someone murmured endearments sleepily beside me. I leaned drowsily into the caress.

My broken arm twinged and I came back with sudden clarity to where I was. I was sleeping on a tiled floor in a grave under a fur cloak with a beautiful holy knight who apparently whispered sweet reverences into my ear as he slept.

The ferocious pain in my broken arm mixed with the ineffable sweetness of this moment that wasn't mine to keep. I let the two sensations twist together, let them hurt and heal, keep me in the moment, and draw me away from it. And I did not know if the pain was my friend or the pleasure, for the pleasure was forbidden and the pain was rightly mine, but both sang hard and sharp and full.

Adalbrand nuzzled blearily against my good shoulder and tears sprang to my eyes. I should wake him and bid him stop. But we'd both removed our armor the night before and stripped down to soft inner layers — modest enough, but they did nothing to prevent the exchange of warmth between us or the softness of his body melding into mine.

My eyes smarted, and not just for the jarring hot pain of my broken arm but for the forbidden sweetness, the gift that was not mine to accept, the desperate, sudden want that filled me from brow to boot buckles and left me trembling.

And it was not lust, for lust is of the body. It was something deeper, something more bitter, something so much more full-bodied than the mere want of physical sensation could ever be. It was the call of soul to soul and the answer. The question and the reply. His arms bid me accept him and his soft murmurs bid me receive his acceptance.

And I did. God have mercy, I did.

I could tell the moment he woke for his nose no longer

stroked my cheek and his delicate fingers froze against my fevered skin.

He let out a trembling exhale.

"Victoriana?" His whisper was so faint I doubted anyone could hear it past the fur cloak.

"Adalbrand." I heard the tightness in my voice, the embarrassing way that it softened his name, even caressed it. My cheeks were hot with the admission.

He cleared his throat quietly.

"I'll heal your arm now, the God willing."

"Yes."

Could a Poisoned Saint choose to love? Did it matter, when I so clearly had accidentally lost my heart to him?

Call me a fool if you want. Call me an inexperienced girl. I was all those things. But I was also honor and fidelity to my core. I had set my feet on the path of the God as a child and I did not turn back through the lashing winds of poverty and the cold chill of friendlessness. I had set myself to serve Sir Branson and I did, right up to the moment I served him by releasing him from the grasp of an enemy. When I set my path, I did not look back.

And now I had set my heart on the man who drank poison for others and ate their pains.

As he set his hand upon my arm and offered his thick-tongued prayer, I felt that firm purpose settle through me, felt that kindled love throb like embers banked in a careful fire, and as the healing took and my arm was whole again, I knew he felt it, too.

I felt how he carefully drew his hands back to himself. Heard him sigh in what tasted like regret. Heard his quiet, self-deprecating curse.

And I dared not say a thing, for now he knew. He knew as no one else ever could, even were I to say a thousand words of confession. My very heart had betrayed me to him.

When he retreated from me, I noticed he only put the smallest distance between us, only put enough to be decent, enough to tell me not that he was disgusted or disparaging, only that he did not yet know the answer to my unspoken question.

His breath took a long time to even out.

Mine took even longer.

It did not help that I heard Hefertus cough in a way I was relatively certain was meant to disguise a laugh.

He should stick to his pearls and fine silks. I wanted none of them. I wanted only a cold, untouched place by Sir Adalbrand's side and a right to call him friend. That was worth fighting for. If he could see through to giving it to me.

When I woke again, my arm no longer hurt, though my heart felt slightly tender.

I crawled out from the cloak into the faint lavender of near dawn. Hefertus sat inches from me, his naked blade across his knees, his eyes staring off into the distance.

"Have you been here all night?" I whispered to him. I could see the others only as lumps across the floor, barely recognizable in the pre-dawn. The golems made larger lumps, their eyes glowing in that terrible way that they always did.

"Why not?" he whispered back. "Adalbrand exhausted himself for a man not worth a minute of his time and then, the moment he could, he healed your arm. Don't think I didn't hear you two under that cloak."

"I didn't think it," I said frostily.

I tested my arm out. It did, in fact, bend and move painlessly. I unwrapped the makeshift bandage. My flesh felt smooth and strong.

I swallowed down a lump. He'd healed me again. Given of himself again. I was forever in his debt.

"You're very voyeuristic for a hedonist aspect," I said sourly.

Hefertus grunted but I could tell it was meant to disguise a laugh. "Ready to take a turn at watch?"

"Yes," I agreed, taking his place and spreading my own sword across my knees as he had.

He snorted at that and then crawled under the cloak to lie

back-to-back with Adalbrand. He must have been more exhausted than I thought. He slipped into sleep before it even occurred to me to check Brindle.

My dog had survived the night. But he was still unconscious, his breath weak and thready.

A spike of fear shot through me. How long could I hold Adalbrand off from healing him? How long could I keep the secret? Were I a more calculating person, I'd smother the dog right here. Instead, I rested a rueful hand on his sweet head and stood my watch, shaking out my arm and inspecting it again every few minutes. The God did as he willed. He gave and he took. I felt like he'd given me a lot more than he'd taken recently. I worried about how that tipped the balance. I had asked the God for so much.

I paused.

The night that I killed my mentor, I had asked the God to help me bury Sir Branson. What had I said? Had I asked that he be laid to rest or that I bury him?

I pressed my lips together, suddenly worried.

The God answered the prayers of the Beggar Paladins — always — but not always in the way you thought. Could the demon have been trapped in the dog because I prayed that? Because Sir Branson's soul yet persisted and I had not found a way to bury him with honor? Was the demon ... was he stuck in the dog because Sir Branson was stuck in it?

Something icy gripped my heart. I thought, perhaps, with trepidation and a great deal of doubt, that I might have found one answer tonight.

"If you exist, Merciful God," I prayed quietly into the darkness. "If you are there and you hear me, please help me to cast this demon out and remove him from the world completely, and with him all others in this place."

It was a good prayer. A righteous prayer. After all, it wasn't for me, and those kinds of prayers were the best kind.

Someone cleared his throat and I nearly leapt in my flesh.

"Did they tell you about the clock?"

It was Sir Owalan, staring at me in the half-light. On one cheek, the first rays of dawn painted his features pink. On the other side, his face glowed a very dull orange. A faint light that I realized was coming from down the hall.

"What about it?" I asked. What was he doing creeping around in the darkness? His sword was out, too, and he smelled metallic, as if he were bleeding.

He lifted one hand to point and his robe fell back, revealing a knife stuck through his wrist.

I hissed a gasp.

Erg.

No. Just, no.

I flinched back without meaning to do so.

"We slotted all the cups in the clock while you were being tended," he said in a low voice, and the intensity of his eyes made my skin crawl. "The hands began to move."

"It tells time?" I asked, stupidly, my eyes locked on his wrist.

"In a way," he whispered. "I was checking on it just now, and it's changed from where it was at sunset."

"Clocks do that," I said steadily.

"It's counting down, I think. And we've used up one-sixth of the time."

"What happens when we run out?" I asked.

He didn't answer, but I followed his gaze up to the ceiling where the demon slept.

"Do you think the monks here left because the Rim moved?" he asked me. "Or did they leave because of something else?"

"I haven't thought about it," I said slowly.

"Funny. It's all I can seem to think about."

If he was trying to scare me out of my mind, he was doing an excellent job. I almost thought I felt my own shadow flinch.

And then he was gone, and as the dawn swelled and light pierced the room through the carving in long, sharp beams, I saw drips of scarlet blood trailing after him.

And Then There was Darkness...

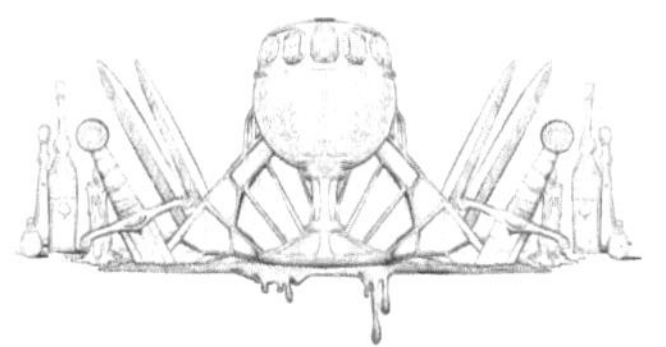

"If he still lives, he needs his cup filled!" Sir Coriand calls down.

They'll have to work that out for themselves. I have no energy for traitors.

We're at the stairs. I'm supporting the Vagabond as she ascends them, stumbling in a way that tells me she's in a lot of pain.

She reaches the top and pauses over her cup.

"I have nothing," she says through her gritted teeth, and her eyes are a little wild as her gaze darts back to the dog. Ha! She'd had the same thought I'd had about him.

"Let me," I manage to say between heavy breaths. I still have angry tears on my face. It's easy enough to let one fall into the broken cup she chose. Why a broken one?

"You're not my adversary." She says it like a declaration, like a queen awarding a prize.

I want to kiss her.

The thought is unbidden. Unwelcome. I thrust it aside.

"Aren't I?" I grit out. "Have I not made things harder for you? Do I not make them harder now? Trust me, Lady Paladin, I am no proper friend to you."

"Are you not? For you are a friend like no other," she says, lips trembling at some emotion I cannot discern.

Her confession tears something inside me, opening me wide. I'm stuck in her gaze. I'm trapped like a fly in treacle. I can't breathe.

"It's not working!" the Penitent calls from behind me. "Why isn't it working?"

Beneath us, our platform begins to sway and the sound of stone on stone rings as the statues throw themselves at our refuge.

I lift my hand up, press the cut in my thumb to her vessel, and squeeze a drop into her cup. Friend or not, I am indeed her rival. Her enemy. Because friendship with me is ruin to any woman.

Her cup glows bright, confirming that.

And as sudden as the sneaking dawn, silence falls. My breath

Chapter Twenty-Four
Poisoned Saint

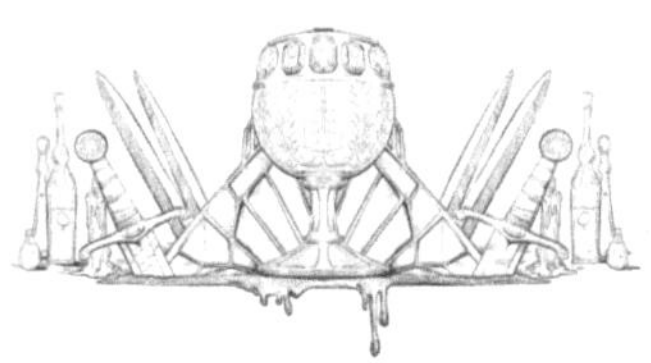

Healing one man from a mortal chest wound and then a woman from a compound fracture is more exhausting than they tell you. There's a reason we're meant to build up our piety before we arrive at battles and plague towns. A reason we're trained rigorously in dedication. That I was already almost drained before my arrival here is doing me no favors. But my heart thrumming every time I see the Vagabond Paladin, and the careful work I must do to deny myself so much as a single touch of her had been helping ... until last night when, despite myself, I slipped. Even so, I sleep until well into the morning.

When I wake, everyone is drinking tea without me.

My eyes find the Vagabond immediately. She's taken time to clean her face and fix her braid; her arm is draped over her dog's body. His rib cage moves enough that I know he is breathing, though his lungs hitch badly. There's tightness right through her posture, and there should be. We are in a hell.

Not *the* hell, obviously, but there are hells and then there are hells.

The problem with hell is that it makes demons. Creates them the way we were so sure that this place could make Saints.

What I don't see, to my relief, is pain in how Victoriana sits. It pleases me even more when her eyes snag on mine. My heart kicks in my chest like a fresh-caught fish.

"It's a code," Sir Coriand insists, opening his hands to the others.

They're in a rough circle — all but Hefertus, who snores raggedly beside me. The Vagabond must have spelled him off when she woke. I'm still not fully myself. I don't like that. I need to be battle-ready and instead, there is weakness in my limbs and fogginess in my mind and this strange lightheaded softness infusing everything.

Last night keeps invading my thoughts — both the good and the bad of it. I must shove it away roughly. I am a knight of the God, not a boy with his first beard. I dare not moon after a woman when there is work before me.

But I feel her beside me, still. I feel the thrill of waking with my hands against the warmth of her clothing and my nose against the softness of her cheek and I do not want to forget that one precious, forbidden moment that was mine. It is the only moment I may ever have like it.

One of the golems lurches in from the side — the hideous one made of rags and bones. Its rags are stuck to it as if they had been dipped in bone glue and stuck on, but then the sea air had its way and the edges of the rags peel and pick up dust and gravel wherever they touch the earth. Some have stripped almost entirely off, hanging shaggily around it and exposing sticky bones beneath — some human, some beast, all bleached or boiled nearly white. I swallow roughly at the sight of it. The exposed bones are not too different from the look of Victoriana's exposed radius last night.

The creature shoves a mug into my hands and I meet its glowing eyes. Is it a soul in hell inside this terrible constructed body of rags and bones? And what would it have of me if it could speak? Would it plead for death to free it — or would it want life poured into its empty spaces?

I take the mug in trembling hands and mouth a blessing over it.

"Once we crack the code, we can turn the room again and open the next space," Sir Coriand says. "And with the clock ticking down, this must be our priority. No more sleeping. No more eating."

Sir Owalan looks up from a light gruel he's eating — likely given to him by the Engineers, as they're the only ones with supplies. He looks thinner and more hollow-eyed than ever, as if he is a candle being burned down. He takes one more defiant mouthful and something flickers in his shadow. It seems to build somehow, as if it is darkening, growing.

I frown and look toward our miserable light source — the bas-relief wall — but I see nothing that would change his shadow. Just his, no one else's. Perhaps a bird flew past the carved-out holes. I don't believe it, but I have no other way to explain what I just saw.

"*Should* we turn it?" the Vagabond asks quietly.

"Of course we should!" Sir Sorken rumbles. "The only way out is forward, my lass."

He is leaning back against the stairs, seemingly at ease as he sips his tea, face freshly shaven, hair brushed back neatly. Both Engineers are brilliant men, but I've known enough brilliant men to know that sometimes practicality escapes them. If your head is too high in the clouds, sometimes you can't see the dirt.

"This place is not making us Saints," she says quietly, and she's not looking at them. She's looking upward, where those hideous statues of us stand.

"We look like Saints in these statues," Sir Owalan argues.

"Do we?" she asks. "Do those even look like us? Or is it just another twist of the mind? Like the door twisted our sin so that the doubt I confessed twisted into terror? Now we've all confessed to murder. What is it twisting us into with that?"

"Metaphysical arguments and the great philosophies are a wonderful pastime," Sir Sorken announces like he's the first to ever have noticed this. "But they are hardly of value to us now. We are trapped in the earth with few supplies. A clock is ticking. We do not know what happens when it runs out, but we do know that the last time we opened a door, this room spun. If we open another door, another wall will twist over this great open space that faces the sea. It has but a series of narrow stained glass windows and we will not be able to escape through them, but if we twist it a third time, then the open door will face the sea, and if nothing else occurs to us by then, we might fling ourselves into it and escape that way, or twist the room a final time and return to how it was set up before, and then stride grandly up the stairs and back into the world. Or, we can sit here and argue until we are nothing but bones and no one but Cleft and Suture will ever know our fates."

I glance again at the golems. What would happen to them if we all died? Would they tunnel through the rock and go their own way? Or would they sit down here and wait for the next party of fools to open the door and slip down below? *Could* anyone open it from above when it was twisted as it was right now?

"Perhaps we could scale the wall and find the open door, even if the stairs don't lead to it anymore," the High Saint says quietly, but he doesn't look like he likes that idea.

Beside me, Hefertus wakes, sits, and stretches like a big cat. He is entirely at his ease.

"We have no climbing gear. We have no other option but to go on," Sir Sorken says gently but firmly. "You all know this. Dithering about it is merely wasting time."

"Besides," Sir Coriand agrees, "Don't you want what we came here for? The Cup of Tears? Sainthood?"

"I do." The High Saint's words sound like a vow. His eyes are too bright. I don't trust eyes that bright unless they're in love. Even then. "I want it with all my heart."

"Well, there you have it then," Sir Coriand says as if he is offering us all a good gift. He's not. "This is a puzzle box. A very large, very clever one, but a puzzle box all the same. And puzzle boxes guard important treasures. What, I ask you, is more important than a relic of the God and possible Sainthood?"

"Nothing," the High Saint agrees. He's staring off into the

distance at some glory the rest of us do not see, his knuckles white around the bowl in his hands. I do not like how his shadow flickers with every breath he takes.

"We still haven't solved the problem of who is killing people," Victoriana says calmly.

I feel a little thrill at her relentless bravery. It is so like her to state this in the open, as if a murderer — if there is one — isn't worth worrying about offending. I remember how her breath hitched when I healed her. How that tidy hair had spilled everywhere. I must look away for a moment before I can look back.

When all eyes turn to Victoriana, she lifts an eyebrow. "The Seer did not kill herself."

"Perhaps the power of the God turned on her as it turned on Sir Kodelai when he abused it," Sir Owalan says, unconcerned.

He slips the sleeve of his robe down where a knife is still sticking luridly through his flesh. He should tend to that before it becomes infected and does irreparable damage. If he thinks that I will heal it...

I pause, guilt washing over me. It is not for me to say who received the God's healing. If he asks, I will not deny him, self-inflicted though the wound may be.

"Some people are not as dedicated to the God as they ought to be," Sir Owalan says gravely.

I snort at that.

"And does that usually result in decapitation?" the Vagabond asks, her eyes wide with feigned innocence.

Sir Sorken laughs, and down here in the bowels of this place, it does not sound like a nice laugh.

"There are no murders happening here," he says as if he is a judge rendering a verdict. "And now, children, we have a puzzle to solve before time runs out."

"What happens when the time runs out?" the Majester asks uncomfortably. I do not think he meant to be a murderer. I think he thought he was a mercy-killer. Or perhaps this place has driven him mad. His hands still tremble and there are green shadows around his mouth and under his eyes.

Even so, I feel my skin creep when I look at him.

"What puzzle?" Hefertus asks, stretching again before standing and working the strap on his sword belt.

"We do not know what happens, Majester, but it cannot be beneficial," Sir Coriand says. "Look at the trial we already faced. Perhaps we have only one chance to solve this box or we will perish here. And if that is true, we ought to hurry. As to the puzzle, Sir Hefertus, we refer to the etching showing the sun moving through its courses."

Hefertus grunts. "Oh, well we all know what that meant. Not much of a puzzle."

He is greeted by stillness and silence except for the whistling of the breeze through the cutouts in the stone.

He looks around slowly, his brow furrowed. I barely suppress a grin.

"Is something wrong?" Hefertus asks.

Sir Coriand sets down his bowl of tea, a slightly bemused smile on his face. "Are you saying you know what the etching means, Sir Hefertus?"

In answer, Hefertus whistles an odd tune, a little breathy and lilting. It does not suit the mood at all, though it reminds me a little of what he was playing on the organ. A dirge if ever there was one.

"Is there any of that tea to go around?" he asks when he is done.

Sir Sorken snaps his fingers and one of the golems lurches into action, attending to a kettle. It is only then that I realize they are burning rags to heat the kettle. Some of them look a little too familiar and my stomach twists. Have … the golems haven't pilfered from the dead to light their fire … have they? That cloth looks very much like the Inquisitor's cloak.

Hefertus accepts the mug and drinks like a man badly in need of a brew, and I stand unhappily, striding away to stretch my legs and clear my head for a moment. I still don't feel quite right. My heartbeat is too fast, my lungs sore, every bone in my body aching — though especially the arm. I think perhaps I am feverish. The whole world feels hot. Far too hot. As if the sun has taken against me, though I cannot see even see his face.

"Is he going to tell us or what?" I hear the Majester's anxiety creeping into his whispered question, but I don't look at him.

I don't look at anyone. I just need a little air. Just a little. I make my way to the cutout bas-relief and put my nose and mouth to a hole too small to even shove a hand through. I feel like a prisoner looking longingly at a floor drain.

"The sun marks are times of day, obviously," Sir Coriand says. "But how did you get musical notes from that?"

Hefertus whistles a single note. It's not his usual clear, melodic whistle but a breathing one that sounds more like the wind than a song. I close my eyes and let the cold air blowing in from the sea wash over my face, and I treasure that scent of salt and pine trees. It feels so far away and yet the same wind washes over them and washes through this rock prison and over me.

Hefertus's whistled note fills my ears, seems to grow.

But that's not it at all.

His note simply matches the wind as it washes into the room.

"Something about the shape of the rocks outside and the bas-relief and the tide must change the sound of the wind whistling in," Hefertus is saying. "Or maybe it's none of that. Maybe it's magic."

"The tune you whistled?"

"It's just the notes the wind makes as it runs through the carving. In the order of the times on that little chart."

In the silence, I hear quiet feet approaching me. I grit my jaw, but even though I was ready, I flinch when a hand drops lightly on my shoulder.

"Are you well, Poisoned Saint?"

The Vagabond's voice is like honey on my tongue and sun on my face.

"I beg you. Remove your hand," I gasp out as quickly as the words can form.

Forsworn, forsworn, forsworn.

My mind chants the word but though I know what it is meant to be, it still sounds like "lost" to me and I want to reach out and take it back. I want to take back her touch that flies away and leaves my shoulder cold. I want to snatch her hand in mine.

"I am well enough," I manage, not wanting to reject her kindness entirely, but I dare not look at her.

"But he already whistled it and it did nothing," Sir Owalan is protesting in the background. "So it can't be the answer."

"I think it's meant to be played," Sir Coriand says. "Would you try to play it for us, Sir Hefertus? On the pipe organ?"

I know my friend will say yes. To him, playing a song is as natural as breathing.

"You could take one of the golems if you like. Suture, perhaps," Sir Sorken says. "You might need to tear out of there very quickly and a golem is a help for that."

"I can trust my own two feet," Hefertus growls. If he hadn't decided before, he has decided now.

"Then do it and do it quickly," Sir Sorken is saying. "And as for the rest of us, brothers, I suggest we say our morning prayers, have a quick tidy, and be ready. Last time a door was opened there wasn't much time to waste, hmm?"

I should wish Hefertus well. I should do exactly what Sir Sorken suggests and tidy up a bit. I do neither of those things. I keep my face pressed to the cold stone. I breathe the scent of freedom from the salt of the sea and the scent of courage from the lady paladin hovering beside me and I pray.

God have mercy on me. God have mercy.

"I will try to heal your dog before we go into the challenge," I tell her when I feel I can speak again. "I should have about enough strength for that."

"No." Her refusal comes too quickly.

I've had no reason to doubt her in all of this.

I have reason *now*.

My eyes flick open and I see the look in her eyes and the way she shutters them to try to hide it. She is afraid to let me heal the dog. She is hiding something.

Queasiness settles in my belly and I feel my face twist.

"Why do you doubt me?" I ask her in an undertone. "Why will you not allow me this?"

In the background, the others have decided on communal prayer. Their chant is like bone broth on a cold morning. It comforts me even from afar. The familiar words wash over my mind; the familiar chanting lines echo in my heart.

"I do not doubt you," she says, but her gaze is held by mine and it is dancing with lies.

"You do. Your dog needs healing but you will not let me touch him. Are you afraid I'll kill him because he bit me? Have you not seen I do not lash out in vengeance?"

"I do not doubt your mercy." Her voice is small. She breaks the hold of my gaze and cinches her breastplate straps a little tighter. She checks the fit and buckling of her boots.

"But you reject it," I say quietly, and still she does not meet my eyes.

Her silence feels like a knife.

"Why have you taken against me?" I press.

I think I might know. She judges me for last night. She knows I have taken pleasure in touching her, denying my calling and staining us both with guilt.

I bite my lip.

She shakes her head in denial, but there is shame all over her face and I know I put it there. It was I who touched her, I who whispered endearments to her in the darkness. My belly feels like I've swallowed a rock. My head is swimming.

"I apologize," I whisper. "Most humbly."

She opens her mouth and her face twists with vulnerability, but just when I think she will confess something to me, she shakes her head again and thrusts a water skin at me.

I take it, angry enough at myself that I grip it too tightly. I do not know what to say. I am awash with disgrace.

She stalks away and begins to tidy her things, wrapping up the cloak, stretching her muscles, checking over her sword. I watch her every movement, my eyes catching on the wear of her straps and clothing. She's ragged and poorly repaired. Impoverished.

I have faith in the God, but why does he require so much from his servants? Holiness, they say, is why he demands it. Sacrifice purifies the heart. For if you have given up riches or physical kindness or freedom from pain, then it is not hard to give up the temptations to evil thrown in your path. Why grasp for power when you've denied yourself riches all your life? You can see how hollow it is, just as you've seen how hollow are the riches that others have. Why steal wealth when you've given up kind touches and gentle closeness as I have? To turn your back on cold silver is easy in comparison, trivial even. That's the theory of it, and in practice, it has worked. Set your feet on the path and start to walk down it and the other path grows more and more distant, more and more inconceivable.

I know all this. And yet I want all the world for her. Even if she is as tarnished with guilt and wanting as I am. Maybe she is right. Maybe there is more evil walking among us than just what is in this place. Maybe we've brought some here with us. The golems, for instance. Murder in the heart of one of our ranks. I suck on my bottom lip and try to think.

I'm surprised when a movement catches my eye. It's the Majester, approaching me with a twisted expression. He's guilt and shame and misery, and he should be. He should be. Plenum Hexilan — the Inquisitor — was a bright, vibrant man. He should not be dead.

I find I'm trembling when he reaches me. It's not for me to judge. But I am judging. It's not for me to say how the God directs vengeance. And yet, I want him to direct it here.

God have mercy on me.

"I can't think," he confesses to me in an undertone, laced with the melodic prayers of the others. "It's twisted my mind, wrung me into a killer. Ruined me. I can no longer be a paladin. I took off the raiment today and I've given the Engineers my sword."

My eyes widen as I see he wears no scabbard.

"I want you to have the map."

He shoves it into my hand and his haunted eyes come so close to mine that I can smell the fear on him rolling off in waves.

"Map?" I ask.

"You healed me. That means you were me for a moment. Surely, you saw. Surely, you understand. I'm tainted, Poisoned One. I'm misshapen right through the marrow. You should have left me dead."

"I did not," I say through gritted teeth.

His eyes look into mine, hollow and furious. "My life wasn't yours to preserve. It wasn't yours. He told me to kill. Don't you see that? Did you see it when you were me?"

He sounds almost like a child pleading with me, and I don't know why I feel tears so close. It makes no sense. I feel no pity for him. I feel no harmony with a cold-blooded murderer — no longer a knight, holy or otherwise. Not now.

And yet I have to blink very hard to hold them back when he pleads, "He told me."

And then he's gone, back turned to me, and hurrying to rejoin the prayers of the others, and I'm left gaping.

I tuck the map into a pocket.

With my heart open and my chest constricted, I look to the Vagabond Paladin. I wasted all the healing on the Majester — insane now, perhaps, or so guilt-ridden he's of no use to anyone. It should never have been for him. I should have swept down to that platform and lifted her beloved dog and healed him right there.

Mayhap that is why she resents me now.

When she bends her head and bows in morning prayer, I can hardly hold my feet back as they move me slowly, obliquely toward her. She has told me she rejects my healing for her dog.

But that is not up to her. I will show compassion on whom I will show compassion and if that is a dog, well then, so be it.

And I know this is unwise. If Hefertus were here, he would hold me back and raise a very distinct eyebrow. If we are to fight again, I should be fit to fight, and I won't be if I do this.

But Hefertus is not here. And within me, something tugs me forward and will not let me go. Something good, I hope.

Because as her sweet voice recites the Prima Dolce morning prayer, I kneel beside heavy paws, and lay my hand on a brindled head, and I feel where the skull is fractured, feel the butterfly breath threading through a doggy nose. And I close my eyes and pray.

God grant your healing to this dog. Let me take upon me his woes, let me take upon me his pain. Knit him together as you have from the first.

Like always, it starts as warmth in my heart and spreads out to my fingertips, and then — for one ghastly moment — we are woven together, dog and man and — God forfend, what is *that*?

My eyes pop open. I'm staring into wide-open, golden doggy eyes. But that's not what I'm seeing. I'm seeing distinctly three different beings. The dog, yes, with the scent of warm grass in his nose and a deep affection for Victoriana in his heart — you and me both, canine. But also the specter of a barrel-chested knight with sharp eyes and surprise highest in his emotions. He opens his mouth in wonder at the same time that I gasp at the third thing. A dark, twisted, painful presence. It bites my mind and heart like molten lead droplets hitting the skin.

I cannot think. I cannot reason. Fear floods my bowels and chases up into my throat and I'm choked by it, I'm gasping with it. I violently throw it away from me. No.

But for that moment — that bare moment — I am the dog who wants nothing more than to run in the grass with the wind in his face.

I am the old paladin with pain in my bones, pain in my heart, and a fierce, protective love for the girl with the brown eyes — a love so strong that he cannot simply walk away.

And I am the demon with a heart full of wickedness and it bubbles up and it boils over, and my mind begins to scream at the terrors it teases out and the horrors it suggests as it whispers and calls to me by name.

I'll flay you alive and eat you, my treasure. I'll gobble you up and smack my lips.

"What have you done?" I whisper.

Her eyes snap open and meet mine, and the faint glow that surrounded her as she prayed bursts like a soap bubble. She looks down at the dog, up at me, and for a moment our faces match.

We wear twin expressions of betrayal.

"What have *you* done?" she asks, and she sounds as if her heart is rent in two.

And then the floor lurches and the walls around us turn.

Her dog leaps to his feet and barks, one sharp yap.

Down the hall somewhere there is shouting, but I hardly care.

She is no Vagabond Paladin. Just as I feared. She is no paladin at all, for no holy knight would permit a demon to live. No servant of God would dwell with it — let it *sleep* at the foot of her bedroll, feed it from her hand, hold its broken body on her lap and shed tears.

I turn to the side, go down on all fours and heave, and then the room stops turning. The darkness of the bas-relief carved picture is gone, facing the dormitories now, the former arrow-slit windows face the corridor to our first trial, and in both their places are long stone slit windows that run from floor to ceiling and are filled with stained glass in yellow and red and blue and green. The thick base of the stairs blocks some of the space that should have been window, but the ones left make up for it. They flood the room with beams of colored light. I crane to look and see the edge of the fountain around the bulk of the stairs, now twinkling with rainbow colors. And when I look back, a golden beam washes over the Vagabond as she beholds me with terrible hurt in her eyes.

"I've seen what's at the heart of you now," I growl. Whatever affection flamed in me before is morphing into horror. Early flickers that I thought were love are now abhorrence. I can't stand the sight of her.

She juts her chin out. "And you've found one more thing that you can't forgive?"

Her tone tests me as if she thinks can challenge me into forgiveness. As if she thinks she can make me bend by declaring the opposite of the truth.

She is wrong.

Beside her, that terrible demon disguised as a dog sinks low, tongue out and lolling, butting her thigh with his head as though demanding affection.

"I will not forgive this," I snarl back, and the hurt in her eyes is no less than the agony in my heart. The way she pales is no less than the way I do.

And then the result of what I have just done washes over me and I collapse onto the floor. My last thought is that I hope I do not land in my own sick.

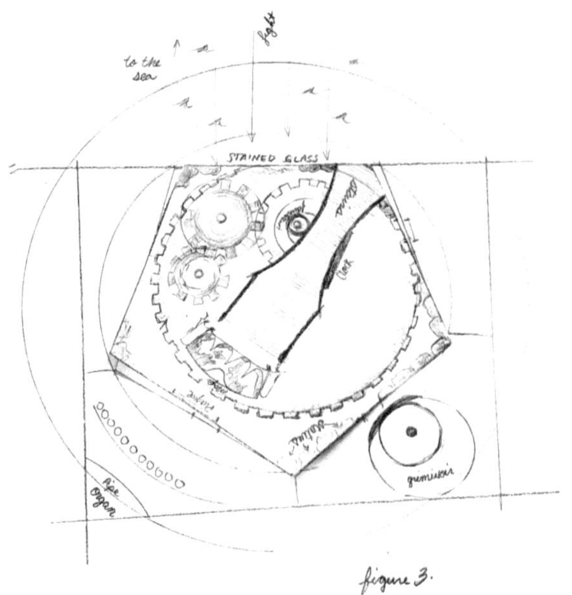

figure 3.

Chapter Twenty-Five
Vagabond Paladin

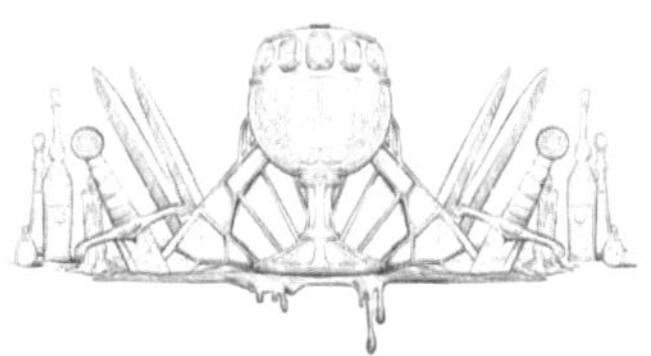

Y*es! We're back!*

I felt the demon's rejoicing twisting through me in the same moment that the breath *whooshed* from my lungs. Brindle barreled into me, round skull smacking into my belly so hard that if I hadn't already lost my breath, I'd lose it now. His enthusiastic tongue washed my hands and arms as I reached to bury my hands in his fur, trying not to crumple.

Adalbrand knew now.

Saints and Angel's blood, he knew.

I couldn't catch my breath. It was stuck in my throat like a barbed hook.

And now we find out. Is Adalbrand the honor and chivalry he pretends? Is he the holy paladin he thinks himself? Is he your love-sworn man as he suspects? Now is his reckoning and we shall discover the answer with him.

Or he'll go mad and murder you, and that should be entertaining at the very least. Do you think he'll cleave you in two with the sword, or will it be the dagger slid subtly between your rattling ribs? I love watching lovers torn asunder. It's almost always their own faults. You two are lovers now, aren't you?

I had said Adalbrand was too forgiving. I had accused him of it. But he said he would not forgive this.

Forgive? Why not ask him for the moon and the stars and all that lies beyond the Rim. This is marvelous. You really think he could still care about you — a tarnished vessel, a ruined blossom. How adorably flawed of you. I like delusion for you. Do continue.

Forgiveness is a real thing.

Is it, paladin? Will your God forgive you when he hears you've been sharing a vessel with a vile one? Will he welcome you to his embrace?

One can hardly help who one must room with, whether it be bed bugs, fleas, or the damned.

I shuddered as I gently pushed Brindle aside to check Sir Adalbrand's prone form. He had passed out but he was still breathing. Grimly, I moved him into a more comfortable position.

Brindle circled him with gently padding paws, sniffing all around him.

You really have a way with the menfolk, sweetling. Do you always make them sick, or is it just this green stick of a man?

I was reasonably sure it was realizing he'd aided a devil that had done him in.

You could try to pretend to be an innocent victim of my malevolence. That might be cute.

I *was* an innocent victim.

The demon's laughter rang through my mind.

You are all complicit in deeds that mock you and ruin you, like puppets danced into a fire making flowery bows and curtseys all the way into the inferno.

Saints bless it. I'd lost him, then. Barely had him for a moment and then lost him. Somehow it felt worse than anything else so far. It twisted and wrenched inside me as if I had swallowed a brick and it was making its way through my insides, the corners of it catching as it went.

I stood abruptly just as Hefertus came running at full speed straight through the cluster of paladins praying. He took in Adalbrand's prone form and my stricken face and then uttered a foul curse.

I nodded my agreement as our mouths twisted into matching frowns.

"What did he do?"

"He healed my dog. And learned something he didn't like," I said grimly. The one nice thing about Sir Hefertus was that he didn't bother with niceties or feelings. I didn't need to spare him.

He grunted. "Fool. That could have waited."

I nodded but I hovered over Adalbrand, not sure how to help him.

"Marvelous work, Prince Paladin!" Sir Sorken boomed out, striding toward us.

Prayers had ended — probably thanks to Hefertus scattering the other paladins like a dog running through a flock of pigeons. There was a note of tension in the room.

"Do we look at the new puzzle to twist the room next, or do we go straight to the next challenge for the cup?" Sir Owalan asked, bouncing from foot to foot. Either he did not notice Adalbrand had passed out or he did not care. "Maybe we can just keep turning it and forget the challenge entirely. We'd get out that way, right? And we could try again later."

"I rather think not," Sir Coriand said, with a cheerful smile. "The challenges are there for a reason and they must be completed. Our cups are only partially filled. Do you want to find the Cup of Tears? Then we must fill them entirely. You've read the words written here. '*Our hearts spoke out our hopes and our souls bore the cost, the man and the spirit and all that was lost. Bold together we race where no others have trod, for we are more than men, we have become Saints. Choose now holy vessel. Be careful, be clear, for the bones of others will root out your fear, wash your cup with sorrow, bathe your vessel with blood, but choose your gift wisely, be it fire or mud.*' Likely, we will find the next stanza of this verse at our next station, and if you want the Cup of Tears, then we must follow it, or fail."

"No," I said quietly, and very deliberately, I stood over Adalbrand's body, facing the others. They drew together in the stained light, a flock of shrieking crows, a gaggle of squabbling gulls. I hated them in that moment for their self-serving heartlessness.

Oooh. Look who likes to defy authority.

Sir Coriand shed his cheerful, dreamy-eyed exterior like a snake sheds its skin. It made him seem to grow before me; certainly his shadow swelled.

"I'm afraid no is not an option, Beggar. We have come for the cup. We will receive it. And you have no choice but to go with us on this quest."

"There's always a choice," I said quietly, and I drew my sword.

Oh, the sweet drama! Trouble in the ranks, holy against holy, it makes my shriveled heart sing! Fight, rip, tear, little snack!

Sir Coriand stepped forward quietly but his eyes were fixed on mine and I felt a thrill of fear settle down my spine. Who was this Engineer really? Behind him, his bone-and-rag golem shifted, reminding me that in any fight, it was not the elderly knight I'd battle but his massive creation.

He lifted two fingers in a mockery of blessing and said, "Those of you unwilling to give up the quest before we've even begun should go now."

Did his fellow Engineer have nothing to say to that? I shot him a glance.

"Yes, yes," Sir Sorken said, still wearing the skin of cheerful acquiescence. His eyes held a glimmer I did not like. "Right you are, come along, brothers. This way."

He strode down the well-worn path toward the clock and the open room, not even glancing back, and without a word, the High Saint and the Penitent followed. The Majester sent one shivery glance backward and then he followed, too. They stalked off like four cats — not quite wanting to walk together but headed in the same direction all the same.

"Sir Hefertus?" Sir Coriand asked quietly as the others disappeared from view.

"The fountain is still working. That's a good thing, right?" I heard Sir Owalan saying. Already his voice was distant.

"If the Vagabond has doubts, then I have them too," Hefertus said, shooting a glance at me that practically screamed, "W*hat are we doing?*"

What are *you doing, Victoriana? Simply throwing yourself into the gears to jam them is no plan.*

This monastery was wrong from top to bottom and I was finished complying with any of it. I'd already lost a friend. I did not want to lose my soul in the bargain.

But must you lose your head, also? Think!

Hefertus cleared his throat, looking between us, one hand twisting through his topknot of golden hair. "The Poisoned Saint has worn himself out and we can hardly leave him here alone."

"If the other trial was any indication, then we cannot leave him here *at all*," Sir Coriand said reasonably. "It will take all of us or none of us in the next task and the clock is ticking."

"And the dog?" Hefertus asked, eyeing Brindle warily.

As well he should.

I laughed — a grim, gallows laugh.

Both the male paladins glanced at me, Hefertus nervously, Coriand grimly, as if I were a mistake he must set right.

"The dog must come along," the older paladin said. "It was there last time. I think you understand, Hefertus, that we must go through this trial. I think you see that."

Hefertus looked back and forth between us.

"This place is evil." I felt so tired. The kind of tired you only feel when it is you against all others.

"A wild assumption," Sir Coriand said, with his big trust-me grin spread wide. "I see no evil here, except the poor lost thing stuck in a trap on the ceiling — and if these monks were evil, why would they have trapped one like a mouse?" His eyes narrowed, and while his easy smile never flickered, I felt the moment that he shifted his emotions. "And of course, Lady Paladin, the one you brought with you."

I felt the blood drain from my face.

One of the voices in my mind — maybe both — spat one curse after another, some foreign to me, others familiar. I tried to block them out.

"What?" Hefertus asked carefully.

I shifted my feet. But I knew myself. And I knew he was seeing the truth of it all over my face.

Be on guard!

Sir Coriand delivered the killing blow. "A dangerous game to play, Beggar. Are you even a paladin? No paladin I've ever known has been so cozy with a denizen of hell."

Hefertus turned his body to me, blocking Coriand out. "Deny his charge."

I swallowed. "I cannot."

He paled. "Treachery," Sir Hefertus breathed out. "Vile treachery."

He made a stumbling lunge toward me and I pivoted out of the way. He was wrong about me. At least, in the way that mattered.

Watch out!

"Hefertu —" I began and then something grabbed my foot and yanked hard.

The room spun upside down. My braid swept back and forth over the mosaic while Hefertus turned abruptly upside down and looked down at me in disgust. I kicked against what was holding me with my free leg but it was solid as bone and after a second, it was manacled in place, too.

Hefertus's boot drew back and kicked, and for a moment all I saw was black and all I felt was pain. I forced myself to stay aware through the pounding in my head. I must not lose my grip on my sword. I must not lose consciousness.

My mouth was full of warm iron. I spat blood. My face was on fire.

"Suture will bring her, and Cleft has the dog," Sir Coriand said calmly, as if he routinely kidnapped other paladins with the help of his golems. "If you would be so good as to carry your friend. He deserves more honor than a golem can offer and we'll be sure he's safe enough in the trial to come."

"Of course," Hefertus said, and I could hardly blame him. Wouldn't I do the same myself if I'd discovered a friend was hiding a demon from me?

The golem holding my ankles began to walk, swinging me side to side with his long strides. I wiggled in his grasp, trying to catch sight of what was happening.

Hefertus collected Adalbrand's unconscious form and shot me a death glare as he slung the man over his shoulders. Behind him, Cleft carried Brindle by the foot. My dog yipped and growled, sounding desperate and panicked.

Well, isn't this a treat. Paladin versus paladin and not a one who wants to be near you, demon consort.

He laughed long and haunting in my mind as I blinked back tears of frustration, carried to a fate I did not want and had not chosen.

The golem's strides sent me heaving back and forth, an angry pendulum. I tried to twist to see what the locked door might reveal, but Suture carried me with my back to the door. Instead, I had a good look at the clock. Our cups were slotted in place in an odd pattern I didn't have time to analyze. What worried me was that they still glowed slightly with an eye-twisting dark light, as if with a power untouched by the God.

We passed it in a moment and found the open door. Cleft went through before me and in my mind, the demon roared out the translation to the next verse of the poem. Or the prophecy. Or the spell. Whichever it may be.

No power is priceless,
No honor unearned,
From storehouse bring wisely,
Add gift to the churn,
A sacrifice given,
An offering made,

What no longer serves you,
Is the price you must pay.

Oh lovely. More sacrifices. I gripped my sword hilt doubly hard, wondering if I'd be able to fight upside down with my feet anchored. If there were sacrifices required, I had a bad feeling that they'd be happy to be rid of me. I would not go like a lamb to slaughter.

And what about Adalbrand? He was in no position to be dragged into a fight. I hadn't expected those golems to surprise me — a terrible oversight, to be sure. I should have known better. It was always the quiet ones.

Well, not always. I knew a man once who sang while he burned cities. He wasn't quiet at all.

And I hadn't expected Hefertus to turn on me after he'd sworn to stand with me.

Yes, well, you didn't exactly tell him that he was making an alliance with two knights, one paladin defuncti and one demon vivius.

Cute nickname, rotting corpse. I think I'll call myself Vivius from now on.

There was a sigh in my brain that sounded as world-weary as I felt.

But there was no time to explore any of this. We rounded the curved hall and came out into the great room, and even from my view — upside down — it was spectacular.

When this room had been carved from the rock, someone had said, "I want a vaulted ceiling and a vaulted floor. Make me islands of bleached white skulls of every creature you can find and the spines of great fish. Then splash some purple light around. You know. For mourning and repentance. And don't forget the books. There should be lots and lots of books. Shelves. Stacks. You know, every way you can think of to include books is what there should be."

Just like in the previous room, someone had drilled holes in the ceiling, but half of these had been fit somehow with purple glass and the light shone down half purple and half white.

In our liturgy, purple was the color of mourning. And my heart was mourning with the purple. I was mourning that eleven paladins had entered this place and only one seemed to still have his honor intact, and that one was being borne into this place whether he willed it or not by a silent servant.

I love this place entirely. Do you know what it is?

If it was a library, it was a terrible one. The curving walls of the cylindrical vault were lined with books, books, and more books on shelves innumerable. But how anyone would access them, or how they could possibly read them all or even find what they were looking for, seemed like an impossible task. There were deep grooves between some of the shelves, but they were too far apart for steps, and wove too strange a track for a moving ladder. Some spiraled high into the shelves above, others dipped low below and still others wove through the center, crossing at times. The books were shelved between them, positioned to adjust to the widening and narrowing of the space. Since some were higher than my forearm and others as short and narrow as my pinkie finger, there were no shortage of volumes for every space. Even so, the uneven shelving only added to the general look of chaos.

At least the books had been preserved. By all rights, they ought to have crumbled away to nothing in the centuries since the monastery ... demonary? ... was lost to the world.

It's a grimivior.

That was entirely unhelpful.

Like a holy repository but the opposite, I would think, my girl.

No, no, that makes it sound so dull. It's a reservoir, like a place to hold a great deal of water, only this is a reservoir for grimoires — books of demonology and the teachings of the arcane. And the swell and rise of the mortal understanding of all things finds its climax here.

So it was a room of evil. And writings about evil.

Overly simplistic, as always, snackling, and that is why you are worth nothing but to be devoured whole. Who are you to discount Viscoth's Soul Anatomy *or Corthasasm's* Holy Dissipation *or even Fragralot's* The Debauchery of the Nine Saints and the Siphoning of Secrets Closely Held?

Based only on the titles, it occurred to me that if I were to light a candle and set it against those shelves, that act alone might elevate me to Sainthood.

Ha! That's adorable. Look down.

It was hard to look down when I was hanging upside down. Much easier to look up into the complicated silver-edged buttressing where the shelves ended in the distant shadows of a wealth of fish skeletons large enough to swallow a whole horse. Easier still to view the central pillar that rose up in the middle of the cylindrical room. It was white and thick with carved statues of men and women who were half human and half creature. They were layered one above the other and all of them reached upward with hands and mouths as if waiting for the heavens to feed them ... or screaming in despair, perhaps. I understood the sentiment. Oddly, the pillar did not contain books.

I tried to crane my neck to look down and only caught a yawning chasm of ghastly books falling away as far as the eye could see.

Exactly. They drilled to the heart of the rock. And what did they find down there in the bones of the earth?

The world was built in the bones of the God. Maybe that's what they found.

Or is it built on the sediment of hell?

Fear quickened within me — partly in horror at his proposition, but mostly because Suture had shambled to the edge of the drop and was holding me over it. Emptiness yawned beneath me. And possibly so did the sediment of hell or whatever we'd just been talking about.

Breathe, Victoriana.

Breathe, my girl. Easy, steady breaths. Fear is not your friend today.

Friend or no, he was bent on having me.

Not before I do. No fear for you, little sweet. You are mine to devour.

Well, at least I was popular among the things that wanted to kill, rend, and tear.

Sooo popular.

The cliff edge was ringed by little walkways that were a touch more narrow than I'd like, and each one ended at an island. I turned my head to the side and realized the walkways were more like arms and the arms fit into the slots between the shelves. The ones that looped and wrapped every which way. So they accessed the shelves in some way, then. That's nice. Maybe I'd get to see them operate before I dropped to my death.

The islands were ringed with railings, contained their own stacks of books — of course — and at the center, each one bore a small altar woven of bone. On each altar were candles. Unlit. But candles all the same. The same magic that preserved this place must have preserved them, too, or vermin would have eaten them centuries ago. There were dozens on each altar.

"When you're all on an island, I can throw the switch and it will begin," Sir Sorken called out, pointing at a complicated mechanism attached to his island on the far end of the semicircle.

I tried to trace the way the mechanism reached to each platform but I found it too hard to follow from where I hung. Sir Sorken leaned casually beside the switch — if that was what it was — and beside that was a handle attached to a gear, carved to look like leaping fish within delicate sprays of water rather than a practical machine. Of course.

"I think it's important to balance out the weight," Sir Sorken announced. "Just a theory, but possibly an important one when we dangle over a drop, hmm? Set the Poisoned Saint on his own platform, Sir Hefertus. I left room down at the end for him and the Beggar, but you're the heaviest and I need you in the middle."

Hefertus looked torn, glancing from the island platform on which he was meant to place Adalbrand to the island he was meant to occupy. They were very far apart. If he agreed, Adalbrand would be completely vulnerable.

As things stood now, the islands were as follows from Sir Sorken on one end to an empty island on the other: one, Sir Sorken on the far right; two, the platform he was indicating was for Hefertus; three, a platform holding the Majester that Sir Coriand was hurrying to join; four, a platform shared by Sir Owalan and the High Saint; five, the one meant for Adalbrand; and six, the empty platform — for me, perhaps?

"What about the dog?" Hefertus protested, hesitating.

"The dog will stay with me," Sir Sorken boomed out as if he were pardoning the canine of his sins.

Ha. He wishes he had that kind of power. And that's the thing with you paladins. You are so convinced of your worthiness that your arrogance trips you up, and oh, but it's a delight to watch. Pure drama! Pure pleasure. Please don't die, snackling. I'd hate to miss all of this.

Because of course I was only living to entertain him.

Cleft brought the dog over to Sir Sorken as Hefertus gently laid Adalbrand on his platform. At least he was kind to his friend, even if he was an idiot for not siding with me on this.

For a moment, I felt hope as Cleft lowered Brindle.

That's right! Let me at him! I could feast on stringy old paladin if required.

But Sir Sorken had been ready. As Cleft lowered my doggy friend, he put his great stone hand over Brindle's muzzle, and lightning-quick, Sir Sorken tied Brindle's mouth with rope and cinched the rope to his belt, which he fitted around the dog's neck. Together, they laid Brindle on the altar and tied him in place.

I make a terrible sacrifice. You need to tell them! Tell them that killing dogs is a crime no one will forgive. Not even the prince of demons himself.

I thought the prince of demons didn't forgive, Sir Branson said curiously.

Now was *not* the time to argue theological technicalities.

I cleared my throat. I couldn't tell if that got anyone's attention. It was Suture who determined which way I faced, not me.

"Brothers," I spoke loudly, carrying. I'm no orator. In fact, addressing them all made me as nervous as dangling over this library hole. I persevered. "We are not finding a holy cup in this place. It is not making us Saints. Surely, you see that. A murderer walks among us and this place is made for an unholy purpose."

There was a silence and then Sir Owalan said a little awkwardly, "You're spinning something out of nothing, Beggar. The Seer died at the hands of nefarious forces — a demon that the High Saint tells me you refused to cast out. Sir Kodelai died trying to rectify that, and the Inquisitor was a nasty accident. You have to expect that any quest worth performing would be rife with trial and difficulty. We cannot all be Saints. Only the worthy."

"And those of us not worthy?" I asked but there was no answer.

I felt like cursing.

Go ahead. Who's stopping you?

I rather hope she's holding back for my sake.

You won't be here forever, wretched corpse. One day she'll be free to be exactly as loose as she likes.

"Let us pray," Sir Sorken intoned, and as Suture carried me roughly to my platform, they spoke together, "For what we are about to receive, we thank you, oh God."

I felt like I was being readied for dinner. Dog and Beggar. What a treat.

If only you knew, snackling, how I've craved you, how sweet your soul would be upon my lips. It would go down like aged wine.

Because that wasn't at all creepy.

The platform rocked as Suture's feet hit it and I got a nice up-close look at my altar. I tried to read the words on it, but I didn't have to — Sir Coriand was already calling them out as the platform trembled beneath me. If it broke, would the golem drop me? Would I be able to catch the edge in time?

"Your altars read, 'A worthy price you'll pay, and on this altar lay, or your soul to us you'll lose, in punishment for your ruse.'"

Wait. Hold on now.

"You put my dog on your altar!" I called out, but inside I was more offended by all this terrible poetry than I was by that fact.

You think my imprisonment and possible slaughter is less offensive than bad rhymes?

I wasn't the one who had rhymed "pay" with "lay."

"Everyone ready, then?" Sir Sorken asked calmly, ignoring my accusation. "Ready yourself, Suture. You'll drop the girl and retreat the moment I throw the switch. There's a good construct."

And then there was a squealing sound and I screwed up my face against it, as if that did anything beyond blurring the spines of the books in front of my nose.

The golem dropped me and I managed to angle my shoulder enough to roll with the drop rather than damaging my face a second time. I felt the platform sway wildly as he leapt from it, and then lurch to one side.

I clawed my way to stand, keeping my sword braced in both hands, and when I was able to find my feet, my island platform was already shuttling down its track around the curve of the cylindrical room. It bore me upward in a spiral. The central pillar was to one side of me and a whirl of books to the other.

All of the platforms were moving at once, some of them spiraling upward slowly, like Sir Sorken's and mine, others dipping quickly downward or ranging in a roughly flat line.

Sir Adalbrand's platform was one of those moving in roughly a straight path, which meant that even though he'd started behind me, my upward trajectory was negating my head start. If I timed things just right and had nerves of steel, I could drop down to his platform when our paths crossed.

Maybe.

I sheathed my sword and started tearing at the buckles of my breastplate and other armor. I needed to be *light.* Any extra weight and this might not work.

My tabard I discarded with its belt, my breastplate followed, pauldrons and gauntlets after that. I'd already been lightly armored, but now I was stripped of all but my leather pants, filmy undertunic, my boots, and my sword. I wasn't giving up the sword.

Not even if it drags you into the depths?

Not even then.

I toast your courage, and if you fail, I'll inhabit those you love best and eat their hearts raw.

Lovely. I'd better not fail.

I clambered up to the top of the delicate railing surrounding my platform and my belly lurched at the great distance below. Carefully, I turned so that I was crouched with my back facing outward, peering down at the space between my boots. I felt wildly off-balance.

Because you are, you fool! You won't make the catch and you'll fall to your death.

But now the platforms were crossing and I had no choice. There was no way I was leaving Adalbrand alone to face this challenge. What if he woke and found himself drifting with no clue as to what to do or where he was? He might judge me now. Might hate me. But he didn't deserve that.

I lowered myself so that I was hanging by my hands, tensed the muscles of my lower back tightly to lever my legs backward, and then the moment I saw Adalbrand below, I thrust my legs forward as I let go of the platform and tensed hard to draw my arms forward, too, stabilizing me in the air.

Books whooshed by. My heart was in my throat. I had eyes only for the edge of his platform.

Here it was. I reached for it, caught it —

— and felt the fingers of my right hand slip while my left found purchase. I swung wildly from my left hand, the newly knit bone in that arm screaming with the effort of holding me in place. Frantic, I clawed up with leg and arm.

Your sword! Unbuckle your sword, it's dragging you down!

It was dragging. I felt the weight of it.

But I didn't dare let go. If any time was a time for prayer, it was now.

I skipped the niceties.

"Merciful God make me strong and sure. Help me up onto the platform. Your healer needs me."

I wasn't entirely sure about that part. But the God must have been. A renewed burst of energy filled me and this time when my right arm grappled for purchase, it held, and I pulled with all the might of my wide shoulders and levered myself up and over the fish-spine edge of the platform to fall in a lump on the other side.

Chapter Twenty-Six
Vagabond Paladin

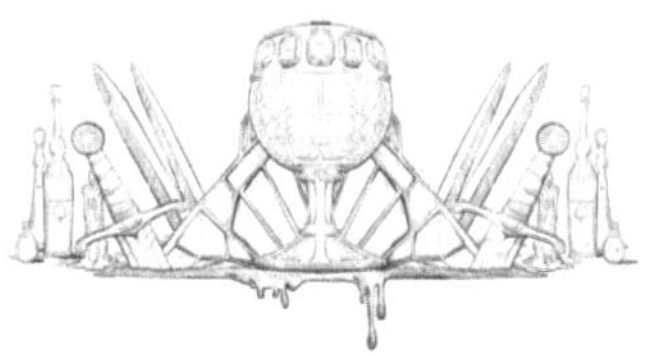

I lay on my back for a long moment, heaving in gasps of breath, watching the lights above me twinkle from white to purple to white while the smell of old leather and vellum filled my nose and with it the sweet, sweet knowledge that I was alive.

Yes! Sir Branson cheered in my mind, and for once I didn't mind the dreadful laugh of the demon because I was there to hear it.

With shaking limbs, I turned on my side and saw Sir Adalbrand slumped where they'd laid him. My heart twinged with guilt. It was healing my dog that stole his strength and finding my secret that ruined him.

Well. Good things never did last. And at least I could keep him from becoming a casualty of carelessness or of malice, the way the Inquisitor had been. At least I could guard him while he came back to his senses.

Gently, I eased him into a more comfortable position, untangling his limbs and settling his armor into places where it wouldn't dig into his flesh — or wouldn't dig as badly. Should I remove it? He likely wouldn't thank me for that.

I pulled myself to my feet and tried to assess our situation. Books were scattered on the floor. I rifled through them but they were written in languages I didn't know. I had knowledge of Deus Grandi, Aurelian, and a few words of Uxanthal. I could read Formal and Ancient Deus Grandi. These books were written in none of those, and some had such an inordinately different script — a flowing kind that looked more like a series of mountain ranges than actual words, and another that looked like pictures of squat little men who wanted to tunnel through my spleen and make a temple there — that I was sure they were all in different languages from each other.

Were I to take any from the shelves, I think it would be safe to say it would be nearly impossible to find a book I could even read, much less one that would be of value to me.

They're all of value, you foolish child, you delectable innocent. They're grimoires. *I told you. They're primers in the arcane — or more detailed tomes. They're manuals for the creation, care, nurturing, and calling of dark souls. Would you like to peer into the depths? Here is your chance. Care to build a jhinn of smoke and despair? Your wish is that creature's command.*

Unless there were some on banishing, I wasn't interested.

The demon sounded disgusted. *Just flip through a few. There might be pictures for fools who have only your limited education and brain power.*

How flattering. I started flipping through the one with the flowing script and as soon as I saw the first picture, I flung it over the side of the moving platform. Hefertus yelled out a muffled curse.

"There are people down here!" he roared up to me.

So there were. And there were madmen who had taken time to painstakingly detail *that.* If I ever met the author, judgment would be swift and brutal. His feet would not take a step before I claimed his head.

The demon muttered a string of curses. *Listen, you poxy milk-*

faced droll, if you throw them all away, you won't be able to use one, and you need one for this rite.

I froze. So he knew what this was.

There was silence in my mind.

Had he known all along? Had he been lying? Blood roared hot and powerful in my ears until I could hear nothing else.

I will find out, my girl. Have a little patience.

And then the voices in my mind were suddenly opaque to me. I could only feel the edges of murmurs that sounded like distant arguing.

I took that moment to look out from my platform. It was slowing a little, though it still moved in a strange up and down spiral. Around me, the others moved on their platforms, too. I caught a glance of Sir Coriand snatching a book from a shelf as he swept by, his hair flowing behind him in strands of gnarled snow. With another glance, I caught Sir Owalan sitting on his altar, feverishly flipping through another book. He was hunched over it like a carrion bird guarding his prize.

"What do you think it means that we must offer up what doesn't serve us?" the High Saint called into the room. "I serve the God. I am served by nothing."

I could almost hear Sir Sorken's sigh when he boomed back. "It means something no longer useful to you, High Saint."

"Like an ear?" the High Saint called back, clearly confused.

"I'd say that would be a safe bet for you, High Saint, as you are indeed a poor listener."

I almost snorted at that.

"Did he mean that?" the High Saint whispered to Sir Owalan, but as with everything else, even his whispering was obvious and overly obnoxious.

"You tell me," the Penitent said, annoyed. "Do you think it will help things to hack your own ear off?"

"It might."

"Then please, be my invited guest. I'll lend you my belt knife if your own is not sharp enough for the task."

"The one in your arm?"

"God have mercy, Saint, you try my patience."

They cycled farther away from me, and then I heard Hefertus sigh and his platform stilled, glowed a soft barely there purple, and began to drift back toward the platform.

"Oh, excellent work, Prin —" Sir Coriand began to say, but his words were cut off by a groan, as a platform — the empty one that I was meant to be in — suddenly ground to a halt, stilled, and then lurched from its track, plummeting downward. It glanced against Sir Sorken's platform, leaving an eruption of curses behind it, and kept falling like the stone it was. It seemed a very long time before we heard it hit the floor. If there even was a floor down there.

My heart was caught in my chest and I was frozen in place as I watched it fall.

This time, it was the Majester who cursed. And he went on cursing. And on and on, and then his cursing ended abruptly in a sigh.

"What was ... should we assume that for every one of us who succeeds, another will fall?" the High Saint asked, his querulous voice rising sharply at the end.

"Or it simply fell because it was empty," Hefertus called down.

While we were watching the original platform fall, his had returned back to the ledge where it had started. He'd already exited the platform — smart man — and was standing there beside Suture. The golem's eyes glowed dully, as if he were a bored child forced to watch a proceeding of his elders. Hefertus leaned easily against him like he was leaning against a tree. Little bits of rag stirred against his shoulder and I shuddered.

"Hurry up, you lot. All you need is to pick a book, make a sacrifice, and light your candle. There's a tinder box in the little drawer at the bottom of the altar." He yawned as he said it, as if he, too, were terribly bored.

I checked my — our — altar. There was, indeed, a small

drawer hidden by carved vines and flowers. When I slid it open, there was a tinderbox within, just as he said.

"You light the candle last," Sir Coriand scolded the High Saint, looking down over his rail to the other man's platform, "and you should choose your tome carefully. These things have consequences."

I caught a glimpse of him as his platform crossed on the other side. He was running a finger along the spines of the books as they passed, clearly noting the titles for those that were marked. I didn't think I could read that fast even if it was all in my own language. Sometimes I forgot how formidable the Engineers were.

I put my head in my hands for a moment to think. What was I to do now?

I felt oddly light with most of my armor gone.

Gone forever, it would seem. The cost to replace that alone ... it would be years before I could beg or borrow enough for a whole set. I might be able to appeal to the aspect. Some paladins kept extra odds and ends. A pauldron only in need of a small repair here. Most of a breastplate if someone could get those dents out and didn't mind that jagged edge over there. They might be willing to part with them. After all, the whole point of our Aspect was that we met the world with open hands. Those who wanted what we had could take it. Those who could, would give to us what they could spare. And the God watched over all of it, his guidance supreme.

I sighed. There would be no more armor anytime soon.

Right now, I needed wisdom more than armor anyway. I had only inklings about this place. I had no understanding of it at all. Should I try to play this game with the others or should I keep refusing? What would be the consequences of refusal? Of complicity?

I bowed my head and put my hands, open, on my knees. Perhaps the God would bring me insight.

I heard a doggy squeal and my head whipped up.

"Brindle?" I called, and there was a snarl and the snap of jaws.

I was on my feet, sword in hand, in the next breath, but I couldn't even see Sir Sorken's platform from where I was. I'd lost track of whether it was above or below me, and the vault echoed so much that I couldn't find it by sound alone. I frantically searched in every direction.

My mind was bombarded with curses. A few were familiar, but most were far more foul and horrific than anything I'd ever heard.

"Brindle?" I called again, more tense. "Sir Sorken? What's going on?"

I still couldn't locate them. There was a snapping sound and a man's grunt and then I heard Sir Sorken's booming voice.

"Back! Sit!"

I felt my eyebrows lift.

The dog lives. Though it was a near thing. I think the demon may have lent him inordinate strength. They can do that when they're very upset.

Sir Branson's words were drowned out by more curses.

"Sir Sorken?" I called out. "What are you doing to my dog?"

More curses.

And then I saw his face appear over the edge of a platform well above mine. "That animal is accursed!"

He tried to kill us. He tried to sacrifice the dog as the thing that does not serve him.

Above me, his platform trembled.

He chose poorly. Both because I plan to eat him alive and because the altar takes inferior sacrifices very personally.

"Sorken, my dear friend," Sir Coriand called from somewhere right below me.

"Present!" Sorken yelled out.

"I'd not tempt fate, my lad. Only real sacrifices accepted."

"It would seem that is true. The altar will not accept a mangy, worthless dog."

"Sorken!" I barked. "That is *my* dog you're trying to kill. I demand you stop at once."

From the ledge, I heard Hefertus snort in disbelief, like I didn't have the right to defend the dog when it also held a demon.

"Tried to kill," Sorken said tightly, as if distracted by something. His head had disappeared but I heard the telltale sound of knife on flint. "I am no longer trying."

The cursing continued as the platform rocked wildly. I tensed my jaw. I did not want Brindle to die — but even I had to admit that the demon within him could not go on living.

Excuse you, but I certainly can, snackling.

If we're about to die, I should tell you what I learned from him, Sir Branson said grimly. *This place is exactly as you suspected. Tell her how you mistranslated.*

There was a long pause and a feeling like a slap inside my own head.

Tell her.

I mistranslated.

Tell her how.

If the demon spoke, it was too quiet for me to hear.

Then I *shall tell. You'll recall he read you a poem on a plaque at the bottom of the steps.*

I did recall that, yes. And now, I was sweating and clenching my jaw as the platform the dog was on shivered again.

Our hearts spoke our hopes and our souls bore the cost, the man and the spirit and all that was lost. Bold together we race where no other has trod, for we are more than men, we have become gods.

I tilted my head to the side. That wasn't how that read. He'd said, "we have become Saints."

Yes, he did. It was a lie.

A lie that the Engineers had gone along with.

Perhaps they are not as fluent in Ancient Indul as they claim. Perhaps they were shaky on the translation.

Or perhaps they found the fiction useful. But what did it mean? To become gods?

Sir Branson seemed to grow more agitated as he explained. *To blaspheme. To rise above the God himself. To play at being his equal.*

The dog's platform lurched forward suddenly and my breath caught in my throat, but it moved backward up along its former trajectory, reaching the cliff edge again in record time. Brindle sprang from the platform to the rock beyond, all signs that he had ever been held captive gone. Despite the weight of two extra souls, he was light on his feet and his tongue lolled from his mouth happily.

That's what I learned, my girl. This place, as you suspected, was never meant to create Saints at all.

And thinking so is as foolish as when you can't tell our voices apart, snackling. What kind of paladins are they making these days? Soft, gooey-centered ones. In my day, you were rage and wrath and the blade of the God coming down in power. Now you can't tell the difference between the dead and the demonic, between an empty monastery and an empty arcanery.

A ... a what?

I flinched at the growl that echoed through my mind, low and rumbling.

One moment.

"Sir Sorken," Hefertus acknowledged from the platform, and my eyes drifted to see him grab Brindle by the scruff and hold him in place.

"Well, I was pushed to hurry a little, but I'm happy enough with my grimoire," Sir Sorken said easily as he reached that space, clapping Hefertus on the shoulder. "What did you choose, Prince?"

Hefertus held up a large, blue-bound book with a hand missing a finger. Where once his pinky had been, there was now only a bloodless stump.

"Gave your finger, hmm? No longer serving you?"

"No longer serving anyone," Hefertus grunted.

"And your book, hmm? *By Light of the Divine, Moon Into Moon*. What is this?"

"I think it's a book of air elementals of the High Snow Desert," Hefertus said easily.

Sir Sorken snorted loudly. "Very fitting, Prince. How did you choose it?"

Hefertus shrugged. He hardly seemed to notice Brindle still growling in his grip. "I asked the God to choose for me and this book fell off the shelf into my hand." He paused. "Why did you call yours a grimoire?"

"Because that is what it is, Sir Hefertus. A grimoire. Dedicated to the calling up of strong demons."

Hefertus flinched backward, his eyes narrowing. "Are you having fun at my expense?"

"Never. Give the dog to my golem. He'll mind him while the Beggar pleads her case. If she doesn't come back, then we'll decide what to do with it. Wringing its neck might be best, given the circumstances."

Suture grabbed Brindle in a huge bearhug and began to stride toward the corridor as the dog tried to lick his rag-and-bone face.

"Come, Sir Hefertus. Let's go see if the door is open or shut. If it's open, we'll brew tea. If it's shut, we'll come back and tease the others for taking so long."

I gripped the lip of my platform as tightly as I could. What would happen when I could no longer see Brindle. Would I hear him still?

He still owed me an answer about what an arcanery was.

A place dedicated to the worship of demons, of course, he said in my mind and my blood ran cold. *But you knew that. Or suspected it. You knew there was no way this place could be of the God. You know that the evils playing out here weren't accidents. Didn't you?*

I did.

But why make so grand a place for this? It seemed to be made for a single purpose and could accommodate no more than a dozen. Why the sublime carving and glorious decoration? Why the beauty everywhere?

Is it beauty, my girl? Is it even there? Or is it a trick of the mind, like seeing your faces on the faces of the statues? Mayhap the beauty you imagine is made in your dreaming. Mayhap this place is nothing but a crumbling grave of bones and horrible traps.

His voice was growing fainter as he was carried away.

But why build an arcanery at all? Why build a house of worship where so few worshippers would ever set foot?

Who ever said an arcanery was a house of worship? You silly little snack. You foolish meal. How do you worship the God?

By devoting myself to him and doing as he commands.

That's a weak, petty worship. Worship is giving yourself entirely over to something. And sometimes it turns into creation. After all, don't you mortals consider the act of love a kind of worship? And does it not create?

But demons couldn't create. That was one of the tenets of the faith. They could only twist what was already created.

Unless you are the hands of the devil.

And his voice faded past hearing, leaving me trembling as I realized what he was saying.

We were completing trials and tasks, solving puzzles, making offerings, confessing sins. What were all those things added up together? He was right that there was worship being done. But more than that, it felt as though we were brewing something. Something made from many parts like the stews they made along the southern shores, full to the edges with spices, meats of such varied sources that it was best not inquire, and more types of vegetation than I'd ever dreamed could exist. I had asked one street vendor what her secret ingredient was after she offered us a half a bowl for free.

"There are eighty-six secret ingredients and the last one is love," she'd cackled toothlessly.

What were we brewing here with our many ingredients and the fear and greed we'd brought with us to this place?

I looked down at my hands. They looked clean enough. And yet my mind insisted they were stained. Stained by deeds done unknowingly.

Did it make a difference if I kept doing them now that I knew? Did that somehow make me *more* guilty?

The world felt as though it was moving in slow motion. That what had come before might not be as it had seemed but rather conjured by my own mind as part of a trap to hook me and drag me into the most evil of deeds terrified me. Could I trust my own senses at all?

Could I trust that I was suspended on a stone platform over a great vault?

Could I trust that I was seeing the Majester fall by, eyes wide, fingers grasping at nothing?

Wait.

I gasped and lunged forward.

I was a second too late to grab at him. A second too stunned.

I caught his eye as he streaked past silently, felt the jagged terror in the black gleam of his pupil, and then he was gone, plummeting past into the darkness below, narrowly missing the central pillar in his descent.

Like with the platform, it was a very long time before I heard him hit the ground. I almost missed the sound behind the hammering of my heart.

My breath was caught in my throat, one of my hands pressed to my chest, the other to my mouth.

God have mercy.

I looked up and saw Sir Coriand looking down, horror painting his expression.

"He leapt," the Engineer said, his voice soft, bereft. "I didn't realize he would leap until it was too late."

My common sense was telling me that was usually the way with suicide. I'd buried so many villagers who'd died the same way that I'd lost count. Usually, it was done with their ragged friends and family clustered around me, wet-eyed and snuffling in the cold and wind while Sir Branson said a prayer and tried to tell them that it wasn't a demon, just despair. As if that were any better. Some people were just never made for this world, he'd say sadly. And then he'd brew tea like Sir Coriand and Sir Sorken did. And he'd offer it around and pray with those who could use a moment's comfort. Offer whatever coins were had to the bereaved and move on.

My common sense was also reminding me that Majester Generals were made to lead armies. Their power from the God had influences over groups, like when he made us acutely aware of our enemies while we were fighting for our lives in the last trial. Did it also go the other direction? Could our suspicions of him and our judgment have cracked his mind? He hadn't been wearing his tabard today. Had he lost the will to go on? Could this place with its fiendish intentions have slid deep under his thoughts and pulled on levers buried deep?

All that sounded logical. Possible.

But as I murmured the prayer for the dead, and heard it echoed around the chamber to me, I thought that perhaps there was more to this story.

Because Sir Coriand's platform was drifting back to the ledge, his candle bright, his tome chosen. And whatever gift he'd made at the altar wasn't one I could see.

Was it possible that it was the *Majester* who was no longer serving Sir Coriand? And if it was, who else would he decide no longer had a right to live?

I shuddered, backed up a step, and then another, and then I sat down hard on the floor across from Adalbrand and I put my naked sword across my knees. Every muscle of my body was tensed. And it all felt dreadful and cold as the decay that comes after death.

"Almost done, brothers?" I heard Sir Coriand call out gently.

"The High Saint can't reply," Sir Owalan called back a little unsteadily. "Otherwise I think he might have screamed when the Majester went flying by, poor broken man. I confess to shaky hands myself. I'm not certain I can light my candle with them, but yes, the High Saint has his book chosen." He laughed shakily. "It's massive and it's bound with metal latches. Serious business. I think he gave his voice. I suppose it no longer served him." He bit down on a hysterical laugh. "Oh, Saints. Oh, Saints." I heard a knife striking flint. "There she is! She's lit. Oh Saints, I don't feel well."

"Did you give your health, my boy?"

"Had to ... had ... had to give someth —"

His words cut off but I heard Sir Coriand call down urgently. "Hold on to him, Sir Joran. You'll be here in a moment and I'll be right here to help."

There was some silence and then the sound of the platform reaching the ledge again and a few grunts. My platform had moved to where the central pillar hid them from me.

"You'd best be working out your offering, Beggar," Sir Coriand called out. His voice was falsely cheerful. "We'll be back for you."

Sir Owalan must have said something, because I heard Sir Coriand's distant voice give a reply. "Oh, she's sulky as a spoiled child for all she's a Beggar. Too young, if you ask me, but I don't suppose anyone did."

I looked at the books scattered in heaps on the platform. And I looked at the books on the wall where our platform had come to rest. And I looked at the altar and made up my mind.

I would not participate. And no, I was not a sulky child unwilling to join in because no one else wanted to play her game. I was taking a principled stand.

Whatever this worship was making, I refused to agree to make it, too. And if that meant I died here on this platform and it fell down into the pit below and my bones were left for all eternity beside the Majester's, well, then that was what was going to happen, wasn't it?

I just hoped Sir Branson found a way out of the dog. Or

maybe that Brindle tore out Sir Coriand's throat just for fun. Or something.

It was hardly my concern anymore since I was going to die right here.

I blinked back hot tears and looked far into this distance as the cold stole my strength in tiny flickers and shreds, and this damned arcanery stole my spirit the same way.

Chapter Twenty-Seven
Poisoned Saint

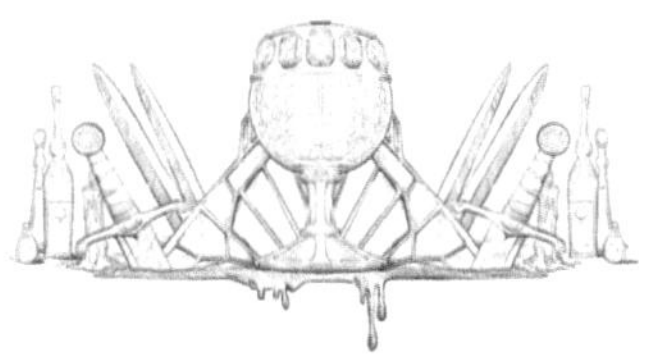

I come awake with a start.

It is night. Darkness surrounds me except for a lit candle in a pool of wax about halfway between myself and a pair of beautiful, treacherous, demon-loving eyes.

I leap to my feet in a heartbeat and have to catch myself against … against an altar made of woven bones? I cringe back from them. I could almost swear some are human.

"What is this place?" I manage to rasp. It's not exhaustion or fear that roughens my voice. It's unmitigated wrath.

Fury and hatred twist up in a pair, writhing through my belly and up to my heart. I'd fallen for her. It was safe enough to admit that now. Now that she is become my sworn enemy. Now that the sight of her twists me right through with hatred and disgust.

I am a devil, for I have fallen in love with one.

An aching sadness joins the rest of my collection of sorrows.

"A grimivoir, apparently." There is an ironic twist to her mouth, amplified by the sharp, flickering shadows of the candle. She sounds resigned, as if she has already read the book of my heart and knows how the story ends.

She stands, with me, as if she can't let me get the upper hand by being taller. Her armor is gone. She is wearing what she slept in last night: leather trousers and a light linen tunic. She's lost her braid entirely and her loose black hair tumbles across her shoulders and down her back. If she wasn't still carrying the sword, I'd wonder if she is the same woman. She looks haunted. Brittle.

Why *is* she carrying a sword? Unsheathed. Naked in her hand.

I draw my own blade with slow care. I want to let her know I will not fall to her sword easily while also trying not to provoke her to immediate attack.

I have told her I cannot forgive. I have seen her soul stained through with the keeping of a demon. She will know what must be done next.

"What is a grimivoir?" I ask, stalling for time, getting my bearings. I will not fail in this. I just do not wish to succeed at once. Could I delay it a year, I would.

I look carefully around us, trying to assess without losing track of her. I do not dare let her strike first. I've seen her fight. I'd be lucky to bring her down along with me if she landed the first blow.

I roll my shoulders as I think about trying to match my strength to her speed, my experience to her ferocity. We will likely both die. Am I ready to meet the God and give an account?

We're neatly trapped on a platform two long strides wide in every direction from the center. The odd stone bench, the books, the candles, and the spine-like carvings that serve as a rail around the edge provide no escape. There is not enough light to see farther than that, though a faint glow above suggests possible starlight and the echo of my words tell me this is a large place. I might be able to climb the bookshelves on one side of us, but to what end?

There is not much room to move here and there is no sign of the others.

"Have we been banished here?" My words echo slightly, as if the room finds them humorous.

She snorts. She is laughing at me. I feel the muscles of my face tighten in annoyance. Her mockery will be her last emotion. Is that what she wants?

"In a way," she says, shifting her weight onto her back foot.

Good. She knows she is threatened. She will not be a helpless innocent when my blade crashes through her. This is right. This is fitting. This is how justice is served. Something tickles the back of my mind. A little voice asking me if perhaps Sir Kodelai had these very thoughts only yesterday.

She is grave as she goes on, "This is the second trial. The room that was behind the door after the walls shifted. You can't see it now, but it's a library — or rather a grimivoir. Books line a cylindrical room that stretches high to the ground above our heads and reaches farther down than I could guess."

"You didn't throw anything into it to check?" I ask, lifting a mocking eyebrow. Bitterness twists my every word. "A loose stone? Your innocence?"

"*I* didn't," she says, and she shifts again, this time uncomfortably. I'm aware of her every twitch and shift. Only because I soon must attack her and slay her, not because she draws me in like the smell of sweet fruit in summer. Not because her every movement lulls me like music well composed. Not because she is enchantingly feminine and lovely in this terrible place. "The Majester tested it by flinging his own body into the depths — or so Sir Coriand would have us believe. I am not so certain."

I flinch back from that.

"The Majester is dead?" My words sound hollow. I still feel his map burning in my pocket.

"I should hope so." She sounds bitter, too. Perhaps I am not the only one swimming in misery. Well. That credits her. She can still feel regret. Is that enough to absolve her? Not nearly. "If he lives, then he suffers. He fell a very long time before I heard his body hit."

I grunt at that. "And the others? Where are they?"

She seems to harden with resolve when she says, "They

completed the task and left. They'll be back. They return every so often to check on my progress."

I pause. My thoughts must catch up to my circumstances.

It is unlikely that the Vagabond would fail at a task the others have succeeded in. She has purposely refused the task — whatever it is.

There are only two reasons she might do that. She could be taking a moral stand against the evil of this place. I dismiss that immediately. No one who fosters demons in their pets would stand on principle against evil.

That leaves only the other choice. She has stayed for me — whether because she vowed to work with me, or out of misplaced compassion, or to keep my mouth from revealing her depravity.

She is a fool.

"You know I have to kill you, don't you?" I ask her, and my deep sorrow flows through my words. "You will not dismiss the demon. You will not kill the dog. You've suffered evil to take a foothold." My voice nearly breaks, but I take it in the grip of my determination and force it to be firm. "I have no other choice."

Her chin stiffens and for a moment I see conflict on her face. And then she laughs — sudden and sharp — and she throws her blade to the floor. It crashes to the ground and I wince. She's certainly notched the blade.

"I'm going to die one way or another," she says, still laughing darkly. In the darkness, I think I make out a bruise on her cheek, but it is hard to be certain. "Whether at your hands, or slowly on this platform, or when their precious clock runs out. Perhaps your blade is a mercy. Are you offering me a mercy, Poisoned Saint?"

She spreads her hands and arms wide, open and ready. I can see her heart beating wildly under her light linen shirt. The candlelight exaggerates the movement, and I have to swallow hard to dismiss the image of her vulnerability. I cannot afford pity.

Do not suffer the witch to live, is one of our tenets. And a witch is not a creature from a story — a poor beggared, bedraggled woman just trying to survive. I'm arrested for a moment at that thought and my eyes flick sharply to her golden-brown ones before my train of thought returns. A witch is not an elderly woman who knows herbology and the curing of ills with plants and poultices, or the art of tricking chickens into laying again, or of finding still waters, or of birthing children stuck in the passage. No, those are common misconceptions. A witch is, and always has been, a man or a woman who plays with the arcane, who draws up demons from under the earth and sets them to dance in fire and cruelty across its surface — who permits them life.

Just as Victoriana has.

I must act before I lose my resolve. Those wry marigold eyes are softening me like butter in the sun. I dare not let them melt me entirely.

My dedication is to the God. My vow is to act and live in his name. No earthly thing has the right to subvert that. I will fulfill my duty, even if it guts me. Even if it drives me to madness.

Everything in me twists painfully and the broken arm I took from this lovely sinner throbs with the pain I borrowed from her. I lean into the pain, into the sorrow. I let melancholy build and froth.

I am poisoned with her ills and poisoned with the thought of her death. I swallow it down and it twists me from sternum to tail. Twists and twists and wracks me but I dare not let it wrench me from my course.

In such attitude are the most valiant deeds always done — in sorrow, but in earnest.

I lunge forward, sword held perfectly for a killing blow. She juts her chin farther out but she does not flinch. The air flows around me, dragging as if to stay my hand. Every sharp moment lengthening out to feel like an hour in passing.

I will plunge my blade through her heart.

I will end her now.

I will — she glows suddenly, a subtle tremor of gold.

I gasp, pulling my strike at the last second.

NO.

The word — intangible and with the distinct flavor of holiness — echoes firmly through my mind and I pull my arms back so forcefully that I wrench them. I've stayed my blow in time, but the momentum of my torso flings me forward even as I drag my arms backward and release my grip.

My sword clatters to the ground with hers, the sound of metal on metal singing out.

My balance has deserted me and my body crashes into her. Breath sawing raggedly, we stumble backward together.

One of her arms wraps around me instinctually. The other must catch us against the rail and turn us, because we do not fall over the side. Instead, she bends our momentum into a spin and we wheel away from the rail, bodies forced together in a clinch. We tumble to the ground to land on a bed of books. She has spun us so that she lands under me. And her chest heaves as violently as my own. Her look of shock mirrors mine. And when shock twists into relief within me, I see it twisting within her, too.

"It seems the God will not permit me to slay you," I say slowly, wonderingly, and my voice is breathier than I expected it to be.

"It seems so," she agrees, panting. "And that is a problem since he has done nothing to prevent me from turning the course of my heart toward you."

Is it braver to admit that now — to me, her would-be murderer — or to have spread her arms to receive my killing blow?

This seals it. She will be my undoing. She is more of a trap than this place ever could be.

I can bear it no longer.

I kiss her.

It is not a soft, hesitant kiss, as perhaps it should be. It is not sweet and savoring as I might have dreamed of in the dark of the night. It is violent and immediate. A confession and an anguished plea all in one. And when I break away from her lips, my eyes smart.

My voice sounds half like a snarl. “If he will not permit me to kill you, then he must suffer me to love you.”

“Must he?” she asks, pushing a hand against my armored chest. My heart seems to thump against my breastplate, my breath trapped between my lips as her tongue had been only a moment before. The whole world is too hot. Her wicked lips curve into a wry smile. “That seems a terribly twisty way to look at things.”

I let out a huff of air as I fight desperately for control, to regain mastery of mind and body from this drunken moment that snatches and claws at both.

“It is the only way I have,” I confess, and then I place my forehead against hers with slow deliberation — a chaste choice amid a sea of lustful ones — and I shudder a gasp when I feel her fingers twist into my hair, tugging lightly.

But she is not content to let things lie.

“And what of my evil deeds? What of the demon I permitted to live?”

I groan in misery.

But I kiss her again before I answer, and this time I am tender about it, mindful, gathering her into my arms as something precious, and sitting us both upright. I am also thorough. And it is only when we are both breathless and gasping that we break apart and meet each other’s eyes. It’s a moment of such painful cherishing. A tiny stolen snatch of life as a drowning man snatches a last breath. I think I’ve put my whole heart into this moment. It’s a pitiful heart, guilt-stained, broken, and rotting in some places, but hot with desire, tremulous with hope.

“What have you done?” she asks me, a little shakily. “Are you not forsworn against affection? First, you fail to kill me, then you confess love to me, and now you do as you have vowed not to?”

I clear my throat, draw back a little farther, though one hand remains on her waist, unwilling to leave her. “Yes.”

“You have kissed me. And you have done it with aching sweetness.”

I feel raw and open as her words drag my actions into the

light. Anyone on the outside would judge me a fool for falling so hard, so fast, and in such circumstances. I hardly understand it myself, but I have learned not to question what is plainly true.

"What does this mean for you?" she pushes.

I open my hands wide. "I have lost all the focus I have built up to heal others — which was little after expending myself as I have these past days and nights. If someone needs healing, I will not be able to help."

She looks at my hand, and is that wistfulness I see when she takes it gently in her own and removes it from her waist and hands it back to me? It is not rejection. She has told me her heart is mine for the treasuring.

"Then I think we dare not do that again."

And I should be glad she is sensible and has saved us both. But I do not feel glad. I feel as though I have been left for dead upon the battlefield. I am bereft.

I pull myself to my feet and turn my back to her.

I do not know what to say. It feels like lying to agree to that. I busy myself with pretending to flip through one of the books on the altar. What is this rubbish? One look at one of the woodcuts within and I toss it from our perch. I don't care if we need it later. No one should ever look at a book such as this.

"Adalbrand?"

My name on her tongue seizes my breath in my chest.

"Mmm?" I dare not permit myself words. They will only trip me.

"Will it come back?" She pauses. She sounds concerned. "You power? Have I damaged you forever?"

I turn abruptly, startled by the choke in her voice.

"No." The word gasps out of me instinctively and I nearly touch her again, my hand rising to cup her face, only to fall away again.

Her hair is tousled from my kisses. And her cheeks are flushed in the candlelight. I realize, as I had not in my passion, that her lip is swollen and the skin just under the corner of it is purpled with a bruise. I cannot heal it.

"Not forever," I say distractedly. "Has someone hurt you?"

She reaches two fingers up to gingerly prod at the bruise.

"Hefertus," she says a little wryly. I don't know what my face does to show my vitriol, but she hurries to add, "The Engineers told him about the demon. It would seem all good men of faith want me dead once they hear that."

I swallow and lower my hand and say very carefully, "I think now would be a good time to try explaining it to me."

A spark of fear shoots into her eyes and her gaze flicks to our swords still lying on the floor, unclaimed.

"I told you we were casting out a demon when it jumped into Sir Branson."

"You did," I agree gravely.

She bites her lip. "I had to kill him. He was trying to kill me and I couldn't get the demon out and I would have died. And then the demon could have rampaged anywhere, hurt anyone."

I nod. That part is all understandable. It is the other part that doesn't sit well. The part where she didn't *also* kill the dog.

"But when the demon jumped into the dog, I was able to subdue Brindle."

"But you didn't cast the demon out," I say carefully, trying not to accuse. It is an effort so great that I should be Sainted on the spot.

"I couldn't."

I wait. If the God did not want her dead for her misdeeds, then he must have a reason. This time it is she who turns her back and drifts to the rail.

"And then Sir Branson's soul was in the dog, too. And I didn't have the heart to kill poor Brindle when that meant saying goodbye to Sir Branson forever."

I feel myself soften with understanding. The old man I'd seen with the dog and the demon. I'd almost forgotten about him.

"Goodbye?" I echo, not sure what else to say.

She spins and looks at me and she swallows hard. "They speak to me. Both of them. All day long."

"Saints." I run a hand over my face. What must that be like?

"Yes." She twists her fingers through her disheveled hair and looks at the ceiling.

She is beautiful, this mess of a woman. Beautiful and clever and terribly troublesome, and my fingers itch to hold her again. Her kiss still burns my lips. I want the taste of her back in my mouth. I want the feel of her back in my arms. What shall I do? I am ruined by her.

"His insights are true sometimes. But he lies to me, too. The demon, I mean."

"He's why you can read Ancient Indul," I say, finally understanding.

"He lied about this place. He calls it an arcanery now. A monastery — but for those who worship demons."

I inhale sharply through my nose.

Her wry smile twists even more. "Exactly. What do you think we're building as we go through each step of this carefully laid out puzzle?"

"I dare not guess."

She takes a step forward and I inhale again, and this time I draw in her musk and sage scent. "Do you believe that men make their own demons, Sir Adalbrand?"

I pause, and when I speak it's with deliberate care. "In war, sometimes. In life, also. We terrorize ourselves."

"I don't mean, do people bring their own downfall. I don't mean it figuratively. I mean in actual living breathing certainty. Do men form and shape and hammer out demons in their likenesses and then unleash them on the world?"

It's a thought worthy of consideration.

My mind is racing through texts I have read, through accounts. There was a war in Ghentav years ago. Before my time. They ran out of food. When they finally were overrun and the attackers found what was behind the walls ... well. One of the scribes who had written the chronicles had died at his own hands. Another had killed and eaten a third scribe even though there was plentiful food by then. After that the records had grown … murky. Our aspect had buried the records in clay pots in a church cemetery, deeming them unsafe for a regular library. Had they made a demon on those fields? Had it fought for them and turned on their attackers? Had it turned on *them*?

"Perhaps," I say, still thinking.

"I think we do," she says in a small voice. "And a place like this makes me wonder if we made all of them."

"All of … what?"

She speaks slowly, her marigold eyes sober and liquid in the candlelight.

"I think that we — humans — we made every demon that ever was. We manufactured them as a bowyer carves out the shape of a bow. We sculpted them as an artist sculpts a bust, with careful attention to every detail. We breathed life into our sins and hates as the Engineers breathe life into their golems."

I inhale sharply at that, too. I do not hold with golems. And what she is saying troubles me.

"Is this why you are still sitting on this platform when the others are gone?"

"Is it more of a sin to craft a demon when I know what I'm doing? Is it more of a sin than not killing the dog the demon is already in?"

"Why don't you kill it? Don't tell me it's to keep the voice of your dead paladin alive. I know that is not all the story."

She looks tired. "If I kill the dog, then the demon will leap, and then I'll have to kill another man. And another. And another. Because until I figure out how to cast this one back into hell, he's a danger to everyone. He's not coming out just with prayer." She juts out her lower lip. "I could keep my hands clean. I could be a Saint. But then who will die for that? Whose soul will be made foul because I wanted to keep myself unbesmirched?"

I am considering this.

"Surely you understand."

"*I* understand?" I can't keep the disbelief from my tone.

"You kiss very delectably for a man sworn against it."

I swallow.

"I'm not ..." I cough, awkwardly, not sure where to put my gaze. "I'm not *entirely* sworn against it."

"You're *not*." She doesn't believe me.

"Are you *entirely* sworn against taking coin offered you?"

"No."

"And yet that is riches."

"I am forsworn from hoarding it." Her smile is wry.

"Even one or two coins?"

"No."

I give her a wry smile of my own. "Then consider this my two coins."

She thinks, tapping her chin with one finger before raising one brow. "I'll consider it whatever you want it to be if you'll do it again."

She is tempting me and it is working.

"Here?" I ask, gesturing tightly to indicate our surroundings. "In an arcanery where we are forced to breed demons or die buried under the ground? Here, in the dark, on a teetering platform? Here, where men might have died in this very trial?"

She swallows and looks away. "The Majester. Whether he fell or was pushed by Sir Coriand."

"He was pushed," I say gravely. I have no doubt about this. "Never underestimate a man who will keep a half-living slave."

She looks back at me and I can tell she wants to say something but she doesn't.

"Say it," I urge.

She shakes her head, laughing ruefully.

"Say it." I am firm this time.

"Fine, let it be so. Here is what I have to say: I ought not to take from you what is not yours to give. You are forsworn affection."

She is correct, of course, in every way. By rights, she should be dead at my hand, and I should have a demon in a dog to contend with. But the God has stayed my hand. And by doing so, he has left me only two paths: ignore her entirely, a thing that cannot be done with her demon dog and her insistence on bucking the course others try to set for her, or embrace her. I have made my choice, the God have mercy on me.

I swallow and commit to it.

"If we live through the turnings of this monastery, then we will both emerge on the other side with a shared problem — three of them, to be precise."

This gets her attention. "What three problems?"

"Firstly, that we have sworn to stay by each other until the cup is returned to one of the aspects. A cup, I might point out, that is not here and likely never has been."

She nods steadily. "Yes."

There is no fear or panic in her eyes, and I feel my brows lift. It's not a paladin thing to fear commitment, but even so, I am essentially revealing to her that we are bound together indefinitely, and she does not recoil from that. Interesting. I am ... a little ... flattered by this.

"Secondly, that there is a demon in your dog which we will need help to remove, and it must be kept a secret until we find that help."

"We?" Her tone is hopeful, and I feel a spark of hope ignite in response.

"We," I say with certainty.

"Thirdly, that you have sworn to never forgive me." Her eyes meet mine sharply and I feel hot again.

I take her hand. "I renounce my vow. I forgive you in all fullness."

"Your resolve was very weak," she teases.

"But only because of the third problem."

"Fourth," she corrects, as she steps closer, and now our breath is mingling. I don't let go of her hand.

"No, that was your problem. I have not confessed to it. I knew from the moment my hand was stayed that forgiveness was granted to you."

"Then tell me, what is your third problem?" Her gaze stays anchored to mine. I am losing myself in marigold eyes.

"My third problem is that I have fallen hopelessly in love with you."

"That *is* a problem." She looks a challenge at me. "What are you going to do about it?"

I draw nearer and nearer to her as I speak, until my lips are brushing hers as I say, "It is especially a problem since I have already kissed you once, and I have had no time to recover from the event, so it harms nothing at all for me to do it again, right now."

This time it is she who presses herself into me and takes my lips in hers. I taste her excitement as if it is my own. I draw in her desire with the softness of her lips and the warmth of her breath and the silkiness of how her long hair tangles around me. Her strong, work-roughened fingers grip my face, and her nose slides against mine. I close my eyes and beg to lose myself forever.

This should wash me of none of my guilt. That is the domain of the God alone. And yet, in some indefinable way, it does. It makes redemption feel possible. It creeps down into my fibers and tells me that my shame need not blemish my honor forever.

I should not find forgiveness in the arms of a woman. I should not find hope in her kiss. That should be tainted with the stain of lust and be tangled up with my failures, my shortcomings, and my broken vows.

It is not. There is something about this that glows like the light that surrounds my brothers when we pray. There is some mystery here that salves wounds and binds broken souls.

I do not question it. I thank the God it exists and melt into the relief that has not been my companion in more than a decade, and into the warmth I never thought I'd feel again, and I try to thank her with how I kiss her. I try to say all the things I don't dare allow to touch my lips. I try to make promises I may never be free to keep.

There's a thump and we spring apart, gasping.

"You can't wait in the darkness forever, Beggar girl," Sir Coriand's voice rings out. "Eventually, you will have to come to your senses and play. Or, if you are very unlucky, one of us will solve this riddle soon, and turn the room, and you will be trapped forever in this empty, yawning tomb."

"Did I hear correctly, Engineer?" I call back. "Did you murder the Majester General?"

There's a silence that is just a breath too long.

Sir Coriand's voice is far too familiar when he replies. "You're back, Poisoned Saint. What a relief! Your friend Hefertus has been worried about you."

"I'm surprised he's not here," I say in a light tone. "I would have expected loyalty from my old friend."

"Oh, you know the Princes," Sir Coriand says lightly. "Lacking common sense. Besides, the Beggar is just like her beast. She stands over you and growls. Did she tell you she leapt from her own island to join you on yours? A brave thing to do, if foolhardy. Maybe you can do the same for her. Make the sacrifice, light the candle, and put it and a book on the altar, and you can come eat the soup that Cleft has brewed for us. It's mushroom. The golems collected a lovely crop of morels before we were all brought down here. We'd nearly forgotten about them in the excitement. I think you'll find it aromatic, hmm?"

It has never surprised me that the blackest of souls have the lightest of voices. They carry no burden for no conscience weighs them down. Some might think that a blessing. I know it is not. My own father flew high and light, free of consequence or shame, until he was burned by the sun and crashed to the depths. I should pity him, but I do not find it in me to feel warmth for a man who treated my mother as he did.

I wonder when Sir Coriand will crash.

"I won't join you," Victoriana calls out. "You know that."

"Convince her, Poisoned Saint. A day and a night have passed and we have but a single day and night left on the clock. What do you think might happen when time runs out and our doom comes after us?"

"No less than we deserve," Victoriana mutters.

"I heard that, Beggar. Think what you will, but you are no Saint, and even if you were, I would not care what you thought."

And then he is gone, his footsteps stomping away across the stone, and we're left in silence again.

"They come every hour by my estimate," Victoriana said quietly. "I think they are growing frantic. They aren't sure if the puzzle isn't being solved because they have the wrong answer or because I won't join their game."

I pause. "They are going to lock us both in here? With me helpless and you dissenting?"

She laughs darkly. "They have killed three paladins and another died for their secrets. What do they care about adding two more?"

"And you think these murders were all done by Sir Coriand?"

"The Majester kept talking about a voice telling him what to do. I thought he meant a demon, or that he was crazy. But what if he was talking about a literal voice? What if it was the Engineers calling down to him in the chaos?"

That was plausible. "And the Seer? The Engineers stayed up top."

"As far as we knew. What would have kept them from sneaking down when no one was watching?"

I grunt. Those are solid points.

"Then we have to decide," I say. "Eventually they will crack the code and they will spin the walls again, and we will be trapped in here while they move inevitably to what must be the last trial."

She's nodding, a look of determination on her face. I must choose my words with care.

"We can stay here and die on principle."

Her eyes take on a dangerous gleam. She doesn't like the "or" dangling in the air. I say it anyway.

"Or."

I wait for her to master her anger, and only when she cocks one eyebrow do I continue.

"Or, we play their game for now, and we look for a way to stop them. And when we find it, we destroy everything made in this place. Because if we don't, then who will? Shall we let them succeed without us and leave someone else to face the demons they create?"

She looks like she's bitten into something sour. "I've already crossed too many lines. I was hoping not to sully myself with this."

I nod, but I stay silent. Sometimes people just need to talk an idea through.

"I don't like compromises." She looks torn. "I know you likely don't believe that after the dog, but I don't want to take another step in the wrong direction. And what about next time? How many times will you say, 'Just one more thing. Then we'll stop them.'"

"Only this time," I promise.

"Likely, that's what the people of the past said the first time. When the first denizen of hell was drawn up from the earth."

I nod. How can I deny that this is a terrible idea when it so plainly is? And yet, here we are.

"Principles are good things. Worth standing on. Worth dying for. But sometimes, if you want to achieve a thing you must be practical."

"Says the man who took a vow of celibacy because a girl died, even though her death was not his fault."

I let out an exhale that is almost a rueful laugh.

"I am no Saint, Lady Paladin," I murmur. "Did I not prove it by kissing you? But I have been in enough sickrooms and on enough battlefields to know that sometimes there are two good things and you may only choose one, and sometimes there are two bad things and you *must* choose one, and today we are faced with two terrible choices, and my brave Vagabond, I fear we must choose one."

"I'd already chosen death," she says steadily.

I nod. I understand. I do. But I would rather have her with me.

"I'm asking you to choose otherwise. Come with me. Help me stop the others. Help me stop what they are making."

"And afterward?" she asks a little wistfully.

"After we are all dead?" I ask wryly.

And this earns me a startled laugh. "Yes, after that."

"Then walk with me in Paradise," I say softly. "I have never been very good at being alone. I fear that even the halls of the God may be lonely places."

"Shush now," she tells me, and places a finger over my lips. "No blasphemy."

"As you say, Lady Paladin." When she removes her finger, I try to be gentle with my words. "I have vowed myself first to the God and now to you. Do not ask me to sit and watch you die."

"You may yet see it, if we fight," she says, but she retrieves her sword from where it lies.

A slight smile edges my lips as I lift my own sword, check the blade — shockingly, it is undamaged — and return it to its sheath.

"We will fight. Side by side," I tell her gravely. And I am both regretful at the thought of what we must do next and excited for the challenge. I've always been like that — pawing the earth at the mere suggestion of a race, sniffing the air at the hint of a hunt. "And I must build back my faith and focus. I dare not let it slip again."

She nods gravely. She knows. I doubt she has a coin to her name. How could she not know?

"After this last kiss," I say, and when I lean in, my breath catching in my throat, I let my lips brush hers as I plead, "Just one more. For a blessing."

"Bless you, then, supplicant," she whispers the formal words and lifts two fingers, but her words dissolve as her tongue meets mine and we taste each other with exquisite slowness. And I know we are both savoring the embrace that is likely our last, drawing from it fortitude for what comes next. When it eventually must end, it ends in her huffing laugh.

"Go with my blessing," she murmurs.

"I feel very blessed," I say somberly. And it is worth teasing her to get a second dose of that laugh. "And now what do we do here?" I ask her. "What ingredients go into this terrible brew?"

She faces the altar with a glare.

"We're supposed to give something up. I think the High Saint gave up his voice."

"For which, I'm certain, the others are grateful."

She snorts. "It has to be worthy and something that no longer serves you. I think Hefertus gave a finger. I do not know what I shall give. I rather like my fingers."

"I have a suggestion," I say, my tone wry. "Why not give up your lies? I would prefer them long behind us."

She looks at me defiantly. "Only if you offer up your guilt. It chafes me. Surely, after all these years, it chafes you, too."

I shrug my agreement.

She grabs a book from the shelf at random and without looking at it, slams it on the altar. It is very thin, the cover ragged and torn. A burned hole goes straight through the front cover. Ironic, that her book looks so much like her. She looks a challenge up at me, and without breaking eye contact, I draw my own book from the shelf and thump it on top of hers. I think mine is thick and gold edged.

She snorts, grabs the candle from the floor, and puts it on top of the books.

I open my mouth, but before I can ask her what comes next or if this will even work with the pair of us bending the rules of sacrifice, the platform rocks, and then a faint glow seems to form around it and we begin to drift along the shelves. It's too dark to gauge how quickly the island moves, but move it does, and I find that against all odds, I am sorry. I will miss that place along the shelves where she bared her heart to me. I should feel guilty for that. But I gave my guilt up.

And now I must show her that the choice we made was worth it all.

"We are of an accord now, Poisoned Saint," she reminds me as our island docks against the cliff face that had been opposite us before. "We are one. Don't let them divide us. I think they will try."

"They don't kiss like you do," I tease in a low undertone.

"How do you know?" she asks me, lifting a scandalized eyebrow. "Perhaps that will be the next trial."

"A kissing contest?" I smirk at the absurdity of it.

"It could happen," she says lightly.

And I like being teased by the Vagabond. I like it enough that I lean in over her shoulder as we disembark from the island and cross single-file to the cliff and I whisper in her ear.

"If that happens, I shall fail, for I refuse to kiss any but you."

"Don't be hasty. Cleft might offer," she retorts.

But though I narrow my eyes and give her a dark look, my heart is far happier than it has any right to be in this God-forsaken place.

Chapter Twenty-Eight

Vagabond Paladin

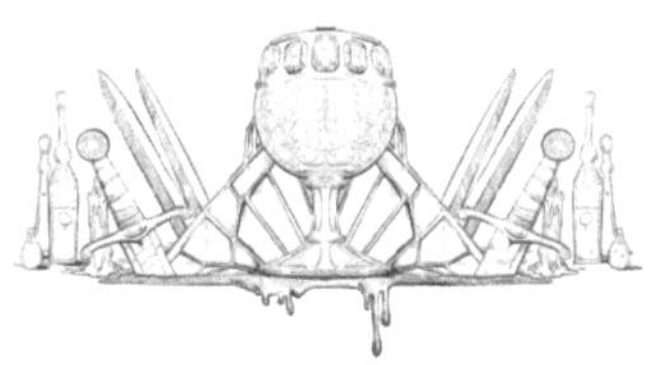

In all my wanderings over the windswept land, I had not thought to have such a gift as this — of soft kisses and warm eyes wanting to work with me, being one with me in purpose, choosing to take up a burden with me. I stole sidelong glances from time to time as if he might disappear if my eyes left him for too long. This harmony was an uncommonly precious thing.

For his part, Adalbrand met my glances with a small crinkling around his eyes and a very slight half-smile.

"We must try to pretend we are willing to go along with the rest," he murmured to me. "I fear you are not well versed in pretense."

"Poverty rarely requires it," I said in a low voice.

"Chastity requires it almost constantly. I have pretended not to see your charms since the moment I met you."

"I am sure it has been an easy face to wear," I said grimly.

I was unused to pretty words and not sure what to do with them. Besides, I had to put aside softness for what was about to come.

Already, I felt the chafe of my conscience. I had sinned. Deliberately. I had added to the creation of a demon. There would be no way to purge myself of such evil without death — either mine or the creature's that I was creating. It made me feel like I had serrated knives under my skin and every movement made a deeper cut. This was not a time for love.

"Trust me, it has not been easy." He sounded a little hoarse.

I turned abruptly to face him.

"I love your teasing," I said a little breathlessly. "I love your kisses and kindness, but I need something more from you now, Sir Knight. I need resolve and purpose, I need all that honor that pours out of you every time you're bumped or bruised. I need you to stand with me — valiant — against what comes next."

He was suddenly serious, teasing put aside. He made a half-bow. "You shall have it from me and so shall the God."

I nodded soberly, tension filling every seam of my being. I didn't know what else to say. I felt dreadfully inadequate to hold his affections. I was the ragged knight riding through the edge of town, not the lady laughing in the center of the dancing. I was the one begging for scraps, not the one fed from the table of a lord. The best I could manage was to draw courage close, screw my face up with resolve, and walk forward.

He seemed to understand, growing quiet and grave, matching my stride so that we emerged into the main room together.

There was a strangled cry when we stepped out of the corridor and Sir Owalan leapt up from a perch on the edge of the clock like a raven lifting off a corpse.

Worryingly, the cups there were brighter with that dark glow and I thought I saw smoke swirling up from them. Owalan practically ran toward us, relief painting his whole face, arms flung wide. His tabard swirled around him, more akin to a monk's cassock than a knight's apparel.

"You did it. You passed the test. I wanted to stay and watch but I couldn't bear to see you fail."

It seemed Sir Adalbrand was correct. I was not adept at hiding my emotions.

"I see your doubt," Sir Owalan said, "but I was of a certainty most worried. The clock ticks down. The time is close. Look. Less than a day remains in the hours it counts down. Already, dawn is lighting the stained glass."

That made more sense than any worry for our safety. He wanted the cup like a dying man wants reprieve.

"Where is my dog?" I asked him carefully.

I'm here. That Sir Sorken is a lovely fellow. Suggested twice that a dog might be nice roasted. I must say it's a relief to hear your voice again.

And the demon?

Oh, I'm here, sweetling. Contemplating my revenge. I think it will involve making someone drown himself in that fountain. Do you think golems drown?

I did not.

What a pity.

Owalan waved an uncaring hand. "The golems are tending your dog. I'm sure you have nothing to fear. Come." His hands clawed toward my arm as if to take it but I shook them off, revulsion filling me at the glimpse of the dagger under his sleeve. He hardly seemed to notice the slight. "You must look at the puzzle. It is stumping us all. It must be attended immediately."

He was trying to draw us to the left, toward where the new puzzle was likely waiting behind the grate and where the bodies we'd managed to recover would be laid out as if in a crypt. I shuddered at the thought of walking past them and then again at the thought of the Majester rotting somewhere below.

"Where are the others?" Adalbrand asked Owalan, peering toward the right. If they were still camping at the base of the stairs, they should be in that direction. I thought I could just make them out with the faintest colored light of dawn through stained glass washing over them.

"Sleeping while they can," Owalan said, motioning to us to hustle after him.

His shadow seemed to be twice the height as usual — looming over him like a monster under the bed finally come to claim its victim. That could only be my imagination, attributing malice where natural phenomena were at play, but imagination or not, it made every hair on the back of my arms stand on end. I kept half an eye on that shadow, watching to see if it were truly anchored to Owalan or if it could slip the bounds and reach out to try to hook me. Fanciful? Perhaps, but this place was making me warier than a rich man guarding his money.

"Sir Sorken is taking a turn at the puzzle," Owalan said, trying to hustle us along. "We've all tried, of course, but no one could manage it. Perhaps you'll see something we missed."

He led us toward the wall where the locked door with the grate covered the puzzle that would turn us one more time counterclockwise.

"Did the High Saint try it?" Adalbrand asked.

"Yes, and you know he's considered a scholar among his people."

"I didn't know that," I said. The High Saint? He was so militant. I did not think one could be scholarly and bloodthirsty at the same time.

The scholars in the capital are even more aggressive. They will fight to the death over the subtle sub-meaning of a word in a passage of text as opposed to its use in a different text with a slightly more nuanced subtext, and friendships will dissolve and kingdoms fracture and then people will die.

All that over a word?

One of the good ones, yes.

And the not so good ones?

Blood will still be spilt. It's why their aspect is ever fracturing and fracturing again into creeds and confessions and distinctions none of us can keep track of. I think Joran Rue is a High Saint of the Castlerock Creed modified by the Year of the Skink Convocation. But I might have miscounted the knots in his belt and if I did, then he's something else entirely.

I shook my head. Madness. I'd rarely thought much further than being sure my hands and heart were pure to keep demons from catching a hook into me. I'd had no time for confessions or creeds and their nuances.

Sir Owalan elaborated. "The High Saint knows Anicani's Catechism and the Confession of the Faith of the Year of Our Lady's Mercy and all five of Prirene's Discourses by heart."

"He does?" I didn't even know what those were.

They don't feed you when you're hungry, I can assure you of that.

"Certainly. He's the son of his aspect's High Elder. They're very devoted to doctrine and the teaching of the fathers. The High Saint has forsworn both riches and marriage for his place in the aspect." Owalan laughed suddenly. "It's like he's both of you at once."

He glanced back and forth at both Adalbrand and me, squinting in the darkness between the glowing clock and whatever glowed up ahead. It was as if he thought we'd laugh, too.

We did not laugh.

Brindle did not laugh.

Give me some credit, the demon complained. *I still have an intact sense of humor.*

Owalan looked around nervously.

"If anyone is to be made a Saint, it will be the High Saint." His voice trailed through the words like he was hoping for the opposite even as he spoke them. "Look at all the others who have failed. You know the reputations of the Seer Ecember — she who moved the populations of cities before the typhoon in the Year of Saint Aspertine and saved thousands of lives — and Sir Kodelai, whose fame preceded him. Did you also know that Roivolard Masamera — the Majester General — was a key negotiator at the end of the Siege of Curan? Or that Sir Hexalan was renowned among the Inquisitors for his kindness and capability in sorting out refugees after the cataclysm struck in High Sartre? He earned a reputation there that could have carried him to the head of his aspect someday."

I frowned, somewhat horrified by his callousness. "If you

know the accomplishments of all the others, why do you care so little about their deaths?"

He looked appalled. "I have the greatest sense of sorrow at their deaths. It is you who trivializes them."

"Me?"

We were almost to the other door. Sir Sorken stood hunched over the grate, fiddling with it, while beside him his golem held up a handful of oil and a burning wick to light his way. It made a strange light that seemed to dance to its own tune. Sir Sorken's shadow towered behind him.

And Sir Owalan's.

And Adalbrand's.

I frowned. But not the golem's. The golem's shadow was long, but it looked correct to my eyes. It was the other shadows that seemed not just long, but overly deep and black, and as I watched, Sir Sorken's shadow bubbled up like a pot of starch left too long on the flame. It rose, building, and then a tendril of it reached out and coiled around the crown of his head like a diadem.

I gasped.

"Yes, you," Sir Owalan was still chiding as if he hadn't noticed that the shadows were behaving as if they were alive. "If you honored their deaths, then you would fight for Sainthood. Is that not why they died? In pursuit of the divine? If you keep refusing to take the trials and make the necessary sacrifices then you spit on their deaths. Thank the God for Sir Adalbrand, who awoke and spoke sense to you."

"Yes, thank the God he awoke," I said dryly. "After you dragged his unconscious form into a trial and left him there to fend for himself."

"I did no such thing. That was Sir Coriand."

"You stood by and watched. Watching an act and doing nothing is giving your approval."

I rounded on him in time to see his stony features flicker with anger, and as they flickered, his shadow flickered, and it built and built up over him, towering and guttering like an uncertain fire when it is only just kindled and not yet set into the bones of the logs that fuel it. Behind those features, his shadow curled up like an animal threatened, trying to appear larger than an enemy. It swayed back and forth as if to charm me into stillness.

Sir Owalan spoke again, this time like a pronouncement. "I do not like you, Beggar. You are neither accomplished nor intelligent. You do not see what we are trying to achieve here. And how could you? Is it not written, 'do not throw thy rubies to the dogs'?"

"I certainly wouldn't throw them to *her* dog," Adalbrand said darkly, dragging us behind him by dint of the pace he was setting. Why did these people have to build this arcanery to such a grand scale?

I shot Adalbrand a look. He'd been silent through this whole discussion. I couldn't tell if his shadow had grown and was lurking low and undetectable, or if it was the same as it always had been.

The look Adalbrand sent back in reply was a wry half smile, as if he found Sir Owalan amusing, or — perhaps — as if he found me just distracting enough that he hadn't quite been paying attention to the Penitent.

He cleared his throat. "No one has to like anyone. We simply must survive this mess without bloodshed and murder. And if that seems like an easy achievement, Penitent," he said as Sir Owalan opened his mouth, "then I bid you look upon those who have already been trampled in our race to the divine."

He gestured curtly to the bodies we were passing. They had not been arranged beyond being laid in a line. Someone had made an effort to kick Sir Kodelai's ashes in a kind of a heap. I wasn't sure if I hoped or feared it was one of the golems. It embarrassed me that they were seeing all of this — silent witnesses to the horrors men and women would inflict on each other when pressed, even those men and women who thought themselves holy. If the golems thought, then what did they think of this? Did they judge? Surely they must. Surely, the God must. We were all stained through to the marrow.

"Decided to join us, did you, Beggar?" Sir Sorken asked, looking over his shoulder at us as we finally approached. "Got over your scruples?"

"How does this door show the puzzle through the grate but then when the room twists, you can walk through the door to the next trial?" Sir Owalan asked crankily, shifting his stance so he wouldn't have to look at me.

"They're offset," Sir Sorken said. "Just by enough that you don't really notice. The puzzles are behind rock when you aren't working on them."

He turned to face us and the light of the makeshift lantern in the golem's hand flickered wildly.

"I am not over the Majester's death, if that's what you're asking," I said in a low tone.

"I had no idea that the two of you were so close," Sir Sorken said in a tone of false innocence, mocking me.

"Must you be close to someone to mourn their passing?"

His voice was purposefully innocent when he said, "You do if it's Roivolard Masamera. The man had no understanding of a good tea. Here, look at the puzzle, what do you see?"

Behind the grate was a series of colored glass slats arranged both horizontally and vertically in a small frame. Sir Sorken reached his fat fingers through the holes of the grate and slid a few with a *clack, clack.*

"It's a common slide puzzle," Adalbrand said from behind me. I liked the way his breath tickled the back of my neck, the way he wasn't nervous about standing close to me, like it was normal now for us to share breath and warmth.

"A slide puzzle with no solution," Sir Sorken said sharply, annoyed. "We tried the colors of the stained glass window, before you ask. We tried them in various orders. We tried the colors of the liturgical calendar in various orders. We tried the colors of the major kingdoms at the time this a — monastery was common, also."

And there's where he slipped, wasn't it? Because I heard the "ah" before the word "monastery." And I knew that somehow, he knew this was called an arcanery. Had Sir Coriand told him that?

"What's that just above the puzzle?" Sir Adalbrand asked, pointing out a tiny etched marking. "Is that a pitchfork?"

Cleft held his thick, rocky hand a little closer to the puzzle and I saw what Adalbrand was pointing to. A small pitchfork etched into the rock above the puzzle. It was missing a tine, broken off a quarter of the way up. And my mind scrambled to remind me that I'd seen that before. I'd thought it was a trident, hadn't I?

"It could be, I suppose. Have you ever seen another pitchfork in these parts?"

Adalbrand shook his head. I didn't think anyone had noticed that window but me.

"Let me try," I said grimly.

"Have at it, Vagabond. And while you take your turn, I think I'll go and brew up some more tea. Stay with the girl, would you, Cleft? You're the only lamp we have, there's a fine fellow. Are you coming, Sir Owalan?"

"I think I'll wait here," the Penitent Paladin said grimly. "Having once abandoned duty, I do not trust the Vagabond not to run off looking for her dog when it is her turn to work the puzzle."

"Where *is* my dog?" I asked mildly.

That's right. Don't forget the nice doggy.

"Occupied," Sir Sorken said briskly. "And so he will remain so until you've taken a turn at cracking the code. Time runs thin."

Adalbrand coughed as I frowned and turned my attention to the slide puzzle.

I could still remember the colors of the original broken triptych. I'd thought it was odd how they'd put the orange and red and blue and green in places I hadn't expected. I thought that — perhaps — I could replicate that pattern if I concentrated.

Behind me, I heard Adalbrand murmuring. "I'd fetch the lady paladin's dog, were I you."

"And why is that?" Sir Sorken asked.

"With the death of the Inquisitor," Adalbrand said, keeping his voice so low that it was hard to hear over the click of the glass tiles as I moved them round and round to slide into place. "I would hazard that Victoriana Greenmantle is the most skilled with the sword among those of us who remain. She is shaken by the death of the Majester — a death she has told me was murder."

"The man who jumped?" Sir Sorken asked darkly. "I'm sure you've seen suicides before. You're no child."

"Even so, I think it would be best not to provoke her."

"Is that why you've been so quiet? I'll not tiptoe around anyone." Sir Owalan had a dagger out and he was carving the stations of the Saint into the skin on his arm, tracing old white scars there that he had clearly traced and traced before. "The God alone is my judge."

"There's also the matter of how you left me in that challenge to die," Adalbrand said in an undertone that suggested he was not eager to bring up this next point.

"Surely you didn't consider the Beggar Paladin to be a threat!" Sir Owalan said plaintively. "She's such a ... crass thing."

"Crass," Adalbrand repeated dryly.

"Not one of us," Owalan tried in a smaller voice.

"Possibly, she is not even a paladin," Sir Sorken said like one trying to break bad news. I almost turned around to look at him at that. "Sir Coriand says there is a demon in her dog."

"A demon?" Sir Owalan sounded alarmed. "Why did no one tell me of this? I must chant a prayer for your souls immediately."

He was ignored by the others.

The cat is out of the bag, dear girl. Or rather the demon is in the dog and everyone knows. The Engineers have been whispering about it all night. They have not yet decided whether to kill Brindle and harvest the demon — those were their exact words — or whether to keep it within the dog so they can blackmail and control you.

And here I thought I liked the Engineers. Their behavior was looking more and more suspicious.

Wellll ... I mean, you are hardly one to judge. You are carting a demon around the place. We must be reasonable in what we ask from others.

"I did not mean that I felt threatened by her, merely that I was abandoned by you."

Sir Owalan scoffed. "We all knew you'd awaken and solve the puzzle. You're no fool."

Sir Sorken made a vague sound in the back of his throat. "Perhaps you should go fetch the Beggar's dog, Sir Owalan. I need to have a word with the Poisoned Saint in private."

There was a pause, as if Sir Owalan might argue the point, but after a moment he made a sound of acquiescence and then his footfalls marched away.

Sir Soken likely thought he was whispering when next he spoke but his whisper carried so easily that I heard every word. I glanced up at Cleft, who patiently held the lamp as I worked, wondering if he heard, too. If he did, he made no sign of it.

"You walk on rotten ice with that one, Poisoned Saint."

"How do you mean?"

Sorken snorted. "Don't think I've failed to notice what game you play. King's bastard or no, you must know you'd be in terrible trouble with your aspect if I were to report you to Bishop Galifarnas. He'd have your tabard."

"Speak clearly, then."

"You're romancing the Beggar. No, don't frown at me. I've seen the longing looks you two trade back and forth and the way you always seem to fall together. I care not what you do here, but perhaps you should. She throws out accusations and makes wild claims. She harbors demons and accuses us of murder. Her madness is dangerous and destructive and make no mistake, it will splash onto you. See that it doesn't. End this foolish alliance." He coughed awkwardly. "She sullies your honor, Sir Knight. And now I must see a golem about a dog."

And then his footsteps were echoing away from us, too.

I gritted my teeth. He did not paint a very flattering picture of me, and I found myself flushing when Adalbrand joined me by the puzzle, leaning against the wall so he could watch my face as I worked.

He had admitted to being drawn to me. Would that change when he saw how I was regarded by others?

"Did you see their shadows?" I asked as I worked, trying to speak of anything but what truly troubled me.

"I did. I do not know what to make of them, but we are on precarious ground. I have tried to lay seeds that might keep you safe, but the others have turned against you. I see how they look at you. If they can get away with abandoning you, they will."

He shook his head ruefully and we shared a look.

"Or murdering me?" I lifted a brow.

He nodded tightly, the lines around his eyes growing deeper.

"And you? Are you regretting being close to such a rebel?"

"Hardly."

I paused. Backtracked two tiles. Tried again. Hesitated, and then just went ahead and asked.

"I didn't really sully your honor, did I?"

"If you did, then I beg thee sully it again," he murmured and I smiled, guessing at the pattern. Some pieces of the window had been too broken to be certain what they'd shown. Nothing. I tried a second pattern.

"Have I ruined you so you may not return to your aspect?" I asked quietly.

His gusting laugh made me pause and look up.

"No. We'd have fewer paladins by half were that true. I could turn back now, return, and my slate would be blank, as if I never so much as touched your lips. That's certainly what the Engineer would like me to do."

He sounded speculative.

I shook my head at myself. I'd known the man mere days, so why did the thought of him walking away from me make me feel as though my nearest kin had been ripped from my arms? It choked me up. It hurt as an arrowhead hurts when it is lodged in the ribs.

I had that happen once. A mistake when a group of us were tussling with a possessed boar, trying to root it out of a clump of thorns. A local man had loosed too quickly and the arrow had struck my rib and wedged there. This bore with it a similar sensation. Every breath brought a reminder that I was stuck and could not be free, for it was in the bone.

"Sir Sorken certainly had a grudge against me. I had always thought of paladins as holy and upright and other from common men," I said sadly.

"We are only men." Adalbrand's voice was wistful. "Perhaps we once were those things when we were few, just a handful of fanatic knights swirling in tiny eddies in the corners of the reach of the church. One here, a pair there, stark in faith, swollen with prayers, surrendered entirely to a force beyond comprehension, to a God both powerful and terrible. Perhaps then, honor grew like a mighty oak, and righteousness flowed like a river, and the good won every battle."

"But now?" I prompted as I tried a third combination. To me, his description sounded just like him. It sounded like his heart whittled down to the quick.

"Now we are bloated with men who claim to be called by the God and sent out in his service, but we are among them now and that is not what I see. I see men blinded by selfish ambition, driven to murder, to exclusion, to the mad allowance of evil thriving in their midst."

"What then shall we do?" I asked grimly, sliding all but the last piece into place. And I meant both about the others here and also about him and I and the tangle of hearts we'd accidentally made.

He leaned so he could look me in the eye when he said, "We shall fight this evil at every turn."

That was good. We were still one in this fight. What more could I reasonably ask for than that? I shouldn't have said more. I knew it. I should have just nodded steadily to let him know I was on his side. Instead, my weak tongue tripped on itself.

"And when we have finished? If we survive?"

He shook his head, his expression torn as if he were fighting a second great war within himself.

"I do not know." He looked up then, his bright brown eyes catching mine in the light of the silent golem's dancing flame. His eyes narrowed with purpose. "But I know I will not leave you, Victoriana. Survive with me, and we will leave this place together and never look back."

An excellent promise. A promise a girl could hold to. Even if it felt like it would not be enough.

I slotted the last tile into place as I nodded firmly to him, turned the key in the door, and then the floor shook again. Exclamations rang out from the other end of the great main hall, and the rumbling, squealing misery of the moving floor began, shaking us both as the world turned.

"Whatever comes next," I told Adalbrand, "whether we live or die, or go wildly mad, I'm not sorry to have met you here. And I am not sorry to have loved you, however insufficiently."

He laughed, a dark, gallows laugh.

"I like how you think, Vagabond Paladin. And I agree." He paused as if he would say more but then he shook his head. "Let us prepare to slay demons and take their blackened hides for trophies."

Excuse you.

"And their shriveled souls for boot leather," I agreed, my tone still wistful, but my words bolstering me.

I'm not sure I like your claws, little snack. Retract them at once.

I grabbed his hand and held it in tight purpose to make our words a promise, but in his eyes, I found a different kind of vow. One that did not fit this grim, terrible place, but was suited more to a land where hopes and mercies still rang true. And it wrung me with a hope I didn't dare keep, but I let it sit a moment like a butterfly resting on my palm. Not mine to keep, but mine for as long as I did not try to keep it.

"Agreed," he murmured, and the rumble of his voice gave me just enough of the taste of that world of hope that my spine stiffened and my heart felt brave.

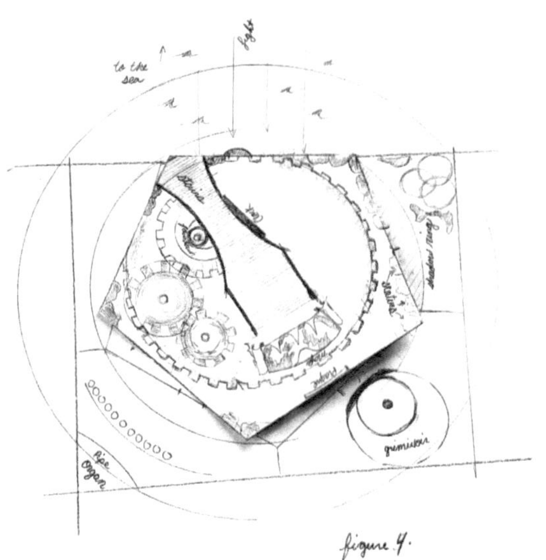

figure 4.

Chapter Twenty-Nine
Poisoned Saint

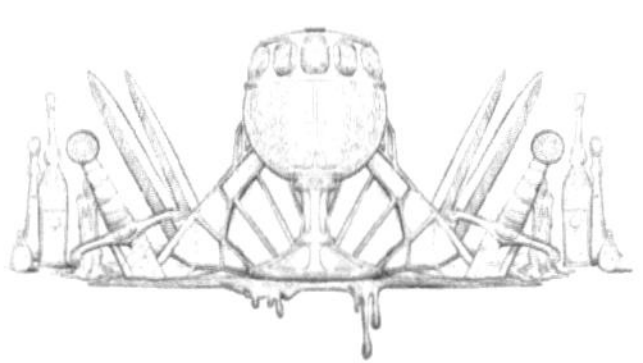

Saints and Angels take it, but I am in trouble. I can feel it breathing down my neck and laughing at me. Things are drawing to a head. There are hours, perhaps, left in this life. Hours in which I must acquit myself well. It is easy enough to waste an hour when you have an unlimited number slipping through your fingers, but when your sum is but a handful? What about then? Each becomes precious and short, and the need to make them gleaming and flawless suddenly feels weighty.

I will die well if I must die. And I will keep Victoriana alive if I can. There are no guarantees.

Either way, I am grateful.

I have been soaked in guilt and shame since my boyhood. Who would think that it would take descending into the depths of hell to finally purge me of it? Who would think that tasting the edges of this poisoned place would be what finally offered me redemption, life ... forgiveness?

I am all tangled through with relief and determination and a kind of raw treasuring of this holy warrior the God brought flaming and all too bright into my life to finally seal my wound with her burning brand. Had I thought he would dip down from above to wash clean one foul paladin, I would have expected a delicate lady swathed in silks with soft white limbs and innocent eyes to be his avatar — one like these statues carved into the ruins everywhere. I would not have expected a doubt-seamed warrior with a hard edge running through her tender heart. I find I prefer the gift offered to the one imagined.

My stream of thought is broken when the floor finishes its rotation, light spills bright and white across the floor, and the dog — Brindle — comes speeding across the ground, claws clicking on the tiles, a sharp aggressive bark slicing the air as he races toward us. I can't help the flinch of the way my body moves to shield hers. I know we have a plan for this dog, but I see him only as a threat. My leg still aches where he tore the flesh.

Victoriana does not feel the same. She crouches down to receive him as he barrels into her, and my eyes widen as his round skull butts into her belly and she leans down to put her cheek to the top of his head and rub behind his ears. I clench my jaw hard as she coos to him.

"There's a good doggy then. Who's a good doggy? You're all wet. You must have been playing in the fountain."

She's scrubbing his fur with her knuckles — as one does with a demon-infested dog, I'm sure.

I very carefully do not say anything. When I look up, it is into the eyes of the golem Cleft and he looks back with those burning hellfire eyes he's been given and says nothing. If he wrote our story, what would it say? The oil in his palm has diminished and his light flickers as the wick grows smaller — though we won't need it here anymore. If Cleft is alive and aware in a real sense, then how does he stomach the insult of being used as a candle? It's inhuman. And if he is not alive, then how does he look at me with such knowing eyes?

I look away sharply and turn my attention to the lattice window. I ache with the scent of the sea and for the first time, a window is close enough and thin enough that if I press my face to the lattice, I can see downward. There are no rough rocks. The sea laps against smooth stone. The window, however, is no wider than my head. None of us could fit through it, even were we to hammer the lattice out. I think even Brindle would be too thick around the ribcage to squeeze his way through. Perhaps the bone golem — Suture — could be disassembled and tossed piece by piece out the window and perhaps there is a way he could reform himself, but I think that unlikely. There will be no escape through this window. And there is no clue as to how to turn the room again, though I realize with unwarranted hope that if we succeed in doing just that, then we could walk right through the challenge door and leap into the sea and swim away from the madness.

My heart pangs painfully with a hunger for that which out-desires any desire I've ever had. Longing, sharp and painful, winds around my bones.

I force my attention back from it with grim determination. If we succeed, then we will breathe free air again. And if we do not, then longing for it will not grant it. I am reminded that wanting a thing is a kind of honoring. I honor free air. I honor it with all my heart.

I am also reminded that I am not a leaf blown by the wind, I am the God's holy knight. I am here with a purpose and that purpose right now is to destroy evil as it reveals itself to me, whether that be in the hearts of fellow paladins, the presence of demons or the constructed golem standing beside me.

What is stopping me, then, from charging my fellow paladins and ripping them limb from limb? I shall tell you what. I do not know which of them is guilty and which is deceived. And until I do, I cannot act in either justice or salvation.

I shake myself back to the immediate moment. I will know soon enough, and then I will act.

The Vagabond Paladin is back on her feet, braiding her hair hastily. Like me, her face is set and firm as she prepares for whatever is to come. Like me, she knows our fight is still ahead of us.

"I think you can probably snuff out that candle, Cleft," I murmur to the golem, feeling a little ashamed that I don't know whether to treat him like a man or a lamp. Soon enough, I will know that, too.

He snuffs out his wick as the clock bongs, a loud, reverberating *bong, bong, bong, bong, bong, bong, bong, bong, bong, bong.* And then the ticking seems to speed up. I don't know if I noticed it before, but I notice it now the way you notice a cloud of biting gnats buzzing around your head. The sound of it slips immediately under my skin, stinging my flesh, biting into my spirit.

I look past the clock to see a frantic Sir Owalan racing toward us, nearly tripping on his own feet. The rest are gathered around the clock face, heads bent together.

"You have to come quickly." He addresses me breathlessly when he arrives, not even glancing at Victoriana. "The clock has sped up and there are only ten hours left. *Ten!*"

He says the last word in a strangled hush, like the clock's hands have wrapped around his throat and are choking it out of him.

"Hmm." Is he part of this? He seems too caught up in the drama of it to also be plotting murders.

"That may not be enough time," he gasps. "And what if it speeds up again?"

"Has anyone learned yet what that clock even does?" I ask, lifting an eyebrow at Owalan.

He's very excitable for a Penitent. I'd always thought them to be a somber, steady bunch. Owalan is young, but at least five years older than Victoriana. One would think he would have calmed after so long in the service. Perhaps that is a reason to suspect there is more here than meets the eye.

"Look up," Victoriana says grimly, and I follow her gaze upward.

It's hard to see more than the gleam of the gilt so high up there. It is dark above and the light from the small window barely penetrates the shadow, but I just manage to see the glint of light off of gilding and ... is it moving?

I shoot her a worried look and she nods. "It's ticking incrementally with the clock. Twisting. It twisted with each spin of the room, and now it ticks with the clock. Is the window ticking, too?"

Is it? I turn back to the window, trying to choose a spot on a cloud to measure by and ...

"I think so," I say eventually, throat hoarse. The words do not want to leave me. "I think the whole room is ticking with that clock."

"Then it is a safe guess that in ten hours the wall will move, that massive demon in the ceiling will drop out of his trap, and the door will face the sea," she says.

"There will be a pause," I say, grimacing at the wall. "Even if the entire side of the inner room is open, and the door slowly traverses it tick by tick, we will need to exit through the door to the trial well before it hits the corner and moves to face the sea."

"Yes." Her eyes track where my finger is pointing.

"And we do not know when in that time frame the demon will drop from the ceiling."

"We don't," she confirms as we both look upward and let the horror of that thought sink in. "But we always meant to cast it out. And we cannot do that until it is out of the cage."

"Either way, we must play this out until it happens. We can't avoid it."

"Sir Coriand!" Owalan shouts suddenly, spinning away from us and darting back down the echoing marble hall. I suppose he needs to pass on that information immediately. His anxiety radiates off him like heat from a cherry-red stove. This would frazzle anyone's nerves. And he was highly strung from the start. Does that mean he is innocent?

I am surprised when a warm palm finds mine. Startled enough that I shoot Victoriana a bemused glance. Her expression is firm and sincere but perhaps she has realized along with me that we are likely in our last hours. Perhaps she wants only to touch another human, to make the most of these last hours.

"Does this count as affection?" she asks lightly.

I squeeze her palm, certain she will pull away when I reply but wanting whatever few moments she will grant.

"Is it meant as such?"

"Yes."

"Then it counts."

She slides her palm away as I predicted, frowns spitefully at the demon in the roof, and strides forward, hands meeting on the hilt of her naked blade. At least her disappointment propels her to action. Mine merely sits like lead within my belly.

We join the others outside the door to the last trial. I am a strange combination of reluctance and determination. The last time I felt this was when I was lined up for the Battle of the Radiant Hills. There'd been little fighting for my aspect. Our healing arts had been more useful on the whole, but before men were wounded and dying and calling for us, we'd made a solid charge, wheeled, and made a second. And it was before that first charge that I felt exactly as I do now. I can almost hear the scream of the horses again and smell how the mud scent changed from fecund to copper laced.

This is surely the last trial, for there are no more hidden walls, no more doors waiting to be unlocked, or rooms waiting to be delved into. Across from us, the clock ticks ominously and the cups there seem to glow brighter, but here where the remaining paladins have assembled, shadows have piled high and unnatural, ballooning up from those who once claimed to be holy — a ragged claim now, too thin to hold up under even the most cursory of scrutiny. The Vagabond's clothing looks to be in better repair than the righteousness of my brothers.

I study them with a new sharpness. Time is running out and therefore the time to act is running out with it. How then shall I judge?

Sir Coriand stands across the entrance with an amiable look on his face. He is sipping tea, using both hands, as if to highlight his harmlessness. This, from a man who likely pushed a brother to his death. My throat twists at the thought, but again, I have no evidence.

"Friends," he says with a gentle, twinkling smile. "Brothers ... and sister."

There's an ironic twist to that last word. I suppose he has decided he will be the required speech-giver.

My eyes find Hefertus's across the group and he squints a question at me. Likely, he's heard rumors from Owalan about the Vagabond. I meet his eyes steadily. I wouldn't expect him to jeopardize himself for my sake. That's why I bear him no ill will for leaving me unconscious and on my own in the last trial. Hefertus is innocent of murder. He's not the one I must seek and destroy.

"Our last trial is upon us," Sir Coriand says. "When it is complete, all riddles will be answered, all doors unlocked, all truths laid bare."

He is far too eager, as if he is savoring this moment. We are silent. What is there to say? None of us has a choice in what comes next.

I am not surprised at all when Victoriana breaks the silence. Her eyes lock onto Sir Coriand. She looks for all the world like her violent dog.

"As a paladin of the Creator God, you are forsworn against lies. I bid you speak now the truth." Her words are soft, but they are soft like a blade sliding through the ribs. Interesting. She will try to draw out a confession. I do not think it will work.

Sir Coriand turns his predatory eyes to her. He no longer looks as if he is simply enjoying a tea. He looks like my schoolmaster once did just before he beat me with his rule stick until I could not see out of my left eye. I was not particularly gifted with numbers.

My hand drifts to the hilt of my sword.

"You'll have your answers, Beggar," Sir Coriand says, to my surprise. "You are right that we are forsworn to lies. We must answer a direct question with the truth. And I will indulge your asking. But not now. Not here. The clock ticks. And ticks. Relentlessly. And she ticks out the seconds of our lives if we do not hurry. Let us not delay. We will enter this last trial. All of us. Your dog, too. The golems with him." I glanced over my shoulder and see the golems are both there, sacks slung over their shoulders. Nothing looks grimmer than a golem. "And when we are all within the trial, then I will answer your questions while the others pursue the highest of callings."

"Highest?" There's a bitter twist to her tone.

"What would you call Sainthood?" he snaps back. But I notice he didn't speak a lie. His question cloaks the falsehood. For I think we all know by now that no one is walking out from this place holy or justified. If we emerge again, it will be as victims or villains. There will be no heroes here.

And without another word, Sir Coriand takes a last sip of tea, hands his wooden bowl over to Suture, turns his back on us, and strides through the open door. Silently, we follow, though I might hear a murmured prayer being chanted under the Vagabond's breath.

Around us, the shadows loom and Sir Coriand's voice echoes back to me as he passes through the door. He moves very slowly, but he and his golems fill the passage so that we all must move slowly with him.

He's chanting that foreboding rhyme that builds on itself with each passing. And his words are highlighted by the rhythm of the golem's feet clomping on the ground as they pound out the beat. The voices of Sir Sorken and Sir Owalan chant out the words with him and they echo and reverberate and send chills through my marrow.

"Our hearts spoke out our hopes and our souls bore the cost,
The man and the spirit and all that was lost.
Bold together we race where no others have trod,
for we are more than men, we have become gods.

I flinch at that word. Idolatry. I can practically smell the brimstone.

"That's what we gave at the door," Sir Sorken calls back. "The sins confessed. They were the first thing we offered up."

Saints and Angels. He knew. He let us do that when he *knew.* That's a tick against him. How much else does he know?

They are still chanting.

"*Choose now holy vessel, be careful, be clear,*
For the bones of others will root out your fear,
Wash your cup with sorrow, bathe your vessel with blood,
But choose your gift wisely, be it fire or mud."

"You took fire indeed when you took the Vagabond's blood, hmmm, High Saint?" Sir Sorken calls back. "Whose blood did you take, Hefertus? I don't remember seeing you do it."

"The Seer's," Hefertus says, surprising me. "I spoke it into the cup as a blessing from the God. Why hurt the living when the dead will do?"

"How very clever. We gave to each other, of course," Sir Sorken says. "We are, after all, each other's only real rivals, isn't that right, Coriand?"

But Sir Coriand is still chanting.

"*No power is priceless, No honor unearned,*
From store house bring wisely, add gift to the churn,
A sacrifice given, a sacrifice made,
What no longer serves you is the price you've paid."

Sir Sorken is still explaining. "I'm sure you've realized by now that what you gave on that altar is now in the mix, too, hmm? The blood and tears of a rival, the sin your heart holds close, the attribute you were willing to give up. I hope your creation has an excellent voice, Sir Joran. You gave yours to it forever, like it or no."

I hadn't realized it before, but now that he has pointed it out, the High Saint's scowl is a silent one. His prayers have stilled and muted forever. I don't like that. They were the only thing about Joran Rue that I ever liked — certainly his most holy attribute. He must think so, too, with the devastation that paints his face when he looks at me. Perhaps he hopes I will heal him. But I clasped hands with the Vagabond only minutes ago and I kissed her minutes before that. I can no more heal him than the golems can. I should feel guilty. Instead, I am weighing whether he is truly as innocent as he appears. A holy front is a good guise for murder and a black heart.

"What did you give up, Poisoned Saint?" Sir Sorken asks.

"My guilt," I say plainly, and am surprised by his startled laugh.

"I never thought of that. Would have been easier than the dog. Did you think of that, Coriand?"

Unsurprisingly, Sir Coriand is too focused to answer.

"I hope you read the books you chose — or at least skimmed them," Sir Sorken says with a nasty smile flung over his shoulder. His iron-grey curls bob as he moves as if we are on an outing and not marching into evil. "I'm sure you've realized by now that whichever one you chose will be the guiding principle for what you are creating."

"Creating?" Sir Owalan pauses in the chant long enough to share his confusion. "I thought we were being made Saints."

"You're being made gods," Sir Sorken says, and his voice sounds satisfied. "If you live through the process. Let's listen to the end of the instructions, shall we?"

Sir Coriand chants them out, and he does not pause, moving from what had been memorized to what is now inscribed upon the ground we pass.

"Now write out your orders. Be patient. Be clear.
For this calling borders the depths that you fear.
Join shadow to vessel, build sinew and bone,
Without conscience wrestle, to carve out a home."

Sir Coriand turns and faces us in the open entrance to the next trial, and his face is twisted in the light of the golem's palm candle. He's backlit by a bright light. The combination makes him look like he is made of wax and melting.

"Alone be triumphant, in solitude shout," he quotes. "*You've made what the heavens themselves cannot doubt.*"

And as the word "solitude" is still ringing forebodingly in my head, he spins around and enters the challenge before us. If he is not guilty of murder, then he is certainly guilty of blasphemy.

Sir Sorken looks back long enough to waggle his eyebrows at us, and then he disappears with his friend.

I brush my hand against Victoriana's and hook my smallest finger with hers — a goodbye, perhaps.

From here in, those who will suffer will suffer. And those who will die will die. And we will likely be both. But if I can find for certain who is responsible for the deaths of the others, I will see they die first.

The dog's tongue licks our joined fingers and I grimace. Great. We have someone's blessing. And I don't know if it's a dog, or a demon, or a moldering old knight.

Chapter Thirty
Vagabond Paladin

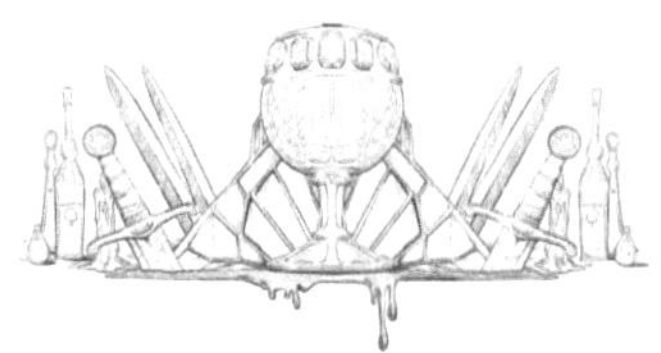

I *think we are close to the end now, my girl, and there are so many things I have not told you.*

I was starting to realize how much he'd protected me from that I'd never understood. It hadn't seemed like it when we were shivering in blasts of cold drifting from village to village eating scraps, huddled in barns, dealing with the kinds of perversion the villagers shied away from. It had not felt it when we wrestled demons in the dark and prayed our way through the twisting turns of evil men. But the world had been simpler then than it was right now under the ground. What Sir Branson had protected me from had not been evil, but it had been the understanding that even those who represent good can be evil, or foster evil, or fight on the side of evil. I had harbored doubts before. In that protected state. He had stood like a shield in front of me and protected me from the worst of it.

I had not realized.

When he taught me to give thanks over scraps, he had not told me it was because greed, when rooted deep, drove the hearts of men to regard murder as a mild inconvenience.

When he taught me to welcome beggars and those who were abandoned by others, he had not told me that they were kings compared to those who wore white and rode in the name of the God.

I also failed to tell you that you were a great comfort to me. A daughter not of my body, but mine to protect, mine to train, mine to love. I loved you, my girl, as a father loves a child. I want you to know that.

I had loved him, too.

The God says you must bury me with honor. Let the honor be that you remember and let the remembrance shine light into the doubts that still endarken your heart.

I swallowed down a desire to dismiss what he was saying just so I could protect myself from what was coming next. I didn't want him to go. And yet I needed him to go and to go soon. Time was ticking down and every demon in this arcanery must be dealt with somehow — including the one in my dog.

Sir Coriand turned and led us into the light of the trial ahead, seeming almost swallowed by it, and then his golems were swallowed next, and then those in front of me one by one.

There is a story from the ancient past of Corinna the Martyr. Corinna — by faith alone — left her family and her home, and dressed in white flowing robes — which, frankly, is a very impractical choice for travel and made me doubt the sanity of her other choices — and walked to the center of a cult of the Heart of the Bull, and there, in their underground lair she had knelt in prayer and asked the God to vanquish her enemies and he had shown her the one weak spot in the structure. Filled with his power, she had struck it a mighty blow, and the temple had collapsed, killing her, and hundreds of worshipers. It had always struck me as odd that we told this tale, because if everyone died then who could tell what Corinna had done?

The God knew and he told his faithful. Abernicus saw Corinna in her Saintly form and made for her a great statue that graces the narthex of the Cathedral of the Three Peaks in Shannamara.

Or, the demon added wickedly. *Or, your pretty girl dressed in pristine white and she ventured out willingly and partook eagerly in the cult's worship, and when the place came down — due, no doubt to poor human construction methods — the collapse took her with it. And then her credulous friends and family painted her as martyr rather than a cultist and you fools pray now to a Saint as twisted as the ones that garnish this place.*

He spun out into raucous laughter in my mind.

And I couldn't have said if his story was true. It had the unfortunate ring of truth about it.

I felt Adalbrand's finger slip free of mine and then he was lost to brightness and I stepped through behind him, blinking in such light as I had not seen in days. My eyes were no longer accustomed to it.

What if Corinna *had* gone to worship false gods? What if at the last moment, she had changed her mind and called on the God and he had both vanquished her enemies and swept her away in the tumult with them, and she was neither Saint nor sinner but merely one more soul in a sea of the broken, the foolish, the uncertain.

Just like me.

Not like you. You, my girl, are destined for better things. Now, shed this doubt once and for all. Walk with me into trouble and let our deeds wash away the tarnish of distrust.

When my eyes finally cleared and I could see, I stood and stared with everyone else.

I should have known by now to expect the rooms of this place to be built to an unimaginable scale. The ceiling towered high above us and was so crisscrossed with light coming down that the room seemed brightly lit. Perhaps it would have felt dull if I had come directly down from above, but I had not. I had been walking in darkness for so long that this light felt blinding. How had we not seen so many holes drilled from above? We must have walked over these places again and again.

Down one wall, water trickled against the flat white marble, growing mold and moss on the wall there in virulent greens and chartreuses. This must be where that stream above had disappeared. And perhaps, it explained why the gears squealed when the room twisted. Had the stream of melting Rim water rusted them? Or did it, perhaps, power them somehow? I was not familiar with water workings, though I was sure the Engineers were. I would not ask them for clarification. I no longer trusted them with anything.

The room was less stark than the others had been. It took me a moment to realize why. There were white statues lining the walls, of course, but these statues were partially crumbled and foliage threaded through them. Vines and shrubs and small trees grew here, stilted and stunted, yes, but alive.

Just the scent of them made my heart feel wistful, longing for the plants above I may never see again. I ran fingers over the leaves closest to me as we slowly made our way into the room, turning to look at everything.

All around the edge of the vault were stone benches set to watch the center and between the benches were lecterns and small writing desks, piled with books and scattered with parchment and ink. Two hundred scholars could easily fit in this room, moving from desk to bench to lectern and still the room would feel too large. The wall behind us, besides one pillar leading from floor to ceiling — which, undoubtedly contained the glass slider puzzle and faced the mesh window — was open to the moveable wall. It was a bit of a relief to see that was so, what with the clock slowly ticking and turning the central room. We would have a chance to escape this room for as long as the door ticked along that open stone wall. Far more time than the mere hour that it would have taken to tick past a single door space.

That established, I turned back to the main room and to the white sand floor in the center. It was clearly placed there intentionally and it was surrounded by a rim of marble carved to look like a swirling line of snakes tangled in on one another.

And above the sand, on pulleys and ropes, were three of the strangest contraptions I think I've ever seen. Already, Sir Sorken was lowering one from a short platform where it was anchored.

"And now, we test!" His voice boomed out.

He could test all he wanted. I felt none of his enthusiasm.

Sir Coriand hurried over. He passed a book, a pot of ink, and a quill to Sir Sorken who fitted them on a small wooden board just large enough for all three. The two of them fussed over it, arranging the red leather-bound book just so and then smoothing their brown tabards and hoary locks as if they were about to present themselves to a bishop.

"You chose the Exclusia Prima, I think?" Sir Coriand said formally, scrawling a note in a second book. I didn't bother questioning how there was still ink in these pots. It was no stranger than that the pages of the books had not disintegrated to dust.

"I did. A fine sample of a great work."

"Blessings on your work," Sir Coriand said, raising two fingers formally.

Having settled his book in place, Sir Sorken eased himself into the leather harnesses, belly down, to my surprise, legs spread out and arms in front to where they could easily reach both the straps of the pulley system and the writing board. With a tightening of his aged muscles, he gave a quick tug, and the contraption released from the platform, swung into the center of the room over the sand, and began to ascend as he tugged the ropes.

The light from above caught him and that was when I finally saw the point of this strange rig that left him helpless and vulnerable, spread-eagle under the ominous ceiling, for beneath him, his shadow built and swirled, seeming blacker and fuller than it had been before he pinned it beneath him to the sand.

We all watched as he ascended to the height he wanted, and then opened his book and began to write and I thought my mouth might drop open when the shadow beneath him altered, billowing here and slimming there, and began to take shape to look almost just like Cleft — his golem creation — but formed entirely of shadow.

"Written," Sir Owalan gasped with wide eyes. "They do say the world was created by a single word, don't they?"

Without uttering a syllable — and no wonder with his voice gone forever — the High Saint snatched up a book and ink pot of his own and hustled to the second of the three rigs. He must have been watching with care, for he was rigged and flying out over the sand in moments, ascending quickly into the air.

I took a moment to mentally measure the space between the rigs. They could not reach each other at the height of their ascension, but I thought they could if they were lowered all the way. Certainly, their shadows could — and would — intersect down below. I had just enough time to wonder what might happen if they did, when Sir Sorken's shadow reached out a clunky arm and swiped at the unformed shadow of the High Saint, scattering it and dispersing it for a moment before it began to coalesce again.

Ah.

So they would be building and battling all at the same time.

How better to test the theories they pour into them?

Brindle nuzzled my hand and I sank it into his friendly fur, drawing in strength for a moment before he wiggled away, left my side at a brisk pace, and trotted around the edge of the room, sniffing everything in turn.

"And now you owe us the truth, Sir Coriand," I said, not rushing to the books as Sir Owalan had, or poking at the sand with my sword as Hefertus was.

I was focused on one thing: discovering who among us had murdered the others. After all, that was the person to stop, wasn't it? The rest could be reasoned with. The rest could be convinced not to make demons. But the murderer had to have known from the beginning what all of this was and had to have planned to use it for his own ends.

"And what truth is that, Beggar?" Sir Coriand asked, rolling his shoulders backward as if bracing for a fight. It was a strange thing to see in a man well past his prime, his hair long and hoary white. But his golem flanked him — Suture — a construct of rag and bone, and somehow the horrible machine looked protective, more bodyguard than beast.

"Did you push the Majester?"

"Of course."

Sir Owalan's head snapped up at that, but the High Saint didn't even look over at him. I heard a low growl from the direction of Hefertus. Adalbrand eased himself against the base of one of the platforms, watching with a keen eye.

"Did you use his death as the sacrifice for the trial?"

"He no longer served me."

"Did you —"

Sir Sorken interrupted me. "If you're going to interrogate my friend, Beggar, I think it's only fair that *your* friend comes up here with us in the sky. After all, we can't have you fighting two against one."

I glanced over at Adalbrand and shrugged. We didn't both need to be down here. Would he go up in a rig if it meant discovering the truth?

He hesitated, frowned, but after a moment he shrugged, too.

"Very well. But I'll examine a book before I ascend. I won't write gibberish for no reason. And I do not scribe in ancient Indul."

"Doesn't seem to make a difference what language you write in. I've written in three languages so far and they all work," Sir Sorken said as if the murder I was trying to discuss was hardly even interesting compared to the task set before him.

The golems shuffled gently around the ring, picking up fallen books and placing them neatly back in stacks. Two against one, indeed. It would be three against one if I tried anything. I would battle them all if I must. I would root out both demons and murderers. I had no doubt that the two were linked.

Ha! As if it is ever so easy. Ask your questions. Find your killer out. At least you'll get one last taste of victory before I rip out your tongue.

It was strange how threats dulled when they were breathed at a constant stream. What would have given me chills only days ago felt insignificant now.

And so the city is taken. With a whisper here, a nudge there, and when no one is looking anymore, when all are drowsing, then we push and we bring down the walls, flood over them with axes and brands ready, and we pillage the city, put it to the flame, and slay every resident. So it will be with your very heart, sweetmeat.

Not if I can help it. And help it, I will, Sir Branson warned.

I did not have the space in my mind to spare for their argument. My mind was focused on Sir Coriand.

"The Inquisitor," I demanded as Adalbrand wandered over to one of the desks and started flipping through the pages. I could tell that he was listening as he worked, his attention divided between me and the books. "Did you tell the Majester to kill him? Was yours the voice he thought he heard?"

"Did he claim to hear a voice?" Sir Coriand asked. "Here, let me help you, Sir Adalbrand. Any of these blank books will do, but you'll need a friendly hand to hold the ropes of the harness for you."

Adalbrand quirked an eyebrow at him. "Forgive me, Sir Engineer, but I fear your hand is not friendly. Did you not just confess to pushing the Majester from your platform? You are a murderer."

Sir Coriand took a step back, wariness in his eyes.

"I did confess that," he said carefully, and my eyes narrowed. He was not flustered or concerned that we had found him out. He was laying out his actions as if they were completely understandable. "And we are all murderers. We confessed it to Sir Kodelai before we entered this place. I suspect we would not have been allowed the trials had we not confessed to at least that. And now think, Poisoned Saint. Have you never killed a man in mercy? You take on ills so great that it almost seems you thwart the will of the God. Did you not save the Majester's life, plucking him from the very gates of death and setting him back into this world?"

"I did," Sir Adalbrand agreed, looking up only briefly before he returned to studying a book.

He drew a parchment from a pocket, smoothed it out, and

folded it into the blank book before flipping through a stack of others. What he was looking for was not obvious to me, but he seemed to have a purpose to his brisk movements and rapid study. Hadn't Sir Branson said that the Poisoned Saints were very well studied? Maybe he was used to combing through a great deal of text very quickly — even in another language.

He opened one of the books wide enough that I could see it from where I stood on the edge of the ring, sword at the ready. The book was filled on every page with diagrams that looked more like engineering theory than like written treatise.

I smell something strange ...

Later. We would deal with strange smells later. Sir Coriand was still confessing.

"And yet you could not restore his mind," Sir Coriand said gently. "Am I wrong in thinking that ills of the mind are not something that Poisoned Saints can take into themselves? Am I wrong in thinking that you did all that you could by the grace of the God?"

Adalbrand glanced up at him with a scowl.

"I think I am not wrong," Sir Coriand said gently. "Let Suture help you with that. The book is heavy."

Adalbrand shrugged off the golem, stalking over to the third contraption with an annoyed set to his shoulders. He arranged his book and ink on the abbreviated table and climbed up the platform.

He was being goaded into that harness. But why?

I glanced upward to where the High Saint and Engineer floated in the air like flies trapped in a web. They had paused in their workings, watching the drama between the Poisoned Saint and Sir Coriand.

It was as if all of them were waiting for Adalbrand, unwilling to keep testing their shadows until he took his place.

Adalbrand paused. "And if you are right, what does it matter, Sir Coriand?"

Sir Coriand's smile might have meant to be a gentle compassion, but I saw it as mockery when he said, "I know how you Poisoned Saints work. What do you call it? Milk of the Reaper? That drink you slip to those whose pain you cannot drink?"

Adalbrand paled.

"That gift you give those whose minds are beyond saving. I've seen it myself, tasted a drop. Not enough to send me to the gates of death, obviously, but you know how curious we are in the Aspect of the Creator God. It smelled strongly of mint and cloves. Do you add them to disguise the bite of death, or are they essential to the making of the toxin?"

The look on Adalbrand's face was pure hatred. He slung himself into the harness violently as if he could get the job over with and rid himself of Sir Coriand's subtle accusations.

"I think you should make your point, Engineer," I said calmly. I was not sure why he was goading Adalbrand and it worried me. I was rightly concerned that the Engineer was more intelligent than I was and likely to spin me to his plans if I was not careful.

Sir Coriand spread his hands wide in a gesture of peace and took a measured step back, almost bumping into Suture who loomed over him.

"My only point," he said slowly as Adalbrand arranged the straps and placed his hands on the pulley ropes. "My only point is that the Poisoned Saint — of any of us — must understand what dealing mercy to a man is like. I dealt the Majester mercy. He was a broken man. He could not live like that."

Adalbrand's lip twisted and he hauled up on the rope so hard I worried he'd break it. Clearly, he was angry, and clearly, he was trying not to let his anger out.

And clearly, he'd forgotten one thing.

"Which brings us back to the point," I said, letting my voice be as dry as the sand under our feet. "Were you the voice he thought was the God? The one that spoke from above and bid him kill the Inquisitor. The one that drove him mad — if he was mad, indeed?"

Sir Coriand's eyes were fixed on Adalbrand, and only when

his harness reached full height, did the Engineer finally turn from him and look at me, and his face transformed from innocence to a look so full of knowing that it twisted my stomach.

"Yes," he said, mildly.

And as he said it there was a sound like slithering. Adalbrand made a startled sound and when I looked up, I realized why the Engineer had been stalling. The straps had tightened suddenly around all three of the people suspended above us. They were locked in place. Trapped.

Whatever came next, I would have no help from the Poisoned Saint. His eyes met mine across the distance and I saw him realizing with me what had just happened. We'd been maneuvered.

He grimaced, but he was a practical man. After a tightening of his jaw, he turned to his book, and started to write, a determined line forming on his forehead.

Carefully, I backed up and to the side, placing my back to Hefertus. I was relatively certain he would not stab me in the back.

"And so you orchestrated the murder of the Inquisitor and the Majester," I said calmly. "Did you know what this place was when you arrived here?"

"You ask me that?" Sir Coriand's voice was mocking. "You, who deliberately mistranslated what was written more than once."

"Not deliberately," I said through gritted teeth, glancing at Brindle.

The game is up then, snackling. Of course, I deceived you. Of course, I lied. How else would I dance you into a trap? How else would I soften you for the blow? But the sin lies with you, because you chose to believe me, knowing I was a demon. You stand accused by your own tongue, for was it not you who said that knowing and doing nothing makes one culpable? You are as bathed in wickedness as I ever was.

His voice faded into menacing laughter.

"Not deliberately?" And now, for the first time, Sir Coriand seemed uncertain. "You didn't do this deliberately? You didn't know ahead of time what this place was? You were not trying to keep it for yourself?"

"What is it?" The words burst from Sir Owalan like he was running out of patience. He'd been watching us, head turning back and forth and back and forth like a bird watching the action. "What is this place? Why is she … why is she blaming you for the things that have occurred here? Surely you don't mean the confessions you've given just now. They were to trap her, weren't they? To keep her from using the demon against us?"

We both turned and looked at him.

"And where is the cup?" Sir Owalan asked, a little uncertainly. "Isn't it here?"

In the silence, all I heard was the ticking of the clock and the scratching of pens.

"It was never here," I said sadly at the same time that Sir Coriand said, "It was always here."

"I don't understand." The Penitent looked stricken, eyes darting back and forth between us. "Where is it?"

"At the base of the clock," Sir Coriand said with a sigh. "Waiting to become the Cup of Tears with what we do here, with what we pour into it, and then drink down into ourselves."

"Just like all the cups, I assume," Adalbrand said from above, his pen still scratching even as he spoke. "The Cup of Tears, Artar's Grail, the Holy Chalice — all the fabled cups are this cup, aren't they?"

I nodded along, certain he was right. They were all holy cups. And none of them were.

"See?" Sir Coriand said, lifting an eyebrow at Sir Owalan. "It has been here all along, waiting to exist. And one of us will complete it."

His golems seemed to loom higher behind him, as if they had grown, the pair of them, as we spoke.

"Do you want to be a Saint, Sir Owalan, Penitent Paladin? Do you want to bring the Cup of Tears back to your aspect that you all might flagellate yourselves before it and honor your God?"

"I did … I do," Sir Owalan said, but his voice was uncertain.

Coriand nodded, a small smile on his lips, like that of a cherub. "Then you will finish this task with us. And you will drink from your cup. And you will bring it back to your aspect exactly as they asked. And you will be a god — not *the* God, obviously. But *a* god — or as we say in the church, a Saint."

I thought for sure he'd reject that. Spit in Coriand's face. Rip the dagger from his sleeve.

He did none of those things.

"Yes," Sir Owalan breathed, and then he lifted his chin and for some reason met my eye as if he expected defiance. And when he spoke it was with power and passion behind it. "Yes."

"No."

The word was spoken so quietly that it almost couldn't be heard over the ticking of the clock, but the scritching stopped as we all turned to look at Hefertus. I felt a weight ease off my chest. I was not alone. Even with Adalbrand stuck suspended from the ceiling. Hefertus would stand against this, too.

He ran a hand over his hair, grabbed the tie, swept it loose, and shook his long, cascading golden hair out in a wave. It glinted with his pearls and his thick beard and he stood just a little taller, a little straighter, spine tall and firm and with his shoulders back he said it again.

"No."

I lifted my own chin, challenging them to come against us, we two who would defend righteousness and goodness together. And how could I possibly lose with Hefertus by my side? The man was a giant. A monster among men.

"I will have no part in this," he said grimly.

I put my hand on the hilt of my sword, ready to draw.

And then he startled me.

He stepped forward, but he did not draw his sword, and he did not take up a defensive stance.

Instead, he raised two fingers in a blessing, and intoned softly, "Bless me, O God, and I will depart from all evil."

A glow like the dawning of the sun erupted from his chest. He smiled a Saintly, pure smile, and then I blinked, and he was gone.

My gasp sounded loud in my ears, almost as loud as the nearly hysterical laughter of the demon.

Your ally! The one person you could count on here on the ground and he — what? He disappears so he doesn't have to get his hands dirty? That's amazing. I'll drink whatever he's drinking.

I could feel the blood draining from my face, sinking so quickly that my head felt light and nausea washed over me.

I glanced at Sir Owalan and saw the murder in his eyes and then to Sir Coriand to see the black humor in his.

"Well, that's one problem solved," he said easily.

There was a strangled sound from the harness where the High Saint was, but I didn't bother looking up. He was as trapped in that rig as Adalbrand was. If he was horrified, then he'd have to wait to act, just like the Poisoned Saint. For now, there was only me and my enemies.

"What will you do, Penitent?" Sir Coriand asked, grimly. "Now that you know you are building a Cup of Tears. Now that you know that the ultimate serving of the God will require ultimate sacrifice?"

"That's not how it is at all," I protested, but Sir Coriand moved to the side, starting to stalk around me and I had to keep turning to stay facing him.

From behind me, I heard Sir Owalan's answer. His voice was torn and ragged, but laced through with sincerity.

"My duty is to serve the God. No sacrifice is too great. No pain too overwhelming. If all is demanded of me, then all will be given, even the lives of those around me."

Sir Coriand nodded to Sir Owalan, somewhere behind my shoulder. It was the nod of one soldier to another. Acknowledgment. Kinship. Blessing.

Saints and Angels.

"Watch out!" Adalbrand shouted.

Brindle barked sharply behind me and I twisted, just in time to see a blade plunge by where my head had been a moment ago. And then a brindled body blurred past and bore Sir Owalan down to the sand, a growl rumbling up from a doggy throat.

Chapter Thirty-One
Poisoned Saint

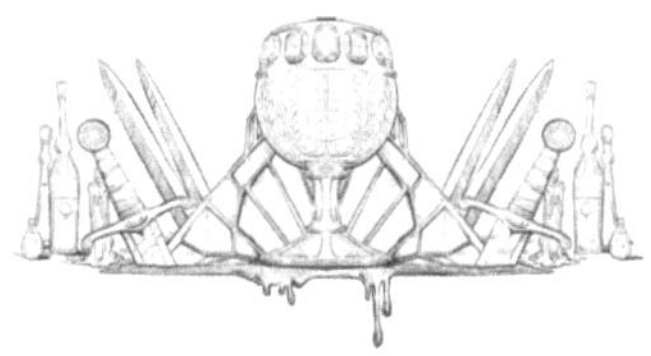

The scholastic facet of the Poisoned Saints had been among the things I liked best about my youth. Pouring over tomes and scrolls both recent and far-flung in the ancient past, dissecting one language from another, translating them both into yet a third, cross-referencing and following ecumenical arguments through the theology of souls that dated back to ten thousand years before my birth and through to the scrappy polemicals of the of our diversified modern time — well, I had happily poured my hours and days into that pursuit, dragged from it only to train my body in the arts of weaponry and battle.

Even now, a Poisoned Saint, galloping from one disaster to the next with barely a hot meal and a breath in-between, I can easily be lured away from duty by the call of a promising tome upon a shelf, or a sage whispering about the latest wisdom they are discussing in the halls of the philosophers.

Though I am made to be a seeker of truth and a lover of the novel, and though this terrible wonder we are experiencing is certainly the most fascinatingly awful thing that anyone will be whispering about for decades — if anyone lives to tell the tale of it — I would prefer to employ my gifts of scholarship another way.

I am crafting a demon. Not quite from scratch. It's already

been fed guilt and murder. My guilt. My murders. My shameful lusts, and my own blood and spit. Now, it billows beneath me, forming, strengthening, churning to the strokes of my pen upon the book. I do not know if I should make it strong and capable to defeat the others already snatching at mine, or if I should make it with a terrible flaw I can twist to destroy it.

I suspect I must do both and I am not pleased with the difficulty of the project. It would be a fun thought experiment in a high tower beside a crackling fire with a cup of mead and a friend to discuss it. It is not so delightful when I know I am dabbling in the dark arts, in a deadly sin that may very well have been the origin of all evil on this earth.

I write down an obscure quote from Nasarithin over five hundred years ago in which he expounded on the idea that evil feeds upon the fear of those around it and thus fear ought to be banished or evil will grow, and as the last words settle on the page, the shadow beneath me expands with a motion like a beating heart.

Too effective. I grimace.

"Have we crafted all the demons that ever were?" The Vagabond had asked. And I do not know the answer to that. Perhaps we have. Perhaps from the very beginning, man has penned his own demise. Perhaps he even used the ideas of the theologians to make it easier for him.

Complicating my complicity further is this: I am bound in this harness as I ply my pen, bound and trapped as Victoriana grills Sir Coriand. I cannot aid her. And I feel shame that I was led so easily into this trap. I should be below helping to unmask the crimes that have been done here.

In my defense, it hadn't felt like a trap when I climbed into the harness. It had felt like maneuvering — like setting them up to confess and putting me up high where I could watch everyone at once.

Sir Coriand makes no excuse for his actions. All the guilt I've been carrying around for years has bent me and yet on his shoulders, it weighs no more than a single flake of snow. He smiles and speaks and he is clearly enchanted by the sound of his own voice.

I have heard the great orators in the capital but I have not heard anyone quite like Sir Coriand who twists murders into sorrowful necessities and makes the Vagabond look crass for asking him to answer for them.

I do not know if I am more horrified by him and his ice-cold heart, or by Hefertus who took one look at this unspeakable choice before us and simply chose it away. Such an escape is not open to me. And even if it were, I do not think I could leave the Vagabond on her own. I am annoyed at my friend. I hope to live to tell him so.

I add to my treatise the argument of St. Flamire who wrote that every evil was vulnerable to the grace of kindness, that a kind word said could still anger and stop up bitterness. I see my shadow shiver and glance up again, divided between the battle below and the task of crafting a monster with a fatal flaw.

The Vagabond stares Sir Coriand down like a brave man stares down a charging bull even though he's flanked by both golems. I both adore her in that moment and think she bears a tragic likeness to real Saints of the past — the ones torn apart by crowds, sawn in half, and beheaded. She has their fire in her eyes, their staunch refusal to quit, their intolerable enemies.

It almost hurts to look at her.

I won't be able to save her if it comes to that.

But I write. As fast and as furiously as I can. And I try to make a monster that can break and yet be broken. I diagram out rules and sketch out plans and if my handwriting is illegible and my sketches much revised, the arcane power of this place does not seem to care.

My shadow is growing.

I write of how sin amplifies itself by curling the spirit in on itself round and round, like a tree stunted by growing within a dwelling. I write that, and the demon billows wide. I write of how anger, when fed, feeds on the one who is angry, and I feel the crack form in the center that I can leverage later.

I glance up and see Owalan move from the corner of my eye. I shout my warning and clench my jaw as his sword splits the air an inch from Victoriana's face. My heart is in my throat as she twists to the side. I thrash against the straps holding me in unconscious reaction, but I can no more leap to her aid than I can fly.

Her demon dog leaps from the shadows. He grabs Owalan by the shoulder, bearing him down to the earth.

A spike of fear shoots through me. Too many buckles hold me in place. And I will not be able to help as long as I am tied into this harness. My fingers fumble with the buckle on my forearm, blunt against the smooth leather.

"If you want to help her, you'd best write," Sir Sorken calls out. "You won't be getting down until you're done. That's how this works, my lad."

His shadow demon shambles over to mine and strikes it with a powerful overhand blow to the shoulder.

I bite my lip, put pen to paper, and scratch until my hand cramps, forcing speed and power into the lines of the shadow I craft. I write of compression and the art of water pumps in the aqueduct systems and as I write my shadow tightens and strengthens. It grabs a strand of Sorken's demon, dragging it a little over the line where our shadows meet before that scrap of shadow shreds away and the demons burst into fragments.

I curse, as my shadow falls to shreds and then slowly starts to build beneath me again. Sorken's is in the same circumstance. I should be throwing all my efforts into my fight against him, but I'm distracted by the sight of Owalan and Victoriana spinning through the space where our two demons were only moments before.

Their blades clash, steel on steel, as they whirl. Victoriana lands a double-handed strike on Owalan's shoulder, but the other paladin still has his armor — I never did ask what happened to the Vagabond's, and curse me for that. I was so fascinated by how I could feel her warmth through the cloth of her clothing, that I forgot entirely that there ought to be steel cladding over it.

With a flick of a pen, I add heat to my demon, writing of how the sear of a guilty conscience is like to a fire that can never be fully quenched, beginning to build him again from scratch.

Beneath me, dancing around my black, filthy shadow, Victoriana ducks under a blow from Cleft, her groan audible as she spins out of the defensive duck and brings her sword up just in time to turn Owalan's blow.

My guts tighten.

She's forgotten Suture.

I cry out a warning as he lunges in from behind her, grasping with bone fingers. At the last moment, the dog leaps, catching Suture's forearm between its canine teeth. The golem tries to shake the dog off, bones rattling, bits of cloth tearing off. Brindle's sleek body shakes with him, teeth rattling but refusing to quit just like his mistress.

It's with the dry-stick snap of a breaking bone that he finally flies through the air, half the golem's forearm and hand still locked in his jaw, to land hard on the edge of the sand rim.

I can't afford to watch to see if he can recover. I write about the tenacity of evil, how a single root left behind can grow again as if it were never razed in the first place. My shadow pops back to strength as if it were never ripped apart — and only just in time. Sir Sorken's demon leaps toward Victoriana, snatching at her foot.

She goes down in a heap, a pained gasp breaking her silence.

I drive my demon forward, using its bulk to push Sorken's back. It thrusts with the power I've scribed into it. And if I did not feel guilty before, it is coming back now. I am creating a monster. I am good at it.

Sir Owalan sails back into the fight, swinging his blade at Victoriana. She rolls, pops up to her feet where her dog stands, still shaking the broken golem arm in his jaws, spittle flying everywhere.

"Don't think I'm done questioning you, Sir Coriand," she says pointing the tip of her blade at him for a heartbeat before turning back to Owalan just in time to slide his strike away. Her eyes flash and her cheeks are flushed with the fight and I force my gaze away and back to what I pen.

"You're a terribly dogged thing, Beggar," Sir Coriand says, annoyed. "I heartily wish Sir Kodelai had succeeded with your demise."

"And why should I not be? We who are poor have only honor and truth left."

"Then enjoy this truth," Sir Coriand says. "Up there in that harness is your friend Adalbrand who spared your life from false accusation only yesterday. And he works studiously to craft a demon. Are you and yours really so different from us? You will do what you must to survive, too."

"Too?" She grits out before leaping so high that she kicks up, pivots on Suture's chest and spins over Owalan's blade to land at his back. He barely makes the turn in time to deflect her sliding blow and the awkward defense makes him stumble at the same time that her dog plows into him and bowls him over.

"Too," Coriand barks. "Do you think you can put this back now? The ability to craft demons to order is out in the world, child of foolishness. You cannot re-cork the bottle. You cannot un-drink the wine. It will be used now by us or our enemies. Better it be us. Better we find ways to use it. To survive. Because someone will."

"No one *has* to," the Vagabond says.

She's dancing to the side, fighting both golems as Sir Coriand tries desperately to keep her dog from his throat. Its savage growling reminds me it's more than just a dog.

I want to help her, but the High Saint's demon is ready for action now, and it leaps at mine, rending and tearing and spinning like a corkscrew made of smoke and I must write and write as I battle foes on two sides.

Mayhap if I change the geometry of the thing, I could use a

double fulcrum to apply force a little more precisely. I sketch a plan out with quick strokes. I feel the sweat forming on my brow and the dull ache in my forehead. My mind is exhausted with how hard I've forced it to think, to draw up knowledge of everything from ancient wisdom to modern engineering, but I must succeed. I must.

The Vagabond is speaking. "We could seal this place up. We could burn it to cinders. No one ever has to use it again."

"Burn it?" Owalan sounds aghast even though his cry bites off his words as Brindle leaps at him. He bashes the massive dog with his gauntlet. Brindle rolls to the side, only to leap to his feet and launch again in a blur of fur and fury.

"You can't. Be. Earnest," Owalan says, punctuating his words with strikes. He must use his off-hand. The dog is too far under his reach for him to use his sword. "There would be no more Saints. No more. Cup. And haven't you seen this place.?The. Art. Alone. Must. Be. Preserved."

I can hear the strain in the Vagabond's voice, but I can't look at her as she speaks next. My demon is all that's holding back the other two from ripping her and Brindle apart and I can't write fast enough. I can't.

If I bend the natural order just here and insist that a flux in gravity could pull this way and a spectral power drawn in through a wind draft just here, I could possibly lengthen the reach ... my thoughts tangle and jumble as I try to design the corporeal form of the demon.

I'm losing ground. I know why. I've shaped and pulled and formed this shadow to fight but I've fed it nothing. And unless I'm willing to channel both power and wickedness into it, then it can't stand up to real denizens of hell.

My demon is too insubstantial. It remains shadow and aping mockery while the others have crafted true horrors. I do not know what the High Saint has fed his but it glows with a bloody fanaticism that must look like his soul in the mirror. The Engineer's demon is as hard and set as his stone golem. There is a ripple of something at the edge of my vision that tells me it's foundation is heartlessness. It will eat the unborn if it must to fuel itself.

My stomach twists. Will I shape such a thing to save the woman below? Will I shape it to destroy the rest? I stare bleakly at it. Honor shakes its head and balks like a war stallion refusing a gate.

Beneath me, the conversation drifts up in snatches as I fight my own battle. A battle of heart and mind.

"You couldn't have murdered them all. You must have had help. You weren't down here when the Seer died."

That's my blazing Beggar. She refuses to give up, tearing every shred of flesh from this bone. Just like her half-demon dog.

"Who do you think has the power to twist a head from a body and a hand from an arm, child? Not any man I've ever known," Sir Coriand says.

"It was someone here. It was no demon," she insists.

Sir Coriand's laughter is thready. I risk a quick glance. He's standing on the shoulders of his golem as it shambles one-handed toward the Beggar, its one good arm scything out as if it will reap her like ripe grain.

"No, it was someone with greater power than any man."

"A golem," she says with certainty. "They could have snuck in later. And they wouldn't even have to confess a sin. Like my dog, they wouldn't be considered contestants in this terrible game."

"Indeed." Sir Coriand sounds pleased that she's drawn the right conclusion.

"But why kill her?"

"She was trying to destroy the key. But she — of all people — should have known. You can't stop fate. What will be, must be. World without end."

I know I must make a choice very soon, or fail in this task. The other two demons have battered mine to nothing but a gasp of shadow. It's faint and weak, a tattered curtain before an armed assault. There's only a breath of it left.

"And Sir Kodelai? An accident? Or planned by you, also?"

"You know, I was hoping someone would ask that," Sir Coriand sounds smug.

"It bothers me that the God would let him be wrong," the Vagabond admits through heavy breaths. She is tiring. They've beat her backward steadily. She's nearly to the wall. Her dog has given up on a limping Sir Owalan and he has backed up with her. "Bothers me enormously. Isn't his same power given to each of us? And yet to me, it flows with goodness, to you it flows with evil, and to the Hand, it flowed in a way that twisted in his grasp and slaughtered him."

Sir Coriand laughs. And I do not like how his laugh makes my throat tight and my heart race.

"It's always the most noble, the most holier-than-thou who are easiest to twist right out of the God's own hand, my girl. The High Saint doubted you. Didn't you, Saint?"

If the High Saint finds his words beguiling, it does not slow his attack. He seizes one seam of my fractured shadow demon and pulls.

"And he whispered in the ear of Sir Kodelai and prepared him as a good wife feeds the yeast in her bowl. And that night, when all of you slept, I came to the High Saint and I confessed all the doubts I had about you, Beggar. Confessed in a heartfelt, wretched manner, and told him too, how you inspired sin within my heart. Not the truth — but he didn't ask me directly if it were true — so I broke my oath and lied. And it was that lie he brought to Sir Kodelai that morning, feeling duty-bound to do so. It was that lie that turned Sir Kodelai's eye away from the golems he was considering as perpetrators, and toward the ragged dirty mud-streaked girl with her filthy mockery of our aspects. That's the power of words, girl. Pick the right one and you can use it like a long lever to twist the heart of man into a knot unrecognizable. I did. And I did it well. Men are just machines, after all. No different than a golem made of rag and bone."

"That's not true," her voice is small, her doubt creeping back.

"The God cares no more for you than poor Suture here. But one of you will soon be dead and the other has never lived at all."

And with those words, he presses his attack. His golem grabs Brindle and throws him so that he smacks a stone Saint statue hard and falls to the earth bonelessly. His other golem leans in, arms reaching with intent, and in that moment I make my choice.

Better to die in the name of the God than to live as creatures turned and twisted. I've always known it, but it is real to me right now.

And for the first time since we've reached this place I really pray.

I pray from deep in my bowels, from the very visceral blood and tissue of my body, from the place at the base of my spine where my soul is knit, from where my heart reaches up like a flowing spring and my brain branches forth like an oak. From *that* place I reach with all I am to the God and I beg him.

"Deliver me from evil."

Perhaps I have also said it out loud. Perhaps I have shouted it. I do not know. But I feel the response.

Light and heat crash over me as if someone has flung a bucket of fire over my head.

It is not pleasant shining glory. It is nothing I might revel in or preen under.

It is like being dredged under by the grip of illness. It is like the fever dreams that wrack you to the bone when they twist and rend and seek to separate a man from his very sinews. It wrenches and wrings me so furiously that I retch down onto the sand. I lose all sense of time and space and the knowledge of my own form, until at last my eyes shoot open and I watch as a great shadow is vomited from my mouth and falls hot and heavy to the ground.

I feel as if a burning coal has been touched to my mouth. My limbs are suddenly free. The book I had written in is aflame, burning with a fire so white I can hardly look. I grab the ash and flame in my bare hands and rip the book apart, flinging it to the sand. I do not even feel the flames. I am already burning.

I stand with superhuman agility in the crisscross of the leather straps, and I leap.

No man should leap so far and live. I have no explanation for why I do not break both tibia and shatter my legs as I hit the ground.

I have heard of the great acts the God allows in times of desperation. My only explanation is that here and now I have been gifted a reprieve from the laws that govern the earth and that for that space of a heartbeat my body and bones belong only to the God and not to any of the rules he buckled 'round the earth when he wove her form.

I land with my feet on the shoulders of Suture and my belly pressing down on Sir Coriand's back. I feel the bone golem buckle under the sudden force, driven to his bone knees on the marble of the floor. There's a splintering sound and then Sir Coriand tumbles out from under me, somersaulting. He rolls upward, dagger flicking from sheath like the tongue of a lizard as he seeks to come up under the Vagabond's guard.

I'm distracted as I find my feet.

A faint bark arrests me and I spin in time to turn Owalan's strike.

Another head strike? Is the man doubly a fool? He certainly seems to revel in such nonsense.

I press my own attack, drive him back, and then backhand him hard across the cheek. My strength must be greater than I remember, because he rolls through the air like a barrel down the hill over and around and over again until he smacks the floor hard, his hands unable to get up and protect his face from the blow. I fear his neck may be broken but I have not the time to check.

Already, I am spinning again. I am leaping just in time to use the weight of my own body to turn aside the stone punch of Cleft as he reaches for the Vagabond.

She's locked into a dagger fight with Sir Coriand, the dagger gripped in her off-hand. She refuses to drop her sword but its bulk is too great for this knife battle and the old paladin is inside her reach.

My breath wooshes out of me and my breastplate crumples painfully into my flesh as I take Cleft's blow, but some of whatever blessing the God has gifted me clings to my body and I drop my sword, grab his stone fist in both hands, and shove with all my strength. He stumbles backward and then freezes.

His sudden motionlessness leaves me off balance and I complete my spin unhindered and crash into him, my backplate into his stone chest. He falls backward, balance lost, stone crashing into stone with a horrendous smashing sound.

I stumble, find my bearings, and look up just in time to see Sir Coriand drop his dagger, an angelic expression on his elderly cherub face as the Vagabond's sword slashes a perfect arc through the heavenly light and cleaves his head from his body. It follows the arc of her blade like a perfectly thrown ragball, spinning ribbons of red out from it in arcs like a maypole at festival time.

I don't have time to react. It comes right for me, smacks my ruined breastplate, and lands at my feet, so that all I have to do is bend forward to look straight into the face of evil.

The face of evil looks back at me, blinks once, and then freezes in a smiling rictus.

Chapter Thirty-Two
Vagabond Paladin

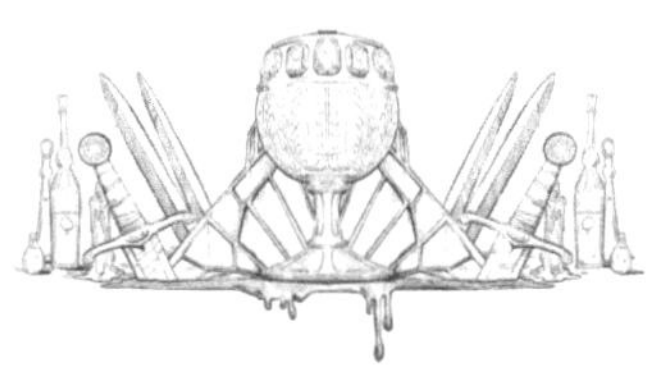

Now *that is* very *satisfying*, a voice said in my mind, and I did not know which it was, but it might have been both at once. *He lost his head. Literally.*

I was panting, every muscle aching after that grueling fight against multiple opponents, my only ally in the brawl a possessed dog.

You're welcome.

My eyes flicked from enemy to enemy. The golems were frozen in place. One had his arm drawn back as if to throw a punch. The other was still on his knees, one bone arm missing. Sir Owalan was panting off to one side, bloody and bitten, looking back and forth between me and Adalbrand.

Run, run, run, little minced meat. You're like a rat in a trap who is chewing off his own leg. It's adorable. Perhaps you'll be my next pet.

I needed this demon out of my head. I was starting to almost find his observations accurate. The idea of a wild-eyed Sir Owalan sitting when told and staying in place seemed fitting somehow.

A quick — and worried — glance at Brindle saw him shaking himself, blood and sweat flinging out from his coat to spray a trembling Sir Owalan. He seemed unharmed. Joyful even.

Nothing like a good scrabble to get the blood flowing. For dog and demon alike.

"You lost your construct, Poisoned Fool!" Owalan taunted. "I shall not be so easily deterred."

He wiped a pink smear of dog spittle and blood from his cheek. Emitting a guttural sound from the back of his throat, he spun, and rushed to the empty harness Adalbrand had abandoned as if he thought one of us would try to beat him to the chance to summon a malevolent spirit.

Well, he had his priorities, I supposed, and clinging to his hope of Sainthood was one of them. It must be terrible to be the kind of person willing to grasp at a thing with no thought of the cost.

Terrible indeed. Remember how when you confessed to doubt and entered this place, it twisted you into a doubter. Forget not how when you all entered a second time, you confessed murder.

I shot a guilty glance to where Sir Coriand lay — headless.

I'd worry about how I was a murderer later.

I had learned a long time ago that the passion of battle fogs the head. I had trained myself to check for wounds the moment it was safe. Fail to do that and you could bleed out without realizing it. I gave my body a hasty check. A few knife slashes. They stung. Only one was serious and it was in the forearm of my off-hand. Adalbrand wouldn't be able to heal it, but he would be able to help me bandage it.

My eyes were drawn to him almost without conscious thought. I found it very satisfying that he was doing the same as I had, a quick check over of his body, a shake of his head as if to clear it, and then a hand running over his face, smearing dust through the sweat there before smoothing across his shorn head. He let out a gusting breath, met my eyes, and offered a wry smile.

"Still alive?"

I nodded wearily. "You?"

His dark laugh heartened me. "For now, it seems." His smile turned bashful. It made my heart melt a little to see such a look of boyish guilt on a face weathered by pain and shadowed by a three-day beard. "I changed the plan."

"No longer interested in building a demon to turn against them?" I asked with a lifted eyebrow.

He shook his head, his mouth twisting into a more serious, regretful expression. When his eyes met mine again they were hollowed by sadness.

"I thought you said we would create evil to stop evil."

He stepped over Sir Coriand's corpse to join me. "I did say that, yes."

His hand reached halfway toward me and then clenched into a fist, as if he were afraid to touch me, or uncertain if he'd be received. I decided for him, crossing the last space between us to press my forehead to his.

"And now?"

His voice was rough when he reached up and brushed a strand of hair from where it clung to blood on my cheek. "And now I will not bend. We will fight evil with good or not at all."

I nodded, my forehead sliding against his with the motion. "And to think you thought your stains could not be washed away. The God reached down himself to burn away your demon."

"To think," he said, and there was wonder in his tone.

"To think you thought errors of youth were enough to ruin your future."

"To think." His laugh now was disbelieving, a man discovering suddenly he was rich only to also discover he must give all that wealth to ransom a friend.

I pulled back enough to meet his eyes so he could see my smile as it warmed my face.

His answering smile brought more comfort than hot tea on a cold shore.

"Bind my arm?" I asked him, and he nodded gently, tiny smile lines forming around his eyes in the dust there. His hands were gentle as he worked.

"If you're done breaking all your vows down there, I have a

small suggestion for you," Sir Sorken called down. "Maybe ask your dog not to defile Sir Coriand's body."

I looked up to where Sir Sorken was carefully penning in his book and then to where Brindle was sniffing along the trail between Sir Coriand's body and his head.

"Brindle," I snapped. "Here."

He looked up at me, hung a doggy tongue from his mouth as if he were laughing at me, and then turned back to what he was doing.

Something smells wrong here. Very wrong.

"I see your dog is well trained, Beggar. Well done," Sir Sorken said. "Whatever you do, don't let him urinate on the golems. They may have frozen at Sir Coriand's death, but they do hold a grudge, and if they awaken, they might take it personally."

"Can't you wake them?" I asked, looking from golem to golem.

"Can I?" Sorken asked. "Do you think that is in my power?"

"I notice you aren't answering direct questions," I said grimly. "Has your plan blown up now that your accomplice is deceased?"

"Sir Coriand was my friend," Sir Sorken announced, loudly but surprisingly dispassionately. "A truth you did not factor in when you beheaded him so dramatically. But we were not conspirators. I came to this place just like you, on the orders of my aspect. I came to seek the Cup of Tears, which I continue to do. If he had other plans, well, that's news to me. A man is welcome to his secrets. I certainly have mine. But you can hardly prosecute me for what you consider him guilty of committing, hmm? Or have you more in common with Sir Kodelai than we imagined?"

I felt my cheeks heat at his words. He was right. I'd prejudged him without knowing.

"Guilt is a cruel mistress," Sir Adalbrand said under his breath as he finished tying the bandage around my arm. He'd had one in his belt pouch, of course. That was just like him. "I would not bend my conscience under the words of Sir Sorken. Lying is not impossible for him, even if he's forsworn against it."

He had removed his gauntlets to bandage the arm and now he reached out and pinched my chin between his finger and thumb. I felt a little shiver run through me as he looked into my eyes as if they were quenching a thirst within him and said, "Forsworn is not the same as impossible. I know it. Mayhap the Engineer knows it, too."

I shivered and his ghost of a smile only made it worse.

"See?" He swallowed and looked away sharply.

"Whatever you're whispering about over there, please keep it down," Sir Sorken said from on high. "The three of us have work to do. Work that may very well take all night. Perhaps it's good you've opted out, Sir Adalbrand. There won't be a place up here for you anyway. Ten hours is very little time to write a thesis that must stand the test of millennia. Don't you think, Penitent?"

"I do think so," Sir Owalan said distractedly. His pen scratched along his paper and his tongue stuck out one corner of his mouth like that of a schoolboy figuring problems. "I will not fail at this task. Do not try to hinder me again, Beggar. I spared your dog once. I am rather fond of animals, after all. I will not spare him twice."

Without another word, Sir Adalbrand took my hand and led me to the wall where the water was running down over the marble. He washed his hands and face quickly in the fecund-smelling water and I joined him, just hoping our horses hadn't relieved themselves into the stream recently. It seemed fine enough, but water could fool you. Just like paladins. That which seems clear and pure could turn out to be poison.

"Will you craft a demon in the harnesses?" Adalbrand asked me quietly as we washed. He had a way of moving his strong hands that seemed too delicate for such large fingers. It charmed me more than I could admit even to myself.

Tell him no.

Again, I could not determine the speaker. And I was worried. Were the two melding together, or had Sir Branson lost his reins on the demon?

"I will not," I said, firmly.

His smile was tired. "If only this were holy water and not runoff from the melting Rim."

I smiled ruefully at that.

"I don't know if these golems may wake again, but you have not slept in a night and a day and I have not slept properly in that same time," Adalbrand murmured. "Let us sit back-to-back and try to sleep, and if one is attacked the other can defend them."

"It's a good idea," I agreed.

We found a place beside one of the benches, neither of us looking up at the mutterings from overhead.

Adalbrand removed his breastplate and backplate and with calm care, we pressed our spines and the blades of our shoulders together, set the swords across our knees, and each faced one of the still golems. In between them, Brindle chewed happily at Suture's arm. And behind him, three twisting shapes grew more and more clear as they were formed from darkness and desire and selfish ambition.

I could see Sir Coriand's head from where I sat. And the sight ate at me. I had killed him. He'd deserved it most assuredly, but even with his confession hot on his lips, the men of my aspect would want an accounting for his blood. I would be trialed. I may even be condemned. I had a thought that likely Sir Sorken would demand such, and if not him then the High Saint, and they would be right to require it of me. I'd killed a fellow holy knight. One did not just get up on their horse and ride away after that.

"Bless me, for I have sinned," I said in a small voice, unable to see Adalbrand's face, but snaking my off-hand back to find his hand.

He twisted his blunt, calloused fingers in mine readily enough. "I cannot be both your lover and your confessor, Lady Paladin."

I shivered at the word "love" but he did not sound as if he judged. He sounded ... tender.

"Must I choose then?" I asked wistfully. For I wanted him to be both. I wanted both the holy Saint and the tantalizing man. Was that too much to ask for?

"Yes," he whispered, and his whisper sounded amused. "You must choose, Victoriana."

And it was how he whispered my name — as if by caressing it with his tongue he could caress me, too — that made me bold enough to lay my heart bare. And why not? What had I left to lose?

Everything?

Why should I not make him both lover and confessor when the hours of my life slipped away like the hours of a winter day — too short, too dark, too pallid?

Do not do this. You leave yourself open to ruin.

Then he could ruin me. I cared not.

I whispered my reply, and if the demon or the dog or the missing knight minded, then they could go chew a golem bone for all I cared.

"I cannot choose one or the other, for my heart has made me yours down to its inmost weaving." I couldn't help but turn my head over my shoulder toward him so that I could catch the edge of his suddenly flushed cheek out of the corner of my eye.

"There is no longer a choice," I went on. "You're beloved or no one is. You're treasured or I can no longer treasure."

His back on mine was warm enough to heat me through — almost warm enough that I wondered if his heart were suddenly beating hard and fast just like mine.

"I was not made for flighty love, for pleasure without allegiance, for enjoyment without cost, for easy affection without eternal loyalty. Draw me close or cast me away, it makes no difference to the direction of my heart."

I heard the sharp drawing in of his breath, caught the edge of his parted lips from the corner of my eye. It made my cheeks tingle, they'd grown so hot.

"I'll love you still even if I go back out to my wandering paths and never set my eyes on your form again. I'll love you in the dark caves and earthen sets of my heart. I'll love you in the silent hours when the world sleeps. I'll love you when I stare long into the heart of the fire in the cold of the night, when the wind sweeps across a world of ocean only to tangle through my hair, when the snow melts and the scents of the hopes of dreaming grasses release into the air, and I'll love you yet when my soul at long last releases from this flesh and wings its way to the God. Even then will I treasure the sweet taste of your name on my lips, of the knowing of you on my heart. You have set me as a seal sets wax. I am changed forever and none but thee can break the seal and open me."

Perhaps that might have seemed an extreme statement to make about a man I'd only met a few days before. But this close to the forces of life and death, to heaven and hell, with our souls and loyalties laid bare and all our secrets out, it felt perfectly natural to leap into life with the same intensity that it was setting upon us.

We were, without consciously meaning to, angling our faces away from the others, and for a moment we were both looking over our shoulders at one another, our breath mingling hot between us, our fingers tangled like roots of two unlike trees, and a mutual understanding hanging heavy and full in the air between us. After a very long moment, he nodded.

"I have thoughts on that," he said quietly. "I have many thoughts. But they are not for this place. Or for the robber ears of our enemies. Go to sleep, Lady Paladin. I will watch your back and pray to the God for a solution to this madness."

I wished he would tell me his thoughts anyway. It felt almost painfully vulnerable to have exposed myself so thoroughly. Perhaps he regretted the things he said earlier. Perhaps he was not so set on me as I was on him.

Perhaps he's looking at a headless corpse and a frozen golem that wants him dead and a demon-infested dog chewing the arm of a living thing and he's just not in the mood to be overly chatty.

Perhaps.

I smiled wryly and settled back in place, facing forward again, and when I shut my eyes the exhaustion of my body overwhelmed the tense longing of my heart. I was asleep in three breaths, but not before I heard the faintest of whispers.

"Doubt anything you like, Victoriana, Lady of the Rejected Aspect, but do not doubt me. Though all the world rejects you, I never shall."

Chapter Thirty-Three
Poisoned Saint

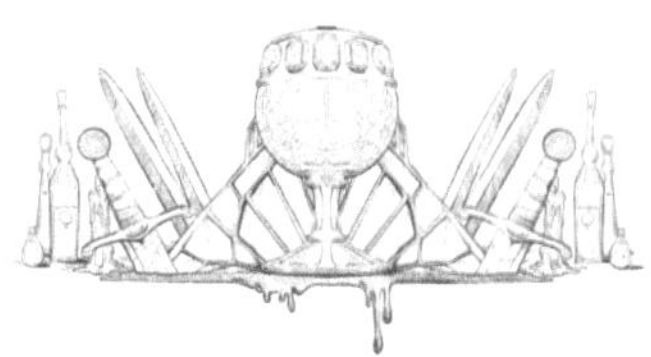

And now I come to the heart of the matter, having danced around the edges for far too long. It is easy indeed to become enraptured by what is before you, caught up in the warp and weft of the weaving of your life and to — as a result of that — lose sight of the pattern as a whole.

I am a paladin, the God's own warrior. And whether he uses me as such or merely tolerates my riding across the hills and plains healing in his name, I am — at the heart of things — his possession.

And so is this place — this arcanery — whether it wills it or not, for all that exists belongs to the God. All that is made is crafted of his flesh and bones.

We are taught from the start that evil is not generated by the God — that it is a rot in the goodness of life. If the Vagabond is right, then it is generated by us — by our grasping and by our guile.

Therefore, if I wish to bring this place down — and I do — if I wish to wash it from the mind of the earth and with it the demons it makes now and the demons it made before, then a simple refusal to make them myself is not enough. I must think of this place as a whole, I must think of how the God looks down upon it, and I must ponder if there is a key — not a key for opening locks, but a key for closing them.

When I think about it, this Aching Monastery is like a lock, isn't it? And our actions are the key, turning the gargantuan stone tumblers one by one. If I do not want the lock opened, then I must seize the key.

I recite my rote prayers — a morning plea that the eye of the God be on me, an evening plea that the hand of the God restore, a noonday plea that the God strengthen my bones for the work ahead. They are out of order and jumbled, just like my exhausted thoughts. But I cannot sleep and they calm me. Even as I hear the Vagabond's sleeping breaths and feel her warmth radiate against my back, I cannot drift with her.

I am also, at the heart, a healer. And if any place needs healing, it is this place. It may not look it, lovely as it is. Looks deceive the eye. I remember being called once — too late — to the house of a lord of the Saracarna. His grown daughter was ill and she was the apple of his eye. I ran my horse to exhaustion after the messenger found me, but still, I was too late. The girl was dead an hour before I arrived. Dead, and lovely beyond any woman I'd ever seen. Perfectly whole on the outside. Infected within.

That is this Aching Monastery. The infection within it is disguised, hidden but strong. Who better to heal it than one possessed by the God for the purpose of drawing out the poison so life might flourish?

That one can only be me.

When I tore up my words and rejected the evil in my shadow, the God blessed me — not just with whatever miracle kept me whole as I leapt from above, but also by filling me again with a reserve of his power. I remained silent about it as I bound Victoriana's arm. Perhaps I should have indicated to her that I had the power to heal it, but chose not to. Her injury is not grave, and I sense somehow that this power will be needed.

Someone must draw the poison from this place. Someone

must take it into himself so that it might be dispelled. And that someone is me.

The Vagabond shifts in her sleep, her drowsy head leaning into my shoulder. I tilt into the weight of it, in the same way that my horse adjusts to take my weight when I ride. It feels correct.

The others considered her a strange choice for the God to call as paladin. I heard their whispers on the matter and I doubted her myself.

But I have learned something down in this grave of a monastery.

I have learned that the God chooses as he chooses and for good reason. Who else would have stood and confronted Sir Coriand as she had? Who stands now, refusing to bend an inch in the face of what has to end in our deaths between the tumblers of this lock?

I had thought her corrupted because she suffered a demon to live, because her heart housed doubt, because her paladincy was not certain. I see her entirely differently now. I see her as a living miracle — a grafting of glory into dust.

It is the rest of us who are not fit by comparison. Who would have thought, in a group that contained the most famous of those who bring justice and a man so devout that he could ask for the blood of another and she would give it to him — in those high circles — that it would be neither of those who passed the test but rather the wild card, the crow, the one swept in with the wind of poverty and subversiveness?

Perhaps the God chose to delight himself with her wildness and bold heart when he made her. Perhaps even now he rejoices in her stalwart spirit and determination. Whether he does or not, I do.

We are such broken vessels — all of us. And what does the God think of that? I am more broken than all the rest. I let my eyes drift over the immobile golems, as close to dead as such things can be. Over the ruined man strewn across the floor — a truly disrespectful sight. Over the three fools who were once holy, now suspended in the air, working hard to undo all the good they've done in their lifetimes.

The broken and those who break. All are accounted for here. I am king among them. King of the Ruined.

And yet the God blessed me.

He could still bless them, too.

I hardly know what to make of such blessing. Surely the Vagabond cannot be right that it is a sign of divine forgiveness. And yet, I cannot help the hope that springs in my heart and tells me it is, that I am tasting the God's own favor on my tongue even now.

If it is, then what I do now means more than it ever has. I have always been willing to die for the God. I am willing now to do it joyfully.

Victoriana shifts again in her sleep. A lock of her hair falls against my neck. I close my eyes that I may better breathe in the scent of her, take this last gift for what it is — the mercy of the God, a taste of what it is like to be washed clean of the past.

If these are my last hours, then I am spending them, moment by moment, *forgiven.* Forgiveness is honey on my tongue. Moves me nearly to tears. I had not grasped so high, had not dared hope.

Bless me, Merciful God, I pray. *I reach for your mercy. This one time, let me find it.*

I do not ask him to let me succeed in my quest to spare the world of this evil. I do not ask for wisdom. I ask only for the one thing I feared I would never have, and it feels like it will crush me under the strength of its embrace.

And it is in this soaring state that the first trickles of a plan start to make paths through my mind. All achievement requires sacrifice. I have now tasted what is good, and I will be the one who will sacrifice. But I will need her help.

Beside me, the dog drops his bone and pads over to me. For a moment we are staring into each other's eyes. Dog to man. Or is it demon to man? Or is it Saint to man? I do not know. One eye burns red suddenly. And the other blue.

A spike of fear shoots through me, but I do not look away. I do not see a big puppy with soft fur and a responsive mind. I see the grapple for dominance behind the facade.

I shiver as the dog walks past me, whines, and puts his head on Victoriana's lap.

I don't quite have a plan yet for him. But I think what I have will work for the rest of what lies here.

And that means these are my last hours on the earth. I will not waste them in sleep.

Above me, Sir Owalan and Sir Sorken toss ideas back and forth as their demons scrap against each other in a friendly manner. They rise higher and higher. Their shadow forms are filled now with flickers of horrors that make my stomach twist if I let myself look at them. Random limbs of man and beast flicker out from them and then are drawn back in. Silent, screaming faces, man and woman, child and beast, reveal themselves and then are torn apart and merge back into shadow. There are other things I cannot describe mixed in with them. Things that scar my mind so badly that I cannot acknowledge what I have seen even to myself.

It is no easy thing to pluck my gaze away or to clear my mind of what I've seen, but I do it. I block them out and let myself drift in the sweet embrace of prayers, the warmth of the Vagabond at my back, and the warmth of the God's fire in my heart. I let it go for about an hour before I know I must wake her.

Time is running out.

I gently run the back of my hand down the Vagabond's arm.

"Victoriana?" I whisper, the sound of my voice cloaked by the murmurs above. And a hissing, snapping, muffled wail that began within the constructed demons a short time ago.

The dog whines as she shifts. I feel her coming awake.

"Adalbrand?"

She's awake suddenly, hand clutching her sword pommel. I smile at my name on her lips.

"I have a plan," I say carefully. I must convince her to help me with this. I know that she will be reluctant. It's understandable. But I must be convincing.

"I crave the hearing of it." Her voice is sleepy. I shift so that now her head is on my shoulder and we are side to side. Her dog looks up at me, his glowing eyes both seeming to wink at me at once.

"In a moment I will plead with our brothers to listen and to stop this madness," I say.

"Oh, so we're going to try futile then, are we?" she says wryly. She looks up and then startles when she sees what they have built as she slept. Her face drains of color and she swallows grimly.

"If they do not heed me then we will move on to the next part, and for that, I need your help."

Her throat sounds dry when she answers. "My help is yours."

She should not have given her word so readily, but I will take it nonetheless. "I will hurry out to the clock and you will watch my back as I bless the water in the fountain."

She's nodding. "You think holy water will help something? That it will purge this arcanery?"

"I think," I say very deliberately, "that all things take power to sustain them — the power of the God in nature, the power of man in maintaining, or the power of evil. And I think this Aching Monastery is powered entirely by the demon in the ceiling. That he is trapped for this purpose, yes, but also tapped for his power, and has been for millennia."

She looks up then and I feel the slide of her hair across my neck. It is a sensation I will treasure and hold on to. Her gaze darts for a moment to the tumbled pain trapped within the shadow demons our colleagues build. She blanches, and then rips her gaze away and back to mine and I see the understanding dawn in her eyes just as it woke in mine.

"You watched them build these demons and realized that whatever pain and misery they are trapping in those things had been fermenting in the one in the ceiling."

I nod, but there is more. "I think the water in the fountain is connected to the water below this place, and it is that water that moves the gears and turns this room. All of it is intertangled with that black creature in the ceiling. Did you see the window when first we arrived?"

"The one where the man and the devil fought and neither seemed to win?" she asks wryly.

"Did they fight? Or were they entangled, one with the other?"

She pauses.

"I think that if I draw on the poison of this place, draw it out of the water, it will also draw the demon from its place above. That I'll be able to draw it into myself. Is that possible, in your experience?"

She looks at me, then, aghast. Her pretty brown eyes are suddenly hard. "It's possible. Maybe."

"Then I must try."

The head in her lap lifts, and the pair of glowing eyes look at me, too. How long have his eyes been glowing like that, and why has no one else noticed?

"What are you saying?" she whispers, and her lips thin in condemnation.

I swallow and force myself to go on. It's a good plan. The only one that will work.

"I will draw the demon in the ceiling into me. And then I will drink the cups these others are filling. And I think that will draw their demons into me, too."

She steals one glance at the tumbled limbs and screaming, helpless faces caught in the swirling shadow beside us and she blanches. She scrambles away from me and backward into a defensive crouch. Her dog growls deep in his throat.

"Adalbrand?" Her eyes are filled with betrayal.

"And then, you will drown me in the fountain — in the holy water I've blessed." Her eyes widen, but I'm not finished. "Drown me and cast out the demons I've drawn in. The God has given you the ability not just to draw them out, but to send them all from this plane." I feel my voice faltering as I try to calmly explain how she will kill me. "There's always the risk they'll hop to someone else, but we both know that can't happen if I hold on to them until I die. I think I can. That's how it works, right? You can cast them out the long way, with many prayers to the God, as you do with humans you encounter, or you can do it the short way and dispatch the host like you do with animals."

The dog's growl grows louder. That's fine. He is not my friend.

"Your proposal is that you'll fill yourself with every demon in this place and then I'll kill you," she says calmly, but she's looking at me like I've gone mad.

"Yes," I say. "It's a solution. Possibly the only solution. And it's the path of honor."

"It's the path of insanity," she hisses.

But the problem is that she's slightly adorable when she's annoyed, and she is very annoyed right now. I smirk a little, enjoying this while I can.

"Don't you dare smile at me," she says, and I'm taken aback to realize there are tears in her eyes.

My smile drops. "Victoriana?"

"How did you expect me to react to your request that I murder you?" she asks frostily.

I am careful when I reply, "With relief. It solves the problem neatly and requires only one death — and that given willingly. You will not be stained by it. Nor will these other paladins. They may yet be saved."

She's shaking her head, looking rather furious for someone presented with an answer to all their problems. I open my mouth to try to persuade her, but I'm cut off by a voice.

"If you're making plans down there, fellow paladins," Sir Sorken's voice booms out, "don't."

He snaps his fingers and, to my surprise, both Cleft and Suture break their frozen postures, pulling themselves up to their monstrous heights with creaks and groans. Suture flexes his unbroken arm.

"You can command them even with Sir Coriand dead," Victoriana accuses him, scrambling to her feet. "You made me believe they were as good as dead."

"It seems I can command them. How wonderful," Sir Sorken says lightly.

She looks up at him for a long beat, her eyes narrowing. Her off-hand drifts down to Brindle's round skull and settles there.

"You lied about not being his conspirator."

She has the mystery between her teeth again and is ready to fight. I hope she remembers this is about more than this now.

Sir Sorken's sigh is so loud that I hear it over everything else. "Do you know, I think I've never met a person so stubbornly pigheaded as you, Beggar. You are entirely like that demon-possessed dog you cart around everywhere with you. Holier than thou one moment, a miserable snapping wretch the next, and never, ever, ever willing to just leave a thing alone."

I shoot a glance to Brindle, who stoops to pick up the golem's hand in his mouth. It's the worse for being chewed for an hour.

Sir Sorken is still speaking. "Pretense is too much trouble with you. You don't deserve it, and frankly, you never have. Saints and Angels, girl. You killed Sir Coriand. Do you have any idea how great a mind he had? And you knocked it from his shoulders like chopping fruit, and left me stuck here pretending it made no matter instead of showing you my ire."

He is writing furiously as he speaks, and his demon is building again. I watch as it slides a toe over the line that used to contain it. If we let this go too far, it will be able to reach us.

"So. I'm done with pretense. All of you are such fools. Who rides for a place having never researched it, with no plan and no goal? Pitiful. Coriand Parterio and I have been waiting for this opportunity for more than a decade. And we came with a plan."

"The opportunity to kill?" Victoriana presses.

He scoffs.

"How did you get chosen by the head of your aspect?" Sir

Owalan asks, distracted as he is swept up in the story. "How did you ensure you were the ones sent?"

"We didn't." Sir Sorken grins unpleasantly. "What a waste of time. We found the man they'd sent, killed him on the road, and duplicated his medallion to give us two. It's amazing what you can make when you're an Engineer. Even on the road with little in the way of supplies."

"But why?" Sir Owalan asks, looking confused. "I understand wanting to be a Saint, I do." His tone turns reverent. "And I want the ancient relic — the new relic — the Cup of Tears. I want to bring it home to the Penitent Paladins. I do not blame you for what you did to ascend to this honor. In this place, I have come to realize that sacrifices must be made. Nothing comes for free. And if the God does not guide, then we must guide ourselves. But you aren't me and you've never seemed to care much about Sainthood or the Cup of Tears. So why are you here?"

Sir Sorken pauses just long enough to look up from his work before continuing to scribble. I edge backward carefully. His demon is still testing its limits.

"Why am I here? Surely you've figured it out by now. I would guess the Beggar has. Go on, ragged warrior. Tell the boy why I'm here."

"You knew this place manufactures demons."

Sir Sorken makes a dismissive gesture and she colors, her expression growing grim.

"You came to put yours in your golem and to find a way to keep on doing it, so you can make as many of those things as you like, but this time there will be no debate as to whether they have souls because you'll be filling them with souls you wrote yourself."

That's ... I feel my eyes widen as I steal a look at her. She must have just fit those pieces together, because she did not mention this before now. While I have been distracted with the puzzle of the demons, she has put together the answer for the murders, the deaths, everything else.

"This is how you're going to become a God, isn't it?" she says quietly. "You're going to make your own living, breathing, soul-filled beings."

"The Aching Monastery is a trap for the unwary," Sir Sorken says grimly. "But I did not come here unwary and neither did Coriand. We came with a purpose greater than you fools ever planned for."

"And that makes the murders acceptable?" Victoriana presses.

"Is murder justified when it's done for a higher cause?" Sir Sorken asks with a bite to his words. "You tell me, Beggar. You're the one who killed my friend."

"You'll have an army of slaves, made by you, filled with demons," she says, her voice hollow.

Sir Sorken looks up. "It's a grand vision. I don't expect an impoverished wanderer to understand it. But then I never had much use for you even when I thought you were on to the plan. You practically wear a sign around your neck that says 'expendable' and yet here you are, delaying, prolonging, and making a mess of everything. If you can't find your own path here like Owalan has, then you might as well just die. You're of no use to the world. You can't even perform your main function and cast a demon out of a dog."

"Then you can't be persuaded to stop?" She throws it out like a challenge.

"Stop?" He laughs. "I will succeed. And when I do, you will see what glory is."

It's finally my turn to speak, and I choose my words with care.

"Brothers," I say, addressing the three of them and letting my gaze meet each of theirs. "I beg you stop this madness. It is not too late to turn back from this course and escape. You were holy once; be holy again."

"This *is* holiness now," Sir Owalan whispers, his eyes haunted.

Sir Sorken merely snorts.

But the High Saint meets my eyes mutely, and in his eyes ripple one emotion after another. He is a fly in a trap. I see it.

Something brushes my arm and I rip my gaze away from Joran Rue to Victoriana. Her eyes meet mine and they roar with sadness, like a storm breaking across a mountainside.

Her words are barely audible, they're so brittle. "We'll do this your way, Poisoned Saint. And the God have mercy on us both."

I nod shakily.

Well then. That's it, I suppose. It is time to go and die honorably. I've always known I would. I just haven't quite come to terms with it enough to keep my hands from shaking.

She starts to stride toward the doors.

"Stop the Beggar, boys," Sir Sorken booms, and both golems shamble forward.

"You can't leave!" Sir Owalan calls down desperately. "There are hours yet before the clock runs out! Who knows what will happen if you go!"

"We aren't playing your silly games, Penitent," I call over my shoulder irritably. I am tense. Not just because I am marching to my own death.

The golems stride past us easily and set themselves between us and the outer room.

"What if it ends the trial if you leave?" Sir Owalan pleads.

"Do you love building demons that much, Sir Owalan?" the Vagabond asks, spinning around.

"I will be a Saint," Sir Owalan says gravely.

"And then what? Will you unleash it upon the world?" she asks him, anguish in her voice when her eyes snag on me. I don't like being the cause of her pain, but I see no other way forward. She may mourn me — as I have mourned Marigold. But I have learned such sorrows can be set aside. Perhaps, in time, she will set this aside, too.

Sir Owalan appears affronted, but before he can speak, there's a commotion and he is forced to scramble to control his demon. He lets out a cry as his pen flies to his page.

The High Saint is writing madly. He looks up just long enough to meet my eye again, and in it, I see determination and understanding and something that sings of repentance. His shadow demon rages wildly as his pen dances, bits of horrors flicking out from it in every direction. Its massive hand reaches out — actually, it's a tangle of multiple hands, some ghastly and pale as slugs — catches Cleft, who had strayed into the demon's circle, grabs him by the foot, and flings him against the wall. The huge golem crashes with a boom like a stone falling in a quarry.

Sir Sorken lets fly a foul curse.

I grab the Vagabond's arm and shove her clear of his range while Brindle barks and dances wildly. He wants in on this fight and the lady paladin is barely holding him back.

Sir Sorken's demon is reaching its own tangled arms. Some of them have tentacles lacing between them and everything — arms, hands, tentacles — are wriggling as they stretch. It tries to grab the High Saint's demon but it can't quite reach, and the sound it makes when it strains for the other of its kind sounds like the gnashing of teeth from dozens of different-shaped mouths.

Sir Owalan's demon joins the fray with a screaming roar that sounds fearful and trembling. Rather than helping, it swipes at Sir Sorken's demon, who stumbles into Suture, and for a moment there is pure chaos. Arms, faces, shadows, and screaming voices tangle one over the other.

I look up to see Joran Rue — the High Saint — scramble in his straps. He's trying to get out. The look on his face is sheer panic.

His pen falls to the sand and his ink is right behind it. His face has the look of a man who has just watched his own knife turn on him. He opens his mouth but no scream escapes.

The shadow beneath him rises up, snatches the book in its insubstantial hand, and — against all reason — tears into it with the teeth of multiple mouths at once. Everyone is shouting and then the Vagabond grabs me by the collar and drags me after her. I am running, following her lead, but my eyes are behind me, watching the High Saint.

Suture goes flying past me and hits the wall in front of us. I stumble at the near miss, my breath rasping in my lungs. We're nearly to the door out — nearly, but not quite.

Sir Owalan starts keening in sharp little high-pitched bursts and I risk another glance over my shoulder.

The demon the high saint was creating is climbing upward using straps from the High Saint's harness. It's a tangle of mouths and fingers and something almost swollen that looks like bodies curling in on one another. It's still chewing — chewing around its own eldritch tangled screams and laughter — when it reaches for the High Saint, snatches his struggling form from the half-broken straps, and opens its mouth wide.

One last lunge and the High Saint disappears down the demon's throat like a baitfish dropped into the mouth of a trout.

I feel like my heart has frozen to ice.

The straps break. A dark light bursts in all directions, blinding me for just a moment, and then it is gone, and so are the High Saint and his demon.

The other two demons are flung backward, away from the disintegration of their fellow, and the harnesses holding Sir Owalan and Sir Sorken in place swing with wild abandon.

The High Saint's harness drifts down to the platform like a fallen leaf on the wind.

I choke on my own breath for a moment and am seized by a fit of coughing, but there is no appropriate response for this and I do not try to find one.

I think that in the end, Joran Rue turned his heart from evil. I think that he was a good man caught in a trap he did not know was there.

But now there are only four of us. And two of us are monsters.

"What ... what in the fires of hell just happened?" Sir Owalan asks plaintively.

Sir Sorken snorts. "He was eaten by his demon, wasn't he? Didn't craft it like he should. What did you think would happen?

We aren't playing games here, no matter what the Poisoned One thinks. We are crafting great souls to enact our dreams."

I don't think he's right. Not about anything.

I think the High Saint sabotaged his devil on purpose. I think he did — to a small degree — what I'm about to do. And I honor him for it. Some things are worth dying to prevent.

Owalan pales. "But Sorken," he starts to say. I want to see what he says but I'm tugged, and when I drag my eyes back to what is happening, I see it isn't even the Vagabond dragging me anymore. It's her brindled dog, tugging my jerkin in his teeth, his claws scrabbling on the marble floor, two eyes blazing at me in two different colors.

I take one last look over my shoulder at the golems gathering themselves, at the dark demon shadows coalescing, at the broken body of Sir Coriand, and then I turn and run with the Vagabond and her dog.

Chapter Thirty-Four
Vagabond Paladin

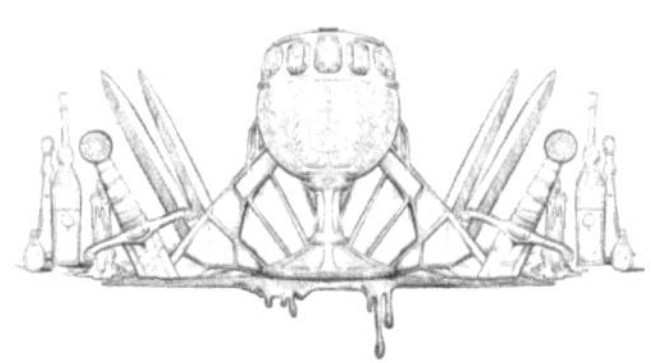

Only a man ... correction: only a man who was also a paladin ... would decide that the way he was going to fix everything was by dying dramatically.

I just wished I could think of a better way to kill a nest of demons and keep them from spreading into the world.

Think! Think hard! This is madness.

But I didn't know if that was the paladin or the demon speaking. It was becoming harder and harder to tell. I could no longer afford to guess wrong.

The dear, chivalrous, noble, holy, *fool* of a man. He'd let me sleep while he concocted this insane plan, and then I'd woken up to find that there were none left but us and two madmen and he had the only plan to fix any of it. And it was a *terrible* plan.

And he'd told it to me with those earnest brown eyes, so wide and innocent, like it would be the simplest thing in the world for me to hold his head under holy water and drown him.

For those who don't know, holy water is meant more as a way to fortify your walls. The practice of casting out the demonic — the primary bent of my aspect — is much more art than science. It's about as reliable and consistent as the rest of our lives — which is to say it's not at all. Every single attempt at it is different, and while paladins claim that they wait for the God to lead them and respond to his will, I think most of the time they're using a combination of instinct, hope, blind faith, and any little tricks they've picked up along the way. I've watched it done maybe a dozen times since I joined Sir Branson's service, and the demons we encountered were weak and had generally already spent the energies of the one possessed in violence to the point that the victim was on the brink of collapse already. But in theory, you could release demons two ways.

One was the slow way, which Sir Branson had been trying with the beggar on the bridge. That way involved a lot of prayer and a connection to the God to essentially make yourself a bridge for his holiness to rush down and burn the demon away through your mortal vessel. It was the way I'd witnessed with every human we'd encountered up until that fateful day on the riverbank. Generally speaking, we had been able to lay hold of and restrain the victim so that we could do the slow work of prayer. It took time because your heart needed to be pure and your desires all attuned to the one result. Or at least, that's what Sir Branson had always said. I don't know about you, but I have trouble flipping my desires off and on like that.

The other way is the fast way. I've referred to this way before when mentioning Brindle. We'd used it on animals who were possessed. While they left their own trail of victims, they were considerably easier to dispatch, even if we'd left one man in such despair over the death of his donkey that his tears still came to mind from time to time. With that method, you killed the victim of the demon, and you prayed while you did it, hoping that the combination would make you an unfit vessel for the demon to hop to, and so with no living home, it evacuates the mortal plane entirely. It's quick and dirty, but it gets the job done a lot of the time.

But sometimes — so rarely that I've never seen it and really only heard about it in the stories Vagabond Paladins tell round the fire when we meet one another — sometimes, the situation is very severe and we fear that even death cannot free the victim or seal the demon to retreat. In those cases, we will use holy water and we will drown the poor desperate person in that water. The water makes it much harder for the demon to leap. The soul it has bound with will force it from the body as the body is killed and bear it to another plane. Sometimes, with a skilled paladin who has done it before, the person can be brought back after death by drowning, and thus the victim is saved even though he has had to die for his salvation. I do not have that knowledge or skill.

But before you speak of cruelty, you should remember that you have not seen the horrors that demons inflict upon their victims, and the horrors they force them to inflict on others. Until you've looked into the eyes of a man so possessed that he has slowly flayed himself with a sharp knife and a mirror, and his soul is weeping within as his body turns the knife next toward those pleading eyes, until you've seen a whole family of tiny corpses and the person they trusted laughing over their broken bodies, until you've tried to patch up living victims so broken and ruined that they are like my tattered cloak inside — there isn't even enough left to mend — until then, do not speak to me of what is cruel. Death — even death by drowning — is a sweet mercy compared to letting them remain in such a state, letting them suffer by their own acts, allowing the demon to twist their every flicker of desire into evil.

I knew why Adalbrand had demanded I drown him in holy water.

I knew what he would be when he let those demons into his body.

I knew, but I was not certain I could do my part. It was not that I wasn't physically strong enough. He wouldn't try to resist me, and I was a strong woman. It was the thought of him thrashing in my arms instead of relaxing into them. The thought of tamping down his bright heart and laughter under cold, clinging water as his soul bled away, instead of nurturing those smiles in him. It was the knowledge that it would be I who killed that bright holy man. I was not a murderer. And the one man I had killed already was the other man I'd loved — albeit as a father. Was I destined then to kill anyone my heart grew close to? It was too much. Maybe even for this cause. Maybe even to save hundreds or thousands of people.

Wasn't it?

Well, wasn't it?

We burst into the main room and I was immediately deafened. The clock began to gong the second our feet hit the mosaic of the main room. *Bong. Bong. Bong.*

It pealed out its crashing warning and when I looked at it — across from us — the face was lit by a narrow beam of light and the hands were spinning wildly around the face of the clock. I traced the light beam from the clock to where the window in the wall was wide open but nearly lost as it moved across the wall. The door to the sea was not yet open, but it was halfway there. Not long now and the demon would drop out of the ceiling and the way would be clear for us to flee.

"The cups," Adalbrand gasped. "Get them."

I scrambled to the loud clock. There was the High Saint's cup, shattered to nothing. The crack in mine had run through and what little had been inside had run out. Adalbrand's was burned so that charcoal coated the inside and not a drop was left. Sir Coriand's was there, still and sludgy like mud. The only cups with steam still wafting from them, bubbling and growing, were Owalan's and Sorken's. I grabbed one in my off-hand and Adalbrand grabbed the other.

And as if that were the signal, the floor twisted, speeding up, and the bonging of the clock went wild. I heard shouts from the trial room and a crash as the door out began to twist past the point where anyone could flee.

I looked up and up, a tickly feeling racing down my spine. My eyes found the dark, gleaming shape immediately, despite the shadows above us. It was easing out from its filigree cage, out the opening made by the turning room, and the very second I spotted it, it dropped. I had a sensation in the back of my mind like a dish shattering, like something sliding down my back, wet and cold, something that was a sibling of dread.

I shuddered.

I did not wait to see how much faster it was than us. I had no illusions that it would be slow ... or kind.

"It's time, Lady Paladin."

I didn't know why he was offering his hand, but there was something in the gesture, as if even now, when he ran as hard as he could toward what he had planned to make his tomb, even now, he would shelter me if he could. Even now, he would offer what comfort he had, were it only a hand.

I took it and hurried with him around the base of the stairs, skidding across the smooth floor as we ran over the orange peel map of the people who had thought the world was both a globe and an ideal place to multiply demons.

I heard footsteps echoing behind me.

Beside me, Brindle's breathy panting was reassuring. I felt him just there, a presence beside me.

But when I glanced at him, I saw flickers of shapes that were not doggy at all.

Flicker, a glimpse of Sir Branson if he were the soft blue of a peaceful summer sky and transparent as a window.

Flicker, an open-mouthed, laughing face that looked half human, half monster, and was just as transparent as my old master had been. It glowed the color of a fire tainted by too much sap.

It's a good plan, the voice in my mind said as I ran, *as good as any.*

But what if that were the demon speaking? What if he were rejoicing already in our failure? Ready to leap once more into a paladin and lure him to his death. Only this time it would be Sir Adalbrand.

There was no ominous laughter in my head. I almost found that more worrying than if there had been.

And then we were steps from the fountain, huffing together as we tried to catch our breaths.

Brindle darted ahead, leapt up the rim of the fountain, and perched there, teeth bared and growling, his eyes fixed on something behind us. There was something odd about his eyes but I didn't have time to note it. I drew my sword the moment we stopped running — though what that would do against an enormous demon, I could not say.

Sir Adalbrand set the cup down on the rim of the fountain and stood with one hand raised, fingers curled except the two he raised in blessing as he spat out the rote words.

"From water we are born, to water we return, may the word of the God bless this water and make it holy, purifying us by it in both body and spirit."

I set the other cup beside his.

I started to turn to see what Brindle was growling at, but I was arrested by the sight of him, because there, overlaid over the body of the dog, were two figures, transparent as cloudy glass and fighting with one another in a tangle of limbs and gritted teeth. I could not truly make out the edges of their bodies, only sense that they fought — two souls in one dog, desperate for dominance.

Hold fast, my girl. Do not surrender. Do not bend!

I completed my spin, lifted my sword arm, and saw the dark, gleaming blackness of the monastery demon bearing down on us.

How did one fight a demon with a sword?

You don't. You're eaten, snackling. And all your adorable ideas about drowning your beloved like some fairytale princess crumble away. Did you really think you could save the world with murder, or was that just a cute excuse for something dark within you?

I wasn't sure how to fight, but I braced myself anyway, kept the sword high, eyes on the target ...

To my horror, Adalbrand shot past me into the darkness.

I gasped, the breath snatched from my lungs, took a step forward, as if I could stop him, and then stumbled back again when I felt a *pop* and the darkness was no more. Adalbrand spun, his eyes wild and too bright in the faint light of the clock, and then he dragged the cup in his hand up to his lips, his eyes locked on mine as he quaffed the entire draught, only a little spilling down his chin into his two-day beard.

I could see how it changed him. How his eyes went harder, the lines of his face sharper, the beauty of his eyes more wild. This was how it was meant to be in this terrible place. He'd drunk down someone's demon, the evil they designed themselves, and now he was possessed by it.

He gagged, choked, clearly made sick by it, and then with a grimace and a slight convulsion, he drank the rest.

"Sorken's, I think. Meant for Cleft," he gasped, eyes swimming with emotion.

My gaze was locked on him, unable to look aside even though Brindle was barking furiously.

Adalbrand flung the empty cup aside and, looking grimly miserable, paused, as if it took all his willpower to still control his own body movements. He heaved twice, broad shoulders bucking, but managed to keep it down, and then leaned over the fountain, gasping.

By chance, he'd landed right beside Brindle.

The dog placed a paw gently on his shoulder, big eyes huge and understanding even as the two specters layered over him tussled and tumbled for dominance.

Adalbrand locked his eyes on mine, his chiseled face wild with the struggle within. He reached for the second cup, but before he could grasp it, a second hand slipped in between us — a hand with a dagger jutting through the wrist between the veins.

Sir Owalan scooped the cup up and drank it down, without so much as a bob of his throat, as Adalbrand's strangled "No!" was still slicing through the air.

Everything felt like it was moving too slowly. I turned slowly, my feet feeling like they were encased in earth though my eyes were registering everything at once.

The room was brighter. The wall must have spun enough

that the entranceway was finally facing the ocean. It poured bright white light across the room, throwing the statues looming over us into stark relief. The one that caught my eye looked like Sir Coriand, and in this light, it looked as though he were holding his own head in place with one hand while he laughed at us.

Here, in the shadow of the stairs, it was still dark, but not too dark to grasp what had happened.

Sir Owalan slowly lowered the cup, a dribble of something faintly dark running from the corner of his mouth. His eyes had taken on an inhuman orange glow. My gaze crossed Adalbrand's just long enough to register his horror — and the red glow behind *his* eyes — and then they moved farther, to behind Owalan, where Sir Sorken had a hand raised. His face was outraged, eyes locked on the cup Adalbrand had drunk and discarded. Suture was picking that cup up from where it fell. Cleft's mighty stone hand was raised like a hammer.

When the next three things happened, I was still moving too slowly to do anything but watch.

Sir Owalan turned to the side and spewed out what he'd just drunk in a streaming arc. Suture, faster than any human could move, caught it in the cup, and then Brindle streaked past me, faster still, and tore out Sir Owalan's throat.

They hit the ground in a wet slap as time caught up, the dog still wrenching and ripping, Owalan's life gone before he hit the ground.

No more demons, Brindle said in my mind, and I thought that maybe I should scream, but the scream didn't come, as if horror had stolen the ability from me.

And then, like water flooding back into a puddle after a rock has been thrown into it, sound returned.

"The cup, Cleft!" Sorken yelled. "Drink the cup!"

Suture handed the cup to Cleft. The other golem froze, confused, possibly, or ... if golems had any will of their own ... reluctant.

I did not have time to watch their tableau because Adalbrand's hand found my jaw and turned me to look at him.

"Victoriana." Adalbrand's voice was heavy, his eyelashes thick on his closed lids. "It is time. Please."

He lurched back toward the fountain, hands braced on the edge of it and face just an inch over the water.

"Put your hand between my shoulders."

I sheathed my sword and placed a hand between his shoulder blades as he leaned out over the fountain.

"I ... I ... I ..." My words were stuttering, the image of Sir Owalan with his throat ripped out still too clear in my mind.

"Please. Victoriana. Most faithful of paladins. Please." Adalbrand's words sounded more like a prayer to a Saint than a plea for death.

So, here we were. At the end of the world, or at least the end of our world. The end of my world.

He turned enough to open his eyes to me, to let me look into the agony and roiling evil behind them. His knuckles were white on the edge of the fountain, his face a rictus. He had taken evil into himself, swallowed it down, and now he truly was poisoned. The most poisoned of Poisoned Saints.

His eyes pled for me to end it as he'd asked, to plunge him beneath the water and to free us all from the consequences.

I blocked out the sound of Sir Sorken similarly pleading with his golem and focused only on Adalbrand.

"You must do this," he said through gritted teeth.

"You're missing one," I said stupidly. "We can't do it with one missing."

He shook his head. "Owalan drank. It can't be drunk twice. His demon leapt to me. And now you must do your duty."

My stupid eyes were watering, making my vision fuzzy.

"Must I?" Not the words I was planning.

His arm reached around, snaking up to grab my other wrist and place it roughly on the crown of his head as if I were blessing him, or baptizing him ... or about to drown him.

His lips shook as he uttered the familiar prayer.

"Bless me, Merciful God, as I cross the waters toward you. Drag me up from the depths to your glories. Consider not my sins for they are many. Take instead this heart which I offer to you now. Bless me, Merciful God."

It was a formal last prayer and I was supposed to say, "Amen," but my tongue would not move. My breath sawed in my lungs as if it were fighting this, too.

Somewhere, far away, the clock had stopped bonging. Somewhere, in another world, I heard a shout of dismay and a scuffle.

I was supposed to press his face beneath the water. I was supposed to let him die beneath my weight. But I could not do it. Not even for this. Not even to save the whole world could I wound him, could I kill him. Instead, I kept my hands where they were but I turned my body so I might take his open lips violently in mine and slide a desperate last kiss over them.

They tasted terrible. Like evil and illness and misery.

But they were his.

His shuddering gasp was all the encouragement I needed, and his answering kiss was pained and hungry, but when he drew back, his mind had not changed. His eyes held in them a depth I could not reach.

"Please."

And the word was so plain, so vulnerable, so open to me.

"Adalbrand." His name seared my lips. His cinnamon eyes bored into mine. "Please don't make me do this."

"I've heard those words before." His voice made it sound like I was ripping out his throat. "And I could no more save her than I can save you. Please, Victoriana."

"But I love you," I whispered, feeling the hot tears spill suddenly down my cheeks.

"Then love me enough to be faithful."

I plunged his head beneath the holy water with a cry of despair and my eyes clenched shut. He tensed beneath my hands. I bit my own lip until I tasted blood.

And this wasn't right. It wasn't right. It —

He was torn from my grip without warning, dragged into the water so that his whole body tumbled into the fountain.

My eyes shot open. My empty hands flexed.

There was a sound half shout, half cry, half gurgle, and the waters swirled pink around the brindled muzzle buried in Adalbrand's neck.

I heard shouts and feet pounding across the marble, but I didn't look back. I threw myself into the fountain.

"Please. No. Please." My words jumbled together as I grabbed for Brindle. All I could see in my mind's eye was the empty gaze of Sir Owalan after his throat was torn out. And I should have been praying as he died. I knew it, but I couldn't stop myself from thrashing through the water toward him.

And then suddenly Adalbrand was free, sputtering, coughing, heaving, finding his feet, dripping wet. Water streamed down his close-cropped hair and stubbled jaw, and his clothing clung to him. I was reminded suddenly that this man I had been about to murder had been the peak of life and health. His body almost sang with the joy of life returned to him.

His hand was clapped to his neck and my stomach rolled at the sight. When it came away, there was blood and three gashes I didn't much like the look of, but compared to the ragged mess I was expecting, it was a relief.

He gasped, bright eyes meeting mine. Something had changed. They no longer glowed red.

He opened his mouth as if he would speak, and then there was a roar from behind us and Adalbrand leapt past me, drawing his sword while he was still in the air.

My head turned, confusion drawing my eyebrows down, but a voice in my head arrested me.

Eyes on me, my girl. Our time is short.

Chapter Thirty-Five
Poisoned Saint

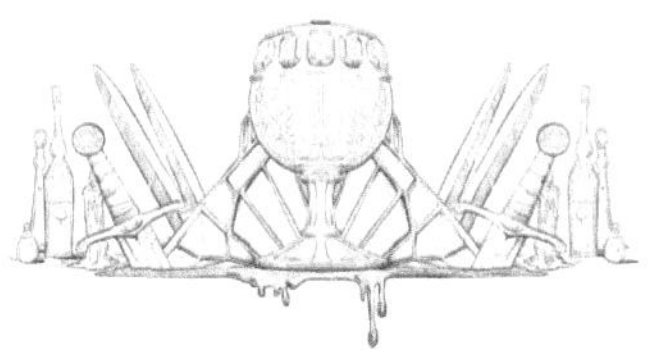

I am staring down death — or rather, breathing it down. And it is nothing, not even the sting of a thorn, compared to the howling, aching emptiness at the depths in me.

Aching Monastery? Ha! Does it go down so far that the pit inside it reaches through the crust of the earth, through her roiling black veins filled with oil and water? Through the meat of her minerals and the bones of her rocks, down deeper still to the beating of her molten heart and through the other side to where there is no earth at all and only the cold, friendless darkness of howling nothing? Does it go to where the soul loses even the understanding of self? To the place where not even a memory of love can yet live?

If it does, then it is only beginning to ache as I am, for in every breath, every blink of my eyes, the demons I drew into my heart play with my mind, feed me on their dreaming, and their dreaming is barbed and drugged, shuffling me unwilling from one damning imagining to another. Each thing they imagine is more deeply wicked, more stained in dread, more ribcage-wrenching, more heart-shredding, more brain-smashing than anything I could conceive. Even if I reach into the most hellish horror I can conjure, it would not rival this.

Can I explain what it is like to be driven through that as cattle are driven through the press with hot irons? Can I explain what it is like to be made evil, dyed with guilt, stained to the marrow with desires you did not ask for and yearnings that make you ill? I do not wish to make you know. The knowing is too terrible.

Shame eats me as the brindled dog ate Owalan's throat. Would that it consumed me entirely. Would that I never felt again.

And then pain flares in my neck and light pours in.

For the second time today, I feel the touch of the God. He sears me. He washes me in flame.

I drink it down, desperate, thirsty, convulsing with my need to be washed of this horror I have let flow into me. I know I am crying. Tears seep from my eyes like rivers overflowing their banks. It's relief, thrown to me like a rope in a storm.

And then I come up, suddenly, choking on the precious burn of holy water, swept clean as the dry desert sands by the power of the God flowing into me. I am, for a bare moment, breathless.

To be in the presence of the kind of creative power that sets the bones of the earth is enough to crumble a man and make him a craving, trembling addict all at once. I am both. To have been just a little near the swirling life, the bright eye of the God as he looks at me and sees, sees, sees, and chooses to wash me rather than crush me, chooses to rip me from the dragging dark rather than watch me be clawed away — I could cling to this forever and never willingly let go.

It's but a moment.

And yet it's forever.

And I return a different man.

The light is gone. Pain laces every breath, a reminder of the holiness and death that swirled into my lungs where air should have been. I feel absently at my neck. If there is pain, it's so minor compared to what came before that I hardly notice.

I find her eyes. And I'm slain.

In all fairness, I ought to be burned by her gaze, too holy to meet after who I've been these last minutes. But I'm not.

She catches my eyes and she's tremblingly beautiful, wracked with the agony I forced her through. Her eyes are bright with tears and her shoulders slump with relief and her lip trembles as something that looks a lot like gratitude washes over her. Her hand still grips her sword and I love her for not bending. She's like a moon to the sun of the God.

I love her for looking at me and not turning away.

I don't know where the dog is. I know I should be looking for him. He's taken into him all that was in me.

But a dark fist reaches for my lady paladin and I do not think. I leap.

I draw my sword as I leap through the air and it comes down hard on Suture's clavicle, driving him back. I spin, grunting hard with the effort of moving quickly enough to dodge blows from two golems at once.

Sir Sorken is behind them. For the first time since I met him, he has drawn his sword.

"Enough of this!" I bark at him. "It's over now. The demons are out of your grasp."

"I've come too far, I'm afraid, my boy," he booms out. "Too far for things to be 'enough.' I'll just have to start the whole process again. Turn the room to the start. It can be done."

I can see stains around Suture's bone and rag mouth where he tried to drink down the demon cup. I know he took nothing into himself. I know because it was all inside me.

He swings at me one-handed, but he's only bone. I deal his remaining arm a decisive blow with an overhead two-handed strike. It snaps his hand off at the forearm and he shudders backward.

"I told Coriand that bone was a poor choice," Sorken grumbles.

He glances up to the man's statue almost superstitiously. Beside it, Owalan's statue's neck has a dark shadow across it. I shudder.

He's maneuvering backward, trying to draw me away from

Victoriana. I spin just in time to thwart Cleft's flanking action and dart between him and the fountain.

Her forehead is pressed against Brindle's. She's not paying attention to this skirmish. I can't help my spike of anxiety at the sight of the pair of them. That should be me. This should be over and I should be dead and drowned in that holy water, having finally redeemed myself, given myself for the good of the world and the honor of the God.

"'Rock,' I told him," Sorken says, lost in the story of his friend who we killed. "It might be heavier and less comfortable to ride, but it's hard to destroy. You'd need a sledge to break Cleft into pieces. This whole place could come down on his head and he'd likely survive it."

I glance back and forth between the pair of golems and Victoriana, and I see their game. I bite back a curse. Of course. They mean to separate me from her and then attack. But I don't dare let them.

A sense of purpose and satisfaction settles over me. Mayhap my first plan is gone, but I can still keep them off my lady paladin's back as she finds a new solution. I hope she realizes that if the dog took my place, then she must drown it as she had been about to drown me. I hope she'll use the time I give her.

I leap into action, gritting my teeth.

Suture first.

I summon what strength I have left and I charge, channeling all my purpose, all my certainty into a series of quick blows to drive Suture backward.

One. Two. Three.

His stubs of arms try to deflect, but that's not the point. The point is to get him off-balance. The point is to find my opening. There it is.

I put the full force of my twisting torso and sinewy grip into the blow and I smash his skull into shards.

Chapter Thirty-Six
Vagabond Paladin

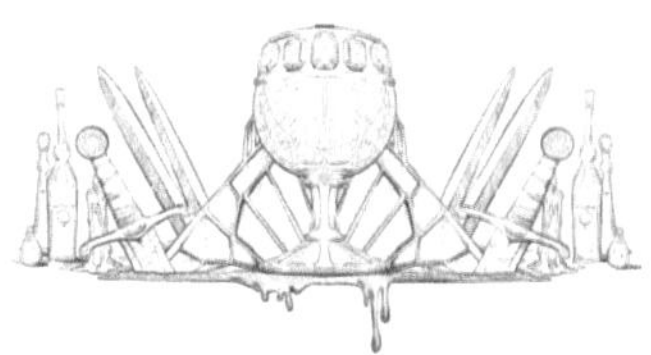

A*nd now you really do kill the dog,* the voice in my head said.

But it wasn't unkind. It was fatherly, and as it spoke, I could see the faint blueish outline of Sir Branson flickering in and out, squatting down in the fountain over the figure of Brindle the dog. His old face wasn't ruined like it had been on the riverbank. It was whole and well and he was looking at me with that kind of gentle musing kindness he always had when I was around him. Behind him, demon figures flickered, arms and eyes and mouths snatching, so wrong that they made my stomach twist. But here, close to me, it was only my friend.

Brindle shuffled his feet in the water. Water dripped from his sad eyes and ran to drip from his ears down his cheeks and back into the fountain. He whined nervously, tail flicking side to side as if he could feel the tussle within him but was as helpless as I was to stop it.

I reached out and rubbed his ears, and he leaned into the affection. It crushed me. Wrenched me.

How was I to meet my responsibility to banish these demons taking refuge in him when before I couldn't banish even one?

How was I to meet these innocent eyes and hold him under the water?

Snackling.

I barely heard the whisper of that demon's voice, though it had become familiar to me. It spooled out into faint, echoing laughter as Brindle whined again and put a dripping paw up on one of my shoulders. He'd taken a long drink from the fountain and his muzzle was clean. If only drinking holy water were enough to dispel demons.

It's not.

Lesson learned.

I told you I still had things to teach you.

I wasn't sure if the sound I made was a laugh or a sob. Whatever it was, it prompted Brindle to start licking my face with his newly washed tongue, and that only made it worse. He was innocent of all this. Why did he have to pay the price?

This is the last lesson, my girl, Sir Branson said. *I've drawn them all in. It took every last bit of effort I could muster. But now you must banish them. Drown poor Brindle, sweet doggy that he is, and dismiss these devils. Learn today that the sacrifice of a paladin is that sometimes we must be used for grim sacrifice if we are to find the path most valiant.*

There were two problems with that proposition. Firstly, that I had already determined I could not drown Brindle. Would not. I could not drown Adalbrand and he'd been less vulnerable, more determined that I do it than I had been.

Then do not drown the dog. Simply dismiss the demons and I will take care of the holy water part of the process. The Poisoned Saint was right to bless this water. Right to try this method. But drowning won't be enough. It's not enough with the really difficult ones.

Then what would be enough? For that was my second problem. I did not think I could banish these demons. I did not know where I would even begin.

It begins as it always does. With prayer. And with faith.

And then what? For I had prayed and prayed and nothing yet had helped.

What have you prayed for?

That I might bury Sir Branson.

Which will be done.

That I might save Sir Adalbrand.

And so you were granted.

That we would be delivered from evil.

A prayer you must now answer yourself along with the God.

But there was the rub. The God had not touched me. Not when I begged for his presence here in this unholy place. Not when I'd spent the night in holy vigil. If he was real and not a trick of my imagination and a twist of my hopes, then he did not care for me. I was a false paladin. An empty suit of armor. A changeling.

The Poisoned Saint did not think so. He saw the glory of the God and was warned from interfering with you.

Perhaps. Or perhaps his attraction to me twisted his mind to believe in things not there. Should I gamble our lives on that?

I heard the sounds of conflict behind me but I did not care anymore. Perhaps one of my enemies would slip through and slaughter me. And if he did then at least I wouldn't have to grasp this thorn.

But I must grasp it. If I did not find a way clear, then we would all be doomed, for if we left this place, and the demons with us, there would be no telling where they would go or what they would do when Sir Branson lost his grip on them.

"What do I do then, Sir Branson?" I asked, defeated.

And his voice was warm in my mind as he answered. *As with all things, open hands. If the God wills, then he will grant your request.*

It seemed too simple an answer. And if he wills not?

Then your soul will be swept away and with it all hope of redemption.

Oh, that was all? I could not help the ironic twist of my thoughts, even now.

It requires faith.

"I've never had faith, Sir Branson," I whispered. "I've never felt its lack more than right now. Is there not something I could *do*? I am good at doing. I am good at daring. I could fight right now just like Sir Adalbrand and he could come down here and have faith."

Brindle whined again, piercing my heart. How could I look into his warm doggy eyes while discussing this?

Adalbrand does not serve the Aspect of the Rejected God. This work is not for him. It is for you, my dear girl. And now you must choose. Will you be brave? Will you choose to reach in faith, though you reject it? Though you fear you will be rejected by it?

Brindle shuffled forward, tail wagging, and I pet his wet head with my trembling hand and kissed his nose with tears in my eyes. He had no idea what we were planning, poor innocent thing. His big doggy eyes met mine and for a moment it was just us three — the ghost paladin, the trusting dog, and the girl who didn't want to lose either of them.

You tried it before without faith. Try again. Try with open hands.

And I knew the moment I spoke it would be over. The moment I agreed, I'd lose them both and possibly myself, too, but I'd been holding Brindle tight this whole time and what had it done but prolong the pain? What had it done but make it even harder to say goodbye?

I sniffled then. Tears were tracking down my cheeks too quickly to wipe away. Brindle's sandpaper tongue licked my cheek and I wasn't ready. I wasn't certain. But then again, I never would be. If I was ever to truly be a knight of the God, then today was the day. And if he showed me favor, he would rid the world of evil. And if he rejected me, or ignored me, or just plain didn't exist after all — which, frankly, I was always a little worried might be true — then I would be swept away.

This took a different kind of courage. A valiant kind. One I didn't have.

One I was going to seize by the throat and demand rise to the occasion anyway.

I narrowed my eyes, gritted my teeth, and I said the hardest words I've ever said.

"Let's do this."

I closed my eyes and I opened my heart.

Chapter Thirty-Seven
Poisoned Saint

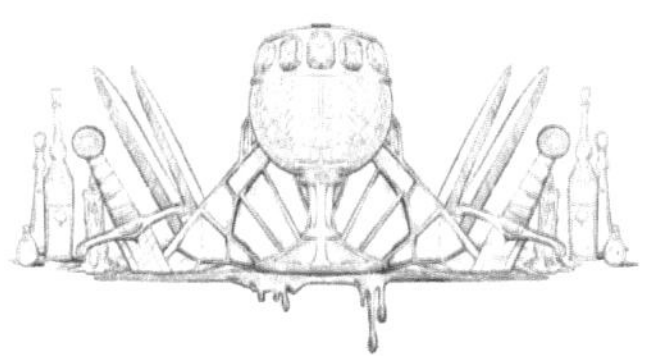

Suture stumbles dramatically away from my blow, breaking apart as he hits the ground, bounces, hits again, rolls, and then unspools into nothing but bone and rag. The magic is gone. Whatever life he had — if he had one — has vanished.

I spin to go after Cleft next and nearly slip on what is left of Sir Owalan.

Poor fool. I have never liked Penitents. But I liked him more than most. And now no one will see him rolled into a white cocoon in his strange hanging tent. No one will see his wide, dramatic eyes, so earnest and needy. He wanted only to be a Saint. It made him a monster.

I force the thoughts away and step over his corpse, ducking easily under a testing blow from Cleft. There will be time for mourning later. This is the part that comes before that.

Cleft isn't trying to kill me. Not yet. I can sense it. He's trying to herd me away from the fountain as Sir Sorken slowly makes his way over to it. They still have the greater numbers while the Vagabond is occupied.

Two can work that game.

I feint a blow toward Cleft and then spin away and into Sir Sorken's path, dodge his startled jab, and come up inside his guard. He's a big man. Built like a barrel. But he's three times my age. I grab him by the sword arm and twist, snaking it around his back. He does not drop his sword despite the grinding of my grip. It's both speed and the strength of youth that gives me the advantage. But he has the big stone golem.

"You could still leave," he says calmly, as if it is common to have me here, breathing down his neck, twisting his sword arm. "Walk away."

I am forcing him before me, keeping him between Cleft and me, keeping myself between Cleft and Victoriana. I can purchase her more time, if I am careful. I hope she is using it. I hope she is not too tenderhearted to do what needs to be done.

"And let you fill the earth with demons? Each one a new soul fit into your created bodies? Is that not the most flagrant of blasphemies?"

"Is it?" Sir Sorken asks. "Is it blasphemy to act as the God? If he created everything, can I not create? If he ruled it, may I not rule?"

"You aren't the God," I say grimly. "What he did well, you mock. What he did with care, you do with no regard for the result."

"I regard the result." There's grit in his words. "I plan it with care."

"You planned that?" I point at Cleft with the tip of my blade. "You planned to make a body of stone — one unfinished and unpolished?"

"It can be refined later. What does he care? He's a block of rock."

The block of rock makes a lunge for me and I turn Sorken as a shield so he cannot hit me. I'm forcing him toward the bottom of the stairs, forcing the golem with us.

"He follows your orders. He made bowls."

"Bowls?" Sorken snorts. "What has that to do with anything?"

"It's a creative pursuit! It's making something new. Only

people and the God do that. You've made him a person!" I can't believe I'm letting my fury over that leak into this moment, but the river can't be turned back now. It's pouring out of me. "A person that you're planning to possess with a demon!"

Sorken scoffs. "The golem is a useful machine but no more a person than your sword is. No more a victim than the dagger buried in Sir Owalan's wrist."

I'm moving him slowly to the foot of the stairs. I meet Cleft's glowing eyes. If he feels anything from Sir Sorken's declaration, he gives no indication.

"If I fill every one of them with demons, what is it to you? It will only make them bolder and stronger and more able to serve. But they will serve *me*. They have no choice. That rock creature has no more control over his actions than an actual rock. He dances only to my tune. You worry about bowls? He made them to my order. That means I made them. And with a demon soul trapped within, he'd be able to do that more effectively — do everything more effectively. And he is only the first."

We're at the foot of the stairs. Cleft makes a lunge for me again and again I pivot, keeping my hostage between us. Is that attack half-hearted? Would I be able to tell?

"I've heard rumors of your holier-than-thou ways, Sir Adalbrand." Sir Sorken is still speaking. I see now how he got where he is. With talk and persuasion. He hopes to persuade me now. To make me as much his creature as Cleft is. "You want an end to slavery? Here it is. You want an end to peasants barely able to scratch out a living? Here it is. Who will benefit when five of these plow every field in town and the men who used to break their backs doing it can finally rest? Who will benefit when wars are fought through hands of stone and clay rather than flesh? Who will benefit when it is stone shoulders that carry the heavy burdens, stone arms that swing the blacksmith hammer, stone feet that cross the endless miles? It will be the peasants you trouble yourself with so.

"Not those peasants. When people no longer serve their

masters, their masters take the very last thing from them — their lives. The peasants will be starved and forced out and left to die when the kings of this world discover they can have all that labor at no cost. And who will stop those kings when they are defended by arms and backs of stone?

"It won't be you, Adalbrand. You're not of the peasant class. And who knows? Mayhap you'll find a way to save all those eating mouths you care so much for."

"What about the slaves you make with your own hands?" I ask quietly as we mount the stairs, slowly climbing them backward. Cleft has taken the bait. He is climbing them with us. "The ones you carve of stone and bone? The ones you haunt with demons from their infancy?"

Sorken scoffs. "They aren't people, Adalbrand. It annoys me that you refuse to think clearly on this point. What we hope to achieve with this is called progress. It's called advancement. You can't stand in the way of it, my boy. You can only adopt it, or be left behind as the rest of us enable a new golden age. It would have happened by our hand or another. If not here, then somewhere else. We were just the ones keen enough to know about this place and to seize the opportunity while we could. Do you know how hard it is to get a good demon in hand these days with the way the Vagabonds are out there casting them all out? If I'd known they were keeping them as pets, that might have changed things."

We've gone ten, maybe twenty stairs up. Cleft is ten steps behind us. Not really far enough, if you ask me. It would take him one hop to be back to the mosaic map on the floor with those long legs. And if he took that leap, he'd just be strides away from interfering with Victoriana. I need to draw him farther.

Sorken seems not to agree. "Ah. Here we are. Time for you to make a decision, my boy."

He twists in my arms and I suddenly realize that the arm I thought was pinned has slipped from its gauntlet, and I'm left holding an empty shell as his sword clatters down the stairs. One minute he's inside my guard. The next minute he has a knife drawn, and I barely manage to twist enough to make it skim across my ribs instead of digging up and under them. Pain flares sharp and insistent. I force it from my mind.

"Saints," he mutters. Just that one word. Small. Almost factual, as if he's stating a number. It's a frank admission of defeat. And he's not wrong. I look him in the eye. See the wry humor behind his bluff exterior. Set that aside.

Without so much as a flicker of conscience, I grab him by the thighs, lift hard and fast, and fling him over the railing.

Chapter Thirty-Eight
Vagabond Paladin

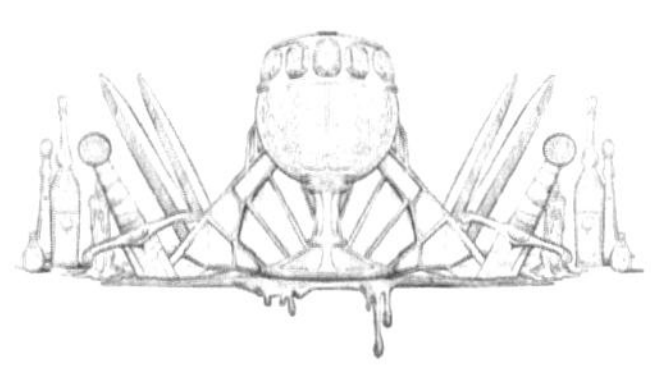

We should say goodbye now, Sir Branson said. *Whatever happens next, there won't be time later.*

My tongue suddenly felt thick. My eyes thicker. I couldn't see Brindle properly as they clouded over but I rubbed his ears and accepted his paw — one last time.

Sir Branson had no paw to accept, and no words could possibly suffice.

Trouble yourself not. I know all that you would say. It has been an honor from start to end. You need not say it for it to be so.

I opened my eyes to share a last look with his blueish spirit. One last goodbye, silent, for I could not bear to speak it. He smiled. My smile was tremulous.

I took a long breath and forced myself to concentrate, closing my eyes again because I could not bear to keep looking.

I knew hundreds of rote prayers of blessing. I said none of them. Nor did I open my eyes when I heard a dull thump behind me and a roar.

If I died, then I would die, and none of it would matter. If I did not die, then this prayer was the most important thing I could do.

I would pray not by rote but from my heart.

Open your hands. It will make it easier.

I held my arms out, palms up.

"Rejected God," I prayed. Best to stick to the aspect I served. I understood it best. I hoped I had faith — any faith. Was hoping for faith a kind of faith? "Rejected by man, ignored, refused. Do not reject my plea now. I hold to you my open hands. I hold to you an open heart."

It had better be open. I was trying to make it open.

I focused my mind on holiness, on purity, on rejecting evil, and on being willing to accept whatever the God gave or took.

I was such a small flicker in a vast universe. Such a tiny voice. I hadn't even the right to make this plea. But the request wasn't for me. And if I didn't ask, then all the world could be lost, for evil bred more evil, and what started here would be only the beginning.

I heard a gurgle and I refused to open my eyes. Refused to watch my friend drown himself in holy water. Refused.

Tears wore hot tracks down my face and I gasped and all that came out was, "Please. Please, if you can hear the prayers of men, then hear this one. If you care what happens to this land, then act. Condemn this evil; throw it far from us. Please."

I had hoped that if he answered me, there would be some kind of indication. A light, perhaps. An overwhelming peace, as the Saints have testified. Perhaps a warm love in my heart for all the world.

I was given none of that.

Instead, there was a sound like something cracking and then a great roar and then light — bright light, too light to look upon, but I opened my eyes anyway. In that moment I saw, or I thought I saw, a great warrior, clad in a light so bright that I could not make out his features or the insignia upon his tabard. In the midst of the brightness, he dragged the demons one by one from the heart of my dog, broke their backs over his knee, and stuffed them into a sack, and last of all he broke the great demon from the ceiling. And when the mouth of the sack was secure, he beckoned with his hand, and out leapt my paladin mentor from within Brindle. He turned and offered me one last wink, and then the warrior slung an arm amiably around his shoulders and then the light was gone, and I was blinking and blinded and all I could see was the warrior and Sir Branson again and again outlined in purple on the back of my eyelids and I thought I heard the echo of a voice in my head and it might have said, "Well done," or it might have said, "I told you so."

And I wasn't sure which it was. But if this was faith, then it was dangerous indeed. Just a flicker was enough to slay me.

My eyes sprang open. And there, beneath the surface of the water, Brindle rested.

"No!" I cried, suddenly unable to breathe.

This wasn't how this was supposed to end. The dog was not supposed to die! Why would he need to die when the God had come and answered my prayer and taken away all the demons?

Was it not over, then? I paused, concentrated, but no, there were no voices in my mind. There was nothing but my sudden sob as I lunged into the fountain and pulled my bedraggled friend out of the water. His fur was sodden, his doggy eyes shut. He looked so small like this.

"No, no, no."

There were footfalls racing toward me — one normal stride and one long, heavy stride. I looked up through a veil of tears to see Sir Adalbrand and Cleft racing toward me. And between me and them, a crack was forming in the floor.

Something fell, striking the side of the fountain and breaking a piece of it off that was about the size of my head. When I looked up, I realized it was the head of Sir Coriand's statue. It stared at me from the ground with one accusing eye.

Only something of great power could hold this place together and keep it from falling apart for a thousand years. And that something had been the demon in the ceiling. A demon that no longer existed.

I hardly cared.

I gathered Brindle up to my chest and stood, lifting him, clinging to him. A hot tear spilled down my cheek and my mind was empty, empty, empty with no Sir Branson to speak into it ever again.

Chapter Thirty-Nine
Poisoned Saint

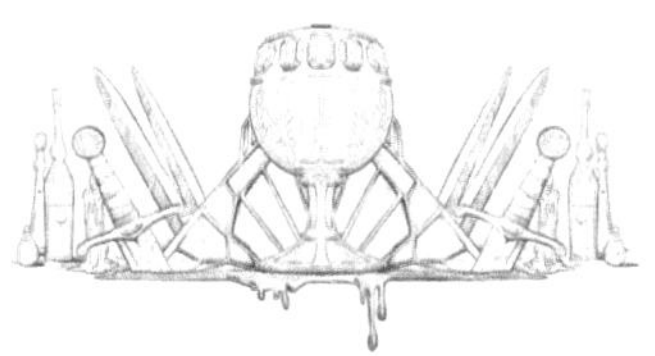

Cleft is moving before I can, running down the stairs five at a time. I don't dare let him get to Victoriana first. Not with her back unguarded. I see him in my mind's eye smashing her with his stone fists and it spurs me to action.

I fly down the first ten steps, nearly tripping in my haste, and then I scramble over the banister and drop over the side. My landing is awkward, my muscles exhausted from being forced to run and fight and run and fight on little sleep and no food.

I see her immediately, standing in the fountain, soaking wet, her hair plastered to the side of her face and tears streaming down as she clutches her massive dog to her chest, awkward with the weight of him.

To my utter relief, Brindle is dead.

Which means the demons are gone.

Which means ... with a mighty crack, the floor splits in two. I glance over my shoulder and I break into a run again. Cleft is behind me, racing across the ground. Whatever he means to do, I must not allow him near my lady paladin. She's earned her right to flee this place if any of us have.

I glance at Sir Sorken's body as I run past it and stumble when he meets my eyes. His legs are dead, unmoving, but his hands claw forward and his eyes are burning.

"Look on what you've done, paladin," he croaks as I pass.

I shudder as his voice claws up my spine.

I reach Victoriana just as she's stepping out of the water, as a piece of one of the statues falls and hits the edge of the fountain. We both look up instinctively.

I want to catch her up in my arms. I want to tell her she's done so well.

I do not. There's no time.

I revel instead in the brief catch of our gazes, on the way our hearts interweave in that intangible touch. I dare not savor it. I spin, sword up. It's only just in time as Cleft brings his fist down.

I barely deflect it. My sword shatters, sending a terrible shudder down my arm.

I find my lady paladin's gaze one more time.

"Run," I say calmly, and then I dance to the side, drawing Cleft after me. "I'll be right behind you."

I have nothing but a stub of a weapon to defend with, but it hardly matters. This is a game of ducking and leaping, a game where stamina wins. And I have none left.

I catch a glimpse of Victoriana as she passes me. She's a strong woman, but she's stumbling and panting with the effort of carrying a dog that surely must weigh as much as she does. I hope she's strong enough. I hope her feet fly with a strength beyond what she has.

"Merciful God, make it so," I whisper as another chunk of ceiling falls down, narrowly missing me.

A second chunk hits Cleft and he stumbles.

"This whole place is coming down, Sorken," I call out. "We ought to flee."

"We?" Sorken laughs, a wracking, coughing laugh. He hasn't moved more than an inch, if that. His back is surely broken.

I look to the golem, meet his glowing eye with mine.

"We must go, golem. Bring your master."

Sorken's laugh is punctuated by wracking coughs again. When he runs out, he wheezes in a gasp and then he speaks very clearly.

"Cleft. Kill him."

My gaze is still locked on the golem. And I do not know if there is a person in that rock. Even after everything, I still don't know. I do not know if he aches as we do, fears as we do, if he realizes how he is being used, or if he is only a mindless tool, but I know that if he redoubles his efforts, I will die here. And he has been ordered to do just that.

He lifts his fist and I draw in a breath, ready to try to leap and run again.

And then — slowly — he lowers his fist and stops.

"Deny your master and you will die," Sorken says in a low voice. "You know this."

But still, the fist does not move.

Cleft turns his head slightly, looking me full in the face, and I feel a rush of cold run over me as I realize what is happening. He has made a decision. He has chosen mercy.

It almost steals my breath away. Not a tool then. Not a tool.

My lips part and I begin to reach out a hand to him.

And then Sorken curses and the light vanishes from Cleft's eyes. Suddenly. A candle snuffed out.

For a heartbeat, I can't breathe.

I'm shocked by how watching that feels just like watching Owalan fall dead to the floor. A person. He was a person all along. I'm so stunned by it that it takes a second cracking sound for me to remember that the monastery is coming down around us.

My eyes linger on Cleft for a moment longer and then I'm moving, running to Sir Sorken, and sweeping him up into my arms. He screams — broken back — and I want to scream with him as the pain in my ribs where his knife scored me and the dog bite in my neck flare with the extra pressure of Sorken's weight. It will have to wait. All pain will have to wait. I can heal him but I will not remain conscious if I try it, and who knows what this madman will do if I am at his mercy. Likely he'll let us both be swallowed by this place.

I run, stumbling, my every muscle screaming. Sorken is old, but he is heavy — my weight plus another half if I'm any judge. And I am exhausted, blood flowing from my side.

Chunks of ceiling fall around us and the cracks of the floor are widening. Who knows how far down this place goes. If it's anything like the rooms the trials were conducted in, then it will be a very long drop.

As I pass them, two of the gears in the floor pull apart. I have to leap over their teeth — well, more like barely stumble over them. My heavy burden is dragging me, pulling my strength, sapping my energy.

In my arms, Sorken lets loose a steady stream of curses, growing more vile the farther we go. I ignore him as I should have all along.

Ahead, Victoriana has reached the door. She looks over her shoulder at me. She is a black silhouette against a light more bright than I've seen in days. It blinds me.

"Go!" I call.

She hesitates, as if she will come back for me.

"Do not wait for me," I order her, but even I can hear the strain in my voice. My strength is failing.

Her eyes widen, looking at something behind me. Likely, she's watching the entire staircase collapse. I stumble two more steps, yelling, "For the love of the God, go, Victoriana!"

She leaps through the door with her dog, tumbles out of sight, and I breathe out a sigh of relief.

I can't help myself; I look over my shoulder.

Where the stairway had been there is a yawning pit. Where the ceiling above it had been, most has fallen through, the ruins that were once above now falling to below. The Saints that ring the room are leaning forward — and once more they have changed. They no longer look like us. Their eyes are haunted. Something that looks like vines ripples through their skin and flesh, entangling them. They have too many mouths. Too many hands. Too many eyes.

I tear my gaze away as the first one tumbles, chunks of it breaking away. I have the most terrible feeling that the hands and feet depicted in stone are trying to claw out and stop its fall.

Looking back was a terrible mistake. The floor in front of me cracks and I trip, falling to my knees, dropping Sorken.

He screams and the crack parts so quickly that his lower body falls with it. His hands cling to the edge of the floor. Beneath him, the gears that turned the floor and the huge axle they theorized about are exposed. He dangles over them, eyes wild. And I do not see the murderer. I see only the man. I reach for his hand.

His eyes meet mine, harden, and deliberately, he lets go.

I do not watch his drop. Perhaps I should. Perhaps it would honor him. But I do not.

He does not scream. His death makes no difference at all.

I drag myself to my feet, my steps slowed by pain and exhaustion. My hand finds my side and comes back slick with blood. I look at it, step into the doorway, and look at the ruins behind me falling away into nothing.

A terrible sense of futility seizes me.

Eleven of us walked into this place. Eight are left in it forever. What madness. What terrible, clawing madness.

I don't think I'm thinking straight. I'm not sure why, but I feel almost like laughing as I turn my back on the yawning space behind me and fling myself into the icy grey water of the sea.

I taste the brine when I enter, and it's life, oh, it's life to me.

Chapter Forty
Vagabond Paladin

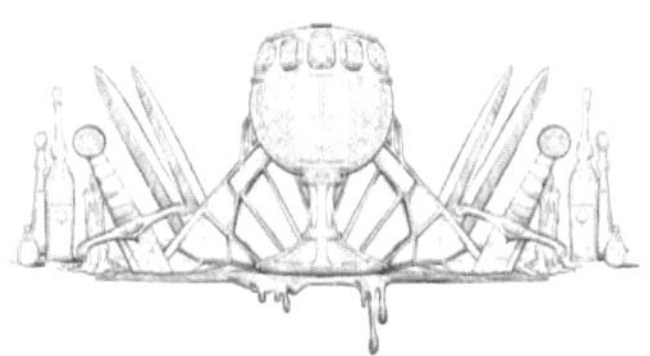

I swam on my back, still clinging to Brindle. My heart was in my throat. I wasn't sure if I should be swimming to shore or trying to wait for Adalbrand to join me.

I kept my eyes fixed on the doorway I'd leapt from. There was no sign of Adalbrand — hadn't been for as long as I was in the water. I blinked hard against tears that would not stop welling up.

Was he stuck? Had he fallen into a hole in the monastery? I should have stayed. I should have stayed and helped him and not taken the dog with me. I was a fool for making Brindle's remains a priority when he was already gone.

A sob rose up and choked me.

And it felt strange not to have two more opinions in my mind. Where was the voice urging me to drown and die? Where was the voice assuring me all would be well?

Gone. Lost to me forever.

A sudden crack split the air and I gasped as I finally caught a glimpse of Adalbrand. He flung himself into the sea at the same moment that the monastery collapsed, caving in with powerful force and sucking water in after it.

The pull of the sudden void dragged the sea backward toward

the collapsing city. Adalbrand swam — frantically — but he was being dragged backward despite his efforts.

And that was too much for me. With a cry, I dropped Brindle, turned around, and began to swim with all my might.

I nearly screamed when something huge in the water streaked by me. I sucked down a lungful of water before I realized it was Hefertus.

"I've got him," he roared, and then returned to slicing through the water as if he were a gleaming fish and this was his bay.

Reluctant, I turned back to Brindle, finding his body and dragging him to my chest once more so that I could swim backward toward the shore. He deserved a respectful resting place. He deserved to be honored.

Perhaps it was best I had not been the only hope for Adalbrand, because before I reached the shore I grew so tired that I was bobbing under the waves, losing hold of Brindle only to grab at him again. I hit the rocky beach breathless and exhausted, clawed us out of the inky depths, and collapsed on a shore that smelled of fecund seaweed and lashed at me with bitter winds.

I was alive.

That alone was the God's own miracle.

I had cast the demons out.

I was free.

And yet I was not.

I clung to my doggy friend — to what was left of him — and sobbed into his fur, stroking the head that would never lift again.

No apology from me could ever be enough. I'd betrayed the great bond between man and beast — the bargain where we promised to protect them if they would follow us.

I gasped in another shuddering sob, but I could not stay here mourning. Not now.

Worry forced me to my wobbling feet, though my vision was blurry with tears. I rose, trembling, just in time to find Hefertus breaking through the waves and hauling himself onto the shore, supporting a sputtering, half-drowned Adalbrand. They rose together from the slate-colored sea, the water pouring off them as if in holy baptism, and my heart leapt with something that sliced through me like hope. Adalbrand was whole — bleeding badly from one side, but whole.

"Adalbrand," I gasped, relief filling me as I looked from him to the angelic Hefertus. That giant who could lure in a thousand maidens just by walking dripping from the waves. I had questions for him later — specifically about why he'd abandoned us — but for now, my heart was full of Adalbrand and I cared not for any answer but his. "Are you whole?"

To my shock, he did not meet my gaze, did not so much as look up as he strode onto the beach with what seemed to be the last of his energy and fell to his knees beside Brindle.

I wanted to fall there with him, to wrap him in my embrace, but his lack of acknowledgment made me hesitate. Perhaps he had only wanted me while we were within the monastery walls. Perhaps all that was over now.

I exchanged a helpless look with Hefertus.

"You drown them because drowning is something you can come back from," Adalbrand muttered, and then he half leaned, half collapsed on Brindle's body.

His beautiful lips, dragging against the soaked doggy fur, muttered a prayer so quietly that I couldn't catch most of it.

I'd seen Adalbrand glorious and burning with light. I'd seen him best enemies who outnumbered him, arms rippling with the fury of the God raining down. But here, praying over my dead friend, vulnerable and broken, here he was beautiful.

He laid his hand on Brindle's head and I thought I heard him mutter, "Amen," before he passed out, his body going slack.

I looked at Hefertus again and the big man looked sharply away, as if this was all too much emotion for him.

Movement caught the corner of my eye.

It was the rise and fall of a brindled fur chest.

A cry escaped my lips and I fell to my knees just as Brindle wriggled out from under an unconscious Sir Adalbrand.

He hardly seemed to know what to do with himself. His tail wagged to an irregular rhythm and he barked sharply before slathering Adalbrand's cheeks in doggy kisses and then jumping up to put his paws on my chest and knock me backward so that he could give me the same treatment.

I was laughing, I realized, laughing in wonder. Laughing with joy. I caught the big furry face on either side of his head and tugged his ears gently back and forth.

"Who's a good boy, then?" I asked affectionately.

"Adalbrand is. Just like always," Hefertus said dryly, but his eyes were glassy and red-rimmed, too.

"Of course he is," I agreed with a grin. "And so is Brindle."

"I won't ask you if he's still full of demons," the golden-haired paladin said, lifting Adalbrand from the rocky shore.

"That's polite of you," I said just as dryly.

He narrowed his eyes and I laughed.

"They're gone," I assured him. "All gone."

And if my voice sounded sad, it was not for the demons. It was for my old friend, Sir Branson, buried now with honor beneath the rubble of the Aching Monastery, just as I'd asked the God to help me achieve.

"I suppose there won't be any more trouble coming from that place?" Hefertus glanced at me.

I shook my head and he let out a relieved sigh as he scratched his beard.

"Survivors?"

I paused. "Sir Sorken still lived when I fell into the sea. Adalbrand was ... trying to help him."

Hefertus grunted. "If he had been salvageable, then the fool would have stayed and died with him. We won't need to go back looking for survivors. Come along, then. The fire should still be burning."

"Fire?" I asked, surprised.

Hefertus frowned at me again. He did that a lot.

"Obviously you were all going to come out in ten hours and you were going to come by sea. Did you really think I wasn't paying attention?"

He held the full weight of Adalbrand as if he weighed nothing at all, not looking even fatigued when I made him pause so I could pull up the edge of Adalbrand's tunic. The slash across his ribs was still bleeding far more than I'd like. I hissed as I tried to probe how bad the injury was.

"We'll take care of him at the tent," Hefertus said.

I nodded and we set out, Brindle trotting out in front of us, nose to the ground.

The shore was rocky and uneven and it took us some time to wend our way around to where Hefertus had set up camp.

It was slow going for all of us except Brindle. Hefertus was being careful with his charge. I was wearied from the journey through the sea and the tumult of emotions that had raged through me at the fountain and the strange, scouring fire of the God that had performed his miracle. I felt as though I'd been scrubbed inside and out and was now a limp rag fit for nothing but drying in front of a fire.

"The God saw fit to set me on the other side of the door," Hefertus explained.

"After you left the battle to us?" I couldn't help myself. No fire or tent was enough to keep the bitterness from my voice.

"It was not my fight," he said simply. It must be nice to have that kind of confidence. "At any rate, it seemed to me that either the demons would win and come screaming out of there, in which case I would be required to spend my life on eliminating them — a thing I'd rather avoid — or someone would defeat them and the place would be a ruin. Either way, I could hardly leave the poor horses there.

"I took them with me. And my gear. And Adalbrand's. If you had something precious to you, I fear it's lost. I didn't want to steal anyone's things. Adalbrand wouldn't care. He is a brother to me."

"You two are definitely very close," I said wryly as we turned a corner in the shore and I saw three horses hobbled beside Hefertus's silken tent and a roaring bonfire.

"Oh no, I mean he's actually my brother. Most likely. My mother claims I am one of King Abrent von Menticure's many bastards, though there's no saying for sure. She's a Duchess of Shannamara. They aren't fussy about bed partners. And they're matriarchal, so I have her name, of course."

I found myself blinking at that. "Does he know?"

Hefertus paused and frowned. "I don't know, now that you mention it. I don't think I've ever told him. He's suspicious enough of me as it is. No need to make it worse." He gestured dismissively. "He doesn't like my devil-may-care attitude. But it's bred in the bone. It's going nowhere."

"Oh." It was a foolish thing to say, but we'd reached the camp now and Hefertus pointed to a pile of blankets on the shore.

"I *did* take the Seer's blankets. She wasn't going to need them. Put them by the fire, would you?"

I arranged the blankets in a pallet and Hefertus set Adalbrand down on it and went to find his kit. The Poisoned Saint would need stitching along his side and possibly in his neck. Brindle had torn him up there, too.

When Hefertus wasn't looking, I threaded my fingers through Adalbrand's hair. He looked so pale. He'd given the very last shred of himself for me.

My gaze strayed guiltily to where Brindle yawned beside the fire. Just Brindle. No demon, no paladin, just an innocent dog again. Behind him, the horses nickered, and when Hefertus returned with Adalbrand's small black bag, I raised an eyebrow at him.

"You only kept three horses?"

"I let the rest go. I don't need nearly a dozen horses."

"But why three?" I pressed as I dug into the black bag to find thread and needle so that I could stitch Adalbrand's side.

"One for me — obviously. One for Adalbrand. I knew he'd make it. He's too tough to kill. And one for you."

"For me?" I looked up, feeling amused despite myself.

"Just stitch the man who might be my brother," he said grumpily. "I'll brew tea."

I didn't ask if he'd stolen the tea. He could keep his secrets. I just stitched Adalbrand, drank my tea, and complied without complaint when Hefertus insisted on bundling both Adalbrand and me in blankets inside his tent.

"Two will be warmer than one," he said when I suggested I help him stand watch. "You can stand watch tomorrow."

I thought that after all that had happened, I should maybe spend the night in vigil. Or prayer. Or just being grateful to have survived.

I watched Adalbrand breathe for a time. Made sure he sounded fine. Marveled that he was alive and not drowned in the sea. His short hair was lovely, plastered to his head by the sea and then ruffled by my fingers, and his lips were soft as they were parted in sleep.

But he hadn't clasped me in relief like I'd expected. He hadn't even shared a single warm glance with me. Though that ached when I turned it round and round in my mind, it wouldn't be fair to hold him to things he'd said when we were both in that dark place. It wouldn't be honorable.

I wanted to try to think about what that might mean and how I should broach the subject with him when he finally awoke, but I was spent and weary. When Brindle padded into the tent and lay down over my legs, a warmth came over me and I couldn't keep my eyes open. I drifted away to sleep to the sound of doggy breath, the gulls shrieking overhead, the pounding of the sea's turbulent breakers, and Hefertus outside the tent humming a tuneless melody.

Chapter Forty-One
Poisoned Saint?

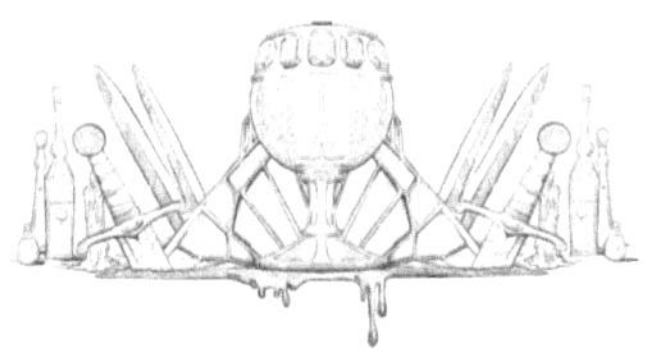

I wake a new man.

Victoriana sleeps just inches from me, her fringe of lashes a fan over her cheeks, her breath soft, dark hair tangled around her face.

She's so beautiful that it hurts. Grips my heart in a fist.

She's layers. The wild woman who streaked herself with mud. The girl too soft to kill her dog even knowing it housed a demon. The stalwart warrior, chin thrust out, refusing to bend when outnumbered. The paladin blessed by the God, shot through with the gold veins of his holiness. She's all these things at once. I love them all.

I reach a hand as if to caress her cheek and then I stop abruptly.

Beneath the ground, she had turned her heart to me. When she was backed into a corner. When she had no other allies. I dare not assume she will choose me here in the open air. It's not that I am insecure, thinking a rival will sweep her away. It's more that I am cognizant that she is a wild creature at heart. A wanderer. A freewheeling bird of the sky. She will not thank me for anchoring her.

Nor will she thank me for pressuring her based on a vow she

gave while under duress. I am no blackguard to hold a woman captive by words spoken under fear and pain.

A doggy face appears from over her shoulder, narrowing his eyes at me. No quarter is given me though I've healed him. He huffs once at me.

I draw my hand back, frown, and rise. Even without additional spirits occupying him, Brindle is a sticky fellow. He has no love for me.

I step out of the tent and find Hefertus cooking a fragrant-fleshed fish by the fire. He has no fishing gear. I can only assume he asked the God for the fish and it leapt from the sea to his hand to satisfy his hunger.

I'm constantly fascinated by how the God deals with Hefertus. Where I am offered pain, he's given plenty. Where I am constantly winnowed to clarity, he is left happily oblivious.

"Pretty girl," he remarks as he turns his fish, not looking up at me. His missing finger doesn't seem to bother him, though it must serve as a reminder forever of the terrible road we walked. "Turned your head, didn't she?"

I grunt. For a man swathed in pearls, his beard oiled and hair brushed until it gleams, he's hardly one to judge another for being too pretty.

"What are you going to tell your aspect about the cup?" he asks, changing tacks.

"Nothing."

His snickering laughter makes me frown.

"Well, my ill-tempered friend, if you say nothing then they'll only have my word for what took place. I think it likely your dark horse in there will only write a letter." He gestures at the tent, where Victoriana sleeps. "Can she write, do you think?"

"Rude. She read Ancient Indul, a thing you could not achieve." I bristle at his insults but they feel good. Like the bracing wind along the shore that bites at my exposed skin, they remind me I am alive.

I look out over the hole in the ground left by the collapsed ruins across the water from us. There's nothing there. Not even the arch or the statue that once graced the hilltop. It's all water now. I shiver. It's a miracle that is not my tomb.

"Her *demon* read Ancient Indul," Hefertus corrects dryly.

I shoot him a look.

He smirks. "What? I keep up. Common sense may not be my greatest strength, but you should be glad for that. A man with any sense would have run the moment he was free of that place."

I grunt again. "I would say rather that it shows your lack of sense that you stayed."

He laughs. "Then you should thank the God that he took my excess sense, for it saved your sopping wet soul from death."

We're quiet a moment and then he sobers.

"If I'm to give the report on this incident, my surly friend, then I will have to make a decision. I can report the incident as it happened, and you might find there are people with many questions to ask you. An uncomfortable thought, no? Some of the Aspects of the Divine God are ... how do I say 'hellishly awful' without being rude?"

"I think you just did," I say, amused.

"They'll do all those lovely things they do to the truly innocent," he continues, his tone dark, mocking, and merciless. "Thumbscrews. Broken bones. Lighting you on fire to be sure your marrow runs out and you aren't a demon. You know. The usual holy work."

"A fate I'd like to avoid," I say with a furtive glance at the tent.

"A fate you'd like your lady love to avoid. Don't play coy with me. You'd revel in all that misery. It's your aspect's way. It's not my way, though. I like to keep things bearable. Which is why another story occurs to me."

"And what is that?" I ask, taking the fish he puts on a leaf and passes to me.

My belly is already rumbling as I reach for it and I have to close my eyes to guard the pleasure of hot food from slipping out where Hefertus might see it. I nearly moan when the first scrap touches my tongue.

Hefertus's voice takes on a charming lilt as he lays out the story.

"We came to this place, all of us, but the door to it stumped us. It would not allow entry and could not be forced. We camped several nights, our tents spread out, and then one night — horror of horrors — the place fell into the ground and was covered by the sea, and everyone camped on top of it was swept away into the chasm, except the three of us, the dog, and the horses, who were camped just far enough away from the actual ruin to be spared. A kindness of the God. A miracle."

"It's a good story," I say after a while as we eat. "But someone might try to bring ropes and go down into the ruin to look."

"Underwater?"

"With pumps and engineers, water can be moved."

"As long as it isn't me, I don't rightly care," Hefertus says. "What could they possibly find down there? The place looks too ruined to generate more demons. And I think that the bodies would be long decomposed before anyone could work their way through the rock. It would take months to organize that kind of endeavor. Years, maybe, at the rate the church works."

"There's the golem, Cleft. He froze when he disobeyed Sir Sorken. But he wasn't dead, I don't think. And he's made of rock. It's possible another of their Engineers could wake him."

Hefertus snorts. "Then it's a good thing he has no voice. Stop fretting, Adalbrand. This is a secret best kept hidden. Your Vagabond will understand that." He pauses. "What will you do with her?"

I shake my head. "I do not know what I will do *about* her. Not with her. She is not mine to direct."

Hefertus snickers again. "Sometimes I think it's you who loses common sense when you call on the God and not me. Either way, it makes no difference. We'll travel together back to civilization and then I'll leave you on the road and ride to Saint Rauche's

Citadel to make my report. You won't want to come. I'll tell them all I speak for you, and deliver any letters the pair of you want to write." He pauses. "But I'll read them first, so don't let honesty get in your way."

"I wouldn't dream of it," I say wryly, and then we eat in companionable silence until the Vagabond wakes.

I watch her come out of the tent, sleep-mussed and so desirable that my whole body aches to hold her no matter my good intentions.

It's too much.

I leap up from where I sit like I've been stabbed and hurry off down the shore on my own, trying to calm my pounding heart and shaking breath with the brisk sea breeze and the difficulty of negotiating a path along the angry sea. My neck and my side hurt enough to steal my breath, and that's good. I lean into that.

She stirs me up like a hurricane. I am unsteady, uncertain. I will not let that instability leave marks on her. Not after everything else.

I seek solace in prayer for what feels like hours. My prayers have never felt so intimate. Probably because I've never been touched by the God like I was in that terrible place.

Eventually, I feel a touch on my shoulder and I spin, hope flaring in my eyes, only to be disappointed by the mocking gaze of Hefertus.

"I've always thought your order had it the worst," he says. "Just drive a dagger through your flesh like a cursed Penitent, why don't you. All this celibate angst is killing me."

The black look I direct at him only makes him laugh more.

"Come on, brother," he says, throwing an arm jovially over my shoulders. "The Vagabond doesn't want to stay here, and neither do I. This whole God-forsaken place is haunted. Let's ride as far as we can and keep on riding until we shake the dust of this place off."

We make our way back to where the camp had been. It's already packed, the horses ready. My lady paladin sits astride hers, looking for all the world like a holy knight, though she is bereft of armor. Even her sword is lost back in the fountain.

I lost my armor, too, shedding what was left of it in the sea as I fought for my life. My sword — more precious to me than any other possession — is gone forever.

We're a pathetic pair, we two.

She watches me intently, as if waiting for something. I do not know what that something is, so I meet her gaze steadily and then mount my horse and am grateful when the road is so narrow that we must ride single file.

I ride at the rear. A terrible choice, as it means my eyes are fixed on her back for the next twelve hours as we ride. By the time we decide to pitch camp, I've memorized her down to the finest hair. And when I retire, wrapped up in stolen blankets, refusing Hefertus's offer of the tent, my mind replays the softness of her curves over and over.

Hefertus sleeps in the tent with her. I wish I could resent him for it. I am, instead, merely horrifically jealous. Would that I dared sleep a foot from her. Would that I dared drown in her scent and allow myself secret glimpses of her drowsy form. I dare not. I am overwhelmed just by this much proximity. I will not force her hand. I will not pressure her with emotional displays. That is not the path of honor. If I slipped even once, all my gates would fall open and I would be as overwhelmed as a city when a siege breaks.

I do not sleep. I do not dream. I spend all the night with my thoughts racing round and round. My arms feel so terribly empty.

At the first hamlet we encounter, Hefertus spends money like water, gathering food and supplies.

It is here that my heart is broken for a new reason, for as we walk through the hamlet, a child runs out and into the side of a barrel. His arm goes backward and breaks with a snap. I'm on my knees in the dust in a second, praying over him, gently helping to set the bone and bind it, but though I can administer kindness and help as anyone with knowledge can do, my prayers for his healing go unanswered. No power flows through me. No miraculous healing saves him the pain of the break.

I know why this is. It's a result I expected. And yet it is a bitter pill to swallow, knowing that by choosing one path, I have lost another. By choosing one good, I have prevented another. I leave the child to his parents with a troubled heart and a twisting belly. He lingers long in my thoughts as I mull on the choice I have made.

At the first good-sized town, Hefertus buys the Vagabond and me both serviceable new swords and what little armor is available. It is not the kit of paladins, but it is as close as one can get in the wild.

We spend an awkward night in a crowded inn with one room and one bed. Word has reached the world that the north is opening and gold prospectors, historians, and hunters set out by the dozens. They are only the vanguard. More and more will pour up into the new space as the days go by. It's a strange thing to see the gleam of opportunity in their eyes as they race to a place I can't abandon quickly enough.

Hefertus takes the bed and that leaves the floor for us. I can barely manage to look my lady paladin squarely in the eye. Even the smallest glimpse of her seizes my heart and squeezes the breath from my lungs. It's too much. It's all too much. I sleep with my back to her and for the first time in years, my thin blanket feels very lonely.

The next morning, outside the town in a wooded glen, Hefertus leaves us. He has letters penned by both of us for our aspects and he wears an irritable frown.

"I'm leaving you both. If you're traveling down the same road as me, give me at least an hour's head start."

The Vagabond Paladin looks confused. "I don't understand," she says miserably. "You don't want to travel with us?"

Hefertus growls. "Girl. Knight. Whatever you are. If I must ride one more day with the pair of you and your angsty silences and longing, desperate glances whenever you think the other is not looking, I will chew through the ends of my own hair and eat my own boots. The tension is turning me inside out and I am not even part of this tangled star-crossed love." He makes a sound that is like an unspoken curse. "I want a pair of warm arms and a willing kiss, or ... failing that ... an empty room of my own where I can clear my head. You've ruined me. Both of you. So yes, I would travel alone. Very alone. As alone as a man can be. If you have any sense of gratitude for the fire, and the tent, and the horses that awaited you when you swam to safety, you will give me that, at least."

There's a long silence as he catches his breath. I do not look at the Vagabond. My cheeks are hot with the knowledge that now everyone here knows the hidden cockles of my heart.

I clap Hefertus roughly on the shoulder. Maybe too roughly. He grunts.

"Thank you for all you've done, brother, and godspeed."

He grunts again.

"Thank you, Sir Hefertus," my lady paladin says stiffly.

He laughs, a dark, dry laugh. "I swear to the God," is all he says, and then he kicks his horse and leaves us in his dust.

I look up at Victoriana and see her huge brown eyes looking at me. Her jaw is clenched with determination. She shatters me with a look.

"I suppose you're leaving now, too." Her tone is grim.

Beside her, her dog laughs at me.

I shift awkwardly in the saddle. "I gave my vow to stay with you."

She looks upset. I cannot fathom why. I have exercised every possible caution to protect her heart.

Without a word, she kicks her horse and leads us back toward the town and then down a side road that wends far into the woods. I follow her grimly all through the afternoon, though she never looks back once.

We reach a small creek as the light is fading. She begins to set a fire without speaking. I remove the horses' tack and bring them to water. When they're taken care of, I join her at the fire. Her dog is already there, spread out beside the flames to catch their warmth. He pants happily, wet from his drink at the creek. I swear he is still mocking me.

Victoriana stands abruptly, that enchanting black hair falling into her eyes. She hasn't braided it once since we left the sea, as though she thinks it might offer the protection her mismatched armor cannot. Like me, what armor she has is packed away. She wears only the sword buckled to her hip and her light travel clothing — purchased for her by Hefertus just as mine was. He claimed to be so rich as to hardly care where the money went, but I know full well he is generous to a fault.

"Enough of this." She crosses her arms over her chest and her gaze snags on mine before she rips it away, and in that flicker of a moment, I see nothing but anguish.

What has happened?

I take an involuntary step forward, but the fire is between us, dancing and smoking wildly as if it is alive.

"Victoriana?" My voice sounds uncertain.

"I release you from any vows you made. Any and all promises made to me," she says roughly.

"None but the God can release me," I growl, annoyed. What is this?

"Then ask him to release you!" She turns to me abruptly, her face taut with vexation.

I rock back on my heels, surprised. "Why would I ask that?" I say, my voice barely above a whisper.

She's glorious and deadly, powerful and potent. I want to be in her presence forever.

She scoffs. "Why? You have barely looked at me since we were drawn out of the sea. Adalbrand, you fool of a man." She runs a hand over her face. "Your heart is not with me, so don't let your honor force you to dog my steps. I'll be no one's duty."

Her chin is high and trembling and her eyes are liquid.

Oh.

Wait.

I step around the fire briskly, and catch her by the waist with both hands, driving her back a step.

"Are you saying my distance offends you? Do you want me yet, Lady Paladin?" I ask her hoarsely. The words tumble from my mouth as if a dam has opened. "Are you still mine? Even now? Even after you've seen me possessed by demons? Even after you've seen me commit black murder?"

"Of course I want you, Adalbrand." She sounds like she's on the verge of tears. "It's not me who has been cold and distant since we left the ocean."

"I healed your dog," I say numbly. "I brought him back from death."

"Thank you." She does not sound like she's thanking me. She sounds like she's slamming a door on me.

"It was your turn to speak," I say stupidly. "If you still wanted me that way then it was for you to say it. I thought your silence meant you had regrets. That you wished to put all that behind you."

She laughs, disbelieving, and it's half laugh and half sob.

"Are you always this stupid?"

"I think I might be," I say as I jerk her waist so that it's flush against mine — we're nearly the same height and her mouth is pleasingly close — and then I lean in and kiss her with all the pent-up passion and yearning I've been holding back for days.

She yields beneath my fingers, softens with my kiss, and it reawakens the desire I've been holding down. I groan into her mouth, overcome with need for her, drugged by the taste and feel of her mouth sliding on mine, her lips catching on mine, dragging them toward her. I want to see where else they could catch and drag.

"You can't kiss me." She is breathless when we break apart, her fist firm against my chest, holding me back from kissing her again. I swallow down the stab of loss at her rejection. I've misunderstood. I've overstepped. "You're sworn to celibacy."

Oh. I search her eyes. Is that her only objection? My honor?

"Didn't you see Hefertus pay for my armor and clothing?" I say, my voice clouded by the harshness of my breath. The rise of desire is not so easy to quell as it is to awaken.

She shakes her head. And her voice is pleading. "What does that have to do with anything?"

She wants me to give her reasons to stay. My heart leaps to offer them.

"I gave him every coin I possessed."

Her tone is dry. "He hardly needs it. He'll just spend it on nonsense."

"Did you not see how I could not heal the boy?" I ask, tentatively, trying not to misread her again.

She looks puzzled. "You bound his arm. I thought ..."

I laugh darkly and then her expression turns the bitterness of it into true amusement.

"Tell it to me plainly," she demands.

I tuck her hair behind her ear so I can revel in this moment before I answer her, but her sharp gaze urges me to explain.

"I've left the Poisoned Saints. Changed allegiances. The letter I sent with Hefertus will confirm it with my aspect."

"But the God came down in glory over you." She looks confused. "Why would you walk away from his service?"

"I would not." I bite my lip, waiting to see what she will say when she finally realizes what I've done. "I'm just joining a different aspect. After all, I'm sworn to follow you and you will be wandering this earth for the rest of your life." I pause and clear my throat a little awkwardly. "And if you'll have me, then I'll wander it with you, honoring the Aspect of the Rejected God. And if you won't have me, then I suppose I will be doing it alone, since it's already too late to change my mind. I've sent all the letters and the God has clearly changed where he'll let me direct his power. As far as the world is concerned, I'm a Vagabond Paladin now."

"You did this for me?" she says, understanding dawning.

"Yes," I whisper, and my hands at her waist squeeze just a little, pressing her harder against me. She fits just right.

"And what are you begging for now?" she asks coyly, but there's a shyness to her prodding that I'd like to tease out.

I lick my lips and take a gamble. "More kisses."

And she's laughing when she kisses me — at first — but celibate order or not, I have the skill to turn laughter into gasps, and gasps into moans, and I do just that under the blanketing darkness of the night.

If I am now a Beggar Knight, and if my hands are open to the God right now, then he's filled them to overflowing with good gifts. And I've never felt so free.

Epilogue
Vagabond Paladin

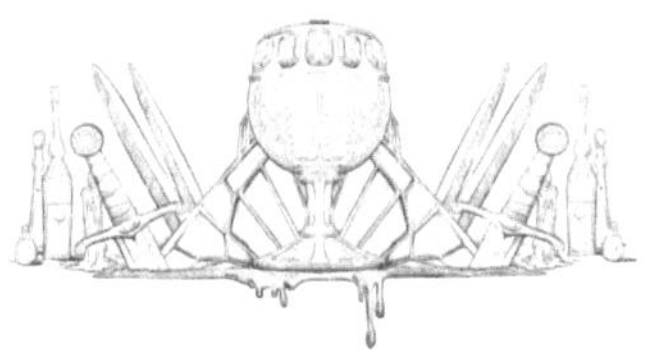

We started out onto the winding forest road from the tumble-down chapel with our hands tightly clasped together.

The old friar had been surprised when we landed on his doorstep in the middle of the afternoon and begged him to bind us in matrimony. We paid his friar's fee with a handful of wild onions we'd found on the way and the old friar, quite taken by us, had gifted me a copper ring that someone had thrown in the plate two Sundays before to stand as my wedding ring.

The God takes away, but the God also gives.

What he'd taken from me was my loneliness and sorrow.

What he'd given me was everything.

There was no warm house waiting for us tonight, no guarantee of a hot meal, no friends to celebrate, but we had our two horses, the dog leaping and jumping as he tried to catch early spring butterflies, and the endless road stretching ever onward.

And above all that we had the kind of love that even the worst of difficulties could not stamp out.

We had the kind of faithfulness that stood a dozen generations.

We had the kind of passion that would keep our blankets endlessly warm.

When I looked into my husband's dazzlingly bright eyes, I saw no more shadows haunting him, no more guilt bowing him down. Instead, I saw the warmth of tender love, and when he looked back into mine, I knew he could see that I had faith now.

It was a faith like I'd never believed was possible.

It was a faith born of love and perseverance.

It was a faith he'd helped create.

And it was all mine.

Acknowledgments

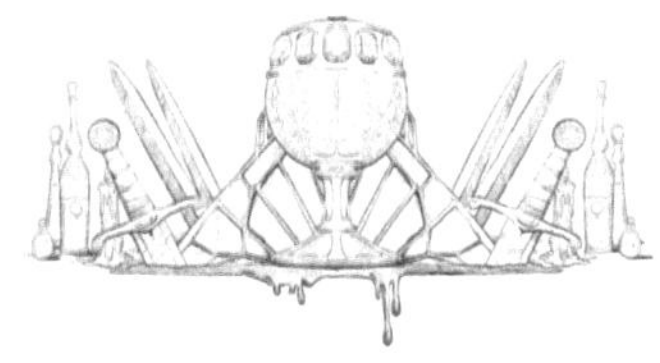

USA Today bestselling author, Sarah K. L. Wilson loves happy endings, stories that push things just a little further than you expect, heroes who actually act heroic, selfless acts of bravery, and second chances. She writes fantasy of various kinds but all of it ends up a bit dramatic and bloody.

Sarah would like to thank **Melissa Wright, J A Andrews, M L Spencer & Eugenia Kollia** for their incredible work in beta reading this book. Without their big hearts and passion for stories, this book would not be the same.

Sarah has the deepest regard for the talent of her phenomenal artists Bastien Jez and Alice Duke who created the gorgeous art that accompanies this book.

A huge thank you to Sarah's editor, Melissa Frain who has polished the language of this book to a burnished shine.

Thanks also to the Noble Order of Female Fantasy Authors who keep her sane – sort of. And to her beloved husband, Cale, and sons Neville and Leif, who are endlessly patient as she talks to them about bookish passions.

Please follow Sarah on social media and subscribe to her newsletter. She has a lengthy backlist and there is so much more to enjoy.

Visit Sarah's website for more information:

www.sarahklwilson.com

Also by Sarah K. L. Wilson

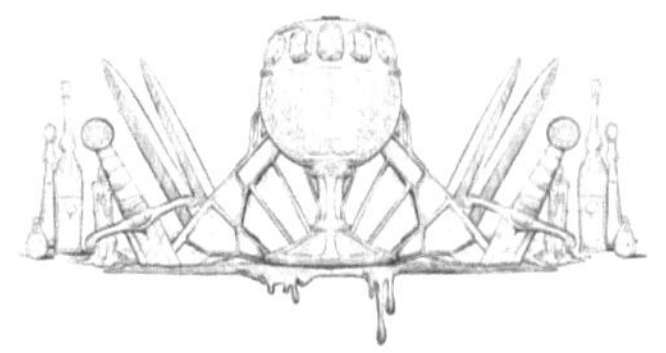

Romantic Fantasy:

Bluebeard's Secret Series

Seven Swords Series

Bridge of Legends Series

Empire of War & Wings Series

Fae Hunter Series

Mayfly World Series

Young Adult Fantasy:

Dragon School Series

Dragon Chameleon Series

Dragon Tide Series

Phoenix Heart Series